MYSTERY OF THE DEATH HEARTH

A Runevision Novel

ALSO BY JACK R. COTNER

Storytellin': True & Fictional Short Stories of Arkansas

MYSTERY OF THE DEATH HEARTH

A Runevision Novel

JACK R. COTNER

Elderstone Press

This is a work of fiction. Names, characters, places and incidents either are the product of the author's imagination or are used fictitiously. Any resemblance to actual events, locales, or persons, living or dead, is entirely coincidental.

ISBN-13: 978-0615671673
ISBN-10: 0615671675

Published in the United States by Elderstone Press

To all those Celts who were, who are, and who will be.

Great Northern Sea
N
The Celtlands
Northern Brendan Valley
Moryn Gweneth River
Highdyn Hill
Carew
Blaire
Brennus Ford
Aife
Doane
Carmel Raif
Elshorn
Cross Abbey
Dynsmore
Gemma
Hierlaneum
Southern Brendan Valley
The Empire
To Rome

AUTHOR'S NOTE

I come from a long line of Celts.

My ancestors came to America in the early 18th century from the Rhineland Pfaltz region. Before the invasion of the Roman Empire that region, like much of Europe and the British Isles, was inhabited by groups of people known as Celts (pronounced *kelts*). Although the language and cultural norms varied widely by group—from Eastern and Northern Europe all the way to the British Isles—there is archaeological evidence that these groups were connected by an impressive trade network which facilitated a healthy exchange of varied cultural, social, and religious ideas. When the Romans spread into the northern lands, however, their efforts to displace Celtic traditions and religious practices with their own led to oppression, dissent, and outright rebellion.

While researching this book, I relied on an extensive body of literature in my quest to learn more about the ancient Celts. I recommend the following: *The Celtic World*, edited by Miranda J. Green; *The Celts: Uncovering the Mythic and Historic Origins of Western Culture*, authored by Jean Markale; and *Who Were The Celts?* by Kevin Duffy. In addition, I recommend *A History of Pagan Europe* by Prudence Jones and Nigel Pennick, *The Druids* by Stuart Piggott, and *The Pagan Book of Days* by Nigel Pennick.

Although I've used the knowledge gained from these and other texts to create the world you are about to enter, this is a work of fiction and not intended to be historically factual. With that disclaimer, I should note that I have taken creative liberties with geographical facts, language, and actual historical events. Any resemblance to Celtic religious traditions, actual people, or places is entirely coincidental. I can assure you, however, that no history was harmed in the writing of this novel.

J.R.C.

The Circle stands upon the Mounds,
Centered on the Highdyn Grounds.
Marks the Rise on Summer's Return,
The Ascent of Winter's Coldly Turn.
Times the Point of both the Solstice;
Smart they are and never miss This.
Planting, Harvest, In-Between,
To those aware, All is Seen.
Look! Laid out, Precisioned Stone,
For Human's sake, they're not Alone.
Cycle In and Cycle Out,
Praise It all and Dance and Shout!
The Patient Oaks, they know it too;
As they breathe for me and you.
Raise your voices to the tune,
Celebrate the Sun and Moon.
Beat the drums, blow the fife,
Happiness for all that's Life!
Mercy, mercy Stars that shine,
The Elder Faith is Old Divine.

Prologue

June 21st in the Roman calendar
Summer Solstice, the Druidic festival of Alban Hefin
Mid-Point marker between the celebrated
Gates of Beltane and Lughnasadh

"This sacred site has been here longer than we can remember," Elder Blaine the Slender told the small group of children clustered around him. They were surrounded by festival vendors in tents bearing colorful flags, all part of the crowd gathered there to celebrate the Solstice holiday. "Heed these stories well, so you may pass them to those who will come after you."

He saw them nod, some smiling, many somber, all attentive.

"Learn your crafts well, listen to your elders, honor the gods, and respect the land. Enjoy the life you have been granted and help others do the same. No other goals should be attempted lest you fall into the evil snare of greed and dishonesty."

A small voice whispered, "He means the Romans, right?"

"Not just Romans, young one. Celts, too, face dark temptations. The two worst enemies we all face are liars and thieves," the Elder continued. "Take nothing that isn't yours. Honor the code of doing what you will so long as you harm no one or their possessions. Have compassion for those less fortunate, help those in need. Follow the path of our Celtic Elder Faith, stay true to its teachings. You will be wise to—"

Blaine's words were interrupted by heavy beating of drums and cheers from celebrants within the inner circle of the standing stones. Before Blaine could continue, a child spoke up.

"What about murderers, Elder? Aren't they an enemy, too?"

Elder Blaine nodded. "Truly spoken young one. Murderers are the worst kind of thief. They steal your life."

Treasure
Theirs or ours
Never argue
It matters not.
Gold and Amber
Sparkly things
Likely a lot.
Minted coins
From the Empire's vault.
Ours, not theirs
It's not our fault.
Earth provides
For us all.
Take it quick
Before the Fall.

1

August 25th in the Roman calendar
Morning
Seven days left in the Celtic Tree Month of Coll (Hazel)
Four days until the Runic Half-Month of Rad (Motion)

Crows—those dark-winged scavengers regarded by Celts as harbingers of death—filled the air above the meadow, diving in and out of the smoke from the looted wagon. They would find plenty here to feast upon, Eiroy thought as he studied the carnage before him. He knelt in the meadow's wet grass and wiped fresh blood from the blade of his deadly short sword.

The smoke rose slowly through the branches and leaves of willow, cane, and alder bordering the meadow. He stood, brushing back a lock of reddish-blond hair protruding from beneath his leather helmet and returned his sword to its scabbard. He watched the three Romans—part of his gang at his employer's insistence—stuff a burlap sack full of the boots, belts, and rings from the bodies of the priest, his acolyte, and the guards. Dragging the stripped corpses down the slope, they tossed them into the river. Eiroy wasn't interested in the booty they'd taken from the bodies; the real treasure was already secured in the barge waiting at the river's edge.

Eiroy and his gang had been ordered to steal the wagon's precious cargo as it was being transported from Cross Abbey to Hierlaneum. The theft would be blamed on others; then, when the time was right, the treasure would be miraculously 'discovered' and the finders would be hailed as heroes by the Great Church. It hadn't been in the original plans for the priest and acolyte to die, but Eiroy had a plan of his own.

The loot from this haul would set him free from this life of crime, give him honor, respect, and a new life in the Celtlands, a life far away from the Romans he despised. He'd planned and he'd plotted and he'd waited for the right chance, the right time. And now the treasure claimed by the Great Church was his. Or soon would be, once he set the rest of his plan into action.

"Hurry! Toss the clothes into the fire and let's get out of here!" Eiroy yelled across the meadow. "We can't waste any more time. We'll have to go now." He didn't want to take the chance an early morning traveler or one of the Empire's soldiers would come along the road and discover the crime. Bad enough his Roman companions, following the original plan, had set the wagon on fire. A stupid idea, Eiroy thought in disgust. It increased their chances of being discovered before they could finish the job.

They'd spent weeks in the Brendan Valley, watching this stretch of heavily forested road west of the old Roman fortress of Dynsmore and east of the small, primarily Roman community of Cross Abbey. It was the perfect spot for an ambush—few dwellings, heavily wooded, little if any early morning travel, with the road running conveniently close to the river. He had known the guards would likely be careless, believing the area held little threat. He'd been right.

Eiroy looked down the embankment to the men waiting on the small barge moored against the bank, the bow facing the mighty Moryn Gweneth River, which the Romans called the River Gwen. The River of Great Blessing was certainly well named, he thought. This morning, it would bring the blessing of escape for him and his own band of thieves.

"Myrdoc, it's time! Send those men up and get your barge ready, we're about to leave." Eiroy watched in satisfaction as four men, wearing the brightly colored leggings favored by Celts, jumped from the barge and scrambled up the bank, short swords and daggers in hand.

One of the men, a younger version of Eiroy, reached his side as the Roman gang members crossed the meadow with the wagon's four horses and the sack of goods taken from the bodies. Watching them, Eiroy removed a bronze item from his belt pouch and passed it to the younger man.

"Here, brother," he whispered. "Take this and place it on your belt. Keep it with you at all times."

"It's heavy," the younger man replied. Curious, he turned it over to examine the decoration. "A rune buckle! This has the glyphs of the sacred—"

"Hush!" Eiroy shot a look at the approaching men before turning again to his brother. "This is our secret, our marker to use should we become separated from each other. You take this one. I will have the other. No Roman can decipher its meaning. Promise me you'll say nothing."

"But why—"

"I'm changing the plan. I'll explain later. Just don't lose that buckle, and don't mention it to the others." He spoke softly as the Romans approached with the horses. The men wore thick-strapped sandals, long tunics tied at the middle with leather belts; each carried long knives.

"Nice buckle. Kind of big and gaudy, don't you think?" said one of the Romans. "Oh, I forgot, Celts like that sort of thing, don't you? Is that part of the treasure? I thought we weren't gonna divide it until later." He stared at the two brothers. Celts.

He wished every last one of them had been driven out of the Empire through the pass at Carew and out into the remaining Celtlands. He would have been happy to kill them all, and often wished his ancestors had done just that. Their language was strange, and even when they decided to speak the language of the Romans, it was with a guttural, strangely slurred, afflicted accent. He knew the Celts hated the Romans for taking their land, their religion, and everything else they valued. And for that, he admitted, who could blame them?

Still, he thought, they should be grateful for the better life, the laws, and the religion the Romans brought with them. As far as he was concerned, Celts were nothing more than a bunch of untrustworthy barbarians. No, he really didn't like Celts in general, but he and these particular Celts had the same merchant employer in Hierlaneum, so he would tolerate them. After all, they were brothers-in-thievery. And it was a Celt who owned the barge which would transport them. So he would tolerate them, but he wouldn't trust them.

Usually, they'd all but fight one another to do the dirty work of the jobs they were on. This morning, however, after helping dispatch the guards, all they'd wanted to do was load the wagon's treasure. He found it strange they had no interest in looting the bodies. That made him uncomfortable considering what they'd just stolen. No, he really didn't trust Celts. And he was getting a bad feeling about this whole operation.

"It's just something I made for my brother. It's a piece of bronze I forged, nothing of value." Eiroy studied the black-haired, dark-eyed Roman. Sergio and his friends had been part of this group of thieves for nearly two years; they'd worked together often. Eiroy admired the Roman's skill with horses, but he did not like him. Like the merchant Pax Catus they worked for, Sergio and his friends weren't to be trusted.

It had been bad enough years ago, Eiroy thought, when the Romans had sent their war machines north and west to conquer this part of the vast Celtic lands. They had brutally forced their religion, society, and their form of central government—Emperor and all—on what remained of the population. It had gotten even worse when the Great Church seized control of the Roman government and instituted their cruel and irrational laws upon the land. The Roman Emperor, still on the throne but his authority castrated by a foreign religion's bureaucracy, now took direction from the Great Church's Grand Religious Cleric.

Eiroy didn't trust any of them. But they were proficient in the art of thievery and excellent horsemen all, so he tolerated them. Now, however, with the treasure securely stowed in the secret compartment below the barge's deck, he no longer had to put up with them. He'd get rid of them, strike a deal with the Celtic Queen, and never deal with Romans or churchers again.

"Let's get these horses loaded and get out of here," Sergio said, gripping the rope halter of the mare. "We need to get the treasure down to Dynsmore as quickly as possible. The priest's representative will be waiting." He took two steps forward, then stopped abruptly as the three Celts from the barge rose out of the brush. "Hey! What are they doing up here?"

"There's been a change of plans."

"What? What do you mean, a change of plans?"

"You take your men and the horses, head south. We'll take the goods on the barge."

Sergio glared at Eiroy. "We're supposed to stay together."

"Like I said, the plans have changed."

"No. We stay together, with the goods. No changes."

"I've been thinking. We should separate and meet up again at the Catus warehouse. You're the expert horseman here, so you and those two," Eiroy said, gesturing toward the other Romans, "can take them back on the road while we take the barge. We'll meet you at Dynsmore."

Sergio scowled. "You've been thinking? Ha, there's a first. Brutovius won't like this," he warned, referring to one of the men who had planned the theft. "And neither will our boss. Whatever's going on here, I don't like it." His scowl grew more pronounced, his eyes darting back and forth, studying those who faced him. He had a very bad feeling about all this.

"Nevertheless, that's how it's gonna be," Eiroy said flatly.

Sergio looked about him, weighing his odds. "We've always followed the plan. You promised, we all promised. You can't go back on your word to Brutovius. Where's your *honor*, Celt?"

"What makes you think there's any honor among thieves, Celt or otherwise?" Eiroy's smile was tight, his cold, blue eyes focused on the man before him.

"Well, if we're going our separate ways, let's divide up the spoils right here, right now."

"No."

Sergio gave him a murderous look. "What makes you think we'll leave the treasure with you, you ignorant, thieving Celt?"

"This!" Eiroy drew his weapon. His brother dropped the bronze buckle and did likewise.

It happened fast. The Roman to the right of Sergio heaved the sack he carried at the nearest Celt and pulled his dagger; the man on Sergio's left did likewise with his blade. Opponents charged, weapons at the ready—everyone but Sergio.

Realizing the odds were against him, Sergio decided to seize the moment to save himself. He swung the big horse he'd been leading around, effectively blocking the advance of his opponents. The animal jumped and stomped as Sergio jerked the rope halter, turning the beast and knocking both brothers off their feet. Leaping astride, Sergio urged the horse into a gallop toward the main road.

Meanwhile, the other men were flailing about and exchanging blows with deadly accuracy, blood spurting from fierce wounds. The crows added their own raucous screams as they abandoned the meadow for the forest. The remaining horses bolted from the meadow and followed Sergio's lead.

In moments, it was over. Both of Sergio's companions lay dead. One of the bargemen lay screaming, his entrails spilling out in a pool of blood. He wouldn't live much longer.

Eiroy helped his brother to his feet. "Are you hurt?" He dusted the dirt and damp leaves from his own clothing.

"I'm fine," his brother assured him, retrieving the bronze buckle from where it lay in the dirt. He placed it in his belt pouch. "Shouldn't we go after Sergio?"

Eiroy put away his blade and gazed across the meadow. "No, he's not important now. By the time he gets back and tells anybody what's happened, we'll be long gone and the treasure will be safely hidden."

"What do we do now?"

"Now we stash the goods and wait until it's time to bargain. Then we negotiate a deal for wealth beyond our wildest dreams. And more importantly, we make a deal that will give us freeman status forever."

Scheme, Connive
Plot and Plan
Lies, Deceptions
Disappointment
Just Reward
For the Dishonest Man.

2

August 26th in the Roman calendar
Early Morning
Six days left in the Celtic Tree Month of Coll
Two days until the Runic Half-Month of Rad

"They did what?" exclaimed Brutovius. He'd been awakened early by the frantic knocking on the door to his small apartment in the Scorpius District of the Roman city of Hierlaneum. When he opened it, a frightened Sergio barged in and blurted out an incredible story of theft and deception on a deadly scale.

Gesturing Sergio to silence, a bleary-eyed Brutovius peered out into the courtyard, making certain no one was there before shutting the door and turning to the man who'd interrupted his sleep. He ran his wrinkled, aged hand through his thick graying hair as he studied Sergio. He shook his head in disbelief. "Tell me what happened. Slower, so I can understand you."

Yesterday, Sergio had fled the scene of the crime full speed on horseback and rode all the way to just west of the small pier at the Dynsmore Crossing. There he dismounted, got a drink from the community well, and rested in a thick grove of trees, trying to figure out what he should do next. Fearing he might be followed, he watched the road back to the burning wagon, all the while keeping an eye on an ox cart and the men guarding it just west of the pier. After waiting there for some time, he rode out of the valley through the Dynsmore Fortress and on to the Roman city of Hierlaneum. He'd made it back to his cheap little hovel of a brown mud-brick one-room apartment at sunset. As darkness fell on the city, Sergio quickly ate a handful of old cheese and two slices of hard, dark bread, washing it down with wine. Exhausted, he collapsed on his sleeping pallet, worrying how he would explain it all, fearing the consequences once the theft of the treasure and Eiroy's double-crossing were revealed. Now as he stood before Brutovius, he wished he was anywhere but there. Taking a deep breath, he began again.

Sergio explained it all, how they'd followed the plan outlined by Brutovius to ambush the wagon at the precise point within the dense forest, dispatch the guards, and load the goods onto the barge. "But when it came time to leave, Eiroy told me he'd changed the plan." He described the brutal attack and everything that happened afterwards.

Brutovius looked skeptical. "So the Celts escaped, the others died, and you managed to get away without a scratch?"

"Hey! I had nothing to do with this. I barely escaped with my life. This is all Eiroy's fault, not mine. I didn't know he was going to steal the treasure for himself." Sergio's head hurt, his eyes bleary from lack of sleep. His hands shook from exhaustion, hunger, and outright fear.

"Calm down," said Brutovius impatiently. "What about the priest at Dynsmore? Did you tell him what happened?"

The Dynsmore priest, Alphonse, had been their contact, the one they'd intended to deliver the Great Cross and other goods to after the robbery. The priest was to have sequestered the treasure until an appropriate time when it would be 'discovered' by the scheming clerics and returned to the Great Church. For that, they would all be rewarded, with the thieves keeping the taxes and other treasure they took off the wagon. That was the plan devised by the Hierlaneum priest, Loxius Scrota.

It was Loxius who'd contracted the notorious criminal leader of Hierlaneum to carry out the plan, and it was that leader who had ordered Pax Catus, Brutovius, and their crew to grab the treasure for the priest. If the plan worked, the rewards would have been great. Now it seemed all that was in jeopardy.

"Alphonse was there as we'd arranged, west of the pier. I hid and waited. I wanted to see if Eiroy was going to show with the loot, but I never saw him or the barge, either. When I left, the Dynsmore priest and his men were still waiting."

"Bad, very bad," Brutovius muttered. "This has ruined everything." He would have to tell his immediate boss, Pax Catus the merchant. Worse, someone would have to tell the one they all worked for and feared— D'Ambrosio, the leader of the criminal element in Hierlaneum. It wasn't something Brutovius had any desire to do by himself if he could help it.

Brutovius was the one who had drawn up the plan to waylay the shipment. He'd planned everything, every detail including the scouting of the appropriate area along the dense forest road near the river where it would all happen. He hadn't counted on or even suspected one of his own turning on him.

"Go over it again," Brutovius instructed. "I want to hear every detail, from the time you took down the wagon to when you knocked on my door. We are going to have to let Pax Catus know, and he'll have to tell the big boss. They're not going to be happy."

Some things go right, others wrong.
Some whistle a tune, some sing a song.
Some dance a jig at the Master's call
Be it private party or public ball.
Some travel the distance, some won't go.
Been like that forever in Life's rodeo.
Get it right or get it wrong
Death still threatens the mortal throng.

3

August 26th in the Roman calendar
Afternoon
Six days left in the Celtic Tree Month of Coll
Two days until the Runic Half-Month of Rad

The meeting with D'Ambrosio did not go very well. Brutovius hadn't expected it would, but at least it wasn't as bad as it could have been, either. The merchant Pax Catus—always the coward when things went wrong—had wailed at the thought of telling his boss the treasure he'd entrusted to the crew had gone missing. Wanting no part of that conversation, Pax had insisted Brutovius and Sergio deliver the bad news.

Brutovius needed to move quickly, lest the crime boss hear of the theft from someone else. That wouldn't be good, because he might think Brutovius and his men were guilty—a thought he hoped would never cross that man's mind.

Sergio, ever the unreliable, slippery thief, had vanished, gone into hiding. He was nowhere to be found when Brutovius went to get him for their agreed upon trip to see D'Ambrosio. Little coward. Good for thieving and nothing else, thought Brutovius as he made his way to the iniquitous Scorpius District and the Delectatio Maximus, a popular pleasure establishment owned by D'Ambrosio, known to all criminal elements as The Holder.

Inside the Delectatio Maximus, colorful plaster wall murals advertised and illustrated in graphic detail the various services available within the vile establishment. As always, the place was crowded with patrons, some drunk, some passed out on the floor, most milling around the long wooden plank resting on two big casks which served as a bar. Behind the bar stood a bartender, a big guard, and numerous casks and containers of alcohol. Beyond them was a curtained doorway leading to the many small pleasure rooms. The rowdy patrons paid him scant attention; they were busy drinking, bantering, and bargaining prices with the pleasure slaves.

Brutovius crossed the front room and moved through the raucous crowd of gamblers in the next room who were wagering money on all manner of games of chance. On the far side of the room, he went through a curtained portal and into a long hallway lit by a series of oil lamps on brass pedestals, their orange light flickering, dancing against the blackish brown, soot-stained stucco walls. He paused at the door at the far end where two armed guards stood. They knew Brutovius from previous visits and one smiled at him as he entered the office of Salvatore Scalia D'Ambrosio.

Brutovius had hoped to be the first with the news about the wicked double-cross of Eiroy and his thieving band of Celts. He wanted to manage the explanation from his point of view, hoping to somehow lessen the negative impact and the potentially deadly repercussions such information was bound to instigate. But his hopes were dashed when he walked into the windowless room and saw the two men waiting there.

"If what Loxius tells me is true, you better have a good explanation for all this," The Holder said. Even when he spoke softly, as he was doing now, the short, barrel-chested old man with hooded eyes in a pock-marked face exuded danger. His hands rested on the table before him, an unsheathed gleaming dagger with a fancy black and silver handle within easy reach.

Brutovius, caught off-guard by the presence of Hierlaneum Priest Loxius Scrota, tried hurriedly to decide what to say and how he should say it. His eyes burned from the smoke of the oil lamps and the priest's thick, sweet perfume.

"Oh, it's true," said Loxius. "Brother Alphonse would never speak a lie to me. He is an honorable man, as are his brothers at Dynsmore." Loxius ran his small, pale left hand along his slick black hair, his beads rattling in his right hand as he glared at Brutovius. "The barge never showed. There had better be a very good reason why I don't have the Great Cross in my possession as we all agreed I would."

The crime boss glanced at the priest, then Brutovius. "Well?"

Brutovius explained the entire situation as he knew it, repeating every detail related to him by the only eye-witness and their sole source of information, Sergio the thief.

"Where's Sergio now?"

Brutovius nervously eyed the other men. "He was supposed to be here, but he's disappeared. He wasn't in his apartment."

"I thought your people were reliable," Loxius said with a sniff and a holier-than-thou look at The Holder. "Otherwise, I would never have approached you for this most important job." He raised his nose in the air. "Celts. You can't rely on them, you know. Not God's children at all. Most untrustworthy."

D'Ambrosio gave the priest an almost amused look. "If your priests and church associates were so much better, why didn't you hire them to steal the treasure?"

The smug look on the priest's face vanished, replaced by one of anger. "Don't make light of such a serious matter. The Great Cross and all the goods taken with it are irreplaceable. They belong to the Great Church. Now, I want that treasure returned and I need it done soon, you understand?"

"Yeah, I understand you. You want the treasure like I want you to pay me all those drinking, gambling, and pleasure debts you owe me." He smiled but he wasn't amused, not in the least. The priest was a frequent visitor to the Delectatio Maximus. He'd run up a large unpaid tab and The Holder was nearing the end of his patience with him.

The priest—surprised, insulted and clearly embarrassed—sputtered, "I've told you, I'll pay you just as soon as I get my hands on the cache you promised to deliver. It will ensure my appointment to the Bishop's post. Don't worry, you'll get your money. And I had better get the Great Cross. I'll give you some time to find it and make this right, or else."

"Or else what?"

Loxius leaned across the table a bit closer to The Holder. "Or else I may have to have the Great Church intervene and shut this operation of yours down for good. Delightfully sinful little place that it is." Loxius laughed out loud and with a swish of his dark silk tasseled robes, stalked out of the room.

Brutovius remained standing in silence, waiting to see if he would be dismissed by the boss or if the guards outside would be ordered to slit his throat. Either option seemed possible. He was getting too old for this, he thought.

D'Ambrosio gestured rudely in the direction of the departing priest. "Shut me down." He laughed. "That's a good one. Well, we'll just see about that. Wonder how interested the Great Church would be in knowing the theft of their precious treasure was all his idea?"

His laughter was interrupted by a loud coughing fit. He reached over, picked up a bottle from the table, uncorked it, and took a long, slow drink of wine. "Any idea where we can find your man Eiroy?"

"Probably still in the Brendan Valley." Brutovius shuffled his feet slightly and dropped his shoulders, relaxing, happy the conversation seemed to be moving toward a solution to the problem rather than retribution for failure. "He has a room nearby, over at the Rodas Villa. We should keep an eye on the place in case he returns."

"Good idea. Where do you suppose he's hiding out? Or where he's stashed the treasure?"

"No idea."

"You familiar with the Brendan Valley?"

"I know a little something about it. I was born there," said Brutovius. It was one of the reasons Pax wanted Brutovius to plan the details of this latest operation, but Brutovius had no wish to remind The Holder of that little fact.

"You were, huh?" He studied Brutovius for some time, thinking. "You'd better get over there and see if you can find him, find out where he's hidden that treasure. I'll send two of my best men along. They can handle any trouble you might get into, but they don't know their way around the valley."

"Yes, sir."

"One more thing."

"What's that?"

"Don't come back here with any more bad news."

Brutovius gulped. "No, sir."

"And don't leave the Brendan Valley until you find Eiroy or the treasure, understand?"

Duty bound, wear the frown,
The orders are well taken.
Tasks at hand wear you down.
Puzzled
Or Worse
Seemingly cursed
We are challenged
But not shaken.

4

August 28th in the Roman calendar
Noon
Four days left in the Celtic Tree Month of Coll

The waning heat of late August was wearing on Orrs, the Roman Commander stationed at the small, primarily Roman town of Cross Abbey. He was tasked with overseeing the activity of its inhabitants and maintaining law and order within the Brendan Valley, serving as a tenuous buffer between the Roman Empire to the east of the valley and the Celtlands to the west. He'd spent the last five years there as an Enforcer of the Great Church and its laws and regulations as directed by the military Prefect in Hierlaneum. He commanded the garrisons at both Cross Abbey and Dynsmore, a job he usually enjoyed.

He wore the gold-trimmed red tunic and black mail coat with inlaid red enamel and trappings of the Roman Commander. Just over thirty years old, he was of average build with thick black hair cut in regulation Roman style. He knew many thought him unhappy because he seldom smiled. At the moment he certainly couldn't think of any reason to smile. Cursing the murdering, thieving Celts who'd stolen the Great Cross, Orrs reached for his water flask and drank deeply before turning his attention back to the parchment scroll that had been delivered by military messenger that morning. Its arrival was no surprise.

The tersely worded missive from the Hierlaneum authorities detailed what was known about the theft, and was highly critical of Commander Orrs himself for not placing sufficient guard on the shipment. The Prefect in Hierlaneum demanded an explanation; Orrs was to report immediately to Hierlaneum and deliver that information in person.

Orrs sighed deeply and looked up as the outer door opened to admit Pluvius, the military Enforcer he'd summoned as soon as the messenger had departed. Absently noting the Enforcer's rigidly correct attire—red cape fastened precisely over a black tunic and a black mail coat inlaid with red enamel—Orrs gestured him to a seat. Grimly, he outlined the orders issued them.

"I can't believe this," exclaimed Pluvius. He'd been a soldier and faithful follower of the Great Church for most of his thirty-plus years, and liked to think of himself as second in command there at the Cross Abbey garrison. The news he'd just received disturbed him greatly. "I still cannot believe the Great Cross was stolen …"

"Our orders are clear. We are to find the treasure, and we are to bring the thieves in alive and question them—"

"Alive?" asked an incredulous Pluvius. "Whoever did this should be executed the moment we find them. Stealing from the Great Church and murdering priests! They cannot be allowed to get away with this outrage."

"Can't disagree with you on that point—"

"We need to catch and kill these blasphemous murderers," interrupted Pluvius. "The very idea of our sacred Great Cross in the hands of Celts—"

"Our first priority is find the treasure. Failing that, we need to locate the outlaws responsible and interrogate them." He paused for another drink of water. "And we need them alive. Getting information will be impossible if they are dead."

Orrs turned from his desk and looked out the window at the courtyard inside his walled, fortified compound. It seemed perfectly rational to him to want the thieves alive. After all, they were their best leads to find the treasure. There would be plenty of time to execute them after the valuables were recovered.

Pluvius snorted. "From the sound of it," he said, pointing to the scroll, "we'd better find something useful to save our ranks or we'll both be cursed with demotions."

"We need to be on the lookout for that barge, too," said Orrs, turning back to the desk and eyeing the list of instructions on the scroll. "Should be an easy thing to spot. Hard to hide something so large. Probably going to find it long before we find the murdering thieves or the treasure."

"And you have to go explain why we did not escort the Great Cross safely back? What will you tell them?"

"The truth, of course." Orrs gazed out the window, thinking hard. He had personally ordered a significant detachment of troops from the Dynsmore garrison to escort the sacred item safely from Hierlaneum to Cross Abbey for the dedication ceremonies of the new church expansion and recruiting festivities. And he'd been waiting for Father Caton at the Cross Abbey church to request an escort back once the festivities ended.

Ever since he'd learned of the theft, he'd been both puzzled and suspicious. Why, he wondered, had they allowed such a valuable shipment to be sent out without his military garrison's escort?

Pluvius had another question. "You don't think they believe we had anything to do with this, do you?"

"I hope not."

"They can't believe we would steal from the Great Church

and murder our own holy men, can they?" Pluvius asked angrily. He worried about what those in positions of power might think about him, fearing they'd think he was unfaithful, disloyal to both his military duties and his church.

Orrs raised his right hand as a signal for quiet. "If I were them, I would be asking some very hard questions of everyone involved." Changing the subject he asked, "When we talked with Father Caton, did you notice anything odd about him?" They had both interviewed the head priest at the Cross Abbey church immediately after being alerted to the crimes.

"Nothing in particular. He seemed nervous and obviously distraught, but then he'd just lost Father Verdonian and one of his acolytes on that wagon. The Great Cross and the other treasure had been stolen. And he's been under a lot of stress these last few months supervising all the stonemasons and the laborers completing the church addition and organizing the recruiting festivities."

"Maybe that was it," Orrs agreed. "But in the three years I've known him, I've never seen him so reluctant to talk. I think he was hiding something. Something important. And I still don't understand why he did not ask for a military escort back to Hierlaneum."

Pluvius was stunned. "You don't think a priest of our Great Church would have anything to do with this, do you? I can hardly believe such a serious accusation is warranted!"

"Then why send that wagon out all but unprotected? I'm not satisfied with his answer. Not satisfied at all."

"I believed him, Commander," said Pluvius, taking a dried mushroom out of his belt pouch and popping it in his mouth. "It's like he told us, he was certain God would protect them after having blessed them with such a fine new building and scores of new members coming forward during the worship and celebration festivities. He didn't think there was any need to bother us for an escort back. He told us he feared God would be angry with him for having such little faith. It's not fair to think he had anything to do with what happened."

Orrs considered that for a moment. "Maybe, but I think there's more he's not telling us."

"Well, they are looking for Celts," Pluvius said, pointing to the parchment scroll on the table. "Not Romans and certainly not priests of the Great Church." He popped another piece of dried mushroom into his mouth.

"I want you to take some men and head out west of here, scout around along the river. Ask questions, see what you can find out. I have to go meet the Hierlaneum Prefect."

"Hrmpt," mumbled Pluvius, "as if any Celt in this valley will willingly give us any information."

"True." Orrs knew it was a tenuous peace they'd managed to keep. They were barely tolerated by the Celts. Some were still outright hostile, but open warfare had so far been avoided for many years. He knew that was due in part to the efforts of one Celt in particular, the Chief Magistrate for Brendan Valley—the one Celt Orrs trusted. "Elder Eghan of Oaks will need to be officially notified of this incident. He and his men may be of some assistance to us in this matter."

The old Celtic system of magistrates had been keep intact to help placate a hostile population, maintain order, and uphold the laws mandated by the Romans. It was much more cost efficient than having to station thousands more military in the area and certainly less stressful for both sides.

"Go with your men as far as the town of Elshorn," Orrs directed. "You can stop there and brief Elder Eghan. Have your men continue west to the Celtlands border and report anything they may learn about these outlaws or the treasure. Then I want you to come back here until I return."

"How much should I tell the Chief Magistrate?"

"Just tell him what he needs to know. We're looking for a group of Celt outlaws or information on their whereabouts.

Give him the names and descriptions we have. Tell him we'll know more after my trip." Privately, Orrs thought the Chief Magistrate probably already knew more of the incident than any Roman.

"I can't wait to see that old man's face when I tell him it's Celts we're looking for." Pluvius laughed, his odd, giggling laugh. He saluted and exited the Commander's room.

Orrs watched him go, pondering the man's strange sense of humor. He looked beyond his garrison's walled enclosure to the distant mountains. The Commander found nothing remotely amusing about the whole affair of murder and stolen treasure. He feared there would be more deaths to come before this mystery was solved.

Harvest Time this month of Muin
When Life's materials are gathered soon
For all below the Sun and Moon.
Collected, processed, made much Higher
Prophetic powers by Lugh's own Fire.
Deity of Light and Intellectual Acquire
'Tis the Month of Spiritual Illumination
Blending with Dreams in Collaboration
To give Life's Mysteries Interpretation.

5

September 2nd in the Roman calendar
Morning
The Celtic Tree Month of Muin (Vine) begins

Murders were unusual for Elshorn and within the Brendan Valley. Murder in and of itself was troubling at any time, but the Chief Magistrate knew the murder of a Roman citizen by a Celt was particularly troubling. The situation could easily ignite the simmering tensions and invite some very unpleasant reactions from the occupying Romans who controlled the area.

This murder happened unexpectedly, in the evening just before sunset in front of Elshorn's tavern and common house. Unlike some previous murders, Elder Eghan was confident he would soon find out the how, why, and who of it all in this case. There was a witness.

Elder Eghan sat on his cool stone bench under the sprawling oak tree in the courtyard of the Magistrates' Compound in the small town of Elshorn, rubbing his chin and fiddling with his long, flowing white moustache as he listened to the man who'd witnessed a Roman's death the night before. The witness was his long-time friend, Elder Blaine the Slender.

"And you don't know what started it, Blaine? No idea why he would have killed this man?" asked Eghan.

Elder Blaine—five years beyond retirement after presiding over his final official initiation ceremony at the Holy Celtic Site of Highdyn Hill and the Standing Stones—scratched his head, belched, and conjured his recollections of the night before. He took a drink from the cup of water he was holding before he answered. "I was talking with the man who did the killing, just before it happened. He asked me about someone he was looking for, his brother I think he said it was. Then the other rider, the Roman who died, came up."

"Start from the beginning and tell me everything that happened," said Elder Eghan, anxious to learn all he could about this murder of a Roman by a Celt.

Blaine ran his hands through his thick white hair, considering how to explain what had happened. Though some parts remained hazy, he recalled some of the awful incident clearly and was likely to have it etched in his memory the rest of his life.

He'd seen the big black horse the moment he stepped out from the Five Fingers tavern, a two-story common house in the center of Elshorn. He doubted he would ever forget the eerie sensation that had come over him as the setting sun spotlighted the stallion's muscular frame and highlighted a large, white cross-shaped blaze on its chest.

The scene was an indelible panorama. Elder Blaine remembered thinking the mysterious mix of light and shadow could not possibly bode well, would somehow issue forth unpleasant things. The churchers might call that superstition, but Celts knew such things were omens. And omens were not something his sixty-two years of Druidic, Celtic upbringing would let him ignore. Yes, the whole vision was foreboding, he thought.

"I knew something bad was going to happen, felt uncomfortable as I stepped out of the tavern and onto the road," he said, wagging a crooked finger at his old friend. "The bright light, dark shadows. Bad omens were afoot. I knew I'd stayed in town too long."

"Omens, you say?"

Blaine shifted on his seat and adjusted his tunic. "Thinking back on it now, I know I'm right. The cross-shaped blaze on the horse is a harbinger of future events, an omen of great import."

"And the man who rode this horse? What of him?"

"He confronted me almost as soon as I'd stepped out onto the road," said Blaine, remembering the black horse prancing slowly along the dusty, wheel-rutted surface, its rider staring hard at him as the horse sidestepped and turned its back to the sunset's vivid glow.

"That's when the rider asked about the man he sought?"

Blaine nodded.

"This man was a stranger to you? You'd never seen him before? Are you certain he was a Celt?" Elder Eghan had hoped there was some evidence that both murderer and victim were Roman, thus taking the pressure off the Celts of the valley. Unfortunately, Blaine's account seemed to prove just the opposite. The only good thing about this murder, if there was such a thing, was the fact neither man involved was from Elshorn.

"That's right. My eyes aren't what they used to be but, yes, I'm certain he was a Celt. He wore striped leggings and I could see light reddish-blond hair, even though he was wearing a leather helmet pulled tight down around his ears. His eyes were blue, his complexion fair. His accent was ours, even though he spoke the Roman language."

Eghan remembered the description the Roman Enforcer Pluvius had given him of the men involved in that business with the Great Cross. Blaine's description was a perfect match.

"What happened next?"

"I am certain he was a Celt, but I decided not to take any chances—not with that gall, that rude stranger. You know how it is, danger lurking everywhere. I reached under my cape and grasped the handle of the dagger I keep in my belt. One can't be too careful these days, you know." He paused and saw Eghan nod in agreement. "I walked over to him, but I was careful not to let him see my dagger."

"And who was it he asked you about?"

Blaine scratched his chin. "He was looking for his brother Eiroy and asked me if I knew him. I told him no."

"Hmm, you don't know anyone named Eiroy? You're certain?" asked Eghan, remembering the names on the list of the outlaws given him by the Enforcer from Cross Abbey. Eiroy was on that list. Coincidence? Not likely, he thought.

"I know no such person," said Blaine. "Do you?"

Eghan shook his head and motioned for his friend to continue. If his suspicions were true about the wanted outlaw, it would be valuable information to pass along to his Roman boss, Commander Orrs.

"There is something else that might be important," Blaine continued. "When I looked up into the Celt's face I saw fear. He was nervous, too. He never stopped looking around him."

"He was afraid?"

"Yes," replied Blaine. He scratched his chin, looked up and considered a memory.

"Maybe he knew this Roman was after him?"

"Perhaps. Anyway, he said he had just returned from the Celtlands and his brother was missing. He thought he might be in town here, maybe in the tavern. He told me he needed to find him quickly." Blaine paused and took another sip of water. "I told him again I knew no such person. That's when he showed me his belt buckle."

The Chief Magistrate was puzzled. "Belt buckle? Why?"

"The man he was looking for wore one just like it, or so he said. It was a big bronze belt buckle with rune designs but with these old eyes I could not make them out."

"Runes? Have you ever seen such a buckle before?"

"No. I told him to go ask someone else. Told him to look in the tavern himself because I hadn't seen anyone inside fitting his description." He turned his cup slowly with both hands. "He was rude. I didn't like him. I had already answered his questions but he persisted. I was tired and wanted to get home."

Elder Eghan waited for Blaine to continue. As the Chief Magistrate it would be his responsibility to investigate and to report his findings to Commander Orrs. If the man Blaine talked with, the one who committed the murder, was the same Eiroy that the Romans were seeking, Eghan knew anything Blaine could remember could be valuable.

"Everything is a bit cloudy in my memory after that."

"Cloudy?"

"Confusion has clouded my recollection, old friend, like the thick fog hanging over the river marshes in the early morning. I do remember raising my hand and motioning for him to be gone, letting him know I had no desire to speak with him any further. But then the other rider came charging up. The man speaking to me turned his head and his mount around to face this rider. It all gets kind of blurry and difficult to remember after that."

"They fought?"

Elder Blaine thought a moment, trying to relive the scene so he could explain it. He remembered stepping back and covering his nose and mouth with his arm, hoping he would not breathe the dust that swirled about them. The galloping horse, its Roman rider dressed in the typical red and white cloth tunic favored by followers of the Great Church, came to a stop facing him and the other rider. The dust cloud enveloped them all. "They didn't fight immediately." Blaine took another drink, contemplating memories.

Eghan waited for him to continue. When he did not, he prompted, "And?"

"Oh," mumbled Blaine, embarrassed. "Well, the dust was so bad I coughed and choked and my eyes burned. I know they were talking but I just wanted to get home."

"I understand," said Eghan, rubbing his chin and nodding. "But you have no idea what they said to each other?"

Blaine struggled to remember. "I think the Roman greeted him by name," he finally said. "He called him Eiroy."

"Strange. That's it? Nothing more?"

"You know how it is after a long evening in the tavern," he said, giving his old friend a sheepish look. "Wine sometimes plays tricks with the memory. And last night, the dark drink pulsed through my veins like the warmth of Arianrod's blessings. Thinking back on it now, maybe the Roman rider said something about a cross. That's why I think the omen of the cross-shaped blaze on the horse is so important."

Eghan compared Blaine's story with the information he'd received about the men who'd stolen the treasure. The man Blaine described as the murderer fit one of the descriptions very well. "Can you remember anything else? Something the Celt may have said to the Roman? Perhaps why they were here? Where they were from? Where they were going?"

"No."

"Anything you can remember might help us."

"Oh, well, I definitely remember what happened next. I'll never forget it. The murder, I mean. The Roman glared down at me, lifted his right foot from the side of his mount and kicked at me. Told me to be gone while I could still walk."

Eghan raised an eyebrow. "He kicked you?"

"I jumped back in time to avoid the worst of it. I kept a tight grip on my dagger and backed up several steps. He turned his attention from me and back to the mounted Celt. I brushed the

Roman's boot print from my cape and began my walk home. I never wanted to see those two ever again. But, as fate would have it, I'd only taken a few steps when I heard the unmistakable sound of weapons being drawn, followed by a clashing of steel on steel and then a loud scream. I heard horses snort and crash into each other, and then I heard the sound of something falling. I tell you, the hair stood up on the back of my neck. I turned and saw the Roman lying still in the dusty street, hands gripping a bloody short sword. His horse was trembling and backing away from his body."

"And the Celt?"

"He kicked his own horse hard and he rode away. He was slumped over a little. I remember thinking he might have been injured. I watched him head down the road and turn at the corner of the Money Lenders. He went out of sight, down through the trees, heading toward the river."

"Are you certain he went to the river?"

"Well, it looked that way. Of course, there's no telling where he ended up going after I lost sight of him. Anyway, I looked down at the body lying in the dusty road, splattered there on the ground like so much bird droppings. There was a lot of blood. Looked like his throat had been cut. Probably died instantly." Blaine swallowed the remaining water in his cup. "And that's all I remember."

Interview terminated, Elder Eghan watched his friend leave the compound. There would be more problems for the people of Elshorn and the Brendan Valley before this unhappy affair was concluded. It was time, Eghan thought, to call his magistrates together.

It comes to us …
Daylight reality, moonlight dreams.
Wonderful things or nightmare scenes.
While awake or while we sleep.
Outward hopes or secrets deep.
Light or dark, manifested above.
It comes to us …
A swirling, churning thing called Love.

6

September 6th in the Roman calendar
Pre-Dawn
Five days into the Celtic Tree Month of Muin

The young apprentice deputy magistrate Weylyn woke from a frightening dream and sat up, sweating, eyes open to the dark room that was his small home. Still early, he judged, certain he'd not slept through the morning bell which rang in the compound an hour before sunrise. Whatever this day might bring, he hoped it wouldn't be worse than the trouble they'd seen in town ever since the murder of the Roman, trouble made worse by the arrival of bounty hunters. Last night's brawl in the tavern had been just the latest disruption of the peace in Elshorn, and Weylyn had a feeling there was more trouble to come.

He lay still, listening. No one was stirring in the compound yet. No sound of shuffling feet in the courtyard, water being drawn, wood being hauled. No scent of morning cook fires in progress. He tossed his cover off, attempting to cool down and forget last night's trouble and the bad dreams that had followed. He stretched to relieve his aching muscles. The brown-haired, blue-eyed eighteen-year-old settled back down and closed his eyes and his memory brought back the nightmare in vivid detail. He was sitting in a surreal version of the Elshorn tavern with the indentured servant and tavern maid, Adrianna, sitting opposite him. In the weird way of dreams, mugs had danced on the table in front of them as fistfights broke out around them. A third mug danced to the side at the end of the table. A small, ghostly figure rose from the mug and, raising his arms declared, "The Celt Weylyn and the dark-eyed Roman beauty Adrianna have reached a stalemate, an impasse."

From an adjacent table another ghostly figure had risen—a frightening, black manifestation of Death itself. It rose higher over the table, growing larger by the second, blocking out the men fighting in the background. Weylyn had recoiled and yelled for Adrianna to run for her life, but she'd only laughed at him across the table as the dark specter of Death raised a hand to strike Weylyn down. Suddenly, a guardian wolf appeared, attacking the dark spirit and saving Weylyn.

Fully awake now, he stood up from his bed and stretched again. He often had dreams like that. While some details varied, every single one included the hand of death hovering above him, poised to strike. And even as death approached, there was always a wolf—his personal Celtic totem—that came to save him.

When he'd told Adrianna about the dreams and the wolf, she would only laugh and mock him for believing in something as superstitious and silly as a personal totem. "Forget all those pagan things and join my church," she would say, flashing those beautiful dark eyes and hugging him tightly.

Dreaming of Adrianna was both pleasant and a nightmare all its own—even if no dark specter of death ever appeared. He thought about the latest dream's ghostly figure from the mug and his proclamation he and his romantic partner were at an impasse. Sadly, it was accurate. He shook his head and rubbed his eyes. He often went to sleep trying to find a solution to the problems between them. As yet, no solution had shown itself. He was angry with the gods of chaos for putting this formidable barrier between them. Of course, it was religious in nature. The gods seemed to enjoy playing this game with mere mortals. Their time together lately almost always seemed to end badly—especially if the subject of religion came up. Neither of them wanted to compromise their beliefs for the other.

"You think your gods are on the earth, in the forests? Ha! Ridiculous! Every civilized person knows God is in Heaven!" Adrianna mocked him.

It was the same old argument. No matter how much time they spent together, there was that seemingly insurmountable obstacle of contrasting religious beliefs which left them in two very different worlds. He remembered his response the last time she'd jeered at him. "God is everywhere, Adrianna. Not just in the sky, but all things. The trees, the grass, the water, the air, in this world, in the Otherworld. God is in all of us."

As usual, she scoffed at his Elder Faith beliefs, ridiculed the idea of anything other than the faith of the Great Church. It was happening more often these days and it was depressing. He didn't want to lose her, but there didn't seem to be any way to resolve this impasse. The Druids at Highdyn Hill had said the star of love, Venus, was in fall this cycle. He winced at the thought of Adrianna's response when he'd told her about that.

"Forget them! They aren't allowed to practice here in the valley any longer. They're nothing but a bunch of mindless, godless pagans. They don't recognize God or they'd join the Great Church. When our forces decree it, our armies will cross over at Carew and destroy them once and for all!"

He hadn't responded. It had been all he could do to keep his temper. He thought how offended and angry she'd become if her churcher religion were forbidden to exist and her clerics and their enclosed buildings were destroyed. She seemed oblivious to how much her hatred of his faith hurt him and angered him.

Weylyn had tried talking to his friend and fellow magistrate, Teg, about the situation with Adrianna but had given up after several attempts, realizing it was pointless. All Teg offered was laughter and ridicule—which he heaped out in huge doses—about Weylyn pursuing a Roman female, and an indentured tavern servant, at that! He'd suggested Weylyn get him a Celt girl, someone who shared and respected his beliefs and culture. After that, Weylyn had never broached the subject again with his friend. He wished he could drop the whole subject and never discuss it again with Adrianna, but he knew that wasn't to be.

Weylyn stretched his arms, rotating his shoulders. His body ached all over, not just from tossing and turning from the nightmare, but from the tavern brawl last night. It had happened right in the middle of one of his depressing on-again, off-again discussions with Adrianna. The tavern had been packed with Elshorn residents as well as with Roman churchers set on giving the Celts a hard time. Adding to the noise were soldiers and bounty hunters—churchers and otherwise—from outside the valley. They'd been all over the lower valley searching for the Celt who'd killed the man last week in front of the tavern. The Roman Prefects had issued a large reward for his capture—alive.

The magistrates, with the help of a few citizens, finally broke up the brawl, but not before it left the tavern in near shambles, Teg injured, and Weylyn himself no closer to resolving his problems with his young love, Adrianna.

Yawning, he made his way outside, splashed water on his face from the water barrel, and hoped things would get better once this new day got underway.

Fate can often deal a hand
Send us out into the land
Seeking that we all must seek.
The venture's not for mild or meek.
Leave the home, the warmth and fire
Seek the future, quench desire.
Hurry, hurry. Don't delay.
Come out from the hideaway.
There is but little time to spend
Before we stop at journey's end.

7

September 6th in the Roman calendar
Midday
Five days into the Celtic Tree Month of Muin

The hearth of gray stone, set in the center of the Great Room of the Chief Magistrate's building, belched fire and midday smoke as food and drink simmered in kettles and pots above the flames. Servants set out the meal before leaving to complete their daily duties elsewhere in the compound, leaving the Chief Magistrate to conduct the meeting with his deputies as they ate.

In addition to Teg and Weylyn, there were three other deputy magistrates working in the Brendan Valley. Elder Eghan had summoned them by runner four days ago from their designated areas: York from Gemma, to the south across the Moryn Gweneth River; Finn of Doane in the fertile upper eastern valley; and Chad from Carew in the west where the fortress stood guard over the entrance to the Celtlands. With the situation growing increasingly dangerous, he'd wanted them together to discuss the situation they faced.

"The death of a Roman murdered here in Elshorn by a Celt

has attracted many outsiders hoping to collect the large reward for the killer offered by the Roman Prefect," he told his deputies. "I fear last night's fight in the tavern won't be the last trouble we'll see. We'll all need to be careful."

"More careful than Teg was, apparently," Finn observed, grinning at his fellow magistrate.

Teg's right ankle was swollen at least twice its size and he had to use a walking stick to hobble around. Swallowing his last gulp of barley and beef soup, Teg responded, "Not too painful I couldn't put a knot on your head with this cane."

The others laughed, including Elder Eghan.

"Maybe you'd like to have a go at me when you heal up, eh?"

"I'd do it now and beat you fair but I'd spill my drink." He raised his cup as if to toast his old friend.

Elder Eghan smiled. "Enough. We need to save our energies for maintaining order and I don't want any of you injured further, especially by each other. This is serious. I don't like how much attention the Prefect has focused on our valley, nor do I like the interest in taking this outlaw alive. Something strange is going on here and we will all need to be on our guard."

The magistrates were the law-keepers and law enforcement of the Celts. Out beyond the walled fortress of Carew where the Celtic Queen resided, her magistrates continued to operate under her supreme direction. But in the Brendan Valley following the invasion and occupation, magistrates took their direction from the Roman military Prefect and military Enforcers assigned by the Great Church's Grand Cleric to keep law and order within the valley. It was at best a tenuous buffer between the remaining free Celtlands and the Roman Empire.

"Most of those trouble makers who caused the ruckus at the tavern last night have moved south across the river," said York, "and look to be heading to my area around Gemma." He got up from his chair and carried his empty bowl to the hearth, then refilled his drink and stood by the fire.

"I expect they will search Gemma thoroughly as they work their way south from the Moryn Gweneth all the way to the mines along the Cliffs of the Dragon and into the southern Brendans," said Elder Eghan. "If they find this wanted man quickly, I'll breathe a sigh of relief. Until that happens, I want each and every one of you to keep your eyes and ears open. If you get any information at all, tell me."

"And if we find him before the Romans do?" Teg asked.

"I want the outlaw captured and brought to me alive, if possible. The Prefect ordered it. If we find him, we will certainly turn him over to them and wash our hands of this affair."

"Well, there's been no reported sighting of him yet," said Chad. "He hasn't been seen trying to get through the pass at Carew yet. Following the instructions you sent along with the summons, I dispatched a runner to the Celtlands to inform them of his description."

The Elder nodded his approval. "Access to much of this valley is quite limited, due of course in large part to our fortress at Carew and the Roman fortress at Dynsmore. He hasn't gone east through Dynsmore or the Romans would have seen him."

"When I get back to Doane, I'll gather some men, make inquiries, and we'll search the northeast, Elder," said Finn.

The Elder set down his empty bowl, drank his hot tisane, and cleared his throat. "We've conducted a thorough search of Elshorn. He hasn't been seen along the Moryn Gweneth River, nor has he been seen along the road to Blaire."

"Maybe he drowned night-crossing the river," offered Finn.

The Elder held his cup with both hands and considered Finn's reply. "The witness we have claims he thought the outlaw was wounded in the fight with the man who died, but we don't know for certain. If he did drown, then his horse should have been found by now. No, I doubt he drowned."

The others considered the Elder's opinion and nodded.

"Where could he be then, Elder?" asked Teg, gingerly

moving his leg to make his swollen ankle more comfortable.

"Perhaps he never crossed the river. It's possible that he might have doubled back toward the Aingeal Mountain north of here," said Elder Eghan, sipping his drink.

"Ah, well then," said York, "with Teg hobbling around like a crippled old woman this could be a job for our youngest deputy, don't you think, Elder?" Returning to his chair, York slapped Weylyn's shoulder and sat down beside him. "Assuming, of course, he can get his mind off that tavern girl long enough." York laughed. The others joined in, friendly and teasing.

Weylyn looked up and grinned but said nothing, his mind focused elsewhere. He was feeling the effects of the tavern fight and the lack of sleep and was only vaguely aware of the conversation around him. He'd eaten almost nothing of his meal as Elder Eghan gave his briefing. He watched the smoke rise up through the central chimney. It slipped away, disappearing into a hazy dark place, seemingly irretrievable. The smoke reminded him of the way his relationship had become with Adrianna.

"With Teg temporarily out of commission, I agree with you," said the Elder, eyeing his youngest deputy. Weylyn had promise. He'd proven himself a loyal apprentice, but Eghan wasn't certain the young man was ready for such a heavy responsibility.

Chad had something other than murder on his mind. "What do you want us to do if we find this missing treasure?"

"Ah, the treasure. Finding the outlaw is one thing. Finding the treasure, however, is quite a different matter." Elder's expression turned serious. He stood up from his seat, turned toward the fire and placed his hands behind his back, thinking.

"They say a lot of coins and gems were stolen," Finn said.

"A valuable haul, if that's true," said York.

The Chief Magistrate turned his back to the hearth and faced his deputies. "Valuable, indeed, and much more. You deserve to know more, because it may affect your safety. You have already heard there was a holy relic stolen during transport from the Church at Cross Abbey. It was on loan for the annual Mother Goddess celebrations the churchers call Saint Mary's. And as you say, York, other valuables such as the taxes and tithes were also taken. But the holy relic they call the Great Cross is certainly the most highly prized of the missing items. My simple order, if you do happen to find this treasure, is to secure it as best you can, tell no one but your most trusted men, and let me know immediately so I can get you help."

"We've all heard of this relic, of course, Elder. It is said to be of filigreed gold, encrusted with a fortune in jewels. Is that true?" asked Finn.

"That is true, but there's much more to the story. The gold in the piece is said to have been poured from the pure gold of a stolen sacred Druidic cauldron taken as the Roman armies overran the area now called Hierlaneum. But perhaps more valuable than the gold itself is a sacred piece of Celtic amber. That, too, was stolen from our ancestors."

"Arianrod's Amber," whispered Chad reverently.

"Yes," said the Elder. "The churchers mounted it on the center of their Great Cross. They claim within this amber one can see the face of their Saint Mary. We Celts know better. Long before the invention of their Saint Mary, this amber contained the face of Arianrod, our Celtic Mother Goddess."

Teg gave a long, soft whistle. "That would be quite a treasure to find!"

"Be on your guard. Safeguard any information you come across, and get word to me immediately. Remember, it's not just Romans who would kill to find this treasure. There are some among us who want to recover what they believe belongs to we Celts. Indeed, it's quite likely there are as many Celts as there are Romans out there searching for the treasure."

New day dawned, tears roll down
Missing maiden out of town
Elder's gone to who knows where
Sun travels the sky without a care
Life of mysteries, daunting, interesting
Challenging and often so unclear.

8

September 7th in the Roman calendar
Noon
Six days into the Celtic Tree Month of Muin

"Missing?" Druce set his traveler's pack on the wooden table, never taking his eye off the woman. "What do you mean Fionna is missing?" He brushed the dust off his blue tunic with the embroidered white tree pattern down both sides, soiled after his ride to Elshorn from the Celtlands.

As a guild runner, a messenger for the Celtic Magistrate's Guild in the Celtlands, Druce was in Elshorn on the Queen's official business. Unofficially, he was here to see Moyna de Aine, a widow he had long hoped to marry, should she ever make up her mind to do so. Each and every visit to Elshorn was a reason to stop and see her.

"All she's talked about is that missing treasure everyone's looking for. It's my father's fault, of course. He's filled her head with crazy ideas. He even told her that he has friends who could help them find it. Crazy talk, that's all it is."

"She's with Elder Petroytrix then?"

"I've been to his house and she's not there." She paused, frowning. "Neither is he. My mother says he left with some friends on a mission he would not speak of and made no mention of when they'd be back."

"And Fionna didn't go with him?"

"No, she was with me the day after my father left. I overheard her talking with her friend Kelwin—he has the cart that takes our goods to market. She was upset my father told her to stay off the mountain. Because of the danger, he said."

"Danger? What danger?"

"I have no idea." Moyna nervously straightened her pale green linen dress with its delicate flower pattern trim and set the cups on the table top, not looking at her suitor. "All I know is she's missing. And with all these soldiers and bounty hunters in the area …" She broke down, sobbing.

He hugged her tightly, stroking her hair. "There, there. She's a bright girl. Fionna can take care of herself."

She pushed away from him, wiping tears from her eyes. "I'm frightened about where she is, how she is." Her voice trailed away for a moment. "And there have been so many strangers in our land since she's disappeared. There's no telling what might have happened to her."

"She's probably out somewhere having fun exploring, hoping she'll find this treasure. The young are like that."

Moyna's dark eyes flashed at him. "Don't make jokes."

He dropped his head, sorry he'd said anything.

"She's always been such a reliable girl, very dependable. If she goes off even for an afternoon she always tells me. This treasure talk has got her thinking crazy things."

"She's also the active and adventurous type," he reminded her. "You've said as much many times."

Moyna collected herself and with an effort regained her composure. Druce was always kind to her, never tried to force himself, and from the very beginning made his desire for marriage known. He would be a good husband and a fine, reliable step-father to her daughter.

Moyna's brother, Glyn, was close friends with Druce, and he had introduced them after the death of Moyna's husband. Glyn, who held a high office within the Queen's Magistrate Guild, would be all too happy to have his sister and his niece move into the Celtlands. Druce's employment as an official guild runner paid well and he would have no trouble supporting the family. The only sticking point was Druce lived in the Celtlands, outside Brendan Valley. While Moyna would have gladly moved, her daughter Fionna cared little for the idea, and Moyna was reluctant to take the girl so far away from her grandparents.

"I should not have burdened you with all this," she apologized. "Now, let's talk about you. Tell me why you have come and how long you can stay." Her smile was warm and welcoming.

Druce smiled in return. "I've been sent to brief the Chief Magistrate about information the guild has gathered on that missing treasure. While I'm there, I can ask the magistrates to look for your daughter if you'd like. In fact, I'm certain your brother would insist I do just that."

She smiled up at him, eyes bright. "Would you, please? I wouldn't dare ask myself. I'm afraid they may not see this as important, not when there's so much else to do."

"Put those fears to rest. Elder Eghan is a fair man and one concerned with the well-being of everyone in this valley."

She nodded gratefully. "Sit. Let's eat. You must be thirsty and hungry after your ride." She served a meal of dark bread, goat cheese, and walnuts as their conversation about Fionna continued. "She's taken Brokan's horse—"

"Fionna stole a horse?" Druce was flabbergasted. Brokan ran the small livery stable where he cared for the horses and chariots of the Chief Magistrate, as well as his own stock and some of the horses owned by several Elshorn merchants.

"Of course not," she said coldly. "She borrowed it, just as she's done many times in the past."

"I didn't mean to imply she was a thief," he apologized.

"She loves to ride and Brokan always accommodates her," said Moyna. "But she always comes back. And she's never left like this, without telling me."

The rest of the meal passed in silence, and finally Druce sighed. "Tell me what she was wearing when you last saw her. The magistrates will need to know."

Instructions given, orders taken
Information important for retention
Be certain now to pay attention
They lay the lines, outline the rules
So everyone knows, even fools
Continence all their worldly conventions
For suspect plans or good intentions.

9

September 7th in the Roman calendar
Late Afternoon
Six days into the Celtic Tree Month of Muin

"You wanted to see me, Elder?" Weylyn latched the oak door behind him and entered the Magistrate's Great Room.

"Yes." The Elder, his back to the hearth, was seated on his bench at the end of the long table. Servants were busy setting out the evening meal. He waved them away and gestured for Weylyn to join him. "Sit. Eat. I have a mission for you."

Weylyn settled into a seat at the table and then reached for a hunk of cheese and some dark bread.

"With Teg out of commission for any difficult work, I've got a big job for you," Elder Eghan said, his voice old but still as strong as his namesake, the oak. "I want you to find this fellow who put the sword to the Roman."

"You want *me* to find him?"

The Elder nodded. "That's what I said."

Since the reward offered by the Prefect, many had entered the valley looking for the outlaw and they had yet to succeed.

And now Elder Eghan was going to set Weylyn to this task, something far more serious than anything the young man had yet been tasked to do as a deputy magistrate. Weylyn felt his excitement rising. This would be a chance, at last, to do something that didn't involve drunken brawls or petty squabbles over property, livestock, servant ownership, gambling debts, or unpaid dowries or taxes.

"I've made some inquires," Eghan continued. "If this outlaw is still in our valley he's likely hiding up in the mountains with his kinfolk. I've obtained the name of a possible relative who lives on the mountain north of Aife, and I want you to go find him. This takes precedence over anything else on your schedule. That includes," Eghan added dryly, "your business with the young servant girl at the Five Fingers Tavern."

Weylyn felt his face flush.

"Given the seriousness of this situation, I would, frankly, have preferred to assign this task to one of the more experienced deputy magistrates. However, Teg is injured and I need the others to cover their areas in the event my hunch is wrong about the outlaw staying in our immediate area. And so, young man, this job falls to you."

"I understand, Elder."

"You must find him quickly. And, Weylyn, be extra cautious with this one. Remember, this isn't some trivial misdemeanor we're dealing with here. There's more than just the murder of a churcher by a Celt involved with this. It is no coincidence all this fuss over the outlaw comes on the heels of the theft of the treasure. The Prefect wants him taken alive, and that tells me he could be one of the men involved. That's why they want him alive, to interrogate him."

"And when I find him, Elder?" asked Weylyn, suddenly concerned he might face a murderer alone, assuming he could even find him to bring him in alive.

The Elder looked thoughtfully at his young apprentice. With

a gnarled old finger he tapped the side of his head and, eyes twinkling, said, "Remember my orders. You find him and notify me. Then we will let the Enforcers handle him. I don't want us any more involved in this Roman intrigue than necessary. Do you understand? I do not need my apprentice deputy taken from me before he's had a chance learn everything there is to learn. Our job, like the Druid magistrates before us, is to keep order in our valley."

"Yes, Elder."

"Make certain of it."

"Yes, sir. It is clear to me."

"This is important. What little I know of this tells me that extreme caution is needed on our part. I cannot emphasize this enough—the man you seek is a killer, and he's wanted by the Prefect in Hierlaneum. That means big trouble."

The Elder rose from the table and paced along the hearth. "You must remember this. It's not just churchers, not just Romans who would kill to have this treasure. There are Celts out there, too. In fact, I've learned of at least two Celts from Elshorn who are actively searching, and they could be just as dangerous as this outlaw if we try to get between them and what they seek."

"I understand, Elder. But if they think he knows where the Great Cross is hidden, isn't it safe to think they will keep him alive until they discover—" Weylyn stopped abruptly, eyes wide. He suddenly realized how dangerous it could be for him to be around this Celt fugitive and the Enforcers—or anyone else—when they learned the location of the Great Cross. He could become expendable once the treasure's location was known.

His look of surprise and revelation wasn't lost on the Chief Magistrate. "So, I see you understand the danger. Remember what I've told you, Weylyn. Take no chances."

About the mountain's serene site
Ribbons tied so neat, so bright
Candles burn 'round melted wax
Good fortune follows many tracks
Sacred pool where deities reside
Both blessed and cursed can abide
Keeping watch about this station
Little spirits with information.

10

September 19th in the Roman calendar
Just Before Noon
Eighteen days into the Celtic Tree Month of Muin

The sacred spring of Carmel Raif was beautiful year round. Its deep, clear pool of water set against the base of the gray-black cliffs was fed from a slow, steady running spring which seemed to magically flow from an opening in the stone, gently cascading down about three feet into the pool. The low rock ledges to the left and right of the pool held many candles. Trees surrounding the immediate area were covered in brightly colored ribbons, offerings to the occupying spirits of the popular sacred site. An arbor of intertwined vines woven across and around three trees formed a protective shelter and safe haven for weary travelers.

Nearly a fortnight had passed since Elder Eghan first put Weylyn on the task of finding the outlaw, Eiroy. Weylyn had wanted to set out right away, but the presence of bounty hunters had again resulted in trouble at the tavern, with fights and arguments becoming a daily problem. The group that had caused the fight in which Teg had been injured had also returned, and the magistrates had been kept very busy working to restore order in the town. It required all their own resources and a contingent of troops from the Roman garrison at Cross Abbey, brought in at the request of Elder Eghan, to subdue all the troublemakers. With order finally restored, Weylyn was free to carry out the most serious task he'd ever been given.

Now, as he made his way up the mountain, he paused to honor the beauty of the sacred spring of Carmel Raif. He saw two young girls kneeling just outside the shelter near the tranquil spring, securing a large bundle of dried sticks.

"Bright day, ladies," said Weylyn.

The girls looked up smiling and returned his greeting.

"I'm Weylyn, a magistrate from Elshorn. How are you two today?"

"We are fine, sir, and thank you. Are you here to make an offering?"

"No, I'm looking for some information."

"Maybe if you made an offering to the sacred pool, the spirits may grant you the information you seek," the young girl suggested, eyes wide, filled with good humor and faith.

"True enough," Weylyn agreed. "But I was hoping one of you might be able to help me. I'm looking for information about a man. He has a big black horse with a large, white cross-shaped blaze on his chest."

"We've seen such a horse!"

Bless Arianrod, thought Weylyn. Even without making an offering, not so much as a prayer at the sacred site, his luck had improved immediately. "You have? Excellent."

The elder of the two stood up and wiped the debris from her hands on the sides of her dress. "It was last week, or maybe it was two weeks, just off the north road from Aife, to the west near the creek. Not sure exactly when, really."

Weylyn dismounted and approached. "Up the Aingeal Hair Trail? This is very important. Are you quite certain?"

"Oh, yes, sir," said the girl. "My sister and I were gathering medicinal roots and tubers in the forest there by the stream when we saw the horse. Yes, just off the Aingeal Hair trail."

"It's true," said the little sister, nodding. "A big black horse with the white cross mark."

"It was tied to a tree near the path leading to the stream."

"Was there anyone with the horse? The man who rides it may have been injured."

"There was a man, but we didn't see him up close."

The older girl took up the tale. "He was down by the stream, drinking. His back was to us but he didn't look hurt or anything. We never went close. There have been many strangers in our mountains lately, mostly Roman soldiers, and our parents have strict orders against ever talking to them. So we just went about our business and walked up the trail to our usual gathering spot. We crossed the stream way north of where we saw the man."

This was incredibly good news, the lead Weylyn had been hoping for. "Can you remember the color of the man's hair? The man I'm looking for may have reddish or blondish hair."

The sisters looked at each other, frowning slightly. It was the older girl who responded. "We couldn't see his hair, he wore a cloak with its hood pulled way up around his neck. He had a helmet on, too."

"The man I'm looking for might have been wearing a helmet, too. Did he see you?"

"I don't think so. We didn't stay but a minute before leaving. He never turned around to look our way."

"He wasn't there when we came back down from gathering. He and the horse were both gone," said the little one.

"Any idea which way he may have gone?" Weylyn thought they probably wouldn't know, but he had to ask.

"We didn't see him again. We just went back home with our gatherings."

"Anything else you can remember?"

The two looked at each other for a few moments, then shook their heads. "Maybe he went to Aife. You should talk with the blacksmith there. I'm certain he would remember the horse," the older girl offered.

"Excellent idea. I'll do that. Ladies, you've both been very helpful." Weylyn reached into his belt pouch and pulled out two copper coins and offered one to each girl. "I wish I had more to offer but here's a little something for you. With gratitude from the office of the Elshorn Magistrate for your help."

Surprised and delighted, the girls graciously accepted the coins. "Thank you, sir," they said in unison.

After leaving Carmel Raif, Weylyn made his way up the Aingeal Hair trail toward the village of Aife, about a mile north of where the girls remembered seeing the man and the horse. Entering the village, he headed for the home of the blacksmith, Angus of the Forge.

A burly, good natured fellow, Angus had moved his family from Elshorn to Aife three years ago to ply his trade following the death of his oldest son, Turi, who was killed by a bear while on a hunting trip. Weylyn still missed his best friend.

As he approached the blacksmith's home, he saw bright ribbons tied about the twelve-foot high Greeting Pole which stood, complete with carvings of glyphs and Celtic deities, in the traditional place to the right of the cottage's door. The colorful ribbons signified a happy and prosperous year for the inhabitants of this home. Turi would have been glad, Weylyn thought.

Angus was busy at the forge, and looked up as Weylyn approached. "Greetings, young magistrate," the blacksmith said cheerfully. "I'm glad to see you, as you've saved me a visit into Elshorn. You've heard of the theft, then?"

"The cross, you mean?"

"Cross?" Angus laughed a hearty, throaty laugh. "Theft of a churcher cross? No, no. We have no need for one of those things here on a mountain owned by the very gods themselves." He continued to laugh as he set down his iron and moved away from his forge. He wiped his hands on his leather apron as he approached Weylyn. "Good to see you again."

"And you. Now, what's this about a theft?"

"It happened on the eve of Illumination. I took a commission for a set of daggers and I'd just finished the first of the pair. The second was nearly finished when it disappeared. We've asked everyone around here if they'd seen it, knew what happened to it but nothing. I was about to take a trip in to see Elder Eghan and report it."

"Greetings, Weylyn!" shouted a young voice.

"Cullen! Greetings to you, too. What's this about a missing dagger?" teased Weylyn. "Haven't you yet learned to keep track of your father's goods?"

The young boy frowned and dropped his head, obviously embarrassed by the question.

Angus smiled at his boy. "Cullen told me I shouldn't worry about it. Said it had probably just been misplaced and we'd find it eventually. But it's been gone too long now to believe that. I've looked everywhere here and can't find it."

"Did you notice anything unusual before it went missing? Any strangers in the area?"

"We had Roman soldiers in the area the day before asking questions about a missing Celt, that fellow named Eiroy everyone's looking for. We hadn't seen anyone fitting the outlaw's description, though. Thank the gods, they didn't stay long. Couldn't get any cooperation from anyone around here."

He shrugged. "They left the mountain the night before the dagger disappeared. I'll tell you, it's got me puzzled. Never had anything stolen like that. Nothing else is missing. I'd appreciate it if you would keep an eye out for it."

He motioned toward the house. "Let's go inside, get something to drink and eat, and I'll tell you what it looks like."

There was good banter during the meal, with much reminiscing about the old days with Turi before the fatal bear attack. Eventually, the conversation went back to the missing dagger. It was a ceremonial one, fancy with inlaid enameled runes along the blade with a heavy, rounded pommel. Angus laid the finished one on the table in front of Weylyn.

"Should be easy to spot," said Angus. "Looks just like this one. A pair just as the commission requested. Now I'm going to have to make another and it's going to cut into my profit. See how the hilt's wrapping is nice and tight and finished? The one that's gone missing is rough, jagged and unwrapped. It would be an uncomfortable thing to wield."

Weylyn examined the weapon and promised to look for its duplicate but thought there was little chance of ever seeing it again, especially if it was taken by one of the bounty hunters or Roman soldiers. He set the dagger back on the table.

"I'll keep my eyes open," he promised. "Elder Eghan has tasked me to find the man who killed the Roman out in front of the tavern, so I can search for your dagger while I'm looking for this Eiroy fellow."

"You think there's a chance he's up this way?"

"I got a good lead from two girls I just spoke with down at Carmel Raif. They noticed a stranger with a big horse with the white cross blaze maybe a couple weeks ago on the Aingeal Hair Trail."

"He didn't come by here. I would have remembered a horse like that."

"And you haven't seen anyone else?"

"Besides the soldiers, you mean? The only strangers we've seen recently were two Celts. They said they were hunting bear up here on the mountain. Nothing unusual in that."

Weylyn thanked the family for their kindness and left Aife, assuring Angus he'd let him know if he got a lead on the missing dagger and promising to visit again soon.

*

Weylyn spent the afternoon checking the dwellings along the road and trails above Aife. It was slow going. He found the house he was looking for just before he lost the sun for the day. Dismounting some distance from the small, round stone cottage with the thatched roof, he remained hidden in the shadow of an ancient oak and watched the house for any signs of the outlaw. If he'd followed the Elder's directions correctly, this should be the home of Fey de Parke, the man thought to be a relative of the outlaw.

Weylyn tied his horse to a lower branch of the oak and crouched down against the trunk of the tree. He studied the area in front of the cottage. He noted a garden plot, each corner marked with a dry stack of stone about three feet high. In the deepening twilight, he could just make out a narrow path leading from the cottage door to the garden plot and down to the main trail. He returned his attention to the cottage. There was a shuttered window to the left of the door. There was no sign of activity, no smoke rising from the chimney.

On the western side of the house Weylyn saw a grove of mountain pine, the high dark peaks of Aingeal Mountain looming in the background. Moving quietly, he made his way along the east side of the house, where he could see part of a corral and a rough shelter of some sort. He eased closer, ever wary, not wanting any nasty surprises by whoever might be inside.

A sudden noise had him drawing back into the shadows. He saw a movement at the corral, then realized he was staring at a horse with a very distinctive white cross blaze. Elder had been right. The outlaw Eiroy must have come here.

The horse continued to graze as Weylyn moved cautiously forward toward the corral, a rough-hewn affair enclosing a grassy area with a trickling stream. Easing open a gate, Weylyn glanced nervously about and moved quietly into the small shed adjacent to the corral. Elder Fey apparently used this space to store small tools and farming implements.

Baskets hung from the rafters and astride a long rail Weylyn found a saddle, dried blood on the leather. It was difficult to see details clearly, but he thought he could see blood on the rails and gate posts as well. Remembering his orders from Elder Eghan, he made his way back to his horse and rode down the mountain in the fading light.

It came to them like wandering Fates,
The lights of Gods through Golden gates.
We must keep the balance, always try.
Like Sun and Moon up in the Sky.

11

September 22nd in the Roman calendar
Pre-Dawn
Eve of the Autumnal Equinox

The pre-dawn air was cold, the sky clear and full of brilliant, sparkling stars. Weylyn hoped the rising sun would bring with it some warmth. He was leading the Roman contingent from Cross Abbey—Commander Orrs, the Enforcer Pluvius, and a sergeant named Virgil—up the Aingeal Mountain trail to the home of Fey de Parke to capture the outlaw, Eiroy the Red. Eghan had dispatched a runner the day before to inform Orrs of Weylyn's discovery at Fey's, namely the black horse with the prominent white cross blaze on its chest.

Weylyn had been reluctant to ride back up the rocky, winding trail—hard going under any circumstances, but even more challenging today with three Romans in tow and no idea what lay in store for him once they made it to Fey's. He didn't want to be here at all; he'd rather have gone outside the Empire to the Celtlands to celebrate the Autumnal Equinox and Winter Finding Festivals with the Celtic Queen.

As Weylyn led the way up the trail, he let his thoughts wander to Elder Eghan who, with many of the residents of Elshorn, were travelling beyond the fortress at Carew to Highdyn Hill for the festivities. He took some small comfort in knowing that Elder Eghan had argued with Orrs about the man's insistence Weylyn lead the Romans to the home of Fey de Parke. Weylyn had overhead enough of that conversation to know that, while Commander Orrs was generally a reasonable man, his tolerance did not extend to pagan ceremonies and traditions. Officially, such ceremonies were now forbidden within the Great Church-controlled Empire. And ceremonies aside, Orrs wanted a Celt with them as they traveled up the mountain to the hideout of the outlaw wanted for the murder of a Roman outside the tavern in Elshorn.

Weylyn studied the trail ahead of him, relieved at least to have company on this trip. Still, trails high up on this mountain held many dangers. A giant bear could jump out of the brush at any moment and crush the life out of them, just as Weylyn's best friend, Turi, had been killed. Shivering, Weylyn pulled his cape up as high as he could around his neck and tugged his tunic tighter. He hated being cold.

Halfway up the mountain, Orrs' horse stumbled. "All this rock," grumbled Orrs. "It's hard on the horses."

"And after a hard, fast ride over from Cross Abbey yesterday, too," Pluvius reminded him.

Orrs sighed and dismounted. "You two go on up ahead. I'll stay here with Virgil and give the horse a rest. Just don't get off this main track until we catch up with you."

"Yes, sir," said Pluvius. He waved Weylyn forward.

They had ridden slowly on. They were out of sight and well out of earshot when Pluvius stopped his horse, arched his back and readjusted the bow and shoulder strap holding the quiver of arrows at his side. "These things are heavy," he complained. "I can't believe Orrs had us march up here without a full contingent of troops. What if something goes wrong? I pray to God we're successful. Can't wait to lighten my load a little by leaving a couple of these arrows in that Eiroy." He chuckled. "I figure if someone's going to die up here on this mountain today, might as well be the outlaw."

"Orrs said we are to take this man alive," Weylyn reminded him. "That's what your Prefect wants, isn't it?" He looked toward Pluvius, waiting for a response. When he got none, Weylyn urged his horse forward and continued on up the trail. He could hear Pluvius carrying on behind him.

"Orrs told me," Pluvius said, "that this Eiroy fellow is involved with the theft of the Great Cross. Orrs said Eiroy and Aod—you remember, he's the one whose throat was slashed in Elshorn—they were part of a gang of outlaws working the roads and the river between Hierlaneum and Rome, waylaying and robbing just about everyone. They stole horses, wagons, coins, gems, you name it. They say they've even taken salt shipments right off the river. Our Prefect believes they're the ones who took the sacred Great Cross, which means they're working in Brendan Valley now, too. Orrs is anxious for us to get the information on the whereabouts of the Great Cross, and find it before the Prefect gets it.

"Our priest at Cross Abby was tasked with keeping it safe, you know. In fact," Pluvius continued, "Father Caton thinks it's all a ruse by the Prefect in Hierlaneum to cover up his Bishop's part in all this. No proof, of course." He reached into his belt pouch and pulled out a mushroom. Popping it in his mouth, he asked, "Can you believe that? A Bishop or a priest involved in stealing from our church? I can't. Certainly not."

Weylyn thought it sounded just like something churchers would do, but decided to keep that observation to himself.

"I've had a premonition," Pluvius confided. "From God. I'll find the treasure and make a great name for myself. I'll find it and receive special blessings from God and my church."

Weylyn stopped and looked down the track behind them. Orrs and his sergeant were slowly making their way along the ridge, but were still some distance back. Weylyn nudged his horse into a slow walk. He was tired of listening to Pluvius, and wished Orrs and his sergeant would catch up soon.

Pluvius reached into his belt pouch and pulled out some more dried mushrooms. "Want one?"

"What is it?" asked Weylyn suspiciously.

"Mushrooms. The best. Go on, have one."

"No thanks." Privately, Weylyn thought those premonitions and ramblings had less to do with the Enforcer's beliefs and more to do with his consumption of those mushrooms.

Pluvius popped another mushroom in his mouth, chewed, and began to sing. "Death will show its dread face cast upon the wooded land and murky bog, but have no fear the Holy Spirit is here, safe we are if we walk with God …" He couldn't remember the rest and hummed the last bit of the song.

Weylyn urged his horse forward, wishing he could block out that irritating voice. He was beginning to think fighting a bear or even the outlaw was preferable to listening to this idiot.

"God works in strange ways, Celt. He knows what's best. He and the Holy Trinity will guide me to my fortune. Yes indeed."

Weylyn was almost a horse length ahead of the Roman. He leaned over and spit off the side of the trail, then took a deep breath, trying to hold on to his temper. The churchers constantly banged the drum of one god even as they reveled in the idea of trinity—a concept they'd seized from the Celts just as they'd taken whatever else they wanted to claim as their own.

Weylyn knew Pluvius was waiting for a reply, but he didn't want to give him one. The Enforcer's emphasis on 'he' was a slam against the Celtic Elder Faith's female deities. Females in the churcher's schema could never reach deity status; instead, they'd been relegated to a subservient role by both doctrine and action. The ancient Celtic Elder Faith knew the way to orderly balance was to recognize, respect, and maintain an equal balance between male and female universal principles.

Weylyn knew it was best if he just kept his mouth shut. It would certainly be safer. Voicing any opinion contrary to the Great Church was a crime, and Weylyn had seen many a Celt be punished, even put to death, for doing so. He also knew if he didn't respond, he'd risk the Enforcer's wrath, and that would certainly get back to Elder Eghan.

"If anyone can find the treasure, Pluvius, I'm certain it will be you," Weylyn finally said with a straight face.

"No truer words were ever spoken, young man," Pluvius said happily. "You Celts don't understand this, but my church will grant me special blessings when I find this treasure. I might even get a transfer, maybe an assignment to be Chief Enforcer for the Pontiff himself. Or maybe even Centurion. Yes. A most suitable job for me."

With an effort, Weylyn suppressed an audible sigh and looked around again, hoping Orrs was catching up. "If you want to find the treasure, we better catch this outlaw first."

Pluvius didn't seem to be listening. "I'm going to find the Great Cross and return it to its rightful place of honor in the Great Church. You do realize that's why everyone's so anxious to find this Eiroy fellow, don't you? They think he knows where the sacred relic is hidden."

Weylyn wasn't surprised about the information Pluvius had conveyed. Celtic magistrates were often kept in the dark about the mission of Enforcers. They only told Celts what was absolutely necessary. The magistrates—once known as Druidic magistrates and long held in high respect by the Celtic community—now served under the Romans as a convenience to the High Prefect and the religious cleric he served.

In the Brendan Valley, the magistrates were a thin buffer between conquerors and conquered. They knew the territory, the people, and the subtle nuances of the indigenous population. They allowed for a calming, familiar social structure which helped control the Celts and ease the friction that came with cultural assimilation. In areas the Romans now claimed as their own, Celtic magistrates and their men were cheaper and more reasonable than having to send in hundreds of military troops to put down any problems. Simply put, the Grand Church leaders thought it more cost effective to leave the old structure in place than to build more garrisons and pay more soldiers. Considering that, Weylyn found himself wishing that Pluvius would get reassigned. Now that would be a blessing all round, Weylyn decided with a grin.

Pluvius was still talking. "You know, I think somebody in the Prefect's office in Hierlaneum is out to get someone in our Great Church. Sounds just like something those ingrates would do." He laughed wickedly.

Weylyn thought it sounded exactly like something a churcher would do.

Pluvius yawned. "You think this outlaw is still up here? What makes you think he didn't flee the area already?"

"The man was badly wounded, we think. I saw blood on the saddle and no one was stirring when I surveyed the area."

"Could have been Aod's blood you saw on the saddle."

"I also found blood on the shed rails. That makes me think Eiroy was wounded in the fight with Aod and was still bleeding when he reached Fey's." He shrugged. "I don't know."

Pluvius grunted and shifted the weight of his weapons.

"I could be wrong," Weylyn said. "I never actually saw him, just the horse." But Weylyn believed the outlaw was in there, hiding, waiting for his wounds to heal. He'd paid the blacksmith's son to watch the main road at Aife, and knew no one fitting the outlaw's description had passed that way during Cullen's watch. And if he was right about Eiroy being wounded, there wasn't much chance the outlaw would have taken one of the rougher secondary trails down to the main roadway.

Orrs and Virgil finally caught up with them. They continued up the trail a short distance before Weylyn halted his horse. He pointed through the trees toward the thatched-roof stone cottage. "There it is."

The young magistrate dismounted and walked to the base of the same tree where he'd stood on his first visit. He studied the house. There was still no smoke from the chimney, no sound of anyone moving about, but something looked out of place, different somehow from his first visit. What was it?

Orrs reached his side. "You're sure that's the house we want?"

"Yes, sir."

Seek, search and logically surmise.
It makes no sense, but even more
To cast bright ribbons from the door.
More mystery than answers
Often await Sunrise.

12

September 22nd in the Roman calendar
Early Morning
Celtic Eve of the Autumnal Equinox

"We want this man alive," Orrs reminded the others. "Don't get too careless with those weapons. We'll move in at my signal." He turned to his sergeant. "Virgil, check the back. Make certain there's no one out there before we go in. I don't want any unpleasant surprises."

The dark haired sergeant drew his sword and made his way around the cottage toward the small corral where Weylyn had found the horse with the white cross blaze.

"Pluvius, you cover that grove of mountain pine." Orrs watched his Enforcer move into position and then turned his attention back to Weylyn. "You think he's still here?"

Weylyn kept his gaze on the cottage. "Yes, sir, I do."

"Just remember our plan. Once Pluvius and Virgil make certain the outer area is clear, I'll give the signal to storm the place. We'll take him by surprise. If he's wounded like you think he is, there shouldn't be much of a fight."

Weylyn nodded absently, his attention still on the cottage. Elder Fey's place was a modest little structure, blending well into the natural landscape. During his reconnoitering on his earlier visit, Weylyn had noticed the dry stacks of stone marking the garden boundary and the ceremonial Greeting Pole, which stood twelve feet high just to the right of the home's entrance. The pole had been in deep shadow during his first visit, but Weylyn could now make out the carvings that decorated the pole. He saw the top of the pole featured a carving of the sacred goddess Arianrod with a headdress of the moon symbol. In keeping with the traditions of the Elder Faith, the pole was carved with various symbols of fertility and personal family runes, and would be decorated in various ways through the year. Decorating patterns differed from Celt to Celt and from region to region. Generally, though, the ceremonial poles were decorated to match the seasons and to identify the important happenings to the families who maintained them.

As daylight advanced, Weylyn kept his eye trained on the front door. Most of the dark blue-violet and red streaks of wispy, early morning clouds had faded away as the sun began another day's journey across the sky. As he studied the small abode, he found himself hoping that Fey wouldn't resist when they captured Eiroy. The plan called for the outlaw to be taken prisoner if at all possible. To the Romans, however, Celts were—at best—a nuisance and certainly expendable. Weylyn knew that Fey wouldn't be an exception if he got in their way.

Orrs was also staring at the house, still in deep shadow beneath the heavy trees. "Remember, when I give the signal—"

He was interrupted by the sounds of a horse whinnying loudly. The noise was coming from behind the house. "God's plague," cursed Orrs. He looked at Weylyn and said tersely, "Wait here." Sword at the ready, the commander ran toward the garden area and crouched against a corner stack of stones.

From the sounds at the back, Weylyn thought it likely that

Virgil had spooked the horse as he came around the house. If it turned out to be the same horse with the distinct markings Weylyn had seen on his first visit, that must mean Eiroy was indeed here.

He studied Fey de Parke's little abode, troubled by the sense something was wrong or out of place. As daylight strengthened, Weylyn could see clearly the roof thatching, the door, the ribbons hanging from the entrance pole. Quiet had once again descended. Virgil must have calmed the animal. Weylyn wondered why the noise hadn't brought Fey de Parke out to check. Was it because it wasn't his horse? No, that didn't make sense. Elder Fey would have investigated any noise so close to his house. Weylyn remembered his first trip up here when he discovered the horse and searched the shed—no one had come out then, either.

He looked over to Orrs, still crouched low in the garden area, poised to give the signal to attack. Weylyn looked up at the remaining thin, wispy clouds and sunlight streaking across the sky like so many ribbons. Ribbons! That's it, he thought. He looked back toward the Greeting Pole. He could see the ribbons more clearly now. They were black. And chalked on the door was a large, blackened glyph of warding. Black ribbons, black glyphs. Death had beaten them to this place.

Weylyn approached Orrs. "Sir, there are black ribbons on the pole and a black glyph of warding on the door."

Confused, the Roman commander looked at the young Celt, and then looked back toward the house. "Are those important?"

"Yes," replied Weylyn. He reached down and picked up two stones. He clicked them together as he whistled nervously.

Orrs gave him a strange look. "Explain all that later. Right now, we move." He stood, sword in hand. "Attack!"

"Attack! Attack!" Virgil and Pluvius echoed.

No need, thought Weylyn. The black ribbons and the Glyphs of Passing—Celtic tradition and an important part of the Elder

Faith's Death Hearth Ritual—signified a death had occurred here. And following Celtic custom, Weylyn knew, the occupants would have abandoned the dwelling for a full seven days. The Seven Days of Danger. This gave the spirits a chance to come and go without risking any of the living.

Following the Seven Days, the Celtic owner would return, have a Healer perform a cleansing ritual and restore the home to its rightful balance in nature. Once the ritual was complete, the black symbols of death would be replaced with the normal, colorful seasonal wreath and ribbon decorations.

Weylyn slowly approached the house, whistling and clanking the stones together to confuse or frighten away the spirits of the Otherworld who would come to view and whisk away the dead. It was believed such spirits could also take the living before their time. Such Otherworld spirits could be confused or driven away by the noise of the living. And while the new religion of the land might think such things nonsense, Weylyn wasn't taking any chances.

He knew Death had not only taken an occupant of this home, it had also killed their plans to capture the outlaw.

Circled about the plans of men,
The Wanderers travel out and in.
While humans seek the wanted knave,
Not knowing all along that Death
Had taken him, knave, to grave.

13

September 22nd in the Roman calendar
Morning
Eve of the Autumnal Equinox

"Nothing," Orrs said in disgust. "If Eiroy was here, he's long gone now."

There was a cool breeze stirring, fluttering the black ribbons on the entrance pole. Taking a deep breath, Weylyn steadied himself by looking out into the dense woods surrounding the south side of the house, appreciating the beauty of the landscape. The foliage, still thick and green, hid the vast view of the river valley below. Soon, though, the leaves would be turning brown and falling, and the wintry season would be upon them.

"No sign of Elder Fey?" Weylyn asked. He'd stayed outside while Orrs and his men violated the black ribbons and the glyphs of warding by smashing open the front door and searching the house. Weylyn had refused to help, even warned against it. He was told not to interfere. Weylyn thought about what he would do if the Otherworld spirits came to carry away these Romans. He decided he would do nothing. While he'd waited, he'd searched the path leading away from the dwelling and had just picked up a small strip of linen when the men emerged.

"It's a mess inside," Orrs said. "Dried leaves and branches hanging from every rafter and beam, and strewn all over the floor. Things thrown all around in there."

"Maybe somebody got here before us, searched the place," offered Virgil.

"Possible," Orrs agreed. "Weylyn, you're the expert here on Celts. Why don't you go in, take a look around? Maybe you'll find something we missed," he suggested with a wry smile.

Weylyn ignored the invitation and handed Orrs the strip of linen. "Take a look at this bandage I found. That's blood."

"You think it's Eiroy's? After all, there were supposed to be two men here, Eiroy and old Fey. Maybe it's the old man's blood." With a shrug, Orrs tossed the linen to the ground. He pulled a piece of dried jerky from his pouch and chewed. "Maybe they had a falling out, and Eiroy killed Fey and got rid of the body. That would explain why nobody's here."

"I believe the blood must belong to Eiroy." He knew Orrs didn't really understand the Celtic culture, but Weylyn knew a person of the Elder Faith would not kill a fellow Celt who was taking care of him. That would be against their code, their religious beliefs. What Orrs was suggesting was something only a churcher would do. "It isn't Eiroy's house. It had to be Elder Fey who placed the marks of death on the home. And we know Eiroy had been injured."

Orrs chewed his jerky and considered this for a moment. "True. But isn't it also possible the old man's relatives were here, found him, and put up the black decorations?"

"Possible, yes, but I think it was Eiroy who died. And it was Elder Fey who marked the house and walked away."

"I still don't understand why you think it was Fey who left

the area alive and not our man, Eiroy." Orrs bit off another piece of the dried meat.

"The horse," Weylyn reminded him. "It's Eiroy's horse. Elder Fey would not have taken it until the seven dangerous days were over, just in case the spirits wanted it to take it to the Otherworld along with the departing spirit of its owner."

Pluvius snorted. "Superstitions!"

Weylyn ignored him. Looking directly at Orrs, he continued on, determined to make the commander understand. "If it had been Eiroy who walked out of the house, he would have either ridden the horse away if he could ride, or led it away to ride later when he healed. Or, he would have let it go some distance from here to help hide the fact he'd ever been in the area."

"Hmmm." If Orrs had any thoughts about the Elder Faith's religious practices, he didn't mention them. "All right, then let's find the body. Where would you Celts bury a dead outlaw?"

They spent the better part of an hour searching the immediate area for signs of a fresh grave. Finding nothing, they made their way slowly up along a trail to the northwest crest of the mountain ridge overlooking gray slate and limestone bluffs. Both men and horses had recently traversed this path. Snagged on a low branch along the trail they found a bloodstained cloth. It matched the one found outside the house. As they pushed further up along the rocky, narrow trail they could see the valley floor far below.

To their left, a small, well-used animal track branched off the main trail and ran down the side of the mountain to the bluffs. About twenty feet down this small path, more pieces of white blood-stained linen cloth had snagged on a large vine of thorns. Weylyn studied the trail carefully. Whoever had passed this way hadn't bothered to cover their passing at all. In fact, it looked as if it was deliberately marked. He saw hard-soled leather boot prints and broken branches along the path. "This way," he said. The others followed him down the path to the gray cliffs.

The stone bluffs rose high on their right. Cluster of green vegetation clung to the rock face. Below and to the left, the valley opened up for miles. The Moryn Gweneth River was a blue glittering ribbon winding through the Brendan Valley on its journey to the sea. Two hundred yards along the narrow trail, they saw the cave. Its gaping expanse of a mouth opened up the cliff for several hundred feet.

Inside the cave, thirty feet from the entrance, they saw a pile of stones, more bloodstained white linen visible between the stones. Weylyn knew it was a Celtic grave, or at least a grave made by a follower of the ancient Elder Faith. On its top, wedged into the pile of stones and ash leaves, was a carved ash wood spirit guardian. Its cloaked and hooded personage bore the long beard and fierce expression of a very determined protector—placed there to help guard the body. It served its purpose well, keeping all predators from the bodies of the dead. All but one, that is—man.

It wouldn't take the other three long to remove the earth and stones and get to the body buried beneath. For Weylyn's part, he would have nothing to do with it and said so. There was always the chance that this was the grave of an innocent, someone who had nothing at all to do with this Eiroy. He did not intend to disturb the resting place of the dead. "I think we should keep looking, check out the area beyond the cave."

Orrs dismissed him. "Those pieces of cloth on the trail and path and the ones on this grave match the ones we found at Fey's. We have to see if this Eiroy fellow is in here. You take a look back through the rest of the cave, see what you can find. Make certain there's nobody here, waiting to ambush us when we start digging."

Weylyn was happy to oblige. These Romans would have no trouble in disturbing the dead. They seemed ignorant of spirits and oblivious to the harm they were doing to their own spiritual health by disturbing a Celtic ceremonial burial site. Of course it wouldn't bother them. After all, they had a history of burning the bodies of their dead. He didn't want to think about what might have become of the poor thousands of Roman spirits treated in such a barbaric manner. It reminded him of the old epics of some far north Celts. In the time before adoption of the Elder Faith, they set fire to their dead and sent them floating across the cold sea into the Otherworld. The Great Church had long ago forbidden anyone to treat the dead in such a manner, although they seemed quite willing to fool with the spirits and the bodies of the departed when it suited their own purposes. Well, they were welcome to it.

He returned from his uneventful exploration to find Orrs' men removing the final stones from on top of the body. He could see the dark brown of the man's leather tunic, the colorful striped leggings. He watched with distaste and repulsion as they rifled through the man's belongings, turning the body over to ensure every possible spot had been searched. Why were they desecrating this body? What were they searching for?

"Look at this!" Pluvius picked up a leather pouch from the stones and emptied its contents. Minted coins, both silver and copper, tumbled across the ground next to the items already removed from the grave. Weylyn saw several polished garnets, a belt, a thong necklace, a leather scabbard about three feet long with sword, a small dagger, and several dried mushrooms.

Orrs let out a sharp whistle. "That's a lot of valuables for a common thief to be taking to a grave!"

The ancient gathering prayer, "September, low, blow soft, till the gathering is in the loft" was completed. The annual autumn equinox had passed. It was one of the four highest days of celebration for the ancient peoples of the world. Both Equinox days and the two Solstice days were celebrated for three days each occasion. The celebrations included festivals, bonfires, dancing, storytelling of the elders, and various feasts and marriages. They were High Druidic Celebrations, as they marked the midpoints between the celebrations of Samhain, Imbolc, Beltane and Lughnasadh. The Autumn Equinox was considered the time when darkness would begin to wrest the days from the light—when soon the nights would be longer, colder. It marks the time of calling, ripening of the harvests. It was the time of Mabon of Celtic tradition, the Tree-month of Coll and Muin; it marked the end of the harvest.

The Great Church proclaimed all these festivals illegal, blasphemous and works of their evil Satan. When the Elder Faith Celts and others of the Celebrations refused to submit, the Great Church took action. It promptly plagiarized the ancient festivals of the Elder Faith and renamed them for their own. The church ascribed their own hierarchy of deities which they called saints to these ancient occasions. Of course, by doing so, they promptly forgot about them being the work of their Satan.

The Celts ignored, as best they could, the recriminations of the Great Church and its Grand Cleric's ranting proclamations and pressed on in the ancient tradition of their ancestors.

14

September 26th in the Roman calendar
Midday
Two days left in the Runic Half-Month of Ken (Illumination)

In the days following Weylyn's journey back down the mountain with the Romans and the valuables they'd looted from the grave, the wintry old gods of the North hurled their wicked freezing winds, blowing snow across the region. Weylyn shivered with cold despite his heavy cape and snug felt hat as he went about his routine duties. It was a relief to be summoned to the Longhouse to brief Elder Eghan on his current assignment.

Weylyn huddled close to the great hearth, still shivering despite the leaping flames and his heavy cape. He was cold from his toes all the way up to his nose. Courtesy and his job both demanded he pay attention to the Elder, but Weylyn was having trouble staying focused on the Chief Magistrate's words. His thoughts kept returning to the mystery surrounding the dead outlaw up on the mountain.

Elder Eghan stood up, tossed another log on the fire, poked it with the iron and turned back to Weylyn. "I asked, have you found the ones responsible for desecrating the old sacred public well yet?"

"Uh, no, Elder. Not yet." Flushing with embarrassment, Weylyn sat up straighter, keeping a firm grip on his fur cape to ensure no warmth would escape. Certainly it was a magistrate duty to keep the sacred well and shrine safe, to guard it in the ancient tradition, but truth told he wasn't interested in the petty vandalism because it was a recurring crime he'd grown tired of investigating. The other deputy magistrate, Teg, seldom got these annoying duties since he was the older, more experienced of the two. But Teg wasn't doing anything right now; his ankle remained badly swollen and he'd contracted a high fever. He'd been ordered to bed by the Elder and a healer assigned to care for him. And in the meantime, it was up to Weylyn to find those responsible for damaging the well.

The old and sacred public well for Elshorn sat in the midst of a large area of ancient trees and temple ruins. It once was in the center of the old village. Much of the ancient earthen and log fortification and the slab stones of the accompanying sacred shrine to the Celtic Horned God Cernunnos remained standing along the perimeter facing the river. It was only a short distance inland from where the small Roman dock was now located.

The ancient well's stone structure was decorated with a larger-than-life stone carving of the deity Cernunnos. Flanking him were two smaller stone representations of female attendants of the deity. Colorful ribbons, urns, and candles for offerings decorated the sacred site. Since the churchers came, the site had been desecrated many times. Always it was one of them; someone drunk, disorderly, and disrespectful of anything Celtic—especially anything sacred to the Celts. Time and again the vases and plates containing offerings were smashed or knocked off the altars, ribbons slashed, and stones damaged. Cernunnos had almost none of his elk horn antlers left on his head and three of the four female breasts were broken away. All the statues had their genitalia chipped off. The Church Prefect refused to take action against the vandals when caught. After all, a Celt water well, sacred temple grounds and a gathering place decorated to honor pagan deities didn't carry any importance to the Roman administration, who viewed all of it as sinful.

After the Eder had assigned him this task, Weylyn inspected the revered site and found an area around the main statue where the earth had been disturbed. It looked as if several drunk and disorderlies had engaged in fights and wrestling matches—as was their wont—and had torn the ground asunder. Weylyn thought the digging was probably for coins that may have been dropped in the area; this was not uncommon since many of the bargemen would occasionally use the convenient location of the heavily wooded area to hold their drunken parties. The thick brush and piles of ruin helped cover distasteful deeds. At least this time they hadn't coated the statues with feces or paint. He did find new churcher vulgarities chalked across the bodies of the statues and had two magistrate's men clean them as best they could. At least nothing else had been broken.

He'd checked the old water well. It looked normal; the long haul-ropes and oaken water buckets were as they'd always been. He really liked this old well; its large opening was capable of serving many at one time. He'd often sit here and think about all the people through the ages who had visited this sacred site, drawn water, rested and conversed under the large trees and left candles and other offerings. When he looked down into the well's opening he could see the ancient handholds and iron rings set in the wall.

Weylyn didn't personally see any reason to continue looking for the perpetrators. The grass would grow back on its own. More disrespectfuls would make their way up from the docks and vandalize the place again. He'd grown weary of interviewing the men at the docks and surrounding area and never learning anything of value. Besides, years ago Elshorn had built a new community well farther inland just off the new square beyond the Five Fingers. It was that newer public well which was most often used these days by all the inhabitants of Elshorn, and had never been spoiled by anyone.

With a start, Weylyn looked up to see his mentor had pulled his own stool close to the fire and was watching him closely. He looked past the Elder's grizzled, pale face with its furrowed brow, bushy white eyebrows, and long, full mustache and stared into the fireplace.

Elder Eghan made himself comfortable next to the hearth, leaning forward and extending his hands to the fire. "What's bothering you?" he asked the younger man.

Weylyn scowled into the flames. "The thing with this Celt, Eiroy and Elder Fey and the Romans. And the way they dug up the grave of Eiroy." He couldn't stop thinking about it. The image depressed him. He was certain the spirits wouldn't forget. He didn't want them to forget he had nothing to do with the desecration.

"Remember, Weylyn, our Elder Faith has been around for ten millennia—the Romans much less and the churchers even less than that. We'll have to get used to the ways of the churchers. They aren't going anywhere for a while, but don't let it worry you. Their time to cycle out of favor with the gods will come." Elder Eghan paused. "Tell me, then, what you think of this Eiroy and what transpired."

"It seems, Elder, like a giant puzzle, but the pieces don't fit together and some are completely missing."

"Ah, you can expect such things when dealing with the intrigues stirred up by the Roman churchers. You see, they think the more complicated they make their lives, the easier it is to deceive—and deceit is a primary tool of theirs. Never forget. Never drop your guard around them. Their plots have more undercurrents than the Moryn Gweneth." He poked the fire with the iron. "But go on about this puzzle."

"Who killed Eiroy, Elder?"

"I take it you don't believe it was Fey?"

"Elder Fey would never have done such a thing, would he?"

"Well, Eiroy was an outlaw, but we both know Fey would do no such thing. It is indeed a puzzle."

Weylyn leaned forward, closer still to the fire. He opened his cape and stuck his hands out to the warmth. "I understand why they wanted Eiroy alive. They wanted information on the treasure. I just don't know why they felt it necessary to search his body after they found him dead."

"They were obviously looking for something. But what? I think if we find the answer to that, we might be well on our way to understanding this puzzle. It's well known, it's no secret, that they wanted to talk with Eiroy. He obviously knew something, had some information they needed or wanted badly. It must have to do with the treasure. But it must be something more than just information, judging from the thorough search they made of Fey's house and the body."

The Chief Magistrate got up, walked over to the water cask, dipped a wooden ladle and added more water to the pot that hung over the fire. "I can tell you this," he continued. "Fey de Parke is best known for his berries and herbs. He uses them in his healing work and to barter for things he needs. They say his herbs are so powerful that he can heal the dead. But, then, that doesn't seem to have helped Eiroy much."

Weylyn was attentive now. He watched as his mentor pulled two cups from the shelf which stood to one side of the hearth. Turning the cups upright, the Magistrate blew into each to clear any evil spirits resting within. He handed the cups to Weylyn and turned back to the small containers on the shelf.

"Hmm …" Elder considered, "which should it be?" He perused the wooden herbal storage canisters lining the shelf. "I picked up a very delicious mix from a vendor up at Highdyn Hill during the Equinox celebrations. He had come up from the placid sea in the far south; an interesting fellow." Eghan sighed. "I tried to persuade Orrs to let you come with me but he wouldn't listen. He wanted you up on that mountain to take him to Fey's."

"I understand, Elder."

"You would have enjoyed the bards singing the old horn dance stories. Superb execution. Full of grace and power, just like the old days." He reached for a canister. "Ah, here it is. A blend of dried rosemary, honeysuckle, and lilac. Guaranteed to warm us up and help us with our puzzle."

The Elder dropped several generous pinches in each cup, then added hot water. "Hmmm, smells great." Elder Eghan swirled his cup, watching the moving herbs.

Weylyn, without thinking, moved his cup likewise.

The Elder continued, "You know, curiosity can be a double-edged sword. Two people fighting each other in front of the tavern isn't unusual. So one of them dies and so what if the other goes to a relative's to recover? Why, Fey, he'd be the one I'd want to be with if I were injured. Quite a healer is what I hear. Nothing unusual about it, is there?" He looked at Weylyn, who shrugged in response.

"Why would Fey move the body up that mountain and bury it so far from his house?" Elder Eghan mused. "Considering his age, it would have been appropriate and easier to have buried Eiroy closer to the house. And where did he go when he finished? I've checked with his friends and those who had business with him. They don't seem to know what could have happened to him or where he might be. Puzzling, puzzling, indeed. It's a problem I need to consider. I will handle the Fey disappearance. Right now, I have something else important for you to do."

Weylyn held his cup steady, waited and watched the Elder.

"I was impressed with your finding Eiroy so quickly. You did a good job—as I knew you would. Even Orrs had favorable things to say about you. Yes, indeed. We were both impressed." Eghan paused for a moment and looked at his apprentice. He cleared his throat. "But that is over now—finished. There's someone else I want you to track down, and I trust you will be just as successful and expedient as on the Eiroy search."

"It may be another important puzzle piece to consider, or it may not be related at all, but we need to find out. A young girl has disappeared. She's taken a horse from the stables of Brokan. She had the stable master's permission, though, so it isn't stolen. The girl is not only the niece of a high ranking respected member of the Druidic Magistrate Guild but she's also the granddaughter of a friend of Fey de Parke. The girl said she was going to find the treasure and make them rich. The mother fears something bad has happened, and I want you to find the girl."

The Elder gave Weylyn the description of the girl and the horse she was riding given him by the guild runner, Druce. "You might want to go talk with her mother, Moyna de Aine. You'll find her over in the artisan area here in Elshorn. She may have some more information for us."

"Yes, sir." Weylyn took another sip of his tisane. He looked into the fire and considered what he'd been told. The more he thought about it, the more questions he had.

The Elder looked grim. "There's something else you need to know. The Prefect's office in Hierlaneum is getting a lot of pressure from the Supreme High Prefect in Rome over this whole business with Eiroy and the missing treasure. Orrs is angry because his Prefect is leaning on him hard. That confirms to me there's more to this than the murder of Aod. It must be the Great Cross and treasure, as we'd suspected and as Pluvius said to you." He chuckled. "It would chafe their backsides if we Celts figured this one out for them."

Weylyn smiled and nodded in agreement.

Elder Eghan sobered. "We need to be extra careful about this, Weylyn. We don't know yet if they were trying to tie the theft to Eiroy because he was involved or because he was just a convenient Celt, but we know Eiroy killed the Roman in front of our tavern. And, according to what Elder Blaine told me, we know Aod mentioned something about a cross. At least, that's what Blaine thinks he remembers. Regardless, we must be extra cautious if this missing girl is linked to the Eiroy incident. For now, your only job is to find her and bring her to me. I want to speak with her before she's returned to her mother. If we find something even remotely connected to the investigation of the High Prefect, we'll keep it to ourselves until we've had a chance to consider our options."

"Yes, Elder." He quickly finished his hot drink.

Elder Eghan stood up and tossed the grounds from his cup into the fire and set the cup on the hearth stones. He stared at Weylyn, his face still grim. "Make certain you do exactly as I say. This is serious business."

Ah, the tasks we have at hand
Some mundane, some quite grand.
Some will wake up, some will snore.
Most will answer knocking on the door.
Chores are naught but lessons learned.
Do them not, and get quite burned.
Elders, they have all the rules
For all of us—even fools.

15

September 29th in the Roman calendar
Celtic Tree Month of Muin ends

Weylyn spent the next several days in the Aingeal Mountain area north of Aife. As he searched, he thought about the information he'd learned from the missing girl's mother when he visited her in Elshorn. Not only was the girl missing, but the mother explained how the grandfather and his friend had talked about the treasure, how they'd hoped to recover it and how their talk of all that had enticed her daughter into the hunt.

It had been an emotional visit.

"I've been frightened about where she is, how she is." The mother's voice trembled. "There's no telling what might have happened to her."

She was concerned for both her father, Petroytrix, and her young daughter, Fionna. During Weylyn's visit, she expressed her belief—her hope—the two were all right and together, but it was clear she felt something was wrong, very wrong. Her story confirmed the information given to Elder Eghan.

Weylyn had departed the home of Moyna de Aine, promising to find her daughter. He'd made no such assurance concerning the grandfather. He had a bad feeling about him because now he had another suspect to add to the list of who might have hauled Eiroy's body up the mountain.

Weylyn trekked back up to Fey's place, hoping to find him or any clue that might lead him to the missing girl and her grandfather. If he were lucky, he might even find a clue to the missing treasure, but the house remained deserted. He hadn't found any indications Fey de Parke or anyone else had returned there. Remnants of black ribbons still hung from the Greeting Pole.

The first cold blast of wintry weather had given way to much milder conditions. The bitter north wind which had been blowing so furiously for two days subsided and the temperature warmed considerably. The sunshine on the landscape of thin ice and the remaining snow patches made the land sparkle beneath a bright blue sky. The pleasant weather wouldn't last long, but for now, it seemed to Weylyn, the land had been washed clean, renewed and scrubbed for its journey through this next season.

The Celtic tree month of Muin had ended, its decorative wreaths of woodland vines removed from display on homes and businesses. In parts of the Celtic world it was time for the celebration of Gwynn ap Nudd, lord of the underworld and the faerie kingdom.

To Weylyn, Aingeal Mountain reminded him of the legends he'd heard of Gwynn ap Nudd's fabled sacred mountain of Glaistonbrai Tor, under which it was said Gwynn ap Nudd lives. He remembered the traditional chant for this time of year. "Harvest rides as long ahead of Gwynn ap Nudd as mountain roses bloom before Midsummer."

Weylyn trudged down the road toward Aife, wondering just how the girl and her grandfather fit into the puzzle of Eiroy's death, Fey's disappearance, and the missing treasure. He considered all he'd been told. Eiroy was a criminal, a horse thief and murderer at the very least. Aod, the man murdered in front of the tavern, was the same, and Weylyn knew the Enforcers believed both Eiroy and Aod were somehow linked to the theft of the Great Cross.

Then there was the matter of Fey de Parke. His present location was a mystery, as was the location of the young girl and her grandfather. Were they together somewhere and searching for the treasure? The more he thought about the puzzle, the more he believed his current assignment was somehow linked to the business with Eiroy.

Weylyn didn't believe in coincidence. He believed the universe was cyclical, orderly, too orderly to have something happen by chance. No, these pieces of the puzzle were related somehow. He wondered if he should go talk with Elder Blaine, the one witness to the incident between Aod and Eiroy.

Remembering the promise he'd made during his last trip to Aife, he stopped at the blacksmith's house to visit with Angus and his family. On their door, the vine wreaths had come down and in their place hung an iron representation of interwoven ivy branches and leaves to mark the tree month of Gort.

The family gave him drink and fresh bread for his journey, but couldn't tell him where Elder Blaine lived. They knew he lived in the dense forest just south and west of Carmel Raif but had no more specific directions. What he did learn, however, was helpful.

Apparently Blaine the Slender, for all his mysterious reclusiveness, had one recurring habit. While there may be many differences between the Elder Faith Celts and other Celt peoples, they all seemed to share a fondness of wine and beer. That bit of information jogged Weylyn's memory; he recalled having seen Blaine at the Five Fingers Tavern in Elshorn on several occasions. The blacksmith's family told him the Elder made his way into town regularly every full moon to meet his friends, a small group of Elders, at the tavern to share drinks, a meal, stories, and a game or two of tiles.

To find the root of the mystery he must go to the ground from which it all sprang. That, it seemed to Weylyn, was the killing of Aod by Eiroy in front of the tavern. He would talk with the one who saw it happen, Elder Blaine the Slender.

Speak upon the Runes so old.
Seek their Mysteries.
Light the light and be so bold.
Without questions, much can go untold.

16

September 30th in the Roman calendar
Celtic Tree Month of Gort (Ivy) commences

"I've told this story many times already," said Elder Blaine the Slender. The old man was busy shuffling small tiles of ivory around the table top in front of him. The rune glyphs of the tiles were face down. Blaine was mixing them up, preparing to do a reading of the runes. A small leather pouch sat on the table next to his large mug of heated wine. "Ayer un tuld ar drus nells, Alder Eghan," he said, speaking in the ancient tongue. Translating, he said, "As I told your boss Elder Eghan." He stopped shuffling and looked down at the tiles as he repeated his account of the murder he'd witnessed. His voice was hushed so only Weylyn could hear his story retold within the confines of the old tavern.

The Five Fingers Tavern and Common House was the only one of its kind in the small community of Elshorn and was a popular gathering place. Its brightly painted facade was flanked by large carved Greeting Poles. Numerous smaller ones lined the outer edge of its wooden sidewalk and large wooden porch.

The main hall was quite large and held a generous amount of tables and benches. The walls were adorned with old dusty mugs, drinking horns aplenty, old hero shields, and animal hides, the largest of which was a huge bear hide tacked to the wall to the right of the common fireplace. The brightest of the wall hangings were various colorful flags representing the guilds of Elshorn. The main hall was flanked by two smaller halls filled with smoky, dark booths. A stairway led to the common house. Large iron lanterns and smoke-blackened oil lamps were on the support beams and tables throughout.

The Five Fingers was a favorite place for visitors of all kinds. And though the average Celts' penchant for overindulgence of wine and beer was greatly overstated by both the early Roman and current churcher historians, the food and drink was excellent and enjoyed heartily by the locals.

The origin of the tavern's name was blurred and a source of much discussion—especially with the right crowd and the right amount of liquid spirits. It was said the tavern was originally named for the glyph of the Oimelc, the first of the eight great Celtic Elder Faith celebrations. It marks the traditional end of the great snows and the beginning of the spring awakening. The Oimelc glyph is a five-branched stave representing the upraised hand with spread fingers.

The other, more popular argument among those who revel at a good story, claims the Five Fingers was so named because of its early reputation as a hangout for the many thieves which passed through here on the river road and the merchant barges. The tavern, the story goes, was the best place to obtain various items—not at full price, but at a 'five-fingered discount.'

Weylyn gripped his mug, stared at the Elder and listened intently at the small table within the Five Fingers. Adrianna crossed the room several times attending to her duties and the customers, but for once he paid no attention to her. He gazed at the Elder sitting across the table, studying the deep lines in the older man's face. Weylyn had first met Elder Blaine at his Initiation Ritual at the Great Celebration at Highdyn Hill five years previous. Even to this day, Weylyn could not shake those memories and the dreams. Just last night, he'd had that same bad dream, a vision that often brought him awake long before the rising sun. The dark blackness of the hand of death reaching out for him, attempting to suffocate him, only to be driven back by his sacred totem, the wolf. He thought back to its beginning, back to his first remembrance of the dream, back to the ceremony with Elder Blaine the Slender at Highdyn Hill.

*

It was the night of the High Festival, the mid-point between Beltane and Lughnasadh and the celebration of the ritual fires. Weylyn was the first of the initiates to see the magnificent figure. The Druid walked into the vast inner circle of well-placed stones and joyous people. He leaped upon the large flat glyph-covered circular center-stone and raised his staff high. Slowly, he turned around and around so all could see. In the center of the circular stone sat a golden cauldron.

Weylyn slapped the young boy to his right on the arm. "There! There he is!" Weylyn said excitedly.

"Yes! I see him!" said Weylyn's best friend Turi. They could both see the white robe of bull's hide, feathered headdress, and long staff of the cleric clearly in the light of the four large bonfires around the outside of the ceremonial rings of stone.

"And look! She's here! Look," shouted Turi. Another figure, a female in a dark robe carrying a large, jewel-laden wand, ascended to the glyph-stone to stand beside the white-robed cleric. The large stones stood in a surreal light against the black, starlit sky, their surfaces shimmering in the yellow-orange glow of the four bonfires. Just that morning, the great monolith's heel stone had marked the Festival of Festivals, the Summer

Solstice, and thus designating the middle day of this annual three-day event marking the sacred mid-point between Beltane and Lughnasadh. The Alban Hefin—in Elder Faith Celt style—was well underway. Thousands of the Elder Faith danced and chanted to the beat of a hundred drums upon the grasses of Highdyn Hill. Undulating in rhythm outside the inner ring of stone, the crowd cheered wildly when they saw the ascension of the Sun and Moon Druids.

Within the inner circle, the twenty-four initiates, young boys and girls, could see the movements, hear the sounds, smell the aroma of burning juniper boughs and cedar incense mixing with the sensuous aroma of roasted pig, beef, and lamb. Inside the ring of stone on a field of grass and clover they sat their bare bodies on neatly folded clothing. They were fresh and clean from the traditional pre-ceremony purification cleansing bath of lavender and cedar. The ritual drink of lobelia, passionflower, and mandrake was well at work. It made them dizzy, euphoric. They felt ecstatic—fully alive—anticipating the ceremony.

The entire hillside and surrounding fields were covered with tents, encampments, chariots, carts and wagons of all types. Individual clan and village Greeting Poles—all painted in various bright colors and carved with name and place-glyphs and symbols in the swirling, intricate patterns of both traditional and Elder Faith Celtic patterns, many decorated with skulls, feathers and animal skins—were staked out in ever-widening rough circles outside the Sacred Ceremonial Stone Monoliths. The stands of large trees and thickets were now temporary home to hundreds of tethered cattle and horses. Pigs and chickens roamed everywhere outside the sacred circles, all hounded and herded by the numerous dogs. Thousands of brightly colored ribbons and banners flew from half as many tall poles to mark individual vendors and events of competitive combat sports, dancing, rune readings, courting, and bardic singing of the traditional Epic Tales held in conjunction with the ritual celebrations. Soon the Elders representing the various villages and areas that were home to the young participants would make their way out and stand before their respective initiates and issue the required ceremonial offerings, chants, and tonics from the sacred cauldron. In celebration of their coming of age, the young within the inner circle would receive their Blessings of Transition—the ritual initiation of acceptance into the adult social structure of the various Celtic groups, including the Brendan Valley Celts of the Elder Faith. Tonight they would have their first ritual visions, testing the prophetic powers within. It had been so for a millennium. It would be so tonight.

Weylyn listened to the speeches, the praise-singings of the many bards but heard only random parts of their telling. His mind was buzzing, his vision blurring in and out of focus. Brilliant colors came and went through his retinas as he tried to focus on the surrounding events. Sights, sounds, all senses, were distorted, out of focus. He was having trouble concentrating. He knew the drums had ceased. He recalled the Sun Druid moving around on the inner stone, shouting to the gathering—his speech echoed by the many sub-speakers around the larger, outer circle so all the crowd could know the words spoken by the Druids. At this point in Weylyn's pre-ceremony stupor, he could only recall some of what the Sun Druid had to say.

"Hear Me! Hear me! Oh, Followers of the Elder Faith, Believers of the Ancient Traditions, Children of the Cyclical Wheels of Nature, Hear me well!"

Weylyn looked around the circle at the other initiates. All were smiling and looking up at the Grand Cleric as he spoke.

"In these days of challenge and trial, the very fabric of our Faith is being tested on the outer fringes of our lands. Even now, participating in these important and ancient ceremonies, are members of our Elder Faith who no longer enjoy the treasured and sacred Celtic rights of liberty and freedom. They travel from their occupied lands, prisoners within their own valley and prisoners within their own homes. Our brethren from within the Brendan Valley know well the plague of the Roman churchers, those purveyors of restriction, pestilence, and hatred who assault the core fabric of Nature itself; the bringers of darkness upon the land; these hypocritical preachers of light who practice darkness; those who profess a great church of goodness, but who do only horrendously dark deeds to us and the earth upon which we live. Hear me, Followers of The Faith.

"We are gathered here for this High Festival, gathered in celebration as we have for all the centuries. The blessed and powerful white eyes of Mog Roith, guardian of knowledge through the ages, shine down upon us. Blessed are we to have the watch of the stones of Mog Roith and those of his daughter, the venerated Tlachtga …"

Weylyn faded in and out, his conscious self struggling against the urge to sleep. When his mind was in the present world, he heard the High Druid going on about the ancient deities and heroes, their deeds and fabled accomplishments. He drifted into the Dreamworld, between this life and the Otherworld, and had the dream vision, a dream in which he was locked in battle with pure evil. And in that dream vision a young wolf—his personal totem—came racing to his rescue.

Weylyn's eyes blurred, distorting the sights around him. His stupor amplified the sounds ten-fold. His environment became a surreal stage filled with wondrous images, sounds, and smells. He lost all sense of time. Eventually, he refocused on the Sun Druid and his speech.

The Druid was calling on the Ceremonial Presenters to make their way to the young initiates and introducing the various Elders as they made their way into the circle. Weylyn looked at Turi sitting beside him. Turi's smile gleamed as he whispered to Weylyn something about the coming of a large bear. Weylyn wanted to ask him about the bear, but the sound of the Sun Druid's voice distracted him.

"... And from the Brendan Valley, the most noble and gifted healer, Elder Blaine the Slender, will help render the ceremony for the honored male youth from that region. We note with sadness this will be his last formal ceremony in the Circle of Stones. He will retire to his home and dedicate his time to his healing practice for the folks of the Brendan Valley region. And rendering the ceremony for our honored females of the valley region, Eldermother Brennarix ..."

Weylyn knew many elders of the valley, but Elder Blaine was not one he could remember ever meeting. He was eager to get on with the ceremony. He leaned over to ask Turi if he knew the Elder. Turi, however, was engaged in a discussion about bears with the young man on his right. An elder wearing a dark robe approached them and ordered them to rise. They could see similar figures around the circle approach the other initiates.

They watched as the robed figure stepped closer to them. He stopped in front of Weylyn and Turi. "I am Blaine the Slender, Blaine the Healer, Blaine the Seerer. I am of the Brendan Range, of the Brendan Valley, of Aingeal Mountain, and of Elshorn. I am your Ceremonial Presenter."

He addressed Turi first. "In honor of your parents and your elders, especially your father, Angus of the Forge, a blacksmith of the village Elshorn and your teacher of the honorable and sacred smithing trade, do you, young initiate, accept the ceremony I'm about to offer you?"

As he had been taught, Turi closed his eyes and bowed his head. "Yes, Elder." He stayed perfectly still as the Elder placed three dots of charcoal upon him—one on the forehead, one on the chest and one on the stomach.

The Elder then turned to Weylyn. "In honor of your parents and elders, especially your mentor, Eghan of the Oaks, Magistrate for Elshorn and Chief Magistrate of all the Brendan Range, and your teacher of the honored magistrate trade, do you, young initiate, accept the ceremony I am about to offer you?"

Weylyn closed his eyes and bowed his head. "Yes, Elder."

After the Elder placed the three dots of charcoal upon Weylyn's body, he stepped back a pace from his two initiates and waited for the other Elders around the circle to complete their duties. When they had all finished, the Sun Druid tapped his staff loudly upon the stone and the Moon Druid waved her wand in a circle around her head. They were the signals to begin the next phase of the ritual. As with one voice, the Ceremonial Presenters spoke to their respective initiates.

The two boys listened as Blaine spoke to them. "It is my duty tonight to prepare you for your journey. With me you will venture into the realm of the Middle Ones and leave the world of the New Ones. You will take your inner journey to see what you will see, to do what you will do. Mark it well, remember it always—the visions you will see. In your seeing, you may be granted sight into the Otherworld.

"Bring back what you can, remember it well, for in your seeing the Otherworld may grant you a vision of your future. With that vision, you will walk into the new world, your future. As it has been for a millennium, let it be so tonight."

*

"Elder," said Weylyn, "you may not remember but you presided over my initiation ceremony at Highdyn Hill, five years ago."

"Ah, my last ceremony. It was a fine one, too. And now here you are, a deputy magistrate. I hope I've been of help to you in this matter."

"You have, Elder, and I am grateful," Weylyn responded. "Is there anything else you can remember about the murder?"

"What do you want to know?"

"You told Elder Eghan that Eiroy asked you about another man named Eiroy?"

"One Eiroy asking about another, yes," muttered Blaine. "You know sometimes the wine can mislead the mind. But, yes, after much mediation on this, I'm certain."

"Did the Enforcers who questioned you tell you that the Celt rider's name was Eiroy?"

"No." Elder Blaine scowled slightly and, turning his head to his left, facing the tavern aisle he half spit, half hissed and said, "Romans, Enforcers, churchers—they have nothing to say." He looked back up at Weylyn. He wiped his face with the back of his wrinkled, gnarled hand. "I heard it from the man who died. He called the murderer by name—Eiroy, as I remember."

He paused and looked back down at the tiles. "I hear many people have the same name these days." He finished stacking his ivory tiles. "Some, I hear, even wear the same rune buckle."

"What rune buckle, Elder?" Weylyn couldn't recall either Orrs or Elder Eghan mentioning anything about a rune buckle.

"The Celt had the rune buckle attached to the front of his belt. He said the Eiroy he sought wore one just like it." The old man coughed, a small dry cough, and reached for his mug.

"And did you tell the Enforcers about this rune buckle?"

"I told them everything." He took a drink from his mug and set it back down.

Weylyn waited for the Elder to clear his throat. "And you told the Enforcers the same story you just told me?"

"Yes," he replied. "But I only told Eghan of Oaks about the rune reading."

"Rune reading?"

The runes were an ancient divining method as well as a means of communications. Many Celts used them. It was a most favored tool of the Druidic Order of Highdyn Hill, the powerful Celtic order headquartered in the Celtlands just west of the Brendan Mountains. They were the order who presided over the young Celts' initiation ceremonies. Highdyn Hill and its fortress city of Carew was now the most powerful of the last remaining true Celtic city-lands bordering the Roman lands and stood as a bastion against further encroachment by the Roman churchers.

Runes—as with nearly everything else in the Great Church-dominated lands—carried a huge penalty for use as a tool of divination. The Celts, however, were smart. They hadn't thrown their bone, stone, clay or ivory runes into the fire just because of a decree by the Great Church. No, they were wiser, more adaptable. They would not give up one of the tools they believed helped in the navigation of their lives.

Since there were no proclamations against games, the Celts soon discovered they could continue to use the runes, carry them openly as long as the Enforcers thought they were using them only for entertainment. Followers of the Elder Faith could not divine openly, but they could legally carry, display and even sell the runes as games of chance and amusement without fear of confiscation by the Church.

"Can you tell me of your rune reading, Elder?"

Elder Blaine the Slender looked to his left, slowly peering around the hall of the tavern. He looked back at Weylyn. He seemed to be considering his answer. The pause was long, but Weylyn knew to wait patiently. The old man took another slow look out across the tavern. He turned back to his young inquisitor. "I will tell you if that is your wish, but you should know this reading was accompanied by a runevision."

They both reached for the drinks in front of them. Each raised their mugs and quaffed goodly portions. When they finished, Elder Blaine continued his tale.

"It was after my encounter with the riders, the Celt and the Roman. I thought a lot about it on my way home that night. It was a long walk for me. At first, I tried to dismiss it, but it would not leave me. I got angry with myself because of what happened and because I could not dismiss it. I kept seeing it over and over a hundred times. I saw it again before I reached my house. Finally, there in my bed, just before I entered sleep, it came to me—the reason why this thing would not leave me. It was the time of Muin. The prophetic powers were working in me. There was something the gods wished to reveal to me about those two men. Lugh, God of the Higher Mind, would light my seeing. I would reach him through the runes."

Elder Blaine took a deep breath, then continued his story. "I rose from my bed in the deep of night, tired from my long walk. I lit the candles on my table. I took the runes from their pouch and shuffled them and placed them in proper order inside the arch of the candles. I was tired; my eyes could barely focus; sleep was doing its best to take me. The runes seemed to rise from the table. I tried to focus but things became covered by a thick haze. I peered into the haze over the runes and focused hard to make it out. I think it was a vision from the Otherworld.

"A large willow tree, a small house, two spirits—one black, one white—were looking at me from the house. A large blue snake moved out front. A short pole bound by iron sat in place of the Greeting Pole. Spirit runes formed in the clouds above the spirit. It was a Place-Marker rune but I couldn't make it out exactly. I think it was the sign of the elk's horn."

*

Weylyn lay in his bed and thought about what he'd heard in the tavern. As Elder Blaine had said, two people having the same name was common. Two people with the same name and identical rune buckles? Maybe. But those same two people involved in a murder? What were the odds of that?

The rune buckle—was that what they were looking for when they searched Fey's house and the body of Eiroy? He couldn't recall seeing the rune buckle among the things taken from the body. Had he just not seen it? Possible, but why hadn't Orrs mentioned it? And why hadn't Elder Eghan said anything to him about the buckle?

Then there was the runevision house in Blaine's vision, the house with the strange pole. To the Elder Faith, visions were always important. It was such a vision that had come to Turi—a vision of a large bear. It was a large bear that had taken Turi's life. Weylyn remembered his own vision—the dark, suffocating hand of death about to strike him only to be saved by his totem, the wolf. With an effort, he pushed that thought away and settled down to sleep.

He lay there and drifted into the realm which exists just between consciousness and sleep. In his almost-dream, his mind saw Adrianna, her dark eyes filled with sadness even as her voice was harsh and accusing. "Why?" he heard Adrianna ask. "Why won't you live in Hierlaneum with me? Why won't you give up your pagan ways? Why won't you give in and become part of my church?"

Why, indeed, he thought as he succumbed to sleep.

Fair she is, the maiden forward spoken,
Low upon the land they cross,
She searches for her history.
The stout oak stands, the willow bends.
The Sun will shine; the Moon will glow for all to see.
The more we find, the deeper grows the mystery.

17

October 1st in the Roman calendar
Midway through the Runic Half-Month Gyfu (Gift)

The day dawned clear, with a southwesterly breeze bringing a hint of warmth from the Southern Brendans—the Dragon's Breath Winds. They blew in from across the top of the Cliffs of the Dragon in the south Brendan range. They would stop as suddenly as they'd started, then cold winds would return. Weylyn took advantage of the mild weather to make another journey back up Aingeal Mountain.

He'd gone to Aife again, intending to visit with Angus, but learned the blacksmith and his family had traveled into Elshorn on business and to restock supplies. Weylyn had spent some time talking with several people who lived in and near the village of Aife, hoping for information about the missing girl Fionna, her grandfather, or Fey de Parke. He hadn't learned anything new and decided to begin searching in earnest around Fey de Parke's dwelling and head farther up the mountain from there.

It was midday before Weylyn found himself once again

staring at the small dwelling. He could see the tattered remains of black ribbons still hanging from the Greeting Pole. It was well beyond the required seven days since the burial. A healer should be summoned to restore the home to its spiritual wellness. Ideally the family, under the direction of the healer, should take the ribbons down. The home should be cleansed of the black charcoal glyphs of warding.

The window was still shuttered tight. He circled around to the back of the house, to the corral and rough shelter where Fey kept his cultivation tools and implements; all were still hanging in place. Gone, of course, was the outlaw's horse and the saddle. Both had been taken by Orrs.

Considering the recent weather and passage of time, any hope of following signs left by Fey in his retreat of this place had all but vanished. Vanished like Fey himself. The young magistrate retraced his steps to the front of the dwelling, thinking about what he'd put together since this whole thing started. It wasn't much. He looked at the home again, the stones, the beams, the Greeting Pole, the black ribbons and glyphs. A nagging feeling something was wrong here wouldn't leave him, but he couldn't understand what it might be.

He completed two trips around the house and the immediate area, circling out ever wider as he slowly searched the woods and slopes for any sign of the missing Elder or any clue as to his or the other missing people's whereabouts. He found nothing.

Weylyn decided, reluctantly, to enter Fey's dwelling. It was the only thing he could think of doing. He needed something, anything to give him a clue to the location of Fionna and possibly an idea of what happened to Elder Fey. He pushed the door open and entered. The place was in the same disorderly, unkempt condition Orrs had described. After an nonproductive survey, he exited and resumed his search outside.

The day wore long, the sun nearing the western peaks of the Brendans. Weylyn picked up the mountain trail behind the dwelling and made his way up to the overlook high above the area he'd led Orrs and his men to in the search for Eiroy.

Weylyn removed his pack and sat down on a large stone. The wind was blowing briskly up from the valley far below, through fields and forests of rich, variant greens, browns and yellows. The wind was blowing the first dead leaves of autumn like so many tiny airborne kites. The blue ribbon of river that was the Moryn Gweneth meandered its way through the valley floor. Far below him Weylyn could see buzzards circling above the jutted edge of mountain which held the cave where they'd found Eiroy's body.

His attention was diverted, distracted from the movements of the large black scavengers by an even larger and more regal sky dweller, an eagle. It soared above the valley and below Weylyn's seat on the overlook. He watched the majestic bird turn and soar in the wind. It glided to the south, then east over the location of Fey's home. Weylyn lost sight of the eagle when it disappeared beyond the trees. If the eagle stayed its current course, Weylyn imagined it would fly to Elshorn and right over the Five Fingers Tavern and Adrianna. He thought of her there, waiting tables, cleaning the floors and mugs, joking with the patrons, doing her best to work off the indentured servitude forced upon her to pay a debt of her legal guardian, her uncle.

The eagle reappeared above the tree line. He watched it fly higher and farther until it once again flew out of sight on its silent journey down the mountain and out over the valley. The thought of Adrianna came to him again. He could see her dark eyes and see the soft curves of her body. His spirit soared like the eagle which just passed on its silent journey down the mountain.

Silent journey.

His mind came back to Fey de Parke and his sudden disappearance. That still bothered Weylyn. It seemed curious he had silently, without any notice to anyone, slipped out of sight without so much as a good-bye to his relatives and friends. And he hadn't made an easy burial of Eiroy, either. Why would Fey have hauled a body up so far from his home when it would have been far easier to have buried the outlaw close? It was all very strange.

"Where oh where are you, Elder?" Weylyn said out loud. A shiver ran through his body, a cold chill ran up his spine. He shook it off. Was it the spirit of a dead Fey de Parke trying to raise him? He hoped not. He picked up his pack, slung the strap over his left shoulder and headed back down the mountain trail toward the Elder's home, whistling softly as he went.

He was tired and he was more than a little frustrated. He was not making any progress in his assignment to find the girl, Fionna. Wherever she was, he hoped she was safely with her grandfather. The more he thought about it, the more he believed the girl and her grandfather were likely on a fool's errand, looking for the missing treasure. Sooner or later they would give up and return home. Unless they were involved somehow in this Eiroy incident, their disappearance didn't seem all that important to Weylyn.

He took another look at the home of Elder Fey as he passed it, heading on down the mountain. For just a moment he considered spending the night there but quickly cast off the thought. He knew the blacksmith and his family would welcome him should he ask for lodging overnight, but he'd intruded on their kindness enough. Instead, he decided to continue on down the mountain past Aife to Carmel Raif. Inside the sacred pool's arbor would be a better choice to stop for the night. No fuss, no bothering others, just a good night's sleep before returning to the Chief Magistrate's compound in the morning. He knew he could make it to the sacred site before total darkness. And he was certain he would rest there much better than inside the home of Fey de Parke.

The shadows were getting longer, darkness well on its way

when he reached the sacred pool. To his dismay, he saw the glow from several lit candles, and a horse tethered at the arbor. Someone had beaten him to the shelter.

He dismounted. It would be rude to bother anyone seeking shelter inside the arbor; he decided to give it a wide berth. Being as quiet as he possibly could, he walked down the trail toward the water, the arbor off to his left across an open area. If he couldn't sleep in the shelter then he would fill his water skin, refresh himself and make his way back to Elshorn in the dark. As he passed the arbor and the horse, he thought he could make out a dark form lying across the floor of the open-fronted shelter. Probably the rider was already fast asleep.

He stopped at the pool and knelt to fill his water skin. A gust of chill wind kicked up and blew dried leaves and debris around. The tethered horse gave a whinny and nicker and then a loud snort. The sound seemed humorous to the young magistrate as he looked back at the arbor and the horse. He laughed softly as he watched the horse twitch his ear, once, twice, three times as if waving.

Water skin filled, he secured it back in its place on his mount. He patted his horse on the head and then, prodded by a memory, he turned back around to look at the horse, its rough-made hemp rope halter tied to a small tree by the arbor. Even in the fading light, he could see it was chestnut brown with one white ear and a prominent white tail. That matched Elder Eghan's description of the horse taken by the missing girl. He decided to take a closer look.

With his own horse secured to a small sapling just off the pool, he made his way back toward the arbor, moving quietly. Blood pounded in his ears, his pulse beat faster as he neared the horse. If this was indeed the horse belonging to Brokan at the Elshorn stables, then Fionna could be in the shelter. Weylyn wondered if she was aware he had come into the sacred site. The magistrate stood very still, listening. Was she asleep? Was it even her? He considered the very real possibility the girl could have been attacked and robbed, the horse stolen and the thief now inside the arbor. He considered his options, standing quietly as the wind rustled through the leaves. In the distance he could hear the rat-a-tat-tat of a woodpecker as it sought out its evening meal. As quietly as possible, he moved to the thicket of small elms at the back of the arbor. Crouching down, he slipped the pack from his back and as a precaution drew the dagger from his belt. As he did so, the mare snorted again. Weylyn stood perfectly still. There was a shuffle of hooves. The animal seemed nervous but Weylyn had no idea if it was because of his presence or because of something else. He hoped it wasn't the 'something else.'

He looked up through the branches of the slender elms to the sky. The evening stars were already shining their lights across the darkening sky as the sun was in its final degrees of descent for the day. When the mare quieted again Weylyn moved into a crouching stance just to the side of the shelter's open entrance. He slowly peered around the side and into the shadowy portal. He held his breath and readied his weapon and strained to see what lay inside.

On the floor, in the shadows, he thought he could make out a dark form lying on the floor on what appeared to be a sleeping skin. Apparently, the person hadn't been awakened by the horse or the young magistrate's approach. Cautiously and quietly, Weylyn made his way inside to the form on the floor. Dagger at the ready, he said a silent prayer to his wolf totem and then, with this right foot, tapped at the form. "Wake up."

To his amazement, the form—a dark blanket stuffed with leaves held up with small sticks to make it appear to be a body sleeping—collapsed. He didn't get the chance to contemplate the deception. At the sound of movement behind him, he spun around, instinctively raising an arm in self-defense even as the first blow struck his temple above his left eye. He staggered as a second blow, then a third, struck him in the head and dropped him to the floor.

A trickle of warm blood dripped from his left eyebrow. His head throbbed. He looked up and saw a shadowy figure run to the mare, turn and throw the club back at him, barely missing his head. The horse with one white ear danced and jumped as the figure began to untie the tether.

Weylyn ignored the throbbing pain in his head and ran after his attacker. He lunged forward and grabbed an arm, but the person twisted out of his grasp and scrambled beneath the horse in an effort to escape. Weylyn followed, reaching out and grabbing leather britches just above the ankle.

His attacker screamed, "Don't! Let go of me! Let go!"

A girl! Weylyn loosened his grip on her slightly but didn't let go entirely. He crawled from under the horse, left hand still clutching the britches leg and attempting to pull her to him.

She was sobbing and frantically attempting to pull a large dagger but it had become caught on her belt and clothing and she couldn't draw it. He looked at her and let go of her leg. When he did, she immediately kicked fiercely at Weylyn's chest with both feet, trying to knock him away from her. She kicked and flailed at him with hands and feet, screaming all the while.

"Don't hurt me!"

Weylyn dropped his own dagger, grabbed for her arms and tried to protect himself from the kicks. She broke away, stood up and ran toward his horse. He chased her down and managed to get a good hold on her but she was strong. She knocked his legs out from under him with a sweeping motion of her right leg against his ankle. Still locked together in struggle, they fell to the ground. He lay on top of her holding her arms down.

"Get off me!" she shrieked. "Get off!"

"Not until you tell me who you are and why you attacked a magistrate," he retorted.

She struggled to free herself from him but this time he had

her where she couldn't move. He felt her relax. She stopped struggling. She turned her head to her right, away from his face.

He gave her a few moments to catch her breath. He raised his torso up without loosening his grip. She'd proven to be strong for such a young person and he didn't want to be caught off guard again. He looked at the dagger wedged in her belt, a dagger with the large, round pommel, inlaid runes and the unfinished, unwrapped hilt. He'd need to examine it in good light to be certain, but he was confident it was the unfinished dagger stolen from the blacksmith at Aife.

She was no longer crying. Her breathing was still heavy but she'd regained most of her composure. She stared at him. "I didn't attack you. You attacked me! And in a sacred refuge, too!" she said with an air of righteous defiance.

"You're a little thief."

"And you're a defiler of sacred grounds!" she screamed. She struggled again, as if testing his hold. She still couldn't move.

He was not going to let her up. "Is that your dagger there in your belt?" asked Weylyn. He'd get her now. He'd catch her in a lie and take her in for attacking a magistrate and stealing the dagger from Angus. He knew where the dagger came from and he certainly knew it wasn't hers.

"No. It isn't mine. It belongs to my friend. He let me use it."

"That dagger is stolen. You took it from the blacksmith in Aife." He grabbed the dagger and after a brief struggle pulled it from its binding around her waist. He stuck it in his own belt.

"I did not steal it. I don't steal."

"Yeah, right." He didn't believe a word of her story.

"Let me up!"

"What's your friend's name?"

"I don't have to tell you. It's none of your business!" she shouted. "If you want that dagger, take it. But don't hurt me."

He could barely make out her face in the darkness.

"Please don't hurt me," she said, her voice softening. He felt her relax completely. She cried softly.

He tested her by loosening his hold. He imagined tears flowing down her face. He slowly rolled off her, stood, and helped her up. She took a moment to straighten her short tunic and re-fasten the brooch holding her short fox cape together, then hitched up the leather britches she wore.

"What were you doing with that dagger?"

"Like I said, it's none of your business." Her voice was cold.

"It is my business. My name is Weylyn and I am a deputy magistrate from Elshorn. I've been tasked to find that dagger, the one with the large round pommel and inlaid runes and unfinished hilt. The blacksmith in Aife reported it stolen."

She stood perfectly still, silent.

"Now, tell me where you've been, Fionna," he demanded.

She gasped and took a big step backwards. "How … how do you know my name?"

"Your mother. She's worried about you, asked us to find you. The Chief Magistrate wants to talk with you."

"Oh." She dropped her head, grabbed a strand of hair and twisted it with both hands.

"And the dagger?" he asked again.

"I needed it for protection." She hesitated, then began again. "I'm looking for my grandfather. He's missing. I needed a weapon for safety. These mountains can be dangerous." She began sobbing softly again.

"You have no idea where your grandfather might be?" He wasn't at all certain she'd tell him even if she knew. At least now he knew she'd been up here in the area around Fey's and it was possible her grandfather had been here as well. Could either or both of them have been involved with the burial of Eiroy, or know anything about Fey's whereabouts?

"I haven't found him." She fidgeted with her cape and brooch. "Are you looking for him, too?"

"Yes. I thought maybe you were together."

"I haven't seen him for days now," she said sadly.

"What makes you think he may be up here?"

She shifted slightly and looked down, not answering.

Weylyn sighed. "Let me tell you something, Fionna. It's dangerous on this mountain. Enforcers were up here with me looking for a man. We found him, dead. He died from a bad cut in the stomach and was buried by Elder Fey de Parke up in the cliffs beyond his home." He pointed back toward the bluffs. "I don't suppose you can tell me anything about that, could you?"

She stood silently, twisting her hair.

Weylyn suspected Fionna—and possibly her grandfather—may have helped Fey bury the body, but he doubted she'd admit anything to him. Elder Eghan would find out, he thought. He felt a sudden urge to get off the trail, but the sun was now completely gone, and the moon not yet visible. Weylyn's eyes had adjusted to the dark and he could just make out the girl's face and her light colored hair. She was looking down and away, as if contemplating what he had said.

"Well, it's too late to do anything more tonight," he told her. We'll move in the morning."

Fionna stopped fiddling with her hair and glared at him. "You're one of us, a Celt. Why are you looking for him? Are you going to give him to the Enforcers?" She stood there defiantly, feet planted firmly, arms crossed.

This was one tough girl.

A gust of chill wind scattered leaves around them, making them both shiver. His head was still pounding from the blows Fionna had landed. A knot had formed on his brow. He needed time to rest and time to think.

"Look, Fionna, it's late. I'm tired. I'll go get my pack and we can eat. Go inside the shelter, where it's warmer. Tomorrow is soon enough to sort everything out." He bent down next to the horse and picked up his dagger and returned it to his belt. Weapon secured, he retrieved his pack and pulled out a cloth bundle containing dried meat and bread. He was hungry and tired and his head was pounding.

In the morning, Fionna could help him sort out this mess with the stolen dagger. She may not have any knowledge of the Eiroy incident, but she certainly was guilty of stealing a dagger and of attacking a magistrate. At least he could tell her mother she was well, that no real harm had come to her. What happens to her now would be up to the Chief Magistrate, Elder Eghan.

He hurried into the shelter, eager to get out of the wind and the coming chill of the night. Three steps inside, he stopped in his tracks as he realized Fionna was nowhere to be seen.

"Fionna! Fionna, come back!" he shouted. Curses to the gods of stupidity, he swore silently. He'd turned his back on her, and she'd run away. Stumbling in the dark, he searched in vain. He stopped, listening for any sounds of movement. Nothing. Not in a millennium would he be able to find her on this mountain in the dark. All he would manage to do is either get lost or killed falling off a bluff in the dark.

"Fionna!" he called again, but only the sounds of the wind moving through the trees answered. He walked back to the pool and got his horse and tethered it next to the one Fionna had been riding. He stroked the mare's nose and rubbed its head. It nuzzled his arm and took a couple of steps left and right testing the hemp rope. "Sorry, girl. You'll need to stay here a while longer. If she doesn't return, I'll take you back in the morning to your stable in Elshorn."

Grab your ankles, kiss the ground
Take twenty lashes like a hound.
Disobey an Elder's rule,
Dance and shuffle like a fool.
But if you move on solid ground,
Even Elders can come 'round.
Logic sometimes bends the rule
And sends the Elders back to school.
Even low points have a rise.
Intelligence will always compromise.

18

October 2nd in the Roman calendar
Midway through the Celtic Tree Month of Gort

Weylyn woke the next morning to discover the mare was gone. Cursing in frustration, he'd mounted his own horse and headed back up the trail, searching for signs Fionna might have passed this way in the night. He'd gone as far as Fey de Parke's place, just in case the girl was hiding there. Nothing.

Back in Elshorn, he stood before the fireplace in the great room of the Magistrate Longhouse and related his experience to Elder Eghan, who sat quietly as Weylyn told his tale. "I'm sorry I wasn't able to apprehend her."

"Well, you did at least find her—even if you let her get away from you."

Weylyn felt himself blushing furiously.

The old man rose from his chair and stretched. He ran his bony fingers through the tufts of long white hair around his ears, and then rubbed the top of his bald head with both hands. He motioned Weylyn back from the hearth with a wave of his hand and paced back and forth with his arms crossed behind his back, hands locked together.

Weylyn watched the Magistrate's restless movements, uncertain what to say.

"I know you said it was dark, but did you see a buckle on the girl?" the Elder asked.

"No, but she did have a stolen dagger on her." Weylyn repeated his conversation with the blacksmith of Aife.

Eghan of Oaks stopped his pacing and turned to Weylyn. "That may be, but the dagger is a trivial matter compared with the treasure and the missing Fey de Parke. No, don't worry about the dagger." He cleared his throat. "I want your full attention. I have things to tell you concerning these little mysteries we have. All, I think, are tied together.

"Angus the blacksmith came to see me. He brought Fionna's mother, his son Cullen, and Kelwin, a wagon boy who used to work with him. They had very interesting information concerning the time just after that Roman was killed here in front of the tavern. Kelwin claims Fionna confided in him. It appears Elder Petroytrix told Fionna not to go looking for the treasure. She was to stay off Aingeal Mountain, stay close to her mother and in Elshorn until he contacted her again. There was something about a rune buckle and warning to stay away from a man named Eiroy—Eiroy the Younger. Fionna said the Elder mentioned a rune place-marker and a runevision. A vision of two spirit men—one black, one white—in a small house under a large willow, an iron-banded totem in place of the Greeting Pole, a glyph of warding and—"

"Elder! That's the same runevision seen by Elder Blaine!"

Eghan looked hard at Weylyn. "Ah, he told you of his vision, did he? Yes, they are same."

"I'm sorry I interrupted your telling, Elder, but I intended to tell you that I visited with Elder Blaine. He said he'd told only you. He didn't share it with the Enforcers."

"Of course he wouldn't!" The Elder's voice raised a pitch or two. "Can you imagine the looks on their faces if he'd talked about his runes and visions? Ha! And looks would be the least of it! Why, they'd have him in irons in the torture chamber in Cross Abbey faster than you could recite the fourteen tree months! They'd have him beaten and his eyes burned out with hot pokers for such heinous churcher blasphemes. Then he'd be taken before the Bishop, forced to convert to their religion. If he refused, he'd be put to death. If he agreed, they'd declare him 'saved' and then put him to death. Either way, he loses!" shouted the Elder. "Of course, he didn't tell them anything of the sort! Hrumpt," he snorted, his face red from anger. He took a deep breath and slowly exhaled, then crossed his hands behind his back and paced the hearth again.

Weylyn sat down and stared at his feet, thinking. It was rare to see Elder Eghan so angry, but he was right, of course, about what would have been done to Blaine had he told the Enforcers of the runevision. But two men having the same vision? What was it Fey and Blaine had in common?

Several minutes went by before the Elder spoke again. "The day I dispatched you to find Eiroy, the girl went missing from her home. Cullen said she was worried something terrible was about to happen to her grandfather. She left to help him."

"Why did she go to Aife?" asked Weylyn.

"Kelwin says Petroytrix had information about Fey de Parke and Eiroy the Red and hinted the treasure may be up there. Fionna knows Angus and his family. They used to live in Elshorn before his son Turi died; but then, you know that already. Her mother told me they were the only ones she knew up on the mountain. I think she was looking for her grandfather and the treasure. She probably thought if she found one, she'd found the other."

The Magistrate returned to his seat and gazed into the fireplace. "There is much to consider."

"So, Elder Blaine heard correctly. There are two Eiroys."

"Yes, so there are. And now one is dead and the other has to be found," mused the Elder. "In my search for Fey, one of his longtime drinking companions said the Eiroys were brothers. He thought they had, at one time—years ago—built a house along the river somewhere west of Elshorn. He couldn't remember where or even if they still lived there. It's possible they moved out of the valley several years ago. That's all he could tell me."

"What's the significance of the vision? The two spirits, one white, one black?"

"It could mean many things. It may reflect two opposing sides of the same thing—the positive and the negative, night and day, or the known and the unknown. If it relates to two people, it usually means one is good, one is evil. It can sometimes mean one is dead, one is living. Maybe it means something altogether different in this circumstance," said the Magistrate. "We should find out. It could be important."

"Is there something else Elder Blaine and Elder Fey had in common besides Eiroy the Red?"

The Elder looked at his apprentice for a long moment. He turned back to gaze at the fireplace once more before speaking. "They had many things in common. But only one important thing, and that was a piece of metal—the rune buckle. Far as I know, it is the one thing related to Eiroy they had in common."

Weylyn thought back to his conversation with Blaine the Slender. He remembered Eiroy the Red was looking for another named Eiroy and both, it was said, had identical buckles. So the other Eiroy was Eiroy the Younger. Where was he? Eiroy the Red seemed to have thought he was somewhere in Elshorn, or along the river in this general area. Why? Because of the old house? Weylyn thought about that and how he might be able to find this Eiroy the Younger.

The Elder was still facing forward, eyes on the small fire and the red, burning embers. He reached over, grabbed the iron poker, and stirred the contents of the fireplace. He continued to play with the fire as he spoke. "Let's consider the facts as we know them. First, Eiroy the Red was here in Elshorn looking for Eiroy the Younger. Brother looking for brother. The Red is confronted in front of the tavern by Aod, whom he kills. Eiroy the Red is wounded and flees to his relative, Fey de Parke, for help.

"At some point, Petroytrix must have learned something important, something that frightened him enough to warn his granddaughter not to come around or to search for the treasure. How or what he learned, we don't yet know. He also told her it wasn't safe to venture from her home and to stay away from this Eiroy the Younger because of the danger. What danger?"

He poked an unburned limb, sending up bright orange cinders. "Then there's this matter of the missing rune buckle. We think it's significant because of the runevision. I believe it has something to do with the Cross and the other treasure taken from the Cross Abbey shipment. According to Blaine, Aod mentioned a cross to the Red that evening he was killed."

Elder pulled the iron from the embers and blew on the end. He set the poker down and placed another bundle of sticks on the fire. "What else do we know?"

"Well, there's the girl," Weylyn noted. "She mentioned the rune buckle to Cullen. If nothing else, it confirms Elder Blaine's story and the information from Kelwin. But we still don't know where it is or what importance it has. If the girl doesn't have it, at least she knows of it. What does the rune buckle have to do with the stolen Great Cross or the rest of the treasure?"

"I don't know yet. Did Fionna have the buckle on her when you ran into her?"

"I don't think so, but she could have hidden it somewhere."

"You think Orrs has it?"

"It's possible. He could have taken it off the body of Eiroy the Red while I looked around the cave. I don't think he found it at Fey's, otherwise why would he have been so insistent about searching Eiroy's body? But why didn't he mention it?"

"Well, there's one possibility—beside their standard practice of not telling a Celt. The buckle may be a clue to the location of this Eiroy the Younger. They can't question Eiroy the Red now that he's dead, so they want the Younger. Could be they don't want us to find the Younger before they do; could be orders from his boss, the Prefect."

"Yes, I see what you mean."

The old man rubbed his chin. "I think I should take a little trip over to Cross Abbey and visit Orrs. I need to give him an update anyway. But I'd also like to see his face when I ask about this mysterious rune buckle."

The Elder stood up, placed his hands on his hips and stretched by bending back at the waist. "Getting stiff just sitting around. Not good for the soul. Go to the stable and tell Brokan to prepare my horses and chariot for tomorrow. I'll be heading to Cross Abbey first thing in the morning. Meanwhile, you search for Fionna, again. Also, I think you need to start looking around for a large willow and a small house with a short, banded Greeting Pole. Could be—in fact I'll wager—this place is more than just a vision. And I'll further venture it has to do with more than just this little Eiroy mystery."

Weylyn stood and headed for the door. "Yes, Elder." He reached the door when the Elder spoke again.

"Oh, Weylyn, one other thing."

"Sir?"

"Angus said to forget about that dagger. It wasn't stolen after all. His son Cullen loaned it to Fionna while she searched for her grandfather Petroytrix."

Willow, Willow by the brook
From the tree we all can look,
To your cure for heads that ache;
We strip your bark for our own sake.
Beneath your branches Runes have seen,
The plots of men both chaotic and serene.
Hiding by your wistful shade
The vision but with Mystery laid.

19

October 3rd in the Roman calendar
Midway through the Runic Half-Month of Gyfu (Gift)

The deeply fissured, dark gray bark and elegant branches of the indigenous willow tree made it a favorite with the locals of Elshorn. The trees were popular for their esthetic beauty and were useful in practical ways. Healers like Elder Fey knew the willow granted the enlightened many benefits. Its stem bark was a painkiller and fever-breaker. It could be used to cure many ailments including sore throats, stomach problems, and even poisoning from eating bad food. Its branches were used by local Celtic weavers to make sturdy, functional baskets. The charcoal made from the wood of the willow was favored by the artisans of the valley. Weylyn knew the warding glyphs of black on Fey's home were likely made with the charcoal of the willow.

Druidic uses were even more elaborate. The branches of the tree were said to be used for the making of powerful ceremonial wands, staffs, and ritual brooms. The Romans called the willow tree salix alba. The name derived from the valley Celts' name sal-lis, meaning 'near water.' The trees were all along the Moryn

Gweneth River area, up and down the many streams which flowed from the surrounding mountains, and were plentiful in the valley around the sacred wells and grave sites. It would be a daunting task finding the right one. Weylyn thought it possible he'd need a cure from the willow before all this was over.

Finding the location of the small house with the carved pole could prove to be even more tiresome. Practically every dwelling in the area fit the description. The exception was the type of pole; it was not the standard twelve-foot pole Celts routinely placed in front of their homes here in the valley. It would be a complete waste of time if the house was merely nothing but a vision, and not a reality of stone, timber, mud and thatching.

He decided to forgo the road up to Aife. He'd been that way too many times recently and hadn't noticed any such dwelling. Besides, the information they had concerning the structure said it was somewhere along the river. So he began his search to the west of Elshorn and the Aife road. He took trails up and down the wooded slopes, followed streams up as far as he could, crossed numerous fields and pasture lands all the way back down to the main road running along and mostly parallel to the Moryn Gweneth in this area from Elshorn westward to Blaire.

He stopped several times to visit briefly with people who lived in the area. None had ever seen a hut or house with a short and metal-banded Greeting Pole. Neither had they seen the elusive Fionna or her grandfather. Weylyn was weary, tired of sitting on the horse. He rode to a high knoll just north of the road and dismounted in a grove of hazel amid the ruins of an old dwelling with a five-foot high carved grey stone with swirling circular patterns.

From this vantage point he could look south. Down below him he could see a large willow next to the Blaire road's main public well. The road was filled with the typical deep ruts made by the many wagons, carts, and chariots which traversed the valley between Dynsmore in the east and Carew to the west. Tying the horse to a hazel tree, he sat on the stones surrounding the old building and pulled bread and dried jerky from his pack.

The sky was clear and blue, the air fresh, cool and clean. The view was spectacular. Beyond the well and the road Weylyn could see the blue Moryn Gweneth River as it made its way slowly westward through the still Celtic-dominated lands and down to the sea far beyond Highdyn Hill. Across the river to the south, he could just make out the north rim of the southern range of the Brendan Mountains called the Cliffs of the Dragon. On the river he could see two barges, headed downstream on the blue water bound for Carew. He chewed his meal and thought about his task. This is going to take forever, he thought. Get smarter about this or you'll be an Elder yourself before you find what you seek, said his inner voice.

He considered what he knew about this house, assuming it really did exist. The idea he was out riding around chasing after an imaginary place was something he refused to believe. After all, runevisions were important. He believed that. If the house came from such a vision, the house must exist and must mean something.

Think. Think.

He finished his meal and considered the puzzle. What was it Elder Blaine had said? "A large willow tree, a small house, and two spirits—one black, one white—were looking at me from the house. The blue snake ran its course out front."

Weylyn looked back at the river, and it came to him, the solution to the puzzle of the vision. "That's it!" he said out loud. He jumped up, put on his pack, untied the horse, mounted, and made his way down to the well at the Blaire road. He dismounted under a large willow, drew water, and let the horse drink.

"You know old fellow," he said to the horse but mostly out loud to himself. "That's the key—the water. In the vision, the large blue snake in front of the house—it isn't a serpent at all, it's the Moryn Gweneth River. The house we're looking for is somewhere along this river and I think I know where. And I'll bet it's the very house Eiroy and his brother built years ago. Maybe that's why the vision was so strong. It makes sense to me." The horse whinnied and shook his head. Weylyn rubbed the horse's muzzle and patted his head before mounting.

Weylyn turned east, back in the direction of Elshorn until he reached the small road leading south to the river village of Brennus Ford. The hillside and immediate surrounding area was once a place of sacred worship to the valley Celts. In those days there was a large, open religious festival area overlooking Brennus Ford. It had been maintained by a dedicated Druidic order of Brendan Valley. That was before the area was overrun, first by Romans, then by churchers. Now an enclosed churcher building sat on the stone foundation of the old Druidic religious Place of Gathering. Only a few of the large willows and other trees which once were sacred to those living around the Druidic site remained. Most all of the older trees—like many of the previous inhabitants—were butchered and burned by the churchers for no other reason than to clear the area to purify their building. There were still several valley Celts in Brennus Ford, but they were few. Most of this part of the river was now inhabited by Roman churchers.

As he made his way down the narrow road to the river, Weylyn paid little attention to the dwellings, only spot-checking those which had promising-looking willows. He ignored all those dwellings which did not have a direct view of the Moryn Gweneth River. If the runevision was correct, the house he sought would be right on the river or very close to it. A hundred yards down the winding trail and just north of the churcher building he noticed to his left a trail leading up a steep knoll. Atop the knoll he could make out a large willow. The surrounding brush obscured the sight of any building which might sit under the large tree. He felt a chill come over him as he made his way up the trail. Halfway up, he dismounted and tied the horse to a small tree. He removed his pack and secured it to the saddle. "Wait here," he told the horse.

As he neared the top of the knoll he noticed the terrain flattened out somewhat and there, under the willow overlooking the blue Moryn Gweneth, was a small house. He crouched just off the trail and studied the area. Though it wasn't round, the house looked very much like Elder Fey's—roughly ten to twelve feet square. Its sides of stone and mud supported a wood and thatch roof. It had a single door facing the river. Was this the house he was looking for? A carved wooden totem with iron banding stood just outside the doorway. This had to be it.

Weylyn saw no sign of anyone. He made his way across the small clearing to a small shed and stall just behind the little house. He raised the wooden latch and opened the door to the shed. A large, dark horse eyed him closely as he closed the door behind him. He held out his hand and said in a soothing quiet voice, "Easy, boy, easy. I'm not going to hurt you." The horse stood looking at him, its only movement the motion of his head up and down. Weylyn moved to stroke its nose as he looked around. Across a rail in the corner lay a leather saddle. It was void of decoration, made Roman plain.

He opened the shed door and then circled the house, searching for tracks as he made his way around. There were several, horse and human. The ground around the Greeting Pole looked recently dug compared to the rest of the ground at the front of the house. The pole itself looked fairly new, without the aged, weathered look most often seen in long-established Greeting Poles across the valley. Weylyn guessed not too much time had passed since it had been carved and put in place next to the home's entrance. A knock on the door produced no answer. He knocked again. Still no response. He considered opening it, then thought better of that idea. Turning, he looked back toward the village. Maybe he could find someone there who knew where he could find the owners of this house and its strange pole.

He walked back to his horse, mounted and then headed down the road toward the river and Brennus Ford. A small stand of trees lined the road left and right among large stones—once part of the sacred Celtic sites now in ruin. The stand of trees and stones ran for a short distance before giving way to tilled fields. The harvest had been gathered, the fodder stored as winter feed for the livestock.

On the right side of the road the small stone churcher building and its adjacent graveyard was now plainly visible. Weylyn saw two men engaged in conversation at the road's edge next to a garden, standing on the path leading from the road to the church. One was a priest, judging from his black robes and beads. The other was dressed in a short leather tunic, a long animal fur vest covering his waist, striped leggings and soft leather boots—attire more traditional to the valley.

Weylyn rode up to them and raised his right hand in greeting. The priest responded but the other man did not. "Greetings, my son," said the priest.

"Hello," said Weylyn, studying the two. "I wonder if you can help me? I'm looking for the people who live in the home back up the road there on the knoll." He pointed in the direction of the large willow and the home with the small, banded pole.

"What do you want?" the man beside the priest demanded.

Weylyn looked at the man, judged him to be about his own height, about mid-life, average build, dark hair.

"Just want to talk, is all. Either of you know them?"

The priest smiled and nodded beside the man standing next to him. "This is the man you're looking for."

With a sour look at the priest, the man looked at Weylyn. "Well, what is it you want to talk about?"

Weylyn shifted on the saddle and studied the man. "I'm a

magistrate from Elshorn here on official business." He pulled out his magistrate's seal. "My name is Weylyn. And yours?"

"Griffyth." The man stared at the magistrate's seal. "Name's Griffyth." He rubbed his chin, his lower lip twitching.

Weylyn explained he was interested in the house because it might be a lead to apprehending a wanted outlaw.

"Outlaw?" The blood seemed to drain from Griffyth's face. "That's ridiculous. I'm the only one who lives there and I'm no outlaw," he stammered and looked at the priest, who was obviously taken aback by the discussion.

"I'm not saying you are an outlaw," Weylyn said calmly. He told them about Eiroy the Red's death and the search for Eiroy the Younger. "Anything you can tell me about these men?"

Griffyth looked sick to his stomach. His face was pale and his whole body seemed to tremble. The priest looked confused as he watched them, trying to understand the conversation.

"Don't know those men, don't know anything about them," Griffyth muttered. "I have no idea why you'd be interested in my house but you'll find no outlaws there. Been in that house most of my adult life. I work on the docks and do odd jobs. That's all. Ask anyone in the village, they can tell you."

Griffyth was surly and nervous, and that made Weylyn suspicious. He had the impression the man was lying, trying to hide something. At the very least, something had upset him.

"Have you noticed any strangers in the area recently?"

"No," said Griffyth.

"Well, I—"

"Bah!" Griffyth cut off the priest. "I don't have time for this, I have work to do. Leave me alone," said Griffyth. He turned and made his way quickly toward the docks of Brennus Ford.

"Go in peace, brother. I'll see you at services," the priest called. Griffyth merely raised his hand without looking back.

The priest turned to Weylyn. "You know, my son, I arrived for my duties only recently, so I'm not familiar with this area or my parishioners. But that was odd."

"Odd?"

"Yes. What brother Griffyth told you wasn't exactly the truth. I'm wondering why he didn't tell you about the girl."

"What girl?"

"You asked if we'd seen any strangers in the area lately and I was about to tell you before he interrupted me." The priest ran his beads through his fingers. "There was a girl here, quite recently. A young Celt girl. A happy soul, though her dress was most un-lady-like. Leather pants, you see." The priest muttered a disapproving tsk, tsk while shaking his head in disapproval.

"Dark brown eyes, light brown hair?"

"Yes, that's her. Wore a red fox cape."

The description matched Weylyn's memory of the girl. "Was she riding a brown horse with one white ear and white tail?"

"That's it exactly" replied the priest. "Is she in any trouble?"

"I need to talk with her. Do you know why she was here?"

"Like you, she wanted to know who lived at the house with the banded pole. Wanted to know where they were. She'd been down to the docks but couldn't get any information and no one was at Griffyth's. She caught me outside here, tending the garden." He pointed to the neatly kept herb and vegetable garden plot running along the road in front of his church. "I told her Griffyth was the man who lived at that house, that he worked around the docks doing odd jobs." He continued to fidget with his string of beads. "He has a boat moored there and does some hauling on the river, I think."

"When was she here?"

"Yesterday. Brother Griffyth must certainly remember."

"Did the girl happen to tell you where she was heading?"

The priest thought a moment. "She said something about Hierlaneum, I believe."

"Hierlaneum?"

Massive, Dense
This Urban Sprawl.
Wind Won't Blow,
Diseases Crawl.
Hateful Men,
Spiteful Women.
Life's Cool Drink
Just Bitter Lemon.
Green Things Grow
Soon Turn Brown
Falling Decayed
On the Ground.
Beggars, Children
With Dark Streaks
Cussin', Pissin'
In The Streets.
Not Much Call
For Registration.
We Can Join
The Congregation.
Welcome All
To
Civ-il-i-zation!

20

October 7th in the Roman calendar
20 days left in the Celtic Tree Month of Gort

The Pandorian Villa section of Hierlaneum was crowded—with people, animals, carts, chariots, and buildings. Following the directions Elder Eghan had given him when Weylyn reported his conversation with Griffyth and the priest, Weylyn headed for the Rodas Villa and Tavern. As he trudged along the crowded boulevard, he remembered Elder Eghan's words.

"If Fionna doesn't know Eiroy's dead, she might have gone to Hierlaneum in search of him. My sources tell me Eiroy had been staying at the Rodas Villa. Get down there and ask around. See what you can learn about Eiroy and with luck find the girl while you're at it."

Picking his way carefully through the wheel-rutted cobblestone street, Weylyn wondered why any Celt would choose to live in such a place. Wild plants and grass sprouted from between the much-used and long-ignored paving stones. Homes, shops and businesses along this once-prosperous boulevard were lacking in paint, their stucco sides peeling away from the mud-brick facade. Graffiti of every description was scrawled and scratched along many of the buildings. It was the churcher time of Our Lady of Victories—formerly the Roman goddess called Victoria—and many of the stores, shops and homes displayed images of the once pagan, now churcher, deity.

This part of the city ran close to the river and the smell of fish and other, more foul odors were strong. The bright sun helped drive the autumn chill from the air but did little to freshen the putrid scents hanging about this part of Hierlaneum.

Beggars—blind, crippled and otherwise—were competing with small children and dogs for the attention of passers-by. The open shops along this road were lacking in the full line of merchandise seen in the shops throughout the finer districts of Hierlaneum. The fruit and vegetable stands were mostly closed but those open had poor selections.

He made his way past the remnants of a pagan Roman temple, its colonnades and statues now in ruin and rubble, stone foundation blocks nothing more than graffiti boards for the churchers to hurl vulgar insults to the deities who'd once resided there. Next to the churcher-sacked temple was the Rodas Villa and Tavern. This two-story structure was surrounded by a high stucco-covered brick wall. Although there was evidence of recent patching, as with most of the buildings, much of the old plaster had fallen away. The large rose garden mural covering the outside of the building was faded, the once brilliant red and yellow roses now pale from age. Two large marble colonnades flanked the iron grating marking the entrance portal.

Weylyn made his way inside along a covered stone patio. Five small tables with wooden casks for stools sat around the patio area. Three men with white hair sat at one of the tables, all sharing a large loaf of bread and drinking from mugs. Through the columns on his left he could see the inner courtyard and what appeared to be about a dozen small living areas. He noticed each door of these small homes was painted a different color. Around these living areas were tiny gardens, their late plantings still growing. In the far corner along the wall with the entrance gate, Weylyn saw a small forge, its smithing tools, casting molds, and fire pit with wood stacked. It reminded him of Angus' forge in Aife. Several people sat on stone benches around these living areas. Children played among the old fountain in the courtyard's center. They were tended by a woman hanging out laundry on the fountain's stone wall. Along his right were three doors with signs hanging over each one, written in the Roman style. Weylyn had no training in reading their language, but he knew from the description Elder Eghan had given him, the third door to his right would be the proprietor's office. The first two doors would lead into the small tavern and eatery serving both residents and visitors. He walked down the patio and entered the proprietor's door.

The smell of garlic and onions was strong. Behind a small table sat a short, rotund man. He wore no shirt and his sandaled dark feet rested comfortably next to a large drinking mug and a shallow serving bowl filled with garlic and onions. Reclining on a sofa in the corner behind the man, a partially clad woman was nursing a baby. Two young boys playing a game with small sticks and rounded stones sat on the floor next to her.

"Come in, come in!" said the proprietor, his Roman language dense and throaty. He took a bite from the onion he was holding and placed the rest in the bowl. He rubbed his hands across his thick black chest hair and smiled. "What can I do for you?"

"I'm looking for a man who lives here. His name is Eiroy."

"Ah, Eiroy. Yes. He's staying in our Blue Rose house. There across from the fountain." He pointed a fat finger in the direction of the fountain. "But I haven't seen him for several days."

"Do you know where I might find him?" Weylyn asked.

"Oh, he could be back any time now. He comes and goes," he said. He belched loudly.

"Actually, I wondered if he might have had a visitor recently, a young girl."

"Ah! A young girl? Well, if, ah, you can't find her, I have young boys available." The proprietor winked and rubbed the gold chain and long, gold cross he wore around his neck.

Weylyn felt his face blush hot. "I need to talk with Eiroy and this girl. That's all."

"Ah, too bad. He'll be back just any time now. I'm pretty certain of it. I bet he'll know where this girl is you're looking for. Eiroy, he's a smart one. A Celt, too. Interesting fellow. You're welcome to wait in the courtyard for him. Or perhaps you'd like to wait for him in my tavern. The wine is very good. I know you Celts—you love your wine." He laughed. "Tell you what, you wait in the tavern for Eiroy to return, and the first drink is on me!" He chuckled, patting his large stomach. "How about it, then?"

"That's generous of you." He pulled his magistrate's seal and showed it to the man. "My name is Weylyn. I'm here on official business. I'm a magistrate from the Brendan Valley, from beyond the Dynsmore Fortress. The girl I'm looking for is Celtic, from the same region. She's about fourteen years, dark brown eyes, light brown hair. She is likely wearing a red fox cape."

"A young Celt girl, eh? She sounds lovely, quite delicious."

Weylyn felt anger flush his face again. He looked at the woman on the sofa; she seemed to be sleeping. "I take it, then, she hasn't been around here recently?"

"I fear she hasn't. Not recently, not otherwise. I would remember such a treat as you describe." He reached between his legs and rubbed himself through his dingy red-trimmed white linen wrap.

Weylyn ignored the man's crude behavior. "Can you tell me

any more about Eiroy? Like where he works, or perhaps where I could find any of his friends or family?"

The proprietor shrugged. "Eiroy has lots of visitors. He's seldom gone too long and he always tells me to have his visitors wait for him. Wait in my tavern, have a drink, something to eat. He'll be along soon." He swung his feet down from the table and turned to the young boys on the floor behind him. "Peterius, run to our tavern and tell the girls this Celt is waiting for one of our guests. He is to have the first drink for free. Hurry, now!" The young boy rushed out the doorway. The proprietor turned to Weylyn. "Please!" He gestured toward the tavern.

"Thank you. I'll take your advice and wait."

"You are most welcome, young sir. My name is Titus. If you have need of anything else while you are here, just come see me. Now, go. Enjoy your drink."

Weylyn made his way outside. He looked across the courtyard and the fountain to the Blue Rose house. He could see the faded mural of a blue rose painted over the door. The home's blue door was closed, its windows shuttered. The grounds around it were bare. No plants, shrubs, or trees. Weylyn couldn't imagine why a Celt would willingly live here. He didn't want to stay here any longer than was necessary but he had little choice if he was to find Fionna. He knew Eiroy wouldn't be coming back, but if Fionna was in this city and still on her own, it was likely she would turn up here. If he couldn't find her here, he'd have to return to Elshorn and hope to find another lead. He walked across the patio and was passing the table where the old men sat as young Peterius came out of the tavern.

"Hail, stranger!" crackled an old man's voice. He sat straight on his stool, his eyes bright, his smile pocked with vacant or blackened teeth. He had a large scar down his left cheek. The other two men flanking him didn't look much better, their garments in tatters. Their scrawny arms and hands lay on the table, guarding their drinking cups.

Weylyn nodded to the men. "Greetings."

"Set yourself down and visit with us," said the old man with the scar. The two others nodded their approval and pointed to a vacant seat opposite them.

Young Peterius crossed to him, carrying a wooden drinking mug. "Here," he said in small, uncaring voice as he sat the cup on the table in front of Weylyn.

"Thank you." Weylyn watched as the young boy shuffled back into the darkness of the tavern. As he reached for the seat, he noticed the second young boy run out of the proprietor's office clutching a piece of rolled parchment. When the boy saw Weylyn, he hesitated, looked back at the proprietor's office, and then hurried out the front entrance of the Rodas Villa. Curious, Weylyn looked around and saw the young mother, baby still at her breast, leaning against the doorway, watching him. What was that all about? He thought about Titus and his insistence he stay and wait for Eiroy's return. Of course, Eiroy would never return, but Titus wouldn't know that.

"Well, then, tell us what brings you to our humble Inn of the Rose?" one of the old men asked Weylyn.

"I'm looking for a young girl."

The three old men howled and cackled. "Aren't we all?" laughed the old man with the scar.

Weylyn grinned. "This girl is missing and I'm trying to find her. I think she knows someone who lives here at the villa. I was hoping I'd find her here."

"Oh, well then, who among us would know her?"

"Eiroy of the Blue Rose house."

The three men looked at each other, then back at Weylyn. They squinted, each of them leaning across the table to get a better look at him with their old, blurry eyes. The one on the right spoke first. "By the Fates, he's a cursed Celt! Just like the other one!" shouted the old man.

"Curses to the Fates," shouted the one on the left. "Told you I could smell them a mile off. I knew there was something about that accent of his."

The two old men both rose up angrily from the table, knocking the bread from its serving tray and spilling Weylyn's drink. They marched off, cups in hand, toward the darkness of the tavern. "Too bad we didn't kill every last one of them!" They continued to swear and complain all the way into the tavern.

Weylyn had jumped up and stood away from the table to avoid the spilled drink. His cup rolled over the edge and fell to the slab stone patio. He stood across the table, looking at the man with the scar.

The old man snorted. "Don't mind them; just old men with long memories. They can't stand Celts. They're a good bunch, just can't stand Celts is all."

"What about you?"

"Tell you about Celts. Hard fighters. Vicious, strong-willed and the devil to bring down. They gave our Legion fits in the battle at Carew. Didn't matter our men were in full armor and armed to the hilt. Heard the drumming and chanting an hour before they got to us. Most of the unit was so scared by the time the first wave came, they near broke and ran at the very sight of 'em. Mind you, they were a frightful sight to behold, wearing nothing but body paint, and carrying all manner of primitive weapons." The old man looked up and away and into his memory, his dark eyes searching for the rest of the story. "They slaughtered half our men before we could regroup. Only reason the rest of us survived and came out victorious was our reinforcements—arrived just in time to pull us out."

The last battle of Carew. Weylyn knew the story, had heard the bards tell the tale time and again. The battle marked a turning point in the Roman invasion of the Celtlands. The

Legion held their line and gained control of the Brendan Valley, but they couldn't push the Celts back through the pass at Carew. The valley now had two fortresses—the Romans to the east at Dynsmore, and the Celts to the west at Carew.

"Yup, lost a lot of good friends to the Celts," the old man continued. "Can't fault 'em though—great fighters. If they'd had equal armor, weapons, and training, we'd all be speaking their language today, I tell you." He chuckled. "Course I reckon you already speak it, don't you?" He pointed to the seat. "Sit back down, boy. Sorry about your drink."

Weylyn picked up the cup and set it upright on the table. He pulled up his seat and sat down across from the old man.

"Name's Calvin, Calvin the Bald they call me now," said the old man. He grinned and ran his hand across the hairless top of his head. "What's yours?"

"Weylyn."

"So you know the Celt, Eiroy, who lives here?" the old man asked. "And who's the girl?"

"I don't know Eiroy, but the girl is someone I've been tasked to find. I was told she might be here. You know Eiroy well?"

"Yup, we talk. He sits and talks with me a lot. He's a good listener. Doesn't let the others get to him when they complain about him being a Celt. Of course, now that I think about it, he never really had too much good to say about Celts himself. He used to say how glad he was to be away from his home in the Brendans. He said his people, as long as they clung to the old ways, would never progress like the Romans. I used to laugh at him for such things. I'd tell him, look around this filthy city. You call this progress?"

"So his people practice the Elder Faith?" When Calvin looked blank, he hastened to add, "It's our way to listen and respect our elders, and to learn from them."

"Ha! Now there's a good one! Was a time when I could name you a thousand Roman elders who didn't get any respect from Celts. Your Celts left all those respected Roman elders dead—dead on the battle field. Then they cut off their heads and paraded around with them. Carried them back to their villages as trophies." The words were sharp, but there was no hate in the old man's voice. "Respect. Ha! That's good. Of course, it was their land we were taking," he said with a sigh. "But it was a long time ago, and some of it best forgotten."

The old man looked at Weylyn then looked down at his empty cup. "Eiroy helps us out around here, you know. My friends and I work here—keeping the outside area cleaned up, the walls and buildings patched and repaired. Plaster, general repairs, that's what we do. Eiroy helps us out for nothing when he's around. He bought me many a round and I've lost track of the times he bought me dinner while we sat and talked. All he ever asked was for us to keep an eye on his place when he was gone. He was gone a lot." The old man paused for a moment. He raised his cup and looked into the empty interior. A frown appeared as he set the cup back down. "He's been gone a while now."

"Yes. He was visiting relatives in the Brendan Valley."

"Did you say he's some relation of yours?"

Weylyn smiled.

"He's in a lot of trouble," the old man confided.

"You know about his trouble?"

"A little." The old man looked down at his cup. "You want another? I could use another."

"No, thank you."

One of the other men who left earlier appeared at the doorway. "Hey Calvin! Get your Celt-kissin' lips in here. We got you another round and we're about to start a game of bones. Come on!" He gave Weylyn a dirty look and went back into the tavern.

"Well, nice talking to you," said Calvin. "Got to go. Never miss a free round and they can't beat me on the bones." He got up from his stool and slowly, with difficulty, made his way to the doorway. He reached the nearest door jam and grabbed the wooden beam for support before turning his head to look back at Weylyn. "Hope you find that girl you're looking for." He shuffled into the darkness of the tavern interior.

Weylyn reached across the table and pulled off a hunk of the hard, stale dark bread. He noticed the woman with the baby still watching him from the doorway. He smiled and raised his hand in polite greeting. Without any response, she went into the office. How rude these people were, thought Weylyn.

He wanted to get Fionna back safely to Aingeal Mountain, back to Elder Eghan and her mother and be gone from this city. He thought about Griffyth and how easily Fionna had found him at Brennus Ford. Had Petroytrix or one of his friends told her where to find him? Griffyth had told Weylyn he'd lived there all his life. Maybe he had, but Weylyn had this feeling something wasn't right. Was Griffyth connected to the murder of Eiroy and Aod? There must be a connection between Eiroy, his missing brother, and perhaps the missing treasure. Certainly Fionna believed there was some connection between the two Eiroys and the house with the stout Greeting Pole. After all, she'd gone out to see Griffyth and confront him.

What if Eiroy the Younger had been hiding in Griffyth's house the whole time? What if he was still there? Weylyn made a mental note to get permission to take Elder Eghan's men out to Griffyth's and look around, inside and out. He started to rise, then became aware of someone standing next to him.

"Can I get you something else to drink?" The dark eyes of the heavyset, matronly tavern maid looked down into his. She picked up his empty cup and wiped the spilled liquid with a cloth. It was something he'd watched Adrianna do a thousand times. "Those old men make such a mess!" she complained.

"Nothing else, thank you. I'll be leaving." He watched her make her way back to the tavern, to the same duties Adrianna had at the Five Fingers tavern. He stood, grabbed another piece of the hard bread, and walked to the street, his thoughts full of Adrianna. If he'd told her he was going to Hierlaneum, she would have wanted to come along. He could imagine her smile, the light in her beautiful dark eyes at the thought of the trip. Not wanting to upset her, he hadn't said good-bye before leaving. But now, even though he knew she wouldn't have been free to travel, he wished he'd brought her. She would want to show him around her city, maybe look for a place to start that tavern she'd always wanted. But this visit was an official one, to find a missing girl. Nothing more.

A group of six Roman army guards marched past Weylyn, their red tunics rustling and black armor clanking to the beat of their pace. They were preceded by two men dressed in the black and gold uniforms of the Enforcers. The two men eyed him suspiciously as they passed. Two guards posted themselves on either side of the villa entrance. The rest of the group went straight into the Rodas Villa. Weylyn swallowed the last of the bread and stepped into the narrow, rutted cobblestone street.

He was tired of Hierlaneum already. It stank with the odor of too many humans crammed into too small a space. A space too void of nature. Too few trees, grass, and open areas. Too many high walls and buildings which blocked the free movement of air across the land. Too many soldiers and bureaucrats in a hurry to stifle the freedom of thought and movement of individuals. He wanted to find Fionna if she was here, but he didn't want to stay a moment longer than was necessary. He stood looking up and down the street trying to make up his mind about what to do next.

"Are you the Celt looking for Eiroy the Red?"

Weylyn turned to see the two Enforcers, flanked by guards, facing him. They were all good sized, with one standing several inches taller than Weylyn's five foot nine. The shorter, stockier man had dark black hair and a grim face. The young magistrate saw the enameled inlay of armor and knew this wasn't just an Enforcer, this was a Centurion. Weylyn saw him stuff a piece of rolled parchment into the front of his tunic.

"Yes, I asked about him," said Weylyn.

"Are you from Hierlaneum?" questioned the Centurion.

"No. I come from the Brendan Valley."

The Enforcer walked around behind Weylyn and stood in the street.

"This Eiroy such a good friend you'd travel all that way to see him?" the Centurion inquired.

"No friend. Just asking about him," Weylyn said. He heard the Enforcer behind him hiss, as if he didn't believe him.

"You don't work with this Eiroy, do you?"

"No. I don't suppose you could give me any information about him? Or maybe where I could find any of his relatives or friends?" Weylyn barely got it all out before the Enforcer behind him grabbed his shoulder. He was spun around with such force and speed that his felt hat went flying off his head.

"Hey! You don't ask the questions around here, Celt. We do!" yelled the big Enforcer. Weylyn looked up into the face of the man. The Enforcer's dark eyes were full of hatred. Two of the guards moved to flank the Enforcer in the street.

Weylyn slowly reached into his tunic pocket and pulled his magistrate's seal out, then stood perfectly still as the Enforcer snatched it from him. "I'm looking for information on Eiroy because I think people familiar with him might know someone I've been tasked to find—"

"Shut up, Celt!" The Enforcer shoved Weylyn back a step as he let go of the grip he had on Weylyn's shoulder. The big man examined the bronze seal he'd taken from Weylyn. He turned it over and studied the emperor's official cast mark on the back. He recognized it as a genuine, official seal. "Look here, Axenus, we got us a for-real Celtic magistrate here in Hierlaneum!" chuckled the Enforcer. He tossed the seal to Axenus.

"Well, this is interesting." He nodded at Weylyn. "Seems we have something in common, Celt," said Axenus. A broad smile appeared. He handed the seal back to Weylyn and raised his hand in greeting. "I'm Axenus, Centurion to His Highness the Royal Prefect. Behind you is Warius. We are temporarily assigned to the Hierlaneum Royal barracks and work directly for the Supreme High Prefect in Rome."

"I'm Weylyn of Elshorn. I work for Eghan of Oaks, Chief Magistrate of Brendan Valley." Weylyn placed the seal in his tunic pocket and retrieved his cap from the street.

"Ah, Eghan of Oaks!" said Axenus, his smile large. "I know him. Ten years ago I took my apprenticeship as an Enforcer in Cross Abbey. We did a lot of work with Magistrate Eghan. How is he these days?"

"Elder Eghan is fine. He is active and in good health."

"Good, good. He is an honorable fellow. Most trustworthy," said Axenus. He scratched his eyebrows and frowned, and then his face lit up with a big smile. "Is that tavern of Elshorn's still there? We spent many a night there, I remember. Why, it sits right on the river. We used to watch all the river traffic while we drank. You could see their lanterns for miles. What was its name again?"

"The Five Fingers." Weylyn knew he was being tested. If this man had ever drunk at the Five Fingers in Elshorn, he would know the tavern's true location. "You must have it confused with another. This tavern sits well off the river."

The Centurion's smile grew even bigger. He slapped Weylyn on his right shoulder and laughed. "Ha! So you say! And right you are. The Five Fingers does sit off the river. Can't see a river barge from there if you wanted to! Let's go inside and have a drink. We need to talk." He yelled orders to the guards, telling them to go in and clear the patio tables of anyone else and to make certain they were not disturbed during their time with Weylyn. The two guards posted on either side of the entry did not move. They would make certain no one entered the villa grounds until Axenus told them otherwise. Two of the guards went inside the tavern and Weylyn could hear much arguing and loud voices from within. Very quickly, however, the tavern shutters and door were closed tight. The remaining two guards stood watch over Axenus, Warius, and Weylyn as they entered the patio.

"Sit, please," said Axenus, gesturing toward the center table. "Our drinks will be out shortly, I assure you."

Warius turned to one of the guards and said, "Go immediately to the Royal Office of Records next to the barracks. Tell the scribe we need verification of a Celtic magistrate named Weylyn from the Brendan Valley. Verify, also, the Chief Magistrate for that region is still Eghan of Oaks. Return immediately."

"Yes, sir." And, with military precision, the guard saluted the Enforcer, turned and quickly made his way out of the Rodas Villa.

Warius sat down at the table with Weylyn and Axenus. "If you're lying to us, your Celtic parts will adorn my trophy case." His tone was matter-of-fact.

"Ha! Pardon my friend. He doesn't like Celts too much," Axenus explained. He turned to his partner. "Now, Warius, just back off this young man, will you?"

"If he's not telling us the truth, I'll—"

"Oh, he's telling the truth." Axenus studied Weylyn for a long moment. The smile slowly relaxed and a somber look came over him. In a much lower and softer voice, he said to Weylyn, "You are of the Elder Faith, aren't you?"

Weylyn felt the blood drain from his face. The deep black eyes of Axenus were looking directly into his but Weylyn said nothing. He just looked back at the Centurion. He could not say 'yes' to the question because it was against churcher law to belong to a faith other than the great church. He would not say 'no' because he would not deny his religion for anyone. This was a dangerous line of questioning he'd gotten himself into here in the heart of Hierlaneum. In a matter of minutes, these men could make him disappear forever from the face of the earth and there would be nothing anyone, including Elder Eghan, could do about it. Worse, thought Weylyn, these men could make him disappear piece by piece over a long period of tortured time. He sat there, barely breathing, and said nothing.

"What in the name of Jupiter has the Elder Faith got to do with it?" Warius demanded.

"Everything," replied Axenus. "I served around the Celts of Brendan Valley. You, Warius, have no experience with them. True, they don't like us one bit, but who can blame them? I learned one thing about them in the two years I served in that Valley. They're an independent, hardworking, honest lot. You may not get an exact answer from them, but you won't get lied to, either, because—except in extreme cases—an untruth is against their religion. And, unless I'm mistaken, this man is who and what he says he is. Am I not right, Weylyn?"

Weylyn couldn't tell if this was a trap or if Axenus was being truthful in his statements. Elder Eghan had warned him about churchers thinking nothing of using deceit as a tool. He continued sitting there, saying nothing. Axenus straightened up on his stool and let out a hearty little chuckle. The smile returned.

"Well, if he's lying—"

"Yeah, yeah. Get off it, Warius. We need to find out what he knows of Eiroy. If it turns out he's lying to us—and I know he's not—you can slowly roast him over a low fire for all I care."

"I'll agree to that." Warius smiled for the first time.

The tavern door opened and a girl carried out three large mugs full of drink. "Will that be all, sir?"

"Yes, thank you." He put coins on her tray. "That will do, won't it? There's a good woman. Now leave us." Axenus waved the server away from the table and turned back to Weylyn. "Now then, just relax. That wasn't a trick question about your faith. You don't have to tell me, I already know and I don't care. Warius doesn't care either. What we do care about is what you want with Eiroy the Red." He grabbed his mug and took a long drink. "Because we've got a job to do also and it involves this Eiroy you're asking about."

Weylyn let his shoulders drop. He took a deep breath and reached for his own mug. His throat had turned dry. His face still burned hot. He drank several swallows before setting it back down. He considered what these Enforcers had told him. He really didn't seem to have much choice. He was in their city, and couldn't get away if he wanted to. The thought occurred to him he might as well at least be cooperative—to a point.

He explained about the missing girl and what he'd done to try and find her. He told them of the warning the girl had been given by her missing grandfather. He did not mention his meeting or conversation with Griffyth at Brennus Ford.

Axenus thought for a moment. "Hmm. Let's see. What we understand of this Eiroy business is that he killed his fellow river scum, Aod, in Elshorn and took a deadly cut in the process. Our men from Cross Abbey later found him dead in his relative's house in Brendan Valley. At least that's what they tell us. That the way you Celts understand it?"

"Close," said Weylyn. "But before he got into it with Aod, he had a conversation with one of our Elders."

"Ah, yes. The old man in front of the tavern," said Axenus. "Tell me what they spoke of."

"Eiroy the Red asked if the Elder knew of anyone named Eiroy. Funny, isn't it? Eiroy asking for Eiroy?"

The Enforcers seemed to ignore his question and, if they found any humor in it, they didn't show it. A few moments passed while they all drank. "Yes, it does seem a bit strange, doesn't it? But never mind that for now. What we'd like for you to tell us is why you think Eiroy the Red went to Elshorn. Got any ideas?" asked Axenus.

"To see his relatives as far as I know." Weylyn took another drink from his cup. "But right now, what I'm looking for is a clue to the location of the girl, Fionna."

"Right, right. Of course, and this girl is so important you'd travel all this way just to find her?" Warius asked.

"Yes. It is the task I've been given by Elder Eghan. It would be nice if I could locate her grandfather, too, in the process. Their relatives are anxious for news of both of them."

"What else did this old man and Eiroy the Red talk about?" Axenus wanted to know.

Weylyn related most of the conversation he'd had with Elder Blaine the Slender. When he mentioned the rune buckle, both Enforcers sat upright and looked at each other.

"Are you certain about the buckle?" Axenus demanded.

"I'm positive." Weylyn could see their interest in this conversation had risen. Warius ran his hands up and down his cup as he looked back and forth between Weylyn and Axenus.

"Do you know why this old Celt never mentioned this buckle to the Enforcers at Cross Abbey?" asked Warius.

"Elder Blaine told them everything, ah, I mean, about the rune buckle, that is," said Weylyn, not wanting to mention the runevision Elder Blaine had kept from the other Enforcers.

The two sat there looking at each other as if conversing on another level. Weylyn took a long drink from his cup and set it back down. Finally, they looked back at him.

"Are you certain?" asked Axenus.

"He told Commander Orrs everything of the conversation and the event on the street, I am certain. Elder Blaine has said it was so," said Weylyn. He saw Axenus smile.

"If that's true, then where is this buckle?" asked Warius.

Weylyn shrugged. "As far as I know, it wasn't on the body when we—they—went through the grave."

"Did the Cross Abbey Enforcers tell you that?"

"Well, no, not exactly. I was there. I was the one who led them to Eiroy. I was there with them when they found the remains." Weylyn shook off that memory. "And of all the things the Enforcers took from the site, the rune buckle was not one of them. At least not that I saw."

Axenus and Warius considered this. Warius tapped his fingers nervously on his cup and looked at Axenus.

"How do you explain the missing buckle?" asked Axenus.

"Well . . ." Weylyn didn't want to let them know he had been pondering this for some time now. He slowly twisted his cup. He glanced over at Warius then back to Axenus. "I can't explain it. I suppose it could have been lost as the wounded Eiroy fled from Elshorn. Perhaps Fey de Parke took it before Eiroy died."

"Ever think Orrs might have taken it?" Axenus inquired.

"No," he said quickly and then realized how that sounded. His face burned as he realized he'd lied. He saw the Enforcers smile. "Actually, I have thought about it. I left for a little while to explore the back of the cave. It's possible he put it away before I returned from scouting the cave. But if he did, why?"

"Could it be a clue to the location of this other Eiroy, or something else? Maybe something of real value?" Warius asked.

The Centurion shot his fellow Enforcer a cold, hard look, obviously not happy with that comment.

Weylyn didn't feel comfortable mentioning the runevision to any Roman, especially Enforcers in the middle of Hierlaneum. He wondered now if he and Elder Eghan were right about the rune buckle having something to do with the stolen Great Cross. He looked down at his cup and said nothing.

"You don't know who the other Eiroy is, do you?" Warius asked. He looked back to his partner and smiled.

"We believe he is known as Eiroy the Younger and a brother to the Red. I think he's one of the keys to finding the missing girl, and right now that's my task. Find Fionna de Aine. And if I can find this other Eiroy, I'll also find out what happened to Elder Fey."

A stir of movement and the sound of boots and weapons clanking on belts came from the entrance of the villa. The guard had returned from the Office of Records. He approached to within three feet of the table, stopped and snapped to attention. "Sir, the Royal scribes confirm the Celt's story."

"Of course, just as I knew they would. Efficient and handy, those government scribes," said Axenus. The large smile returned. He quickly finished his drink. "Good." He stood up from the table and motioned Weylyn toward the villa entrance. "We've already said more than should have been spoken in public. Let's find a private place to continue this conversation."

*

Preceded by two of the guards and followed by the other four, the two Enforcers and Weylyn left the Rodas Villa, made their way down the main street, passed a Roman barracks, and walked through more twists and turns and side roads than Weylyn could count. They came to the outer wall of the city, went through a large open gateway and walked out onto a river pier lined with many small boats and barges. Many flew flags of varying colors and designs. Almost all had the name of their vessels with elaborate pictures in bright colors on their bows.

At the end of the pier they boarded a small barge. The red and black vessel with golden-colored standards flying at each corner was outfitted with rows of padded benches. On its bow was the flag of the Imperial army, its proud, black eagle spread across a red field. Weylyn was offered a seat at the stern. The guards made themselves comfortable up front as the crew navigated the vessel out into the river. The two Enforcers sat next to the young magistrate, one on either side. Weylyn looked over his shoulder and saw the pier and the long line of the ancient city wall stretching out as far as he could see along the river. Back the other way, he saw the city walls extending along the river, curving away and out of his sight, colorful banners and vigilant guards along the wall's top.

Axenus took a deep breath. "Ah, fresh air. I like getting out on the river. Helps clear the mind. Besides, we can talk freely here. No need to worry about who might be listening."

"Yes, we can speak freely now," Warius agreed. "And no hard feelings, Celt, about back there, all right? Just wanted to find out what you're made of. You're the first Celtic magistrate I've run into. I've got this thing about Celts. Nothing personal," Warius said.

Weylyn studied the Enforcer. He didn't know what to make of this big man with the foul temper and his hatred of Celts.

Axenus cleared his throat, briefly surveyed the span of river then turned to face Weylyn. "You must know we're searching for the Great Cross and the other stolen items, but we're trying to find out who planned the theft in the first place. I believe you when you say you don't know where this buckle is. And you don't know much about the theft of the Great Cross, do you?"

"Secondhand information, mostly. We don't get a lot of information from Enforcers, just orders." Weylyn blushed. "What I mean is—"

"No need to explain. I understand how it is, just as you must understand the Prefect's position: tell Celts only what's needed to get the job done. We're just following our orders. That's all—just standard procedure," said Axenus.

"You know why we want that buckle?" Warius asked.

"Elder Blaine said it was just like the one Eiroy the Younger wears, so I suppose you need it to help identify the Younger."

The two Enforcers looked at each other. Warius cocked his head slightly to his left and shrugged at his partner. Axenus replied by nodding his head. He turned back to Weylyn.

"I'm going to break the Prefect's rule for a moment. That

Cross is special. This is a unique situation and has the interest of the Grand Cleric himself. So, understand, what I'm about to tell you must be kept strictly to yourself. Don't discuss it with anyone. Will you give me your promise?" Axenus knew a follower of the Elder Faith would not break a promise.

"Not even tell Elder Eghan?"

"I know Eghan. It can't hurt. Just tell Magistrate Eghan you got this by promise from us. It's important this doesn't become general knowledge. Very important."

"You have my word."

"Our boss, the Grand Prefect in Rome, sent us up here to find the missing Great Cross and recover the other stolen valuables. That part is no big secret. But what we've been able to piece together is guarded information. We tracked down some of the men who worked in the gang of thieves who took the shipment. Turns out they had their own little theft ring going within the bigger ring. When the plot to steal the Great Cross was revealed to the gang, a small group of them developed their own little plans for the shipment. What we uncovered will be of great interest to the Grand Prefect. We don't yet know how high up the original plot went, but we think someone decided if the Cross Abbey priest was implicated in the theft, he'd lose any chance of consideration for a soon-to-be-open high position in the Great Church. His chief rival might very well be the Bishop of Hierlaneum or perhaps a priest in the Great Church here in Hierlaneum. Like I said, whether his eminence was involved directly, we don't yet know. That will be a matter for the Church to settle. We have only two concerns at this point. First, the recovery and safe return of the valuables. Second, we want to find the one responsible for planning the theft."

"Since we think we know who it was, it's only a matter of time before we gather enough information to have the Grand Prefect issue orders to have him arrested," Warius stated.

"Yes, well, we'll see," said Axenus. "On the first point, however, we've hit a dead end. What we have learned is that the original plot fell apart after the goods were taken. As best we've been able to determine, the goods were to be taken to a neutral site and held until members of the Hierlaneum Church could 'find' them, return them to the Great Church in Rome, and thereby thoroughly embarrass their rivals. However, an unknown factor sent the perpetrators' plan awry."

Warius nodded. "They didn't plan on the Celtic factor. When the Celt thieves learned the stolen goods contained the Great Cross, they hatched their own plan to run off with the goods, wrecking the original scheme. They hid the goods well. We learned from talking with a gang member—a horseman named Sergio—that Eiroy the Red was the one in charge of the Celtic plot. They even had, according to Sergio, their own river barge to move the goods. He knew about the bronze buckle and we believe he knew where the goods are hidden. He told us the barge owner who moved the goods worked for a Hierlaneum merchant named Pax Catus."

"Have you talked with this merchant?"

"Oh, we have," said Warius. "We searched his warehouse, took him in for questioning,. That didn't last long."

"Pax was the one who ran the entire gang of thieves. Unfortunately, he's a well-to-do merchant running a very profitable trade here in Hierlaneum," said Axenus.

"If you know that, why—"

"He has the right social connections and is a ranking member in the Merchant's Guild. Even has the ear and the blessings of the Bishop of Hierlaneum," Warius said flatly.

"Because of his connections, he's difficult to touch," said Axenus. "He even gets special treatment from the tax office. Pax was released 'by higher authority' according to the Prefect."

"Pax Catus is a wormy little toad," Warius said in disgust. "He chattered a lot in the short time we had him, though."

"He confirmed the barge operator mentioned by the horseman worked for him," said Axenus. "He freely acknowledged it, said it was all perfectly legal. He denied knowing anyone named Sergio. Seemed insulted we'd believe he'd stoop so low as to associate with mere horse thieves. But that's all the useful information we got before we had to turn him loose."

"Yes, but Sergio, during interrogation, was quite willing to talk about Pax and his little group. A name that kept coming up was Brutovius. Don't let the name fool you," Warius said. "He's not a Roman. He's a Celt who's taken on a Roman name."

"We've asked around, questioned those around the docks. Pax has a good reputation as a skillful and prosperous dealer. His associates, however, have nasty reputations—even among the bad guys. Evidently, this Brutovius character was the one in charge of the shady operations," said Axenus.

"According to Sergio, it was Brutovius who planned the raids and ran the group of thugs working for Pax Catus. Unfortunately, poor Sergio died before we could get any more out of him," said Warius, laughing.

"Why are you telling me this?" asked Weylyn. He grew uneasy with all this information they were so readily giving him, and with Warius' seeming enjoyment of hurting people.

"Simple. We want the Great Cross and the rest of the stolen treasure," Axenus replied. "Celts were implicated in its theft and the forging of the buckle. We've been able to get information from Romans, little to nothing from Celts. If, during your quest to find the Celt girl, you come across any news we can use, we want to know about it."

Weylyn leaned back and began to slowly rotate his head and neck to relieve the tension. He raised his hands up over his head and stretched. The purposeful deceit practiced by the Roman churcher society made him nauseous. Moments passed as he considered what he'd been told. The buckle had some importance. He knew that now without a doubt. Was it also tied to Fionna and her disappearance? He thought about past events, then straightened abruptly. "Why did Eiroy the Red kill Aod?"

"Warius thinks it's all tied together with the missing treasure. The two brothers were part of the group of thieves."

"Yes, but something probably went wrong. It usually does with these types. Can't trust them to do anything right. Eventually, they slip up and we catch them," said Warius.

"Anyway, we think Pax or someone sent Aod to keep an eye on him and the two got into it," Axenus continued. "We don't know why, but we think it's related to the stolen shipment."

"So Aod also worked for Pax Catus?"

"Aod was definitely on the payroll of Pax Catus, but Sergio told us he also hired out to the highest bidder when Pax had no work for him. Notorious as a personal bodyguard and all-purpose problem solver for Pax—one of two—and deadly with a blade," said Axenus.

Warius laughed his cold, hard laugh. "Evidently, Eiroy the Red was better—certainly quicker that evening in Elshorn."

"One of two?"

"That's right, Celt. One of two, and the way we hear it, Aod was the amateur compared to the other one," said Warius.

"It's something you need to know if you're going to be asking around Hierlaneum for information about Eiroy," Axenus warned him.

"There's a good chance with him gone, Catus might send out his best man to find and kill the Younger," said Warius.

"Would that be the Celt, Brutovius, you mentioned earlier?"

"No. Brutovius is too old for such a task. As far as we've been able to determine, he only runs the smuggling and theft operation. The one you need to watch out for is the one they call the Black Hand. Independent fellow. Some say he's done jobs many times for Pax and anybody else who pays the best.

We don't know what he looks like, don't know anyone who admits knowing him, and the ones familiar with him won't talk. But the authorities here have seen his handiwork many times."

"And you, young Celt, never want to meet this man. He is very dangerous," warned Warius.

"The Black Hand? Is that his real name?"

"No," said Warius.

"What is it, then?"

"Parzifal," said Axenus. "Parzifal, the Destroyer."

It hides there where the shadows fall;
This evil Deed that's known by all.
It can't touch the Soul but takes our breath;
This inevitable Force we fear as Death.

21

October 8th in the Roman calendar
19 days left in the Celtic Tree Month of Gort

Parzifal was a master when it came to waiting. In the deep of midnight darkness, he climbed the outer villa wall, crossed over the red tiled roof and dropped—with barely a sound—to the peristyle, the open inner courtyard.

Tonight there was no moon, just the flickering of stars and a stiff breeze. Dead leaves and the branches of the many plants within the courtyard provided excellent noise cover. He sat in perfect, still silence along the row of small trees and dense shrubs growing just off the courtyard's center fountain. He sat this way for almost an hour. It was just like sitting in the small, dark cell where the churcher clerics kept him as a child.

For the last three weeks, he'd surveyed this villa townhouse and the area around it. It had but one doorway for entry and exit and it was always guarded. He looked for the weak spot, noting the guards and their movements, memorizing the comings and goings of those who worked or had business within.

The townhouse, bounded on three sides by busy streets with adjoining businesses, took up most of a block. The street running east of the villa was the Grand Avenue. It ran directly to the front doors of the Great Church of Hierlaneum, less than a hundred yards from the villa. Parzifal noted the marching order and routine of the city guards in relation to the Grand Avenue and the Great Church.

Vendors around the villa were also surveyed. He'd bought bread from the baker along the townhouse's northern wall, wine from the wine vendor along the southern wall, and visited the goods merchant directly across the street from the baker. From subsequent visits, he learned the posts and the movements of not only city guards for this sector but the three personal guards assigned to the villa and its owner. The three were the only security the villa had. They wouldn't be a problem. Even against the most skilled fighters, Parzifal could see their every move coming and these guards weren't anywhere close to skilled. Church-assigned, lazy and careless, they weren't likely candidates willing to give their lives for the sake of the villa's owner—not if push came to shove. Besides, Parzifal learned they each took shifts during the day and night so only one of them was on duty at any given time and on many occasions, for hours, the place would be completely unguarded. This abode of the priest would be an easy nut to crack.

The villa townhouse of Loxius Scrota was a large, elegant one in the heart of Hierlaneum's richest district. Loxius could afford it. After all, he was chief among priests of the several assigned to the Hierlaneum branch of the Great Church of Rome. His fondness for gambling, drinking, and debauchery was well known. Too well known, it seemed.

Loxius—despite all his public and clerical proclamations of goodness and light—practiced that which he did not preach. He had powerful enemies both inside and outside the churcher establishment; further, he was in contention for the soon-to-be-vacant post of Bishop. The current bureaucrat in the job was slated for a promotion to the Central Great Church in Rome. The rivalry for the Bishop position alone would have put him in mortal danger, but Loxius' troubles went deeper than churcher intrigue—much deeper. His forays into the bowels of Hierlaneum's seedier side—the infamous Zone of Scorpius District—had cost him much in the gambling rooms and entertainment venues run by The Holder. However, Loxius seemed unconcerned about owing such a large amount of money to so dangerous a gambling establishment.

As Parzifal had found out, Loxius was in debt to the tune of almost five thousand denarii for gambling losses, goods, and other services. It was a rather large sum, even for a member of the Great Church. The owner of the note was not pleased at so public a figure as Loxius shrugging off his debt. It was bad for business. Parzifal would collect a goodly percentage of the note when he pulled off the contract on Loxius Scrota.

"I want it done soon, and I want a great many people to know about it." The Holder's voice was coarse and rough with hatred. "The pompous churcher bastard had the nerve to tell me to my face he'd have the church close me down if I tried to collect on him. He said priests don't worry about such things because God protects those who serve Him!" The Holder slammed his fist down against the table.

Parzifal listened in silence, staring at his first, often, and now temporary employer. He couldn't see his face clearly in the shadows of this small back room with only one small lamp and its faint glow. It was the way they both wanted it, the way it had always been. Just outside the windowless room's only door stood The Holder's two bodyguards, there to make certain this meeting wouldn't be interrupted.

The Holder's anger didn't faze Parzifal. He was accustomed to angry clients. They tended to spew their rage before sending him out to administer their revenge. He himself had long ago learned to calm such emotional outbursts. He'd learned to suppress them, channel his emotions into strengthening his mind and body. During those long night hours when he'd been locked away by the priests, he exercised his mind and muscles, making himself mentally and physically strong for hauling heavy casks of mead and wine for the clerics. And it helped him endure the priestly perversions forced upon him. His discipline had paid off, leaving him impervious to emotional outbursts.

"I told him his God had better be sleeping with him because I was coming to collect what he owed me, but he just laughed. He laughed in my face, the bastard! I've had men killed for that alone," The Holder said with a snarl. He picked up a flask of wine from his table and filled his cup. He did not offer any to Parzifal. "But I don't want this one killed. No, I want this one left alive. Alive to be a warning not to mess with me and expect to get away with it, church or no church."

"You don't want him killed. What is it you do want?" asked Parzifal. He stood there, motionless, expressionless. His large, muscular frame and dark hooded outfit loomed above the small table and the old man.

"I want you to scare all but the living life out of him, hurt him, beat him all the way to the gates of Hades if possible, but don't kill him. And I want you to hurt him, do it in such a way it will both embarrass him publicly and make him realize there's worse in his future if he continues to ignore his debts. Get that done, and there will be something extra in your payment."

"So, he gets scared, embarrassed, hurt. Whether you ever get your money is not important?"

"Hey, if the bastard is dead, I'll never see it. If he's scared out of his wits, maybe he'll come around. Either way, I think I win. So what do you say? Is it a deal?"

"If I do this the way you want, I could be revealed publicly. It could ruin my effectiveness, my business."

"Don't worry, I'll make it worth your while. After all, you're the best there is. And you should be—I trained you. Besides, I got connections with the Prefect magistrates, you know that. If you get caught, I'll get you off."

He waited for several moments but got no response from Parzifal. "If you do this right, I'll never have worry again about people refusing to pay an honest debt. Know what I mean? All I'll ever have to do is mention the name Loxius Scrota." The Holder laughed and took another drink, slurping the contents of his cup. "So, do we have a deal?"

Parzifal didn't respond right away. He was being offered a chance to hurt and embarrass a priest and get paid for it. Payback for the awful things the clerics of the Great Church had done to him in his youth. He'd thought about such a thing hundreds of times in the past, locked in their dark cells, chained to their beds or bent bleeding against their lashes. He'd sworn revenge, but he'd been too busy surviving in the intervening years. With this job, he could kill two birds with one stone.

His silence was misinterpreted by The Holder.

"All right, I understand your hesitation. You're right. For this special job, I'll pay your percentage and double the bonus. How about I throw in one of my finest black racing stallions? We have a deal? It's my final offer," huffed the old man.

Outwardly, Parzifal didn't move, but inwardly he was laughing. He wouldn't let this old man know the deal seemed more than fair. After all, truth told, he would consider taking the job for nothing at all. No pay, just the pleasure of watching the churcher priest suffer. Finally, he nodded. "It's a deal."

*

He sat there now, silently, in the darkened courtyard. He could hear the wind, the rustling leaves, and the gurgling sound of the villa's fountain as water dripped in from the city's aquifer. He heard laughter, giggling, and other sounds coming from Loxius' private room. The sounds were softening, dying out as the revelers were tiring.

The priest had entertained himself through the night and well into the early morning hours. The young girl and young boy he had with him had left the room on several occasions to relieve themselves and to fetch more wine. In their stupor and distraction, they'd passed right by Parzifal, never noticing him crouched there in the darkness.

It wouldn't be long now. Soon they'd be deep in sleep and it would be time for him to act. He wouldn't rush this. He believed he had the gift of sight, the ability to see things coming before they happened. It was a trait that had helped him thrive in this profession in which he had no equal. He could see the successful completion of this job, too. He would wait patiently for the right moment. He was good at waiting.

He thought about what he would do with the money he would make on this job and the racing stallion—especially the racing stallion. He'd always wanted one. Perhaps he'd retire and raise horses. He wanted to go into the Celtic territories, perhaps even track down his long-lost relatives among the Celts. He had no real idea which village he may have come from, which band of Celts he may be related to, but he wanted to try. It had been a growing desire of his ever since he started his visits with the old Celtic woman.

She was a healer in the Celtarium encampment called High Point, located outside the eastern gates of Hierlaneum. From her, he'd learned much of what they called the Elder Faith, and something had stirred deep within him. He saw the value, the merits of such a philosophy. He wondered if this was the religion of his parents. Would it have been his religion if the churcher armies had never come? He thought so.

They took him when he was four years old, sacked and burned his village and killed his parents in the name of their loving, compassionate, forgiving savior and the foreign, hypocritical religion they professed. Perhaps it was time, in the name of his parents' faith, to leave this life of his and seek out his past, his relatives, and the religion of his ancestors. Time to learn new, more important values. He could take his racing stallion into the Celtlands and start a new life. He could retire, breed racing horses and reconnect with his Celtic past. He might even consider petitioning the Celtic Queen for the status of freeman. He should have enough money saved up after this job; perhaps he could even purchase freehold lands and settle down. The idea was beginning to appeal to him more and more.

He carefully pulled the dark sling pack off his left shoulder, untied the drawstring and reached in. He would spend this time ensuring, once again, everything was in place. He unfolded the small roll of waxed parchment paper covering a large stick of black charcoal then wrapped it again. He checked the strands of rope, the small iron spikes, and small iron hammer, each wrapped in soft skins to keep them from making any noise. There was a small pouch in there as well; he quietly counted out the thirteen copper coins. Replacing everything but the hammer, he set the pack on the ground behind him.

Next, he checked the two long-bladed knives he carried in scabbards, one on each hip. He felt their pommels and took joy in their presence. They were old friends who went everywhere with him and never let him down. He prided himself on his innate ability to foresee trouble coming. These two daggers had always taken care of any trouble he'd encountered.

It would only be a few more minutes before Loxius and his two slaves would be fast asleep. Time now to move against the guard posted at the entrance. He drew a dagger with his left hand and picked up the iron hammer with his right. Slowly and silently he made his way back across the courtyard, through the curtained portal separating the peristyle from the main entrance hall. He moved with stealth as he let the curtains slowly back into their hanging position and gazed about the large room.

There was no light in the hall. He looked to his left and saw nothing but darkness. He peered around a large chest on his right. The small amount of light coming from the north street contrasted with the deep darkness of the hall's interior. Parzifal could make out the silhouette of the guard sitting on his chair facing the street, just as he'd seen the guards do in this open doorway during the day. He crossed the hall. As he neared the guard, he heard the sound of snoring and smiled. He wouldn't need the dagger this time.

The hammer slammed down with a sharp 'thwack' against the skull of the guard, who slumped in his chair without making a sound. It was likely he would never move again under his own power. Parzifal felt the man's neck and wrists. No pulse.

A quick check of the street showed it was empty. Reassured, he put away his dagger and, with hammer in hand, made his way back to the inner courtyard, replaced the hammer in his pack, and listened carefully. There was no longer any sound coming from the private chamber of Loxius.

Across the courtyard's stone walkway, past the fountain, the columned overhang and stone bench, he moved onto a floor covered with large ceramic tiles. Parzifal made his way through the formal sitting parlor to the portal leading to the private pleasure chamber of Loxius Scrota. Below the floor-length curtains of the doorway, he could see a glow of light. Even before he pulled back the lush velvet curtains, he could smell the burning incense, candles, oil, and rich perfumes. He paused again, listening. He could hear the heavy, deep breathing sounds of sleep. Pulling back the curtains, he stepped into the room. A thick haze of smoke gave the candle and oil lamp light an eerie glow. Along the left wall sat a wooden altar table with incense burners and candles. On the wall above it was the Great Church's fetish symbol, a large cross-shaped design with one elongated leg—the most ancient representation of the dagger stuck in the heart of Mother Earth. Across the room, directly opposite the doorway, was the bed. Loxius was on his back, arms at his side. He lay there, head propped up on the long, round pillow, his mouth wide open, snoring. The round, bloated stomach of his puny, white naked body was barely moving. Curled up at his feet in a fetal position was the naked young boy. The unclothed young girl had passed out on a blanket on the floor next to the bed. All three were sound asleep. A pile of silk clothing belonging to the priest lay in a heap on the floor beside pieces of burlap, which served as rough clothing for the slaves. Along the back wall, next to the head of the bed, Parzifal could see the many wine flagons and food plates scattered about. On the wall above the head of the bed was a sign which read: “God is great, God is good, but He couldn’t make us rich like the Great Church could.”

Parzifal wasted no time.

He moved across the room. He placed the hammer on the floor and lifted the girl off the blanket. Her arms and legs dangled like a rag doll. He noticed the copper slave bracelet on her right ankle and the brand on her neck, marking her as nothing more than a possession. He placed her on the floor against the side of the bed. With a swift and violent movement of hands on her head and chin, he snapped her neck. The boy was next; he dropped the lifeless body next to the girl.

He felt no remorse, no regret. He remembered the pain, the humiliations he was forced to endure during long days when he, too, wore such adornment and clothing for the perverted pleasures of the churchers. Those two were now better off than they would have been as perverse pawns of this awful creature.

With the stealth of his profession, he moved to the pile of clothing and picked up a tunic. He used his dagger to strip the bottom into long strands which he used to secure the hands and feet of Loxius. The putrid breath of the snoring priest and the sweet perfume was almost nauseating. Parzifal placed his dagger in its scabbard, retrieved the hammer and picked up the blanket.

He threw it over the sleeping priest, pulling back the upper part covering his head. The assassin pulled his dark cloak over his head to help hide his face. He knew what was coming; he prided himself on his ability to see what was coming next. It helped him survive. He knew the priest would revive. He wanted him to revive. With the remaining strips of cut cloth he bound and gagged the mouth of the sleeping priest. The man stirred toward consciousness, struggling against the constraints on his arms and legs.

"Hrrummpt, ummmp …" Loxius could only mumble as he fought to free himself. His eyes widened in panic as he came to full consciousness.

"Well, well. Awake? Good!" Parzifal straddled the bound and blanket-covered priest. He grabbed the priest's chin and jerked it left and right. "Are you listening? Good. It's time to pay your gambling debts!"

"Aaarrgghhh … no … noooo …"

Parzifal released the priest's chin and flipped the top of the blanket over Loxius' head. With precise moves, Parzifal repeatedly struck the priest hard, but carefully, about the head and face with the little iron hammer.

What we know and what we learn
are often different things.
Like sounds of flutes, or beating drums
or when the church bells ring.
They often bring some things to light,
reorganize the way we see,
or merely darken up the Mystery.

22

October 9th in the Roman calendar
Daybreak
Four days left in the Runic Half-Month of Gyfu

Weylyn woke to the feeling of something crawling on his face. He lay on his right side on the small bed, knees tucked in tight, body balled up in his woolen wrap against the morning's cold dampness as his back pressed against the cold stone of the outer wall of Hierlaneum. He opened his eyes and saw the early daylight peeking through the open portal of the small room. He wiped his face but could detect nothing crawling there and realized he must have dreamed the feeling of bugs on his face.

He rolled over on his back and stretched. His body was stiff and tight, his muscles ached. He shivered and pulled the wrap closer. Through the open doorway, he could see men in Roman army uniforms passing by. Weylyn heard their voices, the rattling of metal, the marching sounds of booted feet on cobblestone. The city's perimeter guards were changing shifts.

He was tired, demoralized. The city was wearing on him. His search so far had yielded little information. He thought about yesterday's tour through the horrid Celtic township around the outer east wall of Hierlaneum and shuddered at the memory.

"The Celtarium!" Warius had announced, waving his hands as if presenting the area to Weylyn. They had traveled down the river as it passed along the southern wall of Hierlaneum. The terrible stench of the river along this stretch was near unbearable. Beyond the southeast corner of Hierlaneum's outer wall, the view opened up to a huge, crowded and ugly shanty town which had grown up just outside the eastern and northern perimeter walls of Hierlaneum. In the distance, Weylyn could see the community rise and extend up from the flat area around the wall to a higher point in the far distance. The higher point contained the only visible large trees.

The Enforcer boat moored at a large wooden pier extending out from the shore about one fourth of the river's width. From here Weylyn could see some of the town, the long Celtic clan and family poles extending up above dilapidated excuses for homes and businesses. A gaggle of women and children were along the bank of the river, a few fishing, some playing, most bathing or washing clothing in the cold river.

The Enforcers' guards on the boat tossed the mooring lines to the men waiting on the pier. The lines-takers, dressed in brightly colored striped leggings and animal fur vests, appeared Celtic. Weylyn noticed there were several Roman guards along the pier and at the building which guarded the pier's shoreline. That building had colorful Roman standards flying from its roof and doorway. He couldn't read the language of the signs on the building but Weylyn recognized it as a Customs Enforcement Office; the Empire was efficient at maintaining government standardization. It was the same as the one at Elshorn.

"I figured if your little Celt girl managed to actually make her way into Hierlaneum, she'd probably find this place," said Axenus. "Besides, this is where you are most likely to find the information you seek on any relatives of Eiroy the Red."

The conditions were deplorable, for Celt or Roman. The streets were muddy, deeply rutted from traffic. Garbage and sewage lay beside the buildings and roads. The smell was even more odorous and putrid than the stink encountered inside the walls; the dirt, the filth, the stench were almost unbearable.

The community had grown with no planning, resulting in a disorganized collection of narrow streets and alleyways which meandered and dead-ended. On several occasions, the accompanying guards had to chase off or silence angry young Celts who hurled curses and debris as they passed. The Romans handled it as if it was a common occurrence.

Warius was disgusted. "We should kick them all out of here, back to the Celtlands. Burn this malodorous village and be done with them. Nobody wants them here anyway. Look at the way they live! Like a bunch of wild dogs."

Weylyn had managed to talk with only a few Celts before the sun got too low for them to remain safely in the area. He learned nothing new. Those who would talk to him refused to say much within hearing of the Romans. He did, however, get a possible lead from one elderly man who thought the people up around High Point might be of help to the young magistrate. The Elder said he could find followers of the Faith there, up among the trees, but the fading light and increasing danger of angry crowds kept them away. High Point would have to be explored another day.

"Come on. We need to get back inside before dark. They'll be expecting us to report back in to the barracks. Do you have a place to stay for the night?" Axenus asked Weylyn.

"Not yet," Weylyn admitted.

"There's a small chamber the city guards sometimes use just inside the east wall gates. You can sleep there. I'll make certain you aren't disturbed," Axenus told him.

He'd accepted the offer, and he'd slept deeply. He couldn't remember even moving, let alone dreaming—certainly no nightmares, only the feeling of insects on his face when he woke. His stomach rumbled from hunger. He tossed off the woolen cover and swung his legs and feet down to the cold stone floor. The air was damp and cold and the odor of mildew hung in the little room. He put on his boots, still damp and muddy from the shanty streets, and tied up the leather string wraps which secured them to his feet and legs. He removed his felt cap, scratched his head, and ran his fingers through his brown hair in an attempt to straighten it out before replacing the cap. He heard the rattle of chains and the groan of the eastern gates opening for another day. He considered exiting through the east gates and getting a quick bath in the river but was already too cold and didn't really want to trudge through the muck again so early. Deciding he would wash later, he yawned, stretched and picked up his pack and headed out into Hierlaneum.

There was a vendor's stand a small distance from the gates. Its owner splashed buckets of water around on the plaza and street around his little business and swept the area clean with a large broom. The smell of beef roasting over an open spit wafted through the morning air. Two soldiers were standing next to the vendor busily eating meat and hard bread from small trays. They and the owner eyed Weylyn suspiciously.

"Good morning. Can I get some of that, please?"

"Depends, Celt," said the owner. He stopped sweeping and leaned the broom handle against his food stall.

Weylyn placed a coin on the counter. "Is that enough?"

The owner picked up the coin and fingered it. He looked at Weylyn, then putting the coin in his belt pouch, reached for a long slender-bladed knife on the spit. Without comment, he sliced a good-sized portion, placed it on a small wooden tray, added a slice of bread and handed it to Weylyn. "Leave the tray on the counter when you finish." He turned and went back to sweeping the area around his business.

Weylyn had just finished his first good bite of hot roast and bread when the loud clatter of bells rang near the city center. He looked up and saw the proprietor stop sweeping. He and the soldiers were looking in the direction of the bells.

"The bells of the Great Central Church announcing the Mass of Saint Felicitas—it's this morning," said the proprietor. "Used to be the celebration of our goddess, Felicitas, bringer of joy and good fortune." He shrugged his shoulders and went back to sweeping. The soldiers put their trays down and walked to the edge of the street and looked in the direction of the church, where the bells were ringing insistently.

Weylyn quickly finished his meal, placed the tray on the counter and washed his hands in one of the water buckets next to the spit. He splashed water on his face and rubbed his eyes. The bells continued to ring. He cleared his eyes and was drying his hands on his clothes when a chariot carrying two Enforcers went racing down the street past the little stand toward the direction of the bells. The proprietor stopped his sweeping again. He and Weylyn were watching the chariot race out of sight when they heard the sound of boots stomping across pavement and saw six armed soldiers in full gear on a dead run, trying desperately to keep up with the Enforcers' chariot.

"Something about those bells," said the proprietor. "They don't sound right. It's the big bells of the Great Church all right, but not the usual ringing of bells announcing a mass. These are bells of warning, of alarm!"

The two soldiers raced back toward the eastern gate.

"Why would an alarm be sounded from the Great Church in the city's center?" asked Weylyn. "What could possibly—?"

"Don't know. Never heard of one before," interrupted the proprietor. "But I don't like it, especially if it involves the Enforcers and the army." He laid his broom against the side of his booth. "I'm closing up."

The blaring of horns sounded from all around the city's

perimeter. Weylyn heard the guards on the wall behind him sound theirs as the eastern gates were pulled closed, and knew his visit out to the Celtarium's High Point area would have to wait a while longer. He listened to the ringing bells. An alarm for an attack would come from one of the city's outer walls, not the city center. He thought about what he should do. He didn't want to return to the room next to the eastern gate. After all, if the city were being attacked, he didn't want to be a Celt caught inside in that little room next to a main gate. He knew he couldn't go to the Enforcer's barracks where Axenus resided, either. He didn't want to stay out on the streets—even the food vendor didn't think that was a good idea and the vendor was a resident. But where could he go? He didn't know the city, just what little he'd picked up since arriving yesterday and the directions to the Rodas Villa given to him by Elder Eghan.

The Rodas, home of the late Eiroy the Red—he wondered if he could talk the owner, Titus, into letting him look around Eiroy's house. Probably not. He didn't want to deal with that man again, but there was the old Roman soldier, Calvin. He was friendly enough and didn't mind a little talk, especially if it involved a free drink or two. And the old man had indicated he knew something about Eiroy's trouble. Weylyn wondered just how much the old legionnaire really did know about Eiroy. It would be worth the cost of a drink to find out.

Age is but a fleeting thing,
As time on Earth goes by.
We gather things as we march on.
Wisdom gathers strength to cry,
"Discount the Elder's knowledge gifts,
And stupid you will die."

23

October 9th in the Roman calendar
Four days left in the Runic Half-Month of Gyfu

Weylyn made his way onto the Rodas Villa Street. He could make out the entrance to the Rodas and saw the iron gates were closed. He hoped they weren't locked. The ringing of the Central Church bells and the blaring of the city guards' horns along the city's perimeter had long since fallen quiet. On his travel from the eastern gate to the Pandorian Villa section of Hierlaneum, he'd seen several groups of soldiers and Enforcers rushing to the city center where the Great Church stood. Occasionally, civilians were running too in that direction, evidently wanting to see what all the commotion was about. But mostly, Weylyn found the shops shuttered and closed and the streets largely deserted.

Reaching the Rodas Villa entrance, he noticed the iron gate was pulled to but not locked or secured in any fashion. He pushed the gate open, entered and shut it behind him. The doors to both the tavern and Titus' office were closed. He looked across the deserted inner courtyard toward the Blue

Rose house, former home of Eiroy the Red. He considered where Calvin might be found. He left the covered patio, walked past the old fountain and approached Eiroy's. The paint on the old, blue door was faded. He wondered if Eiroy had left anything of importance behind when he left for the Brendan Valley. Weylyn knew the chances were excellent the Enforcers had already searched the place thoroughly—especially if they thought Eiroy had anything at all to do with the theft of the Great Cross. He was about to look in the windows of the small dwelling when a voice hailed him from across the courtyard.

"Hail, young Weylyn!" said Calvin the Bald. The old legionnaire was standing in the doorway of the house closest to the small forge and smith in the far corner of the courtyard. He waved to Weylyn, motioning him to come over.

"Greetings, Calvin. I trust your day is a good one?"

The old Roman soldier scoured his scarred face and spat on the ground. "Ha! Good for what?" The old man shuffled out the doorway and shut the door. "Was a lot better before they shut the tavern down this morning. No sooner opened it before they shut it down. Ran us all out, they did. And for what? Turns out it was just a little problem over at the central church is all. Ha! You'd of thought the whole city was under siege or something. From the sound of it, I thought every Celt in the world was armed and at the gates! I came back home and fell asleep after the commotion died down." He rubbed his grizzled old face and looked hopefully toward the tavern. "Do you know if they've opened back up yet?"

"No, but let's go take a look."

"Good idea! Good idea, young man. It's not healthy to miss a good drink to start your day, messes everything else up. You know, these old bones don't move like they used to, even slower without a good morning drink."

They made their way slowly across the courtyard. Calvin took a seat at one of the tables on the patio while Weylyn tried the door to the tavern. It was unlocked. He soon returned carrying two large mugs of beer and took a seat at the table.

"Now that's what I call a drink! A large beer! Woo, hoo! This may turn out to be a good day, after all," said Calvin. "Thanks, young Celt. Here's to you!" His eyes sparkling, he grabbed the large mug with both hands and raised it to his lips. He took a long, deep drink before setting the mug back on the table in front of him. Weylyn did the same.

"You are welcome, Calvin. I hoped I would find you here. If you don't mind, I'd like to ask—"

"Don't know much, I'm afraid. Heard a priest got nailed to the doors of the Great Church this morning before the Saint Felicitas mass. That was what all the commotion, all the fuss was about. 'Least that's what I was told before I went off to sleep. They say it was the work of the Black Hand. Reckon that's all I know. Like I said, I left the tavern, went home and went back to sleep."

Before Weylyn could explain to Calvin that incident was not what he wished to talk about, the maid from the tavern came to their table carrying bread and cheese on a large tray.

"Hey, now what's this, young sir?" Calvin's face showed genuine surprise and delight as he surveyed the meal.

"Well, I was hungry and thought since you had your own morning meal interrupted, you could help me get through this. What do you say?"

"Oh, I'll say yes and thank you again!" He rubbed his hands together, eyes twinkling. He looked from the food to Weylyn, back to the food, then up to the woman. She placed the tray on the table and stood there, waiting to see if there would be anything else. "If you want to know anything about the happenings at the church this morning, if you want to know about the bells and all the commotion, just ask this good woman. She's heard it all by now, I reckon." He smiled and swatted the woman on the buttocks. "Haven't you, young maid?

Tell us what you heard. This young Celt wants to know." The old man laughed and reached for a hunk of bread and cheese.

The heavyset, matronly woman smiled, put one hand on her hip and gently tweaked the old man on his left cheek. "Calvin, you're just full of it, aren't you?" She laughed. "And keep your hands to yourself, you wicked old soldier."

She looked back at Weylyn. The smile disappeared and was replaced by her most serious face. "He's right, you know, I've heard all about it! It was a terrible, terrible sight to behold, I'm told. The priest, stripped down to nothing but his God-given skin and bones! His face all blackened and swollen, must have taken a terrible beating. Oh, it was horrible! His hands and feet nailed by spikes to the Great Church's Cathedral doors. He was bleeding like a stuck pig. His mouth was bound and gagged. When they removed the gag, they found thirteen pieces of the Emperor's coppers stuffed in his mouth! It was awful!"

"Well now, that's interesting, indeed," mumbled Calvin between chewing a hunk of bread and cheese, crumbs falling from the corners of his mouth. "Reckon who'd want to kill a priest of the Great Church?" he asked. He rubbed the bread crumbs from his hands and reached for another drink of beer. His eyes were directly on Weylyn.

"Oh, but that's just it," said the woman. "He's not dead. They say he'll live, but he's in bad shape. They say he was nailed to the door just before the early mass. The mark of the Black Hand was on the door next to the priest, too." She shifted her stance and folded her arms across her chest. "It's a terrible thing to do to anyone, but to a priest! I just don't know what the world's coming to these days. There's just no respect for authority anymore."

She paused and looked at Calvin and Weylyn. When the they didn't respond, she continued, "Well, you men just call if you need something else." She abruptly turned and made her way back into the tavern.

"Hee, hee! Told you she would know what was what. Those girls hear some of the damnedest things!" The old man laughed and reached for more food.

"Yes, you were right." Weylyn had little interest in churcher intrigues and could care less about a churcher priest being attacked, but he didn't want to be rude to an elder. He took a drink and set his mug back on the table and eyed the old soldier as he helped himself to the bread and cheese. "But, Calvin, I wanted to talk to you about Eiroy. Last time we spoke, you said you knew something of the trouble he was in, is that right?"

"Eiroy, eh? Well, yes. I reckon he's up to his ears in trouble, absolutely. What was it you wanted to know, young Celt?" Calvin asked. He continued his meal, not looking up.

"Remember, I said he was out in the Brendan Valley visiting relatives?"

"Ah, yes, I guess I remember you saying that. Yes, visiting relatives, you said." Calvin reached for another hunk of cheese.

Weylyn watched the old man carefully. "He was followed out to the valley by someone, a Roman named Aod. They got into a fight and Eiroy killed him. Eiroy himself was wounded in the confrontation and eventually died from his wounds."

Calvin stopped eating. He dropped his head for just a moment as if looking down at his lap. "Eiroy's dead?" asked the old man, his face blank. After a short pause, he asked, "This Aod fellow he's supposed to have killed, was he a big fellow?"

"No, Aod wasn't a particularly big man, about my size, maybe smaller. But, yes, Eiroy is dead and we don't exactly know why it all happened. I was hoping you could give me information which might help explain—"

"It's that damned cross! I knew it. He was in on its theft. I knew it would get him killed. Dangerous thing to do, steal from the Great Church."

"Calvin, you knew he was going to steal the cross?" Weylyn couldn't believe the old man would admit it outright.

Calvin looked up. "Of course not!" He laughed even as he reached for the mug of beer.

"Didn't know he was going to steal it, young fellow. Just figured that's what happened when he left and news got around about the shipment being stolen on its way back to the Great Church. Put two and two together is what I did."

"But you said you knew he was in trouble?"

"Even a fool would know a man's in trouble when half an army of Enforcer troops break into and search the place you live. That's what they did a few days after Eiroy left. They went through this entire villa. Pulled us all out and wanted to know if we knew anything at all about Eiroy, where he was, where he kept his belongings. They ransacked everything. As far as I know, they never found anything and nobody told 'em anything they could use. They were especially rough with Titus. Told him they'd come for his head if they found out he was hiding Eiroy or any of his things. I heard Titus tell them Eiroy and his friends used the forge a lot, so they tore that place up, too. Didn't find anything though."

He paused to take a sip of beer before continuing. "You see, Eiroy and his friends were good smiths. They used the villa's forge a lot, especially the month before he left this last time. I used to come out and watch 'em work. The forge is next to my house there, you know." He pointed across the courtyard. "Eiroy was excited about something and it showed. He told me one night, after the others had left for the day. He said he was about to do a big job and it would be his last. He'd be able to move out of Hierlaneum and live the life of a freeman, a nobleman. Never told me what the job was, but he was excited about it, said it would make him a hero with his Celtic brethren." Calvin reached for more bread and cheese.

"But he never told you what was going to make him rich and famous? What do you suppose would make him a hero to his people?"

"He never told me. I remember joking with him about it, though. I said a hero to your brethren? What are going to do, take a barge load of churcher heads over to the Celt Queen? We got a big laugh out of that one."

Weylyn took a drink and waited to see if Calvin would add more to the story. When the old man just continued to enjoy the meal, he decided to probe further.

"You said Eiroy and friends often used the forge. What were they were making? Did he ever tell you? Did you get a chance to see for yourself?"

"Well, lately it was metal banding. Big strips. Spikes, too. He said they were for his friend, a barge operator up at Dynsmore to reinforce his barge. Nothing mysterious there."

"Do you remember the barge operator's name?"

"Don't think it was ever mentioned."

"It would be a big help if you could remember his name."

"Reckon I never knew it, but if it helps you any at all, I do recall the name of his barge. It was the Elvira Domino, the White Lady. I remember because my wife's name was Elvira." Calvin got a faraway look in his eyes and seemed to drift away from the conversation. He pulled himself out of his memories and quickly took another drink.

"What about other visitors? Do you know their names?"

The old man took a bite of cheese, clearly enjoying the food. "Seems like I did, but can't recall any of their names. Of course, Eiroy's last visitor I saw, I wouldn't want to know his name. Hope I never see him again."

"Eiroy's last visitor?"

"Was the night before Eiroy left for the last time; it was just getting dark out. Eiroy was finishing up at the forge. Me and my two buddies headed back to my place with a flagon and were about to enjoy a round of bones before we turned in for the night. Like I said, Eiroy was still at the forge. I asked him to join us for a game, but he said he couldn't because he had to get ready for his trip the next day. Anyway, we went into my house and left him at the forge and it wasn't long before we heard an awful loud argument outside. Eiroy was giving somebody a fit about something. Couldn't make out what, but he was mad." He reached for his mug.

"Did you see the other man? Was it someone you'd seen here before?"

"Nope. Never seen him before. Did get a look at him though. You know, my eyes aren't what they used to be, but this one wasn't hard to spot. Big man. Dark clothes. Wore a black cloak with a big hood, the kind like priests wear, you know. Wasn't a priest, though— more like the devil himself."

"Anything else you can remember about him? Would you know him if you saw him again?"

"Don't want to see him again," said Calvin. "I remember later thinking back on it. There was something about him. I don't know." The old man hesitated, thinking back on the incident. "Got this feeling I'd seen him before, but the more I thought about it, the more I realized I'd never seen him before, just men like him. It was the way he carried himself. The way he stood up against Eiroy. You know, there's a certain way a man handles himself. If I was a betting man—and I am—I'd say the fellow was a Celt warrior. Just like the ones we legionnaires used to face. Big, mean and dangerous."

"So the two had an argument? Do you know what it was about?"

"No, not really. When the yelling started my friends and I opened my door to see if Eiroy needed any help. That seemed to catch the big man off guard. He turned toward us real quick and when he did, that's when Eiroy stuck him." The old man grinned.

"Stuck him?"

"Yup, stuck him—with a red hot poker from the forge. When we opened the door, Eiroy lunged at the man, jabbed him in the face with the poker and pushed him down right over there onto the wood pile." The old man pointed in the direction of the stack of wood against the side of the small forge. "Then Eiroy ran out of the villa like the Hounds of Hell were on his trail. The big man fell over the wood and when he did, the hood fell back. Seems like he had light colored hair, but I can't remember. He was holding the left side of his face like he'd been cut or burned—burned I imagine from the hot iron. Anyway, he jumped up, threw the hood back over his head and raced out of the villa, trying to catch Eiroy, I think."

"So you figure it was that night Eiroy left Hierlaneum and made his way to the valley? And this big man in black followed him?"

"Nope, that's not what I figure at all, young man." Calvin smiled. He reached for the last piece of bread and cheese and chewed.

Weylyn looked at the man. There was a twinkle in his eye as if he still had more to share. Weylyn took another drink and waited.

The old man swallowed at last and brushed the bread and cheese crumbs from his hands. He placed his hands around the mug in front of him but didn't lift it. "I know it didn't happen that way because, just before daybreak, I heard Eiroy come back. So I snuck a peek. He took a lamp into the forge and picked up some things he'd been working on and then went to his house for a few minutes. Just at sunrise, I watched him leave. That's the last I saw of him," Calvin said. The old legionnaire raised his mug and finished the beer.

Death had knocked upon the door,
Its workman stood most weary.
Tired and spent and without rest,
From labor in the dark so dreary.
Time, he felt, to quit this job,
His muscles knotted, tired and sore.
Just one more thing he had to do:
Answer the knocking at his door.

24

October 9th in the Roman calendar
Four days left in the Runic Half-Month of Gyfu

The small, windowless room reeked of body odor, smoke, and candle wax. The dim oil lamp, its wick purposefully set low so as not to expel too much light did not reveal much in the way of detail for the two men in the room. Parzifal finished tying the heavy pouch of coins, partial payment for the job on the priest, to the belt beneath his cloak. It felt good hanging there.

"Well, well! I'm pleased!" said the old man. "More pleased than I thought I'd ever be. By all the damned gods of Hades, you've certainly outdone even yourself." The Holder laughed and coughed, his voice as coarse as ever. He drained the cup in one long gulp and poured another. "Ha, ha! Thirteen pieces of minted copper stuffed down his sorry, slimy throat, too. By the gods, that's good. Ha, ha. Never thought of you as one who'd be tithing to the church! That's really good. They'll be talking about this one for the next one hundred years!" roared the old man. He laughed vigorously until interrupted by a vicious cough. He hacked up phlegm and spit it on the floor.

Parzifal was pleased that he'd been able to finish the job on the priest and get back to his place before sunrise. He'd stripped off his clothing, cleaned himself and the tools of his trade, placing the bloody clothing into the fireplace for disposal. He rummaged through a large chest full of wigs and clothing, male and female, Celtic and Roman. He quickly changed into some fine clothes he kept handy for disguise, put on a fashionable, distinguished hat and made his way back to the Central Church. He arrived just as the attendees discovered his handiwork with the priest, Loxius Scrota. Parzifal mingled long enough in the frenzied crowd to know the word had gotten out. He'd only mentioned it once, in little more than a whisper, to the closest couple as they gazed upon the sight of the priest. It was the same message scrawled in charcoal on the front of the church next to the hapless priest hanging there. "He wouldn't pay his gambling debts."

Shocked, but willing to believe it because of the sordid reputation of Loxius Scrota, they quickly spread the information through the crowd. It spread like fire across a field of dry grass in a high wind. The Holder would be pleased. It had gone better than planned. Satisfied, Parzifal had made his way back to shelter and much needed rest. Before he retired, he took the last of the green tinted salve the Celt healer in High Point had given him for his face and applied it to his burn. Following the healer's directions, he tied a white linen cloth loosely over the wound. He'd slept through the day, rising just before the sun dropped from sight.

The fireplace was stoked and lit and into it had gone the bloody clothing from the night before. The damned priest had the audacity to bleed like a stuck pig. He wouldn't keep the soiled outfit. That task completed, he'd made himself a dinner of bread, beef, and onions. He'd uncorked a bottle of honey mead he'd been saving for a special occasion and enjoyed the strong drink with his dinner. He'd considered venturing over to

High Point to visit his Celtic acquaintances, maybe get advice on horse racing and horse raising in the Celtic style, whatever that might be, but thought better of that.

After he concluded his business with The Holder, Parzifal had a late-night appointment with the slimy little merchant, Pax Catus. But first he'd have to finish this visit.

"And the horse, when will he be delivered?" asked Parzifal.

"The black racing stallion? Well, I don't keep my horses inside the city walls, you know. I've sent one of my men to fetch him from my country villa stables up north. He'll be here tomorrow."

Parzifal stared down at the shadowy face of the old man. He'd always been paid in full immediately after a job, but then, he'd never taken a horse in payment before either. He decided not to argue the point. The Holder had always kept his end of the bargain when it came to payments. Parzifal didn't want to get into it with the old man. After all, it was The Holder who long ago had bought out his slave tenure from the priests of the Great Church. It was the old man who, in the strictest sense, gave Parzifal his freedom from churcher servitude. For that, he owed him much, served him well. He could trust him. Besides, there'd be time enough to deal with any non-payment for services should the old man renege on the horse.

As if reading his thoughts, The Holder said, "Don't worry about the horse. He'll be here, just in time for your trip." He reached for the flagon and refilled his cup.

"My trip?"

The Holder picked up his cup and leaned back in his chair. "I've got a little problem I need you to handle."

Parzifal had intended the priest to be his last job. The gratitude and loyalty he felt was wavering, dwindling further each time he visited the Celts at High Point. The longing for a new life in the Celt territories was growing stronger. He would not tell the old man he was planning to leave Hierlaneum to finally retire from this line of work, to finally be completely free. It wouldn't set well with any of his employers, but especially not The Holder. Parzifal had planned to just vanish without so much as a good-bye to anyone and move on to rediscover a life he'd briefly shared with his father and mother, the good life before the hellish invasion of the Romans and his enslavement by the churchers. No, another job had not been in his plans.

"How little is this problem?" asked Parzifal.

"Actually, little is a good description but its importance is large, very large. It's something that could become very uncomfortable for me. On the other hand, it could turn out to be a saving grace. There's a young Celt girl from the Brendan Valley looking for Eiroy the Red. Seems Pax or someone working for him paid off Titus at the Rodas Villa to inform them if Eiroy or any of his friends came by. Fortunately, my men got to Titus first with a bigger payoff. He's been keeping me posted on the comings and goings at the Rodas. The girl showed up at his villa asking questions. Most important of all, she mentioned a rune buckle, and my sources have confirmed to me that buckle has something to do with the treasure. This girl may have it or know where it is. I want you to get her."

"Get her? You mean bring her to you?"

The old man took a big swig from his cup and swallowed it as he leaned forward in his chair. He scowled. "What you do with her is your business, but I want two things. First, I want a guarantee she'll never talk to anyone again. She found Eiroy's place and is asking around. That's going to draw attention. I've been told a Brendan Valley magistrate was at the Rodas looking for her. Fortunately, he's been picked up by the Enforcers so I don't have any worry about him, but that's too much attention already. I don't want that girl too close to my business." He put the cup down on the table, sat back in his chair, arms folded over his chest. "I don't ever want to know what happens to her, understand? I don't care."

"Sounds like this job would be better left to your street ruffians. Less expensive, too."

The old man coughed. He sat up in the chair again and reached for his flagon and cup. "No. I need someone I can trust. I need you to do it. You're right, those street thugs could easily do away with the likes of a young girl but I can't trust them for the most important part. If she's got the rune buckle, I want it. If she doesn't have it, find out how much she knows about it. Find out if she knows where it is."

Parzifal didn't move, didn't respond. He watched the old man refill the cup and take another drink. The lamp smoke in the room was beginning to burn his eyes. He was anxious for this meeting to end, to get out and get some fresh air. He knew the old man's bottle was running low and The Holder never stretched one of their meetings beyond an empty wine bottle.

"She's a young girl, maybe about fourteen years more or less, light brown hair. Wild and unkempt, average build, wearing a red fox cape. A felt hat and ridiculous leather britches. Leather britches on a female. Ha, ha. No accounting for the Celt's lack of sophistication," said the old man. He laughed until his cough took over and forced him to spit again.

Parzifal ignored the old man's condition. "That description pretty much matches a lot of young people outside the gates."

The Holder fought to clear his throat. "Won't be hard. If she's still in the area, she should be easy to find. I understand Titus sent her over to High Point." He coughed again, trying to clear his throat. "You'll need to take a little trip out there I imagine." The cough got the best of him. He hacked and spit phlegm onto the floor. "I do not want that girl asking any more questions. But I want that belt buckle, understand?"

"I understand."

"Make certain you do. I won't put up with those Enforcers getting back to Pax. He's become a real liability. He and his pathetic little band of thieves really messed this one up, and I intend to make myself look good with the Bishop because of their screw-ups, but I can't do that without a certain little buckle or a great big gold cross. If the Enforcers lean on Pax again, he's likely to break. That means he could ruin my operation. I'm hesitant to do anything to him now for a couple of reasons. First, I don't know if he's found the buckle or if he knows where it is. I can't do anything with Pax until I know.

"Besides, there are things my friends in the office of the Prefect just can't ignore. There's only so much looking the other way they can do, just so many bribes they'll take. I don't want a spineless, worthless merchant-thief like Pax hurting my livelihood." He slammed both hands down on the table top. "But right now, I want that buckle and I want the girl silenced." Once again, he coughed furiously.

Parzifal watched The Holder fight to regain control. The old man's health was failing. Parzifal had seen it coming these last few years. Soon, The Holder would be no longer.

The old man gained control of his cough again and looked up from the table at the big hulking assassin. "Well, what is it? That's all I've got. Usual pay—that all right with you?"

Parzifal nodded. "One more thing,"

"What?"

"Do we know who she's seeing in High Point? Maybe where I'd find her there?" asked Parzifal. "And what if she's left the area and gone back home? Do you still want me to take care of her?"

"Track her to the Gates of Hades if you have to. If she's gone back to her homeland, then you'll have to plan on another trip out to the Brendans. But Titus says he sent her to High Point to see some old Celt woman, a healer they call Brennarix," said the old man. "I suppose you could start there."

"All right," agreed Parzifal. He turned and made his way out of The Holder's office. He would set off for High Point just as soon as he paid a visit to a certain merchant.

Cast upon the seas of good or evil,
Souls must pay—and we should know—
Universal Power's rising Spirit level,
All must reap just what they sow.

25

October 9th in the Roman calendar
Four days left in the Runic Half-Month of Gyfu

The huge log building sat in darkness. Its back faced the merchant docks along Hierlaneum's southern wall on the banks of the Moryn Gweneth River. Under the thatched roof, above the locked and bolted entrance door, hung a sign which read: "Catus Trading-Import/Export—Pax Catus, Merchant."

Beneath the massive roof beams inside the structure sat numerous piles of barter in varying degrees of neatness—all goods waiting for pick up or delivery, all waiting in darkness except those in the very front. Those were bathed by the soft, yellow glow of a burning oil lamp on a makeshift table of wood slab set across two large wine barrels. Pax Catus paced back and forth next to the table that served as his office.

"Where in the name of all the demons of Lucifer is he, anyway?" screeched the pacing man. "He's late, I tell you, and he isn't coming. He's sided with those Celts, I know it. Or maybe he's been taken by the Enforcers. Yes, that's it! He may be leading them here this very moment to arrest me again!" The pitch of his voice grew higher and higher as he became more and more agitated. "Can you see anything yet?"

A man, his back to the large warehouse interior, stood looking out a small sliding peep-window in the main door. He answered the question without taking his eyes from the window. "No, sir, nothing. The street still appears to be deserted except for the city guards occasional passing. No sign yet."

"No, of course not! He's turned on me, too, I'll wager." He continued to pace back and forth along the table in the dim light, rubbing his hands together as if washing them in the air in front of him. "I never should have agreed to this. I knew it would be too dangerous. Salt and iron shipments, horses, petty goods and spices from other merchants is one thing, but stealing from the church! I should have known this would happen. That's reserved for clerics, not merchants. Churchers stealing from churchers. Ha! Maybe it was them who set me up. Yes, maybe they intended for me to take the fall for this all along. It would be just like them, wouldn't it? They should have said, Pax, would you mind stealing the Great Cross from the Church so we can get it back and make points with His Highness, the Grand Cleric? Oh, and of course Pax, you won't mind taking the blame for it, you won't mind losing your head over it, will you?" His voice reached fever pitch.

Pax stopped pacing, sat down on a keg at the table. He held his bowed head with both hands and closed his eyes. "It's God's punishment on me, for certain." Hands shaking, he reached into the folds of his blue tunic and pulled out a gold church fetish on a chain worn around his neck. "Please, I pray, let Brutovius sort this out for me. Let him find that cursed buckle or the treasure itself." He kissed it longingly then hid it away back inside his clothing. Vigorously rubbing both sides of his head with his hands, he made huge clumps of his thick black hair stand out in little spiked tuffs. He jumped up from the table and hurried to the door.

"Get out of the way!" He pushed his guard to the side and stared out the door's small window. He nervously scanned the street in both directions. "Damn it, damn it! Can't trust them. Can't trust clerics, can't trust Enforcers, and you better not trust those worthless, tree-hugging Celts! It's all his fault, anyway—if he'd only stopped Eiroy from leaving. I think if the bastard shows his worthless pagan butt up here now, we'll just take one of those long poles back there—" he slammed the small window shut, pointed a thumb back in the direction of a stack of long wooden poles in the center of the room and looked over at his companion, "—and shove it up his big Celtic—"

Pax stopped talking when he saw his guard's face. Even in the dim glow of the lamp, he could see the guard staring into the room.

The hair stood up on the back of the neck of Pax Catus. He turned and saw a large, sinister mass of black robe and hood standing beside the makeshift table. "Parzifal! Ah, uh, you made it! How long have you been … ah, well never mind! Thank God and the Great Church! I was getting worried. Where's Brutovius? We haven't seen or heard from him in days."

Silence.

"I thought Brutovius would return to Hierlaneum with you, like we planned? He, ah, well, never mind about him!" Pax Catus laughed nervously and shuffled a few paces toward the table. When he spoke again, his voice was up two octaves as he all but screeched, "But I would like to know where in Hades that scoundrel Myrdoc got off to. Do you know? Can you tell me? Have you heard from him? My goods are backing up unmercifully without his barge to transport and no one else will haul for me after the cursed Enforcers took me in. It's all over town. My friends at the Prefect's told me they could no longer protect me. There's a Centurion from Rome here investigating this. The Guild is refusing to speak with me. The Bishop won't even see me now. I'll be ruined, ruined I tell you!"

Pax nervously waved his hand toward a seat. "Sit! Sit down. We have to talk. We have to plan a way to get revenge on those double-crossing swine who are trying to put me out of business. If we can't figure this out, I'm going to have to go directly to the Prefect and tell him everything—and I mean everything—and maybe work out a deal with him and the Centurion to get me, ah I mean, us out of this mess." Pax smiled a tight, nervous smile as he took his seat at the table.

Parzifal didn't move but stood there silent, contemplating only one solution to the problem that was the merchant, Pax Catus.

Revealed to those who seek the Truth,
A man-hewn mark upon the stone,
Answers Truth for those who see,
A telltale mark that solves a Mystery.

26

October 10th in the Roman calendar
Late Morning
Seventeen days left in the Celtic Tree Month of Gort

Weylyn made his way through the grimy, muddy, cold streets of the Celtarium, its filth and odor clinging to his boots and clothing. The horrid conditions were barely tolerable for beast, let alone mankind. Steel gray clouds hung low and threatening. A cold breeze blew out of the north, and the residents had closed and shuttered their buildings against the coming storm. Weylyn drew his cape up tighter around his neck and pulled his cap down tight to cover the top of his ears. He knew whatever the Old Man of the North had in store, it wouldn't be pleasant.

The road out of the eastern gates of Hierlaneum twisted and turned, winding in and out of small side streets, alleys, and cul-de-sacs of merchant shops, shanty homes, and market squares. All were laid out in a haphazard, first-come-first-served basis and totally unlike the majority of the symmetrically designed areas within the walls of the large city around which the Celtarium grew. Weylyn concentrated on the small map of parchment Axenus had drawn for him to help navigate the maze of tacky urban slum sprawl outside Hierlaneum.

As he moved through the dilapidated expanse of the Celtarium's buildings, he constantly checked his position against the massive eastern city walls far behind him and the large trees on the high knoll which marked the location he sought. He was thankful the day had dawned cold and threatened bad weather. It was less crowded in the Celtarium—just a few merchants, beggars, and a few hungry canines patrolling the streets and alleyways, the first two hawking their wares or beseeching passersby. This was a bad dream, Celts living in such conditions. The very nature of things seemed surreal, out of place and out of time with his way of living. In the Brendan Valley things seemed in harmony, in balance with the natural forces. The conditions through which Weylyn trudged seemed like a wildly horrible, unbelievable nightmare. Garbage in the streets, the stagnant smell of too many people living in close quarters, the land almost void of trees and growing things, small groups of animals penned up in small, cramped filthy pens and corrals.

A few of the Celtarium's dwellings were fairly well kept; some even displayed Celtic decorations in the old style, but the majority of shops and homes were in dire need of repair. Many were missing doors, shutters and sometimes even roofs. Many more were nothing more than stone burrows packed around with sod and mud. The thick smoke of numerous chimney and outdoor fires swirled about him, blowing through the narrow streets and alleys, choking his lungs and burning his eyes.

He stopped walking for a moment and studied the small, makeshift map and its crude pictures marking certain key landmarks. A light snow was falling as he'd reached a small town square with four intersecting streets. He noted the square's position on his map. The street on his left led up the slope toward the tree-covered hill area of the Celtarium called High Point.

A large cart filled with firewood was parked to his right just off the intersection. Two Celts were off-loading firewood for a merchant. The merchant gave orders to the younger Celt about where and how to place the wood, complaining about the price he was being charged. Finishing with his orders and ranting, the merchant went back into his building, slamming the door behind him. The young boy seemed to pay no attention to the incident but the older man laughed and made a vulgar gesture in the direction of the merchant's door. "Greed is your devil's right hand!" mumbled the old wood merchant. He and the boy exchanged grins.

Greed indeed, thought Weylyn. It was greed that got Titus to talk. He looked back down at the little map Axenus had made for him. He saw the round outline of what the Enforcer had said indicated High Point and the many small squares drawn to approximate key buildings around rough sketches depicting large trees. On one of the small squares was a dark 'x.' Next to that was a pole with what would pass as the outline of a bird. "The raven pole," Titus had said. "You'll find who you're looking for there." That's what Axenus and Warius had forced Titus to admit. Actually, it had been a combination of fear and greed that got Titus in a position to reveal the information. Weylyn thought back to the incident with Titus and remembered how the Enforcers handled it.

*

Weylyn had finished his meal and visit with the old legionnaire, Calvin the Bald. On his way out of the Rodas Villa, Titus had called him into his office to say he did seem to remember a visit by a young Celt girl a while back.

"Maybe it's the very girl you were asking me about earlier," Titus had said. If Weylyn could come up with the right amount of the Emperor's coins, Titus' memory just might return.

"I don't have that kind of payment but if you can remember anything at all about her, what she said, who she was looking for, maybe where she might have said she was going, it would be very helpful," Weylyn had said.

But without the prospect of payment, Titus' memory of the girl apparently vanished. "Sorry, young sir, perhaps when you can come up with something to jog my memory—say, maybe two silvers—I might be able to recall something for you."

Weylyn hadn't come up with two silvers, but he did come up with two Enforcers. He'd left the Rodas Villa and immediately went in search of Axenus. The Centurion, anxious to get any information which would help him find the missing Great Cross, gathered up Warius and two of their men and with Weylyn made their way back to the Rodas Villa and the office of the proprietor, Titus. The two soldiers had been posted outside the office. Weylyn and the Enforcers entered and closed the door behind them. Titus, his sandaled feet up on the table, sat back in his chair eating roasted pork. He'd feigned surprise at their arrival.

"Ah, if it isn't my friend, Axenus," Titus had exclaimed in his friendliest proprietor's voice. "And the young Celt, back again so soon. Come in, come in!" He tossed the bone upon a tray on the table, licked his fingers and wiped his greasy hands on his tunic. He did not acknowledge Warius, but gave him a distrustful look before addressing Axenus and Weylyn again. "What brings you gentlemen to my humble business today?"

Warius took an intimidating step toward Titus and bellowed out, "We're looking for a head to put on this Celt's trophy pole. We thought yours would look real good hanging up there!"

Titus' smile disappeared as the blood drained from his face.

"Don't give us lies, Titus," Warius told him. "We want to find this Celt girl. We know she was here and talked with you."

The proprietor laughed nervously. "Celt girl? Did I say I saw a Celt girl?" He reached down and clutched the gold churcher fetish on his neck chain. "By the pure grace of the Savior of the Great Church, I don't think I remember seeing—"

Warius moved quickly and kicked the end of the small table out from under the legs of Titus. Food and wine went flying. The shopkeeper's legs hit the floor hard and he rolled off his chair and onto the floor. The big Enforcer reached down, grabbed Titus by the hair of his head, lifted him up on his feet and threw him up against the wall where his head hit the stone wall with a 'pop.'

Titus screamed in pain, grabbed his head and fell across the top of his table, moaning. Blood was oozing from a cut on the back of his head. He struggled to keep his feet under him as his upper body lay across the table.

"Did that help your memory return?" Warius demanded.

"Ahhhh, ohhh," moaned Titus. "You broke my skull!" Blood seeped between his fingers as he clutched his head.

Warius had laughed an evil-sounding laugh. "Yes, but we haven't cut it off—not yet!"

"All right, Warius, that's enough. Titus just needs time to remember," Axenus said calmly. "Don't you, my friend?"

"I … I … guess, well, I only wanted a little something for my information, that's all. It's probably nothing; probably won't do you any good," Titus had moaned. His voice turned angry as he removed one of his hands from his head and looked at the blood. "But now I don't think I can remember—"

Warius drew his sword from its sheath, the hissing sound of blade against scabbard sounding like a deadly viper. "Well, no memory, no head."

"No, no!" the shopkeeper yelled as he rolled off the table and backed up against the wall, cowering there as the Enforcer approached. Apparently dizzy, he grabbed his head with both hands and slumped to the floor. "No!" he begged.

"Now look here, Titus. You've been good enough in the past to remember to let us know when Eiroy's friends came around.

You sent us word when this Celt magistrate, here, came calling for Eiroy—and you've been paid well for your services. Don't let this little incident spoil our working relationship, all right?" Axenus spoke softly, politely. "Here, let me help you up." The Enforcer helped Titus to his feet and settled him on his chair.

"Yes, all right. She was here. A young Celt girl looking for Eiroy's home and relatives."

"When? When was she here?" asked Axenus.

"Three days ago."

"Are you certain?"

"Yes," replied Titus. "It was the day of the Celebration of Our Lady of Victories. The girl was trying to find an old relative of hers and she seemed to think Eiroy could help her or something. I remember telling her on the Day of Our Lady she might be blessed with opportunity and victory over what she sought." Titus seemed ready to faint away as he looked at the blood flowing down his tunic.

"Is that all?"

"Well . . ." He paused, pressing his hand against the bleeding wound. "She asked if I knew of any Celts named Parke or something like that. I told her I didn't. She said they would be healers. I told her Celts weren't allowed to practice the healing arts in Hierlaneum. The only Celt healers I'd ever heard of were out in High Point. I sent her out there."

"Exactly where out there did you send her?"

"To the old Celt woman they call The Raven. I forget her real name." He eyed Warius then looked down at the floor.

He couldn't remember the woman's name, but he was able to describe to Axenus the way up through the Celtarium to High Point to the healer's place. According to Titus, her home and place of business was marked by a Celt pole of Celebration whose top carving was of a black, seated raven.

"Thank you, Titus. You've been most helpful. Now get that head of yours looked at before you lose any more of your precious blood. The Bishop wouldn't be happy to know a loyal follower of the Great Church was bleeding all over his city," said Axenus. He tossed a few copper coins on the table in front of Titus as they departed.

*

It was from Titus' description that Axenus drew the crude map to the Raven's house, the map which Weylyn now held in his hands. No Romans accompanied him on this trip, knowing it would cause more trouble than was necessary. They also knew Weylyn stood a better chance of gathering information in High Point if he were alone. "Just let us know if you find anything of interest," requested Axenus.

Weylyn examined the map one more time before turning his attention to the wood merchant. "Excuse me, there! Greetings!"

The old man turned toward the road, looked Weylyn up and down but said nothing. The young boy continued to stack the wood they'd just off-loaded.

"I'm looking for the home of an Elder, a healer. I believe she is known as the Raven. Have you heard of her?"

The old man squinted through the falling snow at Weylyn. "The Raven, huh?" He raised his right arm and pointed toward the hill to Weylyn's left. "Up that road, to the top of the hill. Look for a large pole with a raven carving on the top. Not another like it up there. It'll be on your left, to the west."

"Thank you." Weylyn tucked the map into his tunic and made his way up the hill. It took him about thirty minutes to reach the lowest portion of hilltop before the vegetation took on a comfortable, familiar appearance. The cramped, close-quartered, haphazard building construction of the Celtarium's central area thinned considerably. The road narrowed to half its width and soon became more of a wide, rocky trail as opposed to any road built and maintained by the Romans. Its angle also increased, becoming steeper and more difficult to traverse. Shrubs and small trees and numerous meadows appeared next to many of the dwellings along both sides of the roadway. The further along this road he traveled, the more he noticed the appearance of Celtic decorations on the doors, windows and buildings. Many of the private dwellings and several of the merchant areas sported familiar Celtic Greeting Poles. Weylyn felt more comfortable as the surroundings took on a familiar feel. The snow was falling heavier now.

As he topped the hill he saw the tall Celtic Greeting Pole, its carved, black raven gathering the falling snowflakes as it sat at the very height of the pole. The pole was just where Weylyn knew it should be, to the right of the door as one faced the dwelling. It was adorned with many bright, colorful ribbons tied here and there along the length of the pole. The house was of stone, mortar, and thatching, and faced east to greet the rising sun. A wreath of ivy, the Celtic representation of the tree month of Gort, hung on the wooden front door. The building, sheltered beneath a huge oak tree, was surrounded by smaller trees, bushy herbs, and underbrush. Each of the trees had been encircled by stones. The Raven's home was flanked by several similar buildings about forty yards either side. Weylyn was relieved the buildings in and around the immediate area of High Point weren't constructed so close together as their counterparts in Hierlaneum and the chaotic lower Celtarium. In Weylyn's eyes, this looked more like acceptable Celtic living. Snow was already settling on the roof. A steady plume of grayish-white smoke rose gently from the home's chimney.

He walked to the oak door and knocked three times. The young boy who opened the door and greeted him looked about the same age as Fionna. Like Weylyn, he wore a long wool tunic over his bracae' and high-topped soft leather boots.

"Greetings! You are here to see Brennarix, aren't you?" said the boy in the Celtic language.

"Yes, I am."

"Please, come in. Make yourself comfortable by the fire and I will summon her for you." He motioned Weylyn toward a small wooden table and four surrounding chairs in front of the fireplace hearth. The table held a stack of runic tiles, cups and a wooden tray. A large white candle sat in the center of a carved stone holder on the table. "May I tell her who you are and why you seek her out?"

"I'm Weylyn. I'm a magistrate from Elshorn in the Brendan Valley and I'm seeking information on—"

"You seek information on the whereabouts of a young girl, Fionna de Aine, I believe." A woman stood in the doorway in the back of the main room. "Sorry to have interrupted your telling. I am Brennarix."

Weylyn watched the woman make her way to the table. She was a stout, heavyset woman wrapped in a brightly colored floor-length tunic. A multicolored shawl covered a mass of thick white hair; around her neck hung a large intricately detailed golden torque. It complimented the large gold raven cloak pin on her tunic. Her dark brown eyes held a light of interest but the beautiful and aged face showed a good deal of fatigue and more than a trace of sadness.

Weylyn stood and waited for her to take her seat at the table. He thought he'd seen her before, but couldn't remember where.

She motioned him to sit. "Owyn, get us some drink, please."

The young boy bowed slightly and proceeded to the hearth to prepare the drinks.

"I am indeed looking for Fionna," Weylyn told the woman.

"Why do you seek her?"

"I have been tasked by the Chief Magistrate to find this girl for her mother. I am to bring her back to the Brendan Valley." He pulled out his bronze seal and laid it on the table for her to inspect.

"Fionna is not here."

"Have you seen or spoken with her?"

The woman's dark eyes stared at Weylyn as if trying to penetrate his thoughts. He could not read her expression. He waited, giving her time to consider her response. Glancing around the room, he admired a colorful woven wall hanging, large drinking horns, herb bundles, and assorted candles.

She cleared her throat and he turned his attention back to her. "There was a time when our magistrates had no need to carry an Emperor's seal. Only the appointment of the Celtic Queen was enough to ensure his power and authority." She looked down at her hands and examined her nails. "Sad how things change, or so it would seem. But as we of the Elder Faith know, change is inevitable. Change is a necessary part of the world. Without it, things would not progress through their natural cycles. You are of the Elder Faith, are you not?" She looked at him.

"Yes," said Weylyn. "And I would appreciate you telling me what you know about Fionna." He picked up the seal and put it away.

"Will you turn her over to the Enforcers?"

"No. As I said, I'm ordered to bring her back to her home, to her mother." Weylyn squirmed just a little in his chair. He didn't want to discuss the Enforcers' interest in the girl.

"She was indeed here. Although it was a surprise, it was good to see her again. It's been over a year since I performed the initiation ceremony for her and others of the valley at the Standing Stones in Highdyn Hill. It was nice to see and speak with someone from the valley."

Weylyn remembered now where he'd seen Brennarix before. She had attended the festivities when he and Turi had their initiation ceremony five years ago.

"I sent the girl home. It is where she needs to be, where she will be safe. She needs to stop searching for her grandfather. His whereabouts would reveal itself in its own time. That is the way of all things in their cycle, a fact known for more than a millennium to those of the Elder Faith." She paused again, seeming to catch her breath or maintain her composure before continuing. "Tell me again, why it is you seek her?"

The young boy, Owyn, placed two cups of hot, steaming herbal drink on the table, and then went to sit by the fireplace.

Weylyn began his story with his trip up the mountains to Fey de Parke's abode, the condition of the house, the subsequent discovery of Eiroy's body and the burial site, and his brief meeting with Fionna at Carmel Raife. "Elder Eghan sent me here to Hierlaneum, believing Fionna might come here seeking information about her grandfather." Sitting back, he sipped his tisane and waited for the woman to reply.

Brennarix had listened intently to his tale. Although her hands trembled as she set her own cup on the table, her voice was calm. "Then it is true. My brother Fey must be dead," she said. A far-off look came over her as she gazed out into a space beyond the room. "Perhaps I should have kept her here, safe with me."

"Fey de Parke is your brother?"

"He is my older brother and considering what you and Fionna have told me, he is dead."

Weylyn tried to place this new information in context with what he already knew, to somehow make sense of it. "How can you be certain?"

"Fionna's grandfather is a longtime friend of my brother. She believed if she found Fey she would find her missing grandfather. She was most insistent, and so I did a reading for her. I saw the truth. I saw that he was hidden in the dark realms, perhaps secluded away from us in the Otherworld. I foresaw he would not be revealed to us until the true nature of this mystery was revealed. This incident has but one ending for Fey and perhaps her grandfather—their passing to the Otherworld. I told her this, but she did not believe me. It is normal for many—especially the young—to ignore the truth of the teaching because acceptance can mean pain."

"I think your brother is alive." Weylyn searched his memory, picking out the relevant facts. "The blood on the saddle was Eiroy's, the horse was still there, Fey marked the house, performed the burial. I told Fionna—"

"No! I believe he's dead. You can confirm it," she said. She spoke as if to herself more than to Weylyn.

He stared at the woman. Her expression was unchanged. "I don't understand. How can I confirm the death of Fey? I don't even believe he has died."

"Fionna said her grandfather had warned her to stay off the mountain, to not go anywhere near my brother's place." She paused, twisting her cup on the table. "Tell me, how well do you know the ritual of the Death Hearth?"

Weylyn described the charcoal glyphs of warding on doors and windows, the black ribbons and the Seven Days of Danger. "These I saw at your brother's house. I know that much about the ritual."

"You are a magistrate, an investigator of crimes, an enforcer of the laws, not a healer. You know only that which is known by the average person, the general knowledge available to all." She gazed into the fire and crossed her arms across her midsection. She sat there, not speaking, not moving. After several minutes she adjusted her shawl, then turned back to Weylyn.

"Did you look to see if his rune sign, his personal mark, was placed upon the hearth?"

"I didn't even know of such a mark."

"The master of the ritual, the one who performs it or supervises the work, will always leave their mark upon the hearth so the spirits will know who is responsible for the ceremony. We healers believe these spirits can grant favors for a ceremony well done, or cast misfortune on those who act improperly. This is what Fey believed. He would have left his mark upon his ceremonial hearth."

"How would I recognize this mark?" Weylyn asked.

"Across the top of the hearth or upon some prominent stones around the hearth, is written the glyphs of warding and a ceremonial prayer glyph. In the center between these two inscriptions will be a small circle. Within that circle will be the master's rune sign. Most all are familiar with the glyphs of warding and anyone can scribe a prayer glyph appropriate to the circumstances of the passing. However, only the master of the ritual will know his sign for the center circle. It is the master who places it and seals the building. It is the master who breaks the seal and removes the writing following the Seven Dangerous Days. This must be done before anyone else can enter the area. This protects the ritual and makes it whole and strong."

"Can you tell me what Fey's mark would be?"

She hesitated. "You are not a healer, I should not tell."

Weylyn took a deep breath. He knew Brennarix was searching for a way to tell him without breaking her secret order of healers. He watched her wave her servant Owyn from the room, and waited patiently for her decision.

Finally, Brennarix spoke. "If my brother is dead, I suppose my telling you this will not matter. But you must keep this in confidence."

"Agreed."

"The healer can choose a set of glyphs to represent their person on the circle mark. I do not know all the marks Fey would choose, but I do know one which must be there. It is true for every master of the healing arts. It is the sign which represents their date of birth. Fey was born on the beginning of the runic half-month of Tyr. If the circle is there between the glyphs of warding and the prayer, it will contain at least the Mark of Tyr. That mark is the arrow upward pointing. There may be others within the circle, but that one mark must be there. If it is missing or if there is no circle between, then you will know Fey did not perform that Death Hearth Ritual. It will also mean, I believe, he has passed to the Otherworld."

Weylyn wished he'd known this when he was up at Fey's. He thought about his time in the house. He remembered the hearth, remembered the glyphs. Had there been a prayer glyph? He thought so, but now he honestly couldn't remember. Was there a circle with glyphs inside? He couldn't remember if there was or not. He hadn't been looking for such things. He'd been looking for the rune buckle. He would just have to make another trip up to Fey's but before he could do that, he'd have to pick up the trail of Fionna.

"When did Fionna leave here?" he asked Brennarix.

"Why, it was only just a short while before you arrived. She was going to the docks to see if she could purchase a passage this evening down river to Elshorn."

Reach us all for helping hands
To guide us through to our small plans.
When our own steps stumble out of place
To the Universal grinding race,
We pound it out, flesh and bone,
Having wandered far, we go back home.

27

October 10th in the Roman calendar
Late Afternoon
Seventeen days left in the Celtic Tree Month of Gort

The clouds dropped lower and turned darker with the falling temperature. The snow, heavier now, rode fast on the increasing wind. Weylyn heard the loud pounding of hooves on wooden planking the same moment he saw the charging beast. The large black horse rounded the corner pier-head building on the Celtarium docks. He had no time to get out of its way. Weylyn caught a glimpse of the dark robe of the hooded rider as he was knocked head-over-heels into a pile of wooden casks.

"Hey! Hey!" shouted one of several men gathered outside the customs building. He ran over to Weylyn. "You all right?"

"I think so." Weylyn touched his forehead and discovered he had a cut across his right eyebrow. His legs trembled. Pain shot through his right shoulder and leg. His chest was sore, his vision blurry. He leaned down to retrieve his hat.

"You don't look so good. Maybe you better sit down for a while. We should get that bleeding stopped." The customs man guided Weylyn to a seat on the pier and waved to the small crowd of men at the customs building. A man ran over and handed him a piece of cloth. They wrapped it around Weylyn's head. "There, that should do it."

Weylyn struggled to focus. "Has a boat or barge recently left for downriver? To Dynsmore or Elshorn, maybe?" Weylyn's speech was slurred, his vision unfocused. When he coughed, his chest, his entire upper body hurt.

"Yes, a barge with wine and goods for Cross Abbey. It will stop in Dynsmore twice before it makes its way back. Left a moment or two before you nearly got yourself killed just now." He pointed through the falling snow out beyond the far end of the wooden pier. "There it is out in the center of the river. You can barely make it out. Why? Did you have passage on it?"

"No. I ..." Weylyn paused for breath. He felt dizzy and his body ached all over. He could feel a painful knot coming up on the back of his head. "I'm looking for a young Celt girl. She might be on the barge. She's trying to get home to Elshorn."

"Is that right? A young Celt girl, eh?" The customs man stood up and looked down at Weylyn.

"Has she been here? Did she get on that barge?"

The customs man didn't respond. His face was rigid, his jaw tight. He seemed to be thinking. Weylyn saw him glance toward the group of men watching them. "I think you'd better come with me," the man said firmly. It sounded more like an order than a request. "We'll get this all straightened out over there."

"Get what straightened out?"

"The girl you're looking for is wanted by the Prefect. So, I reckon you are, too. Now don't you give me any trouble. I've got plenty of men here who can bust your head open. We'll just wait in the office while I send one of them to get an Enforcer."

The customs man reached down and grabbed Weylyn's shoulder and hauled him upright. "He said there's a nice little reward for her. Might be one on you, too."

"Reward? Who told you there was a reward on the girl?" asked Weylyn. He felt disoriented and the conversation seemed surreal.

"That Enforcer who just ran you down. He was here looking for her, too, and said there was a reward if anyone could get him out on the river to catch her. But we've got nothing moored here that could catch the barge. He rode to the end of the dock to see if the ferryman had a private float to haul him. Guess he didn't, because the Enforcer rode hard out of here, right over you and back to the city gate fast as the devil. He will be heading for Dynsmore, if I'm not mistaken, to intercept her."

Great Cernunnos! thought Weylyn. He'd lost her again! Desperate to regain some sense of control, he reached under his cape and pulled out his Emperor's seal. "There's no reward on me! And there isn't one on the girl, either." He felt increasingly dizzy. "I'm a magistrate from Elshorn," he managed to say, trying to sound firm and in control. As he tried to stand, a sharp pain shot up from his foot to his head. His couldn't see clearly, his whole body ached, and he thought he might vomit at any moment. "The Centurion Axenus will verify what I say. Now I've got to get to Dynsmore."

"We'll see about that."

It falls just short of the Otherworld
Into that void where minds are hurled.
Blanked upon a clean, cold slate
Pondered meanings left to Fate.
As it is with Spirit Fire
Friends will come to damp our pyre,
To pull us from our morass bed,
To heal our body, clear our head,
Bring to conscious the precious hearth.
They are part of why we're put on Earth.

28

October 12th in the Roman calendar
Early Evening
Fifteen days left in the Celtic Tree Month of Gort

Weylyn heard voices. The chattering filtered through the darkness. His eyes were closed against the pain inflicting his body. The knot on the back of his skull throbbed, and every muscle ached. Warm from the blankets covering him, the smell of smoke from the hearth filled his senses with a feeling of well-being. The voices sounded familiar. He rolled his head to the right until a sharp pain stopped him. He groaned.

"He's awake! Mother Brennarix, he's awake!"

"Well, it's about time," boomed a deep male voice. "You just going to lie around the rest of your life? Or do you want to get up and get the man who did this to you?"

Weylyn opened his eyes to see Warius standing over him. Beyond the big Enforcer he could see Axenus seated at a bench next to the roaring fire of a hearth. Brennarix was crossing the room toward him. The young servant of hers, Owyn, was seated on the floor at the end of Weylyn's bed pallet.

"I feel like I fell off a cliff." He tried to sit up, but quickly realized his mistake as pain shot through his body.

The healer reached his side and gently felt his forehead. "You've beaten your fever, good. Now, all you need do is let time pass and your body heal. You still have a bad cut on your head, though nothing life-threatening as far as I can tell." She straightened the blankets covering Weylyn and tucked them in around him. "I'm making soup for us. You'll have some, then you'll feel better."

"Thank you," he said. He realized his jaw hurt, too.

"Be still for now. You can move when it's time to eat," said the healer. "Do you know where you are?"

"Your home in High Point?"

"Good. Your memory did not take itself to the Otherworld." She left him and returned to the hearth.

"Did you get a look at the man who ran you down?" asked Warius.

"Ran me down?" Weylyn struggled to remember. He tried to think, to see through the deep mist hiding his memory.

"You were run down on the Hierlaneum pier," Warius informed him. "You tracked Fionna to the Celtarium docks. She'd boarded a barge for the Brendans. Before you could get to her, a man riding a black horse ran you down on the pier. The rider was dressed like an Enforcer and claimed to be one. He wore a dark, hooded cloak over his armor. That's what the customs men say, but we know he's not one of us. No Enforcer from Hierlaneum was outside the gates then. We checked. And none fit the description given by the dockers. They reported a large man, light hair and a bad scar on his left cheek. Anyway, after you were run over, the dockers called us. You were in pretty rough shape and kept mumbling the name Brennarix, so we brought you up here. That was two days ago. We've just come back to check on you."

"Two days ago? I've been out for two days?"

"Out cold. Well, except for the fever and the ramblings," said Warius. He leaned closer, dropped his voice to a whisper. "Look, I guess you never talked to the girl, so I don't suppose you ever got a lead on the whereabouts of the rune buckle, did you?"

The rune buckle. Fionna. These Enforcers want that rune buckle. Why? "No. No leads." His head was pounding. "I don't suppose you've found the Enforcer who tried to trample me?"

"Like I said, he wasn't an Enforcer. At least, not one from Hierlaneum, not as far as we can tell. And, no, we haven't found him, but we're trying. We sent messengers via the boats to Cross Abbey, Dynsmore, and Elshorn telling them to look for him. We think he's heading that way. The dockers told us he was after the girl, wanted her real bad. Bad enough to offer a big reward. They think he followed her back into the Brendans. The weather turned bad, though, making travel difficult for the last few days. Hopefully, our messengers we sent by boat will beat him to the area and the Enforcers down there can catch him before he finds the girl," said Warius.

"That's right," said Axenus. He'd made his way over to the bedside. "We haven't caught him yet, but we think we know who he is. We believe it's the Black Hand."

"Parzifal? What would he be doing chasing Fionna?"

"Well, it gets pretty complicated and we aren't certain of all the details yet," said Axenus. Like his partner, he dropped his voice. "This little intrigue concerning the stolen cross has gotten completely out of control. We now believe the seedy underground here in Hierlaneum is making a bid to obtain the stolen goods and return them to the church in exchange for permanent protection from the Prefect and higher authorities. We think they're turning on each other, all of them trying to get the upper hand."

"When Fionna turned up at the Rodas asking questions about Eiroy," Axenus continued, "they thought the girl had some connection to Eiroy. That makes her a target. Eiroy was involved in the theft of the Great Cross, remember, and he cast that bronze buckle. Eiroy the Younger is missing, too—probably in hiding with the goods and waiting for his brother, the Red, to show up. With Eiroy the Red, Aod, Sergio and the rest all dead, Fionna and her grandfather are the only non-gang leads we know of who may have information concerning the location of the treasure. That's why we think they are after her."

Weylyn shook his head, then wished he hadn't. "What about that merchant—the one you said was recruited to steal the cross in the first place. The one Eiroy worked for. Why don't they go after him? Seems he'd be the one most likely to find Eiroy the Younger and the treasure."

"Pax Catus won't be speaking or revealing anything to anyone. Not anymore," said Axenus.

"He was found dead outside his place the morning you left to come up here to look for the Celt girl. Parzifal cut his head off and stuck it on a pole outside," added Warius.

"How do you know it was Parzifal?"

"The mark of the black hand of charcoal was left for us to find. It's the same mark seen from him before, the same signature he always leaves. He did it here and he did it with the priest, Loxius Scrota, when he nailed him to the doors of the Great Church in the city square. The night he killed Pax, he also killed one of the slaves of Pax—cut his throat. That's his style."

"That tells us that Pax had outlived his usefulness to the underground. It also makes us certain he didn't have a clue to the treasure or they wouldn't have killed him," Axenus added.

Weylyn thought for a moment. "Or he told everything he knew before they killed him. Do you think Pax had the rune buckle, or knew where it was?"

"Not likely. We think Pax was killed because he became too much of a liability to those who ordered the theft. They had to know he'd get pressed harder by us and might turn on the others. They could take a chance on lying low and being safe with the Hierlaneum Enforcers and the local Prefect, but with us up from Rome to investigate this for His Highness, they couldn't take the risk."

Axenus paused before continuing. "However, there are still some loose ends with connections to Pax. There's his partner, Brutovius, for example, and Eiroy the Younger. And don't forget the barge operator, Myrdoc. None of them have been accounted for. No one admits to seeing them since Eiroy the Red disappeared. We believe they either have the treasure and are hiding it, or they've got a clue to its location and are searching for it."

Warius smiled. "Maybe we'll find their bodies in the river."

Their conversation was interrupted by Brennarix. "Soup's ready. Leave all the chatter for later. Let him eat something and get some rest. You two come and get it." She ladled up the hot broth, handing her servant to carry a bowl to Weylyn.

After the meal, the two Enforcers thanked Brennarix for her hospitality, donned their heavy, hooded capes to hide their uniforms, and stopped at Weylyn's side. "When you get up and around," Axenus told him, "come by and see us. Maybe by then we'll have news about Fionna."

Brennarix waited for the Romans to leave, then said, "I heard what they said about the big man, the killer they are seeking. I think I know him."

"You know the Black Hand?"

"Not by that name, but he calls himself Parzifal. He, too, has light hair and has worn a similar dark cloak during his visits with me. And I recently treated him for a burn on his face, on his left cheek. I gave him some salve and linens and dressed the wound. It was during one of his many visits with me."

"Visits?" Weylyn asked skeptically.

"He's become a regular, asking questions concerning the ways of our people. He's not a Roman, you know." She looked sad as she related the story. "He's a Celt taken by the churcher armies when he was very young and sold into slavery. He's much confused, but very interested in learning the ways of his ancestors." She paused. "I had no idea he was such a man as the Enforcers describe."

Left alone, Weylyn struggled to keep his mind on the mystery at hand. His head hurt. His body ached even when he didn't move. Well, if he couldn't move, he could at least spend some time thinking things through. He forced himself to concentrate. He thought about his trips up the mountain, his search of Fey de Parke's house, and the discovery of Eiroy's body. He thought about Fionna, the mysterious rune buckle, and the missing treasure. The gang of Pax Catus stole the cross, and then the gang double-crossed Pax, who became the fall guy for the theft. Eiroy apparently knew where the treasure was, so Pax or someone sent Aod to the Brendans to find it or bring back Eiroy. And there was Eiroy the Red's brother, Eiroy the Younger, who also knew the treasure's location. But finding Eiroy or locating the treasure had backfired on Pax. What did he do then? Had he sent someone else out to finish the job Aod botched?

Where did the Black Hand fit into all this? Was it Parzifal Calvin saw that night in the Rodas Villa confronting Eiroy? A large man wearing a black robe, Weylyn remembered Calvin telling him, a man who'd been injured in the fight with Eiroy. That certainly seemed to fit what he knew of Parzifal.

And what was the importance of the rune buckle? Why was everyone looking for a belt buckle?

Weylyn exhaled and felt pain in his bruised chest. He closed his eyes. The missing rune buckle didn't make any sense. What could possibly make it so important people were being killed for it? He hoped to find Fionna before she became another victim. It was his last thought for the evening before sleep claimed him.

Life's answers.
Such discovery!
I think them out.
Some are told to me.
But mostly, they're just
Ser-en-dip-ity!

29

October 13th in the Roman calendar
Early Evening
Fourteen days left in the Celtic Tree Month of Gort
The runic Half-Month of Wyn (Joy) commences

The day's sun rose bright in a clear blue sky, its rays bathing the snow and ice-covered landscape with a glassy glitter dazzling to behold. It was as if Lugh, the god of Light, had placed his own hand across the landscape. But Weylyn had trouble enjoying this slice of winter beauty. He was too busy gingerly and painfully making his way down through the cold, slushy, muddy streets of the Celtarium. The bright sunshine merely compounded his headache. His felt cap covered a bandage wrap placed on the cut across his forehead. He moved stiffly, joints and muscles still sore and weak. He'd left the home of Brennarix at High Point late in the morning after receiving her blessings as well as fresh dark bread and jerky for his journey. She'd also given him a small pouch of dried herbs to aid in healing.

"You should stay and rest a while longer to give your injuries more time to heal," she'd admonished him. "But I understand you must continue your quest to find Fionna. I pray you will reach her in time. May Lugh light your way."

He paused in passage halfway through the Celtarium, shifting his pack on his shoulder. That done, he thrust his hands under his tunic and discovered the map Axenus had given him for his initial visit to High Point and the healer's home. He smiled as he looked at the crude etchings again. They have odd ways, these Romans. Still, a map like this would be handy to point the way to unknown places. It certainly had helped him when looking for the home of Brennarix.

That was it—the reason the buckle was so important, why people were dying over that piece of metal. It must have been used by Eiroy to somehow secretly mark the location of the stolen cross and other goods taken from the shipment from Cross Abbey. But why? To hide it, perhaps, until they thought it was safe to move it?

Then something else came to him. Not all the thieves were Celts. Perhaps the Celts involved hid the booty from the others, perhaps waiting for a chance to get into the Celtlands and restore the gold and amber to its rightful owners. That makes sense, he thought. He increased his pace as best he could. He wanted to confront Axenus with this idea, wanted to see if the Enforcer would confirm his suspicions about the rune buckle.

*

"Well," said Axenus. "Glad you're feeling better. But I think the bump on your head may have shook up your thinking a little. It's an interesting theory you have about the rune buckle, but you really don't need to worry about it. Let us do that. All you need to do is let us know if you find out where it is. We'll do the rest. That's our orders, and that's the order I must give you."

"Yes," said Warius. "Your job is to find the Celt girl and her grandfather. Nothing more."

Weylyn studied them both. Maybe they're afraid if Celts find the Great Cross first, it will end up back in the Celtlands instead of hanging over one of their altars. He'd hoped to learn more, but Weylyn knew it was as it had always been: never tell Celts more than they need to know.

Weylyn knew he was right, but he was willing to play along. After all, he was still in their city, under their good protection. "Well, you're right. I need to focus on the task I've been given." He paused for a moment and looked at the two Enforcers. "What about the assassin, Parzifal? Have you been able to find him?"

"No," replied Axenus, "but we're still looking."

"The Prefect of Hierlaneum assures us his Enforcers are doing everything they can to find this man," said Warius. "But remember, the Black Hand has operated in this area for years now and no one has yet to apprehend him."

Axenus nodded. "True. Of course, the stakes are higher now. There's a huge incentive for Parzifal to be found."

"I'm concerned because he was last seen pursuing Fionna," Weylyn explained.

"I understand. We haven't yet heard from the messengers we sent out to Dynsmore and Cross Abbey, so we don't where or when she would have gotten off the barge. However, we believe the Black Hand may still be within our reach somewhere here in Hierlaneum. We asked around at the docks and nobody reports having seen such a man after that night. Enforcers everywhere are on the lookout for him. So you continue with your quest to find the girl, and we'll do our part here to find the assassin," said Axenus. "Just let us know if you find anything about the buckle. We wish you well."

Weylyn didn't know if the Centurion had meant "wish you well" on finding Fionna or if it meant he hoped Weylyn would lead them to the rune buckle. He supposed it didn't really matter.

Home, sweet home
There's nothing like it.
Not some large, grand mystery.
Our bed, our fire,
Our longtime friends,
Our family greets us joyfully.
Necessary when we're young.
By half-grown we all are gone.
But to escape life's catacomb,
Watch us shuffle, all,
Back again to home, sweet home.

30

October 14th in the Roman calendar
Thirteen days left in the Celtic Tree Month of Gort

The boat trip along the Moryn Gweneth River from the Imperial docks at Hierlaneum to Elshorn had been a pleasant enough experience, giving his body time to heal. The weather warmed enough so the daytime temperatures were well above freezing. The high bluffs surrounding Dynsmore along the eastern entrance to the Brendan Valley were glistening sheets of sparkling ice, especially those in perpetual shade beneath the overhanging bluffs. The huge peaks of the Brendans were snow covered with the ragged winter tops of leafless hardwoods and the evergreens of the tall mountain junipers and pines rising through that white blanket.

He loved this valley. It was his home, where his very being felt at one with the universe. The world was in balance for him here. It was a world away, both figuratively and literally, from the crowded, filthy, overregulated Roman city of Hierlaneum. Everything about that place went against his upbringing and his religion. It also reminded him of Adrianna. She relished the city where she'd grown up. For him, it was a constant reminder of the differences between him and the woman he loved.

He could see her in the tavern the last time they'd discussed the possibility of moving to a Roman city, of making a life together. He should have said something to her then, made a commitment but he just couldn't bring himself to do it. In his mind's eye he saw her sitting there, fuming, swirling her mint leaf around inside her cup of hot tisane with a small cherry wood stick. She'd stared at the leaf and not at him.

"I can tell you've already decided. I know you're not going with me to Hierlaneum when my servitude is over, are you?" Her tone was accusing, hot and hateful. Her dark eyes flared. Adrianna's lips and jaw were trembling. She was about to cry. "You won't even commit to marrying me in my Great Church, will you? You think your gods are out there in the forests, out in the land! Well, they're not, and the sooner you Celts realize that, the better!" She threw the wooden stir stick down on the tavern table and glared at him. "If you loved me, you'd change your ways. But you don't care about me, do you? I'm nothing but a convenience for you. I'm an outsider, just somebody to spend time with until some local girl strikes your fancy!" She dropped her head to the table and sobbed.

The time he'd just spent in Hierlaneum had highlighted the huge gulf between the two of them. They wanted to be together but neither was willing to give in to the other's point of view. He put Adrianna out of his mind for the moment and focused on the information he'd gathered since the death of Aod. Eiroy the Red's rune buckle—where was it? It hadn't been at Fey de Parke's, or at least he'd not been able to find it. If Brennarix was right, Fey wouldn't have it and if he did, it wouldn't be of any use to him now. Maybe it was still with Fey, or maybe Fionna or her grandfather had it. Thinking of Fey, he reminded himself to journey up the mountain to the Elder's home and test the information given him by Brennarix. If the Elder's mark were missing from the hearth, at least part of the puzzle would be solved.

Then there was Eiroy the Younger and his rune buckle, said to be the same as the Red's. If the rune buckle marked the site of the treasure, was it one buckle, or did one need both buckles to find it? This type of deceptive intrigue only exacerbated the pain in Weylyn's head. He forced his mind onto something making a little more sense.

The information from his visit to Hierlaneum at least seemed to fit together, pointing to a not-so-glorious churcher scheme gone awry. One group had apparently arranged to steal from another in order to gain political advantage. Eiroy the Red and his friends stole from the thieves what they rightfully thought belonged to the Celts—the Great Cross of Celtic gold and the Amber of Arianrod, the Earth Mother. But what had they done with it? Where was it now? That, of course, was what everyone wanted to know.

From the information he'd gotten from Brennarix, it seemed Parzifal was certainly involved. According to the healer, Parzifal knew enough of the ritual of the Death Hearth to have faked it to the casual observer. He would also have known it would have been at least a full seven days before any Celt would have entered the dwelling to see the glyphs of the ritual. That would have given him time to look for the rune buckle and, more importantly, search for the valuable Great Cross and the rest of the treasure.

*

Weylyn briefed Elder Eghan late that afternoon on all that had transpired during his visit to Hierlaneum and High Point. He'd also related his belief the man called Griffyth at Brennus Ford, the one living at the house from the runevision, could be hiding Eiroy the Younger.

"I was planning a visit to the guild at Highdyn Hill, so I'll just take a few men with me and on my way back we'll see what this Griffyth is hiding in his house," said the Elder Magistrate.

"You're going to visit the Druidic Guild?"

"If the missing cross is in their possession, they will let me know. And if they don't have it, then we might assume it's still hidden somewhere in this valley of ours. Also, they may have word on Fey de Parke. In the meantime, you find Fionna and bring her in. Hog tie her this time if you have to, but get her in safely and find out what she knows about the rune buckle. And keep your eyes and ears open for her grandfather."

Weylyn assured Elder Eghan he would do his best. His head and body still ached and he was tired from the journey. Before retiring for the night, though, he'd visit the Five Fingers Tavern and see Adrianna. Tomorrow, he'd ride up Aingeal Mountain to search for Fionna. And while he was at it, he'd go by Elder Fey's to see if he'd left his mark upon the hearth.

Do the dead call?
If they did, could we hear?
Would the voice be from afar?
Or would it seem quite near?
Would we listen with our minds?
Or would we run in fear?
Would we open to the chance?
Or would we jump and swoon?
Would we think it summer breeze?
Or howling at the Moon?
Do the dead call?
You tell me.
I wonder if you know?
Do they call on summer days?
Or whisper in the snow?
You tell me.
I'd really like to know.

31

October 15th in the Roman calendar
The Roman Ides of October
Twelve days left in the Celtic Tree Month of Gort

The early morning air was crisp, clean, and very cold. Weylyn watched his breath flow out in front of him as he exhaled. The fresh air of the Brendans rejuvenated him. His headache was finally gone, and his aches and pains were fading at last. He'd stocked his pack with bread and jerky and filled his water flask. With his heaviest fur cape and felt hat, he stopped by the stables and procured one of the Magistrate's horses and made his way slowly up the rugged trail to Fey de Parke's, arriving about the time the sun neared its high point for the day.

Weylyn tied the horse to the small shed out back then made his way around to the front. The ground was crisscrossed with the tracks of deer and smaller wild game and birds. There were no signs of recent human activity. He took a deep breath, said a silent prayer to his totem, the wolf. Weylyn opened the door. The small home had the musty, dusty smells of a building left too long closed to the light and fresh air. He left the door open behind him, wanting as much light as possible inside the place. He stood for a moment looking around the packed earth floor littered with a small table, broken pottery, a bench and piles and bunches of dried herbs and flowers. A movement caught his attention as several mice scuttled their way across the debris and into a hole in the wall to the left of the fireplace. Fey had clearly not returned, nor had anyone—healer, family, or friend—come to cleanse the home.

Weylyn shivered and pulled his cape tighter around his neck and nervously whistled a little tune. He studied the hearth and across its stone work he saw the glyphs and runes of the ritual of the Death Hearth. These were the marks left by the Master Healer, the one who performed or supervised the ritual. It should be the markings of Fey de Parke. He moved closer for a better look. If Brennarix was correct, he would not find the personal mark of Fey. The markings were in both chalk and charcoal. The chalk marks pronounced the usual ceremonial prayer, common to most Celtic rituals. He didn't see a glyph or annotation, however, marking this specific occurrence, or any mention of the one who passed here. Odd. Weylyn did see the glyphs of warding, their bold markings in the black charcoal, warning of the death and the pronouncements of the ritual. Leaning over, he peered closer to the marks. Between the chalked prayer and the charcoal glyphs would be the circular boundary. Inside that circle would be the mark of Fey de Parke but there was no circle separating the two annotations, no personal mark of Fey, no master's rune glyph, no mark of any kind. It was then Weylyn knew the fate of the Elder Fey de Parke, probably lying in some cold, damp hole in the earth waiting to be found. Brennarix had indeed known the truth.

He exited the home and secured the door behind him. He took a deep breath of fresh air and exhaled. Another piece of the puzzle solved, but now he had another in its place. From the beginning it had been a mystery where Fey had gone and why he hadn't returned. Weylyn had believed Fey was in hiding to avoid the very danger about which he'd warned Petroytrix. Now it looked like he'd never return. Who killed him, and where could his body be?

Eiroy couldn't have killed him; otherwise, they'd both been found inside the house when Orrs and his party searched the place. By all accounts Eiroy was in bad shape, in no condition to kill Fey and hide the body. Even if one stretched the imagination to believe such a thing, who was it that buried Eiroy when he died? It wasn't the elderly Fey, who could never have carried a body such a distance. Could it have been Parzifal, the Black Hand, who killed and buried the two men? Had he been in the valley? If so, why hadn't anyone noticed him?

There was no evidence of a body or burial around Fey de Parke's house. If the same person killed Fey and then buried Eiroy, perhaps the clue to Fey's whereabouts could be found near Eiroy's grave. Weylyn walked back to the horse, his steps crunching over the snow and ice-covered ground. He made his way northwest up the steep mountain trail toward the cave and the grave of Eiroy the Red. The bluffs and small streams were covered here and there with ice flows. Across the overhangs of the rugged stone outcroppings, icicles longer than Weylyn hung down like glass stalactites. Weylyn dismounted and led his horse up the trail until he came to the track which branched off down toward the cave. He tied the rope halter to a juniper, secured his pack on the saddle and, whistling a little tune, made his way down toward the gray cliffs and the resting place of Eiroy the Red.

Bluffs rose high on his right and the valley, more than eighteen hundred feet below, opened up for miles to his left. Weylyn could see the Moryn Gweneth glittering as it flowed through the snow-covered valley. Reaching the cave, he saw the pile of stones marking Eiroy's final resting place. He'd checked the entire cave while Orrs and his men had performed the unspeakable at the grave site, and he'd found nothing then resembling a grave into which Fey could have been deposited. He considered another check of the cave, but this was the season of hibernation. He remembered the death of his friend, Turi. Weylyn's dagger would be no match for an irate bear.

He turned and surveyed the area. He looked out over the valley then scanned the area around the cave entrance. Another small trail followed a tiny ledge around the end of the bluffs. Slowly and carefully he pushed through the dead branches, leaves, and vines and made his way along the slick, rocky ledge. He should have explored the whole area when they'd been here before, but Orrs declared their search complete once they'd discovered Eiroy and retrieved the possessions buried with him. Now Weylyn gingerly moved along the narrow trail, keeping his eyes on the tenuous route before him.

He stepped on it the same instant his eyes focused. It was barely on the narrow path, sticking out from an opening in the side of the mountain—a leather boot, a leg still jutting from its top. Startled, Weylyn stepped back quickly, his heart racing. He instinctively dropped his hand down to his side and touched his dagger, its presence somehow making him feel more secure even as he realized this person could bring him no harm. He stood, breathing heavily, too heavily to even attempt to whistle.

With an effort, Weylyn got himself under control. Taking a deep breath, he took a closer look at the disintegrated boot. He could see it was actually what remained of a thick-strapped heavy sandal. The small bones of the foot, exposed through the torn leather, had been picked clean of flesh by predators. Up this high and along this narrow end of the bluff, it was likely buzzards. The leg itself was covered by a sheet of ice and icy patches of snow. He drew his dagger and chipped away at the ice covering the leg. There were buzzards over the point circling when he sat on the overlook high above the cave, watching the eagle. He should have thought to check this area then. He was angry with himself but he knew the outcome would have still been the same—the person would have still been dead, albeit discovered much sooner.

It took him nearly an hour to chisel the thick ice and snow down to a layer of debris covering the remains. There, in a jumbled, broken position almost upside down, on his back and shoulders, lay the body of an elderly man, unceremoniously dumped into the crevice and covered with branches, sticks and leaves. He had been partially covered about the waist with a bloodstained burlap blanket. Weylyn saw the man's face had been beaten badly. The throat had been cut.

Mystery found, Mystery Made.
Mystery Sun, Mystery Shade.
Mystery Forest, Mystery Glade.
Mystery Pole, Mystery Stave.
Mystery lies beneath the Spade.
Mystery Honor, Mystery Knave.
Mystery lives within the Grave.
Mystery Mountain, Mystery Cave.
Mystery Bless both King and Slave.

32

October 15th in the Roman calendar
Late Afternoon
The Roman Ides of October
Twelve days left in the Celtic Tree Month of Gort

Weylyn made his way back down the mountain to the narrow main road which served Aife and the rest of this side of the mountain to Elshorn and the valley below. He'd covered the body again as best he could to discourage predators until others could give it a proper Celtic burial. He realized he couldn't be certain if the body he'd discovered was actually that of Fey de Parke. The face had been beaten severely, possibly during an interrogation about the rune buckle. Of course, he probably wouldn't have recognized the Elder if he'd seen him alive and in good condition, but considering his throat was cut and the body dumped so close to Eiroy's grave, he had little doubt it was Fey.

On his way down the mountain, he stopped and talked with his friend, the blacksmith of Aife. The task he had for him was not a pleasant one, but Angus would be able to verify if the man found in the crevice was Fey. Angus agreed to take some men and bring the body in for a proper burial—regardless of who it might be. And Angus would send word to the Magistrate with the identity of the body, assuming he could recognize the remains. That agreed to, Weylyn continued on to Elshorn.

He pulled his provisions from his pack and ate on horseback as he made his way down the mountain. His mind raced along, sifting through the layers of information he'd gathered since the beginning of all this. Aod, dead, killed by Eiroy the Red. Eiroy, dead from the wound which had been inflicted by Aod. Beyond that almost rational set of circumstances, everything else seemed cloudy. For instance, who killed Fey de Parke—if, in fact, the body he'd just uncovered was that of Elder Fey?

He thought he'd worked that part out, at least to his temporary satisfaction. It almost had to be Parzifal. But he still couldn't explain how the assassin had slipped into the valley, completed his dirty work, and then slipped away again unnoticed. He knew it was possible, but in his mind, unlikely. But if it wasn't the work of the assassin, who then? And why kill Fey?

The only obvious answer was the cursed rune buckle. But again, why? Did it really mark the location of the stolen goods? But then, where was the thing? Who had it? Eiroy the Red's friends and accomplices who helped him in the theft and the subsequent hiding of the loot were, as far as Weylyn knew, all dead. Well, all but maybe one, Eiroy the Younger. After eliminating several names from his mental list of those who likely did not have the Red's buckle or any information on its whereabouts, including Pax Catus, he realized Fionna and her grandfather were still on the list.

Fionna! He cursed the murky puzzle given him by the gods. For him, it always seemed to come back to finding that girl. Each time he found her, she managed to slip away. If he ever completed this task, he'd be free to focus on other things. He smiled, imagining what it might be like for him and Elder Eghan to find and return the missing Great Cross and the other stolen valuables. First, though, he had to find that girl.

But where to look? He ran through the known possibilities. Aife? No, Angus and his family had not seen her. Fey's place? He'd found no trace of her there, nor had he seen any sign of her around the high mountain cave and the grave of Eiroy the Red. It occurred to him he didn't even know if she'd made it into the valley from Hierlaneum. Then another bad thought crossed his mind. What if the assassin had found her before she made it back to the Brendans? That wasn't a very good thought. In fact, he didn't even want to think about that possibility. He decided it was much better to believe she'd made it back safely, that Parzifal, if he was in fact still pursuing her, hadn't yet made it into the valley.

Where could she be? Where would she have gone if she had returned to the valley? According to Teg, she'd not been seen at her mother's home in Elshorn. Weylyn knew Teg had been tasked to keep watch on the place and daily went to ask Moyna if she'd heard from or seen her daughter. Weylyn grew weary thinking about it. The stress of the day had brought back his headache; his skull was pounding, as if the inside wanted out. It had been a very long day already.

He wanted to tell Elder Eghan about his discovery on the mountain, but when he arrived at the Longhouse in Elshorn, the first person he saw was Pluvius, the Enforcer from Cross Abbey.

"Greetings, Weylyn." Pluvius sat astride the wooden bench outside the building, cleaning and sharpening his blades. The Enforcer's dark cape, soaking wet, was hanging across the huge barrel at the end of the Longhouse. He put his blades away and moved to gather his cape as he spoke. "Is Magistrate Eghan with you? Or perhaps Teg?"

"Teg is close by, but I don't know just when Elder Eghan will return. Is there something I can do for you?"

"I'd prefer to speak with Eghan since that's my orders." Pluvius moved to his horse and threw the wet piece of clothing over the back of the saddle. "You'll do just as well, I suppose. Our Prefect received information from Hierlaneum and wanted to pass it on to your boss. Orrs was going to personally deliver this but he had to wait in Cross Abbey. The Grand Prefect's Centurion and his men are coming this way for a visit." Pluvius smiled. He seemed to be in an unusually good mood. "Anyway, I have a description to pass on to the Magistrate from the Centurion concerning a rather nasty person they call the Black Hand. His real name is, uh … let's see …" Pluvius perused a sheet of parchment he'd pulled from his tunic.

"His name is Parzifal," Weylyn said flatly.

"Well, may the spirit of the Great Church continue to shower you with blessings, young Celt. Now you have the ability to read minds?"

"No. I have personal knowledge of this man." He thought about the incident on the pier, when he'd been run over by the black horse and its rider, the assassin. He saw himself flying through the air, slow motion, as he slammed against the casks and fell, face down on the wood and iron banding used to reinforce the pier's wood beams.

"Well, blessings on the Grand Savior! Then perhaps it is you who should be briefing me."

Weylyn stood thinking, seemingly oblivious to Pluvius. The Enforcer said something else to him, but he didn't catch it. He was thinking back to the Celtarium pier and the iron banding. He should have thought of that sooner; it was where he should have looked for Fionna. The small house under the runevision willow by the river—Griffyth's place—the one with the strange, iron-banded Greeting Pole. She'd been there before, looking around and it was the Younger who was said to have the other rune buckle. Weylyn knew he had to get back out there. Perhaps, as the old Celtic saying went, he could kill two birds with one stone. If he got lucky he'd run into Elder Eghan on his way back from Highdyn Hill and he could brief him about the body on the mountain. If he got luckier still, he'd find Eiroy the Younger and get the rune buckle. And if the gods truly favored him, he might even catch the elusive Fionna. He came out of those deep thoughts and looked up to see the Enforcer looking rather quizzically at him.

"You all right?" asked Pluvius.

"I have something of interest you should hear. If you would like to come along with me, we can exchange information on the way."

"Where are we going?"

"Brennus Ford."

Sprinkle words with Spirit dust.
Watch the lies begin to crust.
Into the Mystery, Truth gets thrust
Careful, careful who you trust.

33

October 15th in the Roman calendar
Late Afternoon
The Roman Ides of October
Twelve days left in the Celtic Tree Month of Gort

They rode rapidly through the late afternoon. The sun was still a few hours away from reaching the tops of the western peaks of the Brendans, but a stiff, chill wind had begun to blow off the northern range. This time of year, that usually meant a storm was moving in. Weylyn didn't want to waste any time, especially if Fionna were there. It was still speculation on his part, but if it had been the Black Hand after Fionna, if the assassin were set on finding her and the rune buckle, he'd had enough time to make it into the valley and search for her.

He knew, too, if Parzifal had killed those two men on the mountain, it meant the people who sent him out here knew of Eiroy's relatives. There was a good chance they also knew the location of the runevision house, the house where Griffyth lived and where Weylyn believed he would find Eiroy's brother, the Younger.

As they rode west down the Blaire road leading to Brennus Ford, Weylyn told Pluvius about his earlier confrontation with Griffyth. He explained how Fionna had also been out there, supposedly to find Eiroy the Younger and possibly locate her grandfather. He also told him about finding the body on the mountain and his belief it was the missing Fey de Parke.

The Enforcer made no comment on Griffyth, instead going straight to the subject of Eiroy. "That means old man Fey was there the whole time we were searching the body of Eiroy the Red?" asked Pluvius.

Weylyn nodded. "It also means the murderer made his way up there, killed and buried them both, and left the area without raising any suspicions. So, I'm wondering, how he did that?"

"I see your point. As I know from experience, it's hard for any non-Celt to traverse most courses in this valley without being noticed by at least some of the population. This Black Hand fellow must be really good."

"Yes." Weylyn was frustrated. There was something in his memory he couldn't quite pull out. Something about Parzifal, something important. He searched his memory for the information but could not retrieve it, whatever it was. His mind shifted back to the more important matter at hand, Fionna.

He'd nearly caught her in Hierlaneum. He thought about the assassin, and how close Parzifal had come to finding Fionna first. The thought made Weylyn shiver as he told Pluvius about the incident at the pier and the Centurion's belief it was Parzifal who ran Weylyn down with the horse.

"Why is this assassin after your little Celt girl? Was she a witness to what he did to Eiroy and the old man?"

"I don't believe she witnessed anything like that. The first time I found her, all she talked about was her grandfather. I don't think she even knew about Eiroy's death until I told her."

"The first time? How many times were there?" Pluvius asked, smirking.

Weylyn blushed. "Never mind," he muttered.

They'd ridden on in silence for several more minutes. Finally, Pluvius spoke. "So, you still haven't told me why this Black Hand character wants your little girl."

Your little girl? Weylyn thought. Not on your life! This one has been trouble since the very first time he heard her name. He wanted to correct Pluvius, but he kept those thoughts to himself. Instead, he addressed the question he'd been asked. He turned to look at the Roman. "We haven't exactly worked that out yet but we think it has something to do with the missing rune buckle you Enforcers were looking for in the grave of Eiroy the Red."

The Enforcer's smile vanished. Face red, jaw set firm, he stared straight ahead as he rode, not looking at Weylyn.

Weylyn knew Elder Eghan had already discussed the rune buckle with the Enforcer Orrs. He couldn't think of a reason not to mention it to Pluvius, and he just might learn something of value in return. "You see," continued Weylyn, "Eiroy the Red was wearing a rune buckle on his belt when he killed Aod. Elder Blaine saw it. The Red had even asked Elder Blaine if he'd seen a similar one on Eiroy the Younger. That buckle wasn't in Fey's house and it wasn't in the grave of Eiroy because you and Orrs searched them both."

"We were looking for the stolen treasure. That's all it was. In fact, we believe the garnets and coins we took from the grave came from the stolen church offerings for the sacred and holy Ceremonies of the Day of Saint Mary. But what if they didn't? What good would they do a dead Celt thief like Eiroy anyway? Nothing! Better to put these valuables to God's work than let them rot in a hole with a mere pagan. Besides, Orrs and I have received personal blessings for returning those items to the Church at Cross Abbey. It was a blessing of honor for us to find and return them. Father Caton told us so. And it will be a miracle of miracles when we find and return the Great Cross."

"Maybe it is as you say. You're certain it wasn't the rune buckle you were looking for?"

"I told you, we were looking for the stolen treasure."

"I guess I had it wrong," Weylyn said. He wanted to give the Enforcer a chance to explain himself or maybe dig himself in deeper with his story. Perhaps he would, perhaps he wouldn't. Why wouldn't he come clean about the buckle? Probably had his orders not to mention it to a Celt, thought Weylyn.

They were only a short distance from the turn south to Brennus Ford and the house of Griffyth. Pluvius had set his jaw again, looking straight ahead as they rode. Weylyn waited but Pluvius did not respond.

"You know, Pluvius, as I think this through, I'm even more confused. It's been confusing from the first, and pieces of it still aren't clear. But some of the puzzle has come together." He looked at the Enforcer. "You might find this interesting. When I was in Hierlaneum, I talked with friends of Eiroy. They told me of his metal working abilities. I even saw the forge where I believe the rune buckle was made. Now, that may not be of interest to you, or perhaps you weren't even aware of it. But there's something else I learned, something which doesn't seem to fit with what you are telling me.

"The Centurion Axenus and his Enforcer Warius confirmed the importance of the buckle," Weylyn said. "And, although they weren't specific about why everyone was looking for it, they gave me the impression all Enforcers—including you and Orrs—had been alerted to find that buckle. Why? Well, I have my suspicions." He glanced at the Roman. "Maybe you could help me fill in the missing pieces of this little mystery?"

Pluvius' face changed. The seriously grim look was suddenly replaced by a big smile. He laughed heartily. When he regained his composure he said, "What a blessing! A miracle, even. The spirit of God certainly does work in marvelous ways! The force of the Great Church is powerful, indeed, even when it moves pagan Celts! You, young magistrate, daring to interrogate an Enforcer of His Majesty! A bold move for you, and were it any other Enforcer but me, I'd dare say it was a dangerous one. But performed well—you are to be congratulated." He laughed again. "However, even if I wanted to, I could not discuss that matter with you. Magistrate or not, you are just a Celt, and I have my orders."

Into the fray, the honored ride
bolstered by their swelling pride.
Collided there and cast aside
the evil-makers do abide.
Humble home in countryside
pulled here and there about the tide
of warriors clenched and fortified.
Can all the duties be so justified?
Witness now and then decide
The mystery solved or opened wide?

34

October 15th in the Roman calendar
Very Late Afternoon
The Roman Ides of October
Twelve days left in the Celtic Tree Month of Gort

The small house appeared just as it had the last time Weylyn saw it, nestled under the large, looming willow, guarded by the strange, stocky little Greeting Pole. He'd dismounted and knocked on the door several times but there was no answer. The windows were shuttered and Weylyn could not see anything except darkness when he tried to peer in. Pluvius suggested he continue knocking while he rode around the house, checking the corral and immediate area.

There wasn't much need to wait for Elder Eghan and his men, Weylyn decided. Pluvius was back-up enough. Weylyn pulled his dagger, opened the door, and went in. He found no one, even after he'd thrown open the shutters. Just the usual hearth, cooking utensils, sleeping pallets and a long bench in front of the fireplace. The place was in shambles, things tossed all about.

Pluvius returned to the front door as Weylyn completed his search and exited the house. "Anything?" asked the Enforcer.

"No. How about you?"

"Nothing I could see. Plenty of fresh horse tracks, but no sign of anyone. There's nothing here that needs our attention. What do you say we check the river area? He could be down there in Brennus Ford."

Weylyn mounted up and they made their way south down the sloping road, past the churcher structure to the small village of Brennus Ford. The road continued straight south just a short distance to the small wooden pier and docking facility which serviced the old Brennus Ford area. Nothing resembling the large Emporium of merchant trade such as Weylyn saw in Hierlaneum. This wasn't as large as the Celtarium docks or even the small docks at Elshorn. This was just a short, straight pier extending into the river. There were several small two- and four-man fishing boats. Fishing nets and assorted fishing paraphernalia littered the flat, wooden surface of the pier.

Two men were busy mending nets at the far end of the pier. Weylyn watched them for a moment before his eye wandered to the right. There between a small building and the dock he noticed a barge tied up at the angled bank to the right of the dock. The thought crossed his mind there was something unusual about the barge but, before he could decide what it was, Pluvius spoke.

"Let's go talk with those dockers down there. See if they've seen anyone resembling your Griffyth."

The two fishermen looked up as they approached. When they recognized the Enforcer Pluvius, they stopped work on the nets and tossed a friendly greeting his way. The manner of their greeting, the accent they used with the churcher language and their willingness to speak freely with Pluvius told Weylyn these two were Roman churchers. Much of Brennus Ford was these days. Pluvius questioned them on Griffyth. Did they know him?

Had they seen him recently? Did they know where he could be found now? They were cooperative and friendly. They did know him, confirmed he'd been a resident at the Ford for as long as they remembered. He was a Celt and so they had little to do with him, but they did know him. No, they hadn't seen him for a day or two and didn't know his current location. The three carried on bantering about fishing, trading, cursing both Celts and the weather. Weylyn was not included in any of this. In fact, the dockers didn't so much as acknowledge his presence.

While the Enforcer was busy with the fishermen, Weylyn decided to get a better look at that barge. As he got closer, he realized why it had drawn his attention. This vessel had been completely whitewashed. It wasn't unusual for the vessels along this river to be painted—most were—with various designs and colors, flags, pennants and identification markers including name plates. Even the mammoth carriers he'd seen docked at the merchant facility at Hierlaneum were marked in such a manner, but he couldn't ever remember seeing a boat, ship or barge completely covered in the milky off-white stain. Pegged to the bow of the ship he could make out an identification marker in the Roman language. He couldn't read it, but assumed it was the owner's name for his vessel.

He heard Pluvius give his farewells to the two fishermen. As the Enforcer approached him, Weylyn nodded toward the barge. "Unusual marking, don't you think?"

Pluvius looked at the barge and smiled. "You're right. That's so horrid and garish, it must be owned by a Celt." He looked at Weylyn and laughed. "Oh, no offense."

Weylyn clenched his fists and was about to reply when he saw a chariot with six outriders head toward the small house with the unusual Greeting Pole. "That's Elder Eghan!"

"What's the Chief Magistrate doing out here?"

"He's been over to—" Weylyn stopped abruptly. He didn't know if he should tell Pluvius that the Elder had gone to see the

Druidic Guild at Highdyn Hill. Probably not. Thinking quickly, he improvised. "He's been over to Carew to see if he could get a lead on the young Celt girl and her grandfather and discover any new information. I'd already told him about Griffyth. The Elder said he'd stop here on his way back to Elshorn."

Pluvius, jaw set under a slight frown, said nothing as they made their way to greet the Elder and his men at the home of the elusive Griffyth, where Pluvius quickly assured the Chief Magistrate there was nothing of interest to be found there.

Taking Elder Eghan aside, Weylyn briefed the Magistrate on what little they'd found since their arrival at Brennus Ford. He also briefed his boss on his grisly find atop the western shoulder of Aingeal Mountain.

"Good work, Weylyn. I'm sad to hear of Elder Fey's passing. I was hoping you'd find otherwise. But we've feared it for some time now. As for coming here, your timing is excellent." Elder Eghan glared at Pluvius. "We will see if there is indeed nothing to be found here."

Making no mention of the rune buckle, Elder Eghan tossed orders to his men, dispersing them into the house, the corral and outbuilding and the immediate area around the house. The men had orders to thoroughly search everything, inside and out. All contents of the house were to be taken outside and shown to Elder Eghan, regardless of how trivial the object might seem to them. With a flourishing wave of his hands, the Chief Magistrate ordered them to their tasks.

"Sir," said one of the men from inside the house. "This place is a mess; looks as if someone's searched the place already."

"That's the way I found it," Weylyn confirmed.

"Ah!" said the Elder. "Well, get on with it. Bring everything out here anyway."

As the objects were brought out, he commented on the short, stubby Greeting Pole. "I see what you meant by strange when you described this to me, Weylyn. It is indeed unusual."

Elder Eghan looked at his young apprentice and winked. "But it does bear a striking resemblance to a certain description we got early on, doesn't it?"

Weylyn knew he was referring to the runevision described by Elder Blaine the Slender. He knew the Elder wasn't going to give that information to Pluvius. As for the Enforcer's part, he stood behind the two Celt magistrates, not saying a word, not taking part in the search or any discussion. Weylyn looked at the silent Enforcer and thought he seemed preoccupied, perhaps even nervous. About what, Weylyn had no idea—probably worried a Celt would find the treasure before a Roman did. That would be something Pluvius would find distasteful, even embarrassing, especially since he'd arrived here to search before the Elder and his men.

The Elder walked to the short, stubby pole, looking at the rust marks left by the iron banding on the wood. "Now that is strange, don't you think?" He rested his hand on the pole. "This has to be the ugliest Greeting Pole I've ever encountered."

One of the men brought out a rolled sleeping pallet for the Elder to examine. "Place the items over there on the ground, go through it. Call me if you find anything unusual. I'm especially interested in anything made of bronze. But bronze or not, leave nothing unturned, nothing unexamined," he ordered.

The Elder directed his attention back to the pole. "I've been thinking about this item. Why would anyone use such a thing as a Greeting Pole? It isn't the traditional height or diameter, and there's no carving, no decorations except those iron bands. And it's placed right against the house, instead of the traditional placement. Certainly not your typical pole, is it?"

"Well, Elder, from all accounts neither Eiroy nor Griffyth were traditional. I don't think either one of them—" Weylyn glanced over at Pluvius. Dropping his voice, he continued. "I don't think either of them were followers of the Faith. Griffyth didn't even speak our language, or so he told me."

"So you said." Eghan moved closer to the pole, rubbed the ground with the toe end of his boot. "More to the point, Weylyn, I've been thinking about what you said you learned in Hierlaneum about Eiroy and his friends making iron bands. And here we have exactly that on a Greeting Pole which is itself far from typical. It's certainly out of place in a mostly Roman village like this, and in a home occupied by people who don't even follow the Elder Faith. And didn't you say the earth around this pole looked recently dug when you were first here?"

"Yes, sir. It looked freshly dug, like the pole had recently been placed here."

"Well, well. We have a missing treasure. We have a location we know is somehow linked to the people associated with the theft. A strange Greeting Pole with iron bands which have been made by one of the thieves." The Chief Magistrate looked at his apprentice. "What would you conclude?"

"The treasure's buried here," Weylyn suggested with a grin.

"Let's find out." Elder Eghan called orders to his men in the house. "I want this pole up and out of here now!" shouted the Magistrate. He backed out of the area to give his men room to work. The first of the three men had already drawn his short sword and was chipping away at the earth around the base of the pole. "Weylyn, get my staff from the chariot, will you?"

As Weylyn made his way to the chariot, he noticed Pluvius looked stunned, as if he were having difficulty keeping up with what was going on. He can't believe it, thought Weylyn. Celts have solved the mystery, found the Great Cross. Pluvius was going to lose out on the glory. No wonder he was just standing there with his mouth open!

Weylyn had just reached the chariot when he heard a loud exclamation from the man digging at the base of the pole. Weylyn picked up the staff and ran back in time to see the man jump up and away from the pole.

"Great Cernunnos! Look! Look!"

The other diggers had leaned down and were moving the soil away from the base of the pole with their hands. Both Eghan and Pluvius had moved in closer. The man who yelled was standing beside them, shaking his head.

The diggers began whistling.

"What is it, Elder, what have they found?" asked Weylyn. He tried to peer around the others. "Is it the treasure?"

"I'm afraid not, but we do seem to have found the missing Griffyth. Evidently he was home after all," said the Elder.

The men partially uncovered a body lying face-up in the earth. The face was a horrible color, decomposition already at work. The reddish-blond hair was matted with dirt and bluish-white eyes stared vacantly up into the darkening sky.

"Great God!" exclaimed Pluvius. He crossed himself in the manner of the churcher's superstitious ritual.

Weylyn worked his way close enough to get a good look. "What? There's some mistake, Elder. This isn't Griffyth. This isn't the man I spoke with! This is …" He struggled to speak what his mind knew couldn't be true, but it was Pluvius who finished for him.

"It's Eiroy the Red! But how? I don't understand."

"Eiroy?" Elder Eghan ran his fingers through his white mustache, twirling the long hairs. A moment of quick contemplation passed, and then he yelled new orders to his men. "Forget that poor soul for now. There's nothing we can do for him. This must be the Younger—off to the Otherworld to be with his brother, the Red, long before we arrived. Get the pole out of the ground. Now!"

They backed up again to allow the men room. The diggers set to work, whistling nervously as they dug. The wind picked up, blowing stronger from the north. Heavy, ominous clouds were forming over the mountains. The sun would soon drop over the western Brendans and real darkness would be upon them. They must hurry.

One of the men sent to search the outbuilding ran around the corner of the house. "Magistrate, sir, we've found a man, just inside the woods behind the corral."

"Well? What's wrong with you? Bring him here!"

"Sir, it's a dead man. We think you should come see."

The Elder didn't look too pleased as he looked from the messenger to Weylyn and then to Pluvius.

"I'll go see, Elder." Weylyn volunteered.

"No! We'll all three go." He turned to the men working on the pole. "I want that thing out of there by the time I get back."

"Yes, sir!" the three shouted in unison.

It didn't take the four of them long to reach the spot where the body had been discovered. One of the men clanked two stones together, making a rhythmic sound to ward off spirits.

"Is this the way you found him?" asked the Elder.

"Yes, sir, we didn't touch anything. We'd finished searching inside as you ordered. Nothing unusual there. Then we searched around the woods north of the garden and worked our way up here. That's exactly how we found him."

The dark haired man lay on his back, his brown leather tunic split in three places, two in his stomach and one near his heart. The tunic and his striped leggings were all soaked in blood which had not completely dried, suggesting he'd been recently murdered. A portion of the front of his belt had been cut away on both sides. Whatever had held his belt around his waist—belt knot, buckle or belt brooch—was missing.

"Well," said the Elder. "Do we know who this might be?"

Pluvius stood back, not saying anything and evidently not very interested in getting a closer look.

"I know him," Weylyn said. "At least, I know who he said he was."

"And would you be kind enough to share that information with the rest of us?" scolded the Elder.

"Yes, sir. It's Griffyth."

Revealed to those who think and wait
Answers from unlikely real estate
Resting there upon the ground
Guarding secrets to be found
Signs & Salient, Silent Sent-a-ries
Often through the Centuries
Pass down meanings to us All
Tree Bones. Iron from the Fire
Cast us All our own Desire
Earth & Air & Wood & Water
Even Iron from hot Fire fodder
But Talk too much, tempt the Fates
And they will slam your Wishing Gates.

35

October 15th in the Roman calendar
Nearing Darkness
The Roman Ides of October
Twelve days left in the Celtic Tree Month of Gort

They struggled to pull the Greeting Pole from its resting place against the house as the Elder, Weylyn and Pluvius returned to the front of Griffyth's home. The two bands of iron near its top and bottom added to the already heavy, dense wood. The three men wrestled it out of its hole next to the body. They released their grip and it fell with a heavy 'thud' and the unmistakable clinking and rattling of coins.

The Elder examined the pole and pointed to the small iron spikes holding the iron banding in place. "Break these free. And be careful when you do."

Two of the workers went to work prying the spikes away from the metal banding. Murmurs rose from the group—all expressing surprise and disbelief—as the bands popped free, revealing two compartments carved and cleverly hidden behind the iron bands encircling the Greeting Pole.

"The treasure!"

"By the Holy Graces of the Great Church, I've found it!" Pluvius exclaimed. "Miracle of miracles, I've found the stolen treasure!" He dropped to his knees, crossing himself, then plunged his hands into the nearest chamber, his fingers playing with the coins, gems, beads, gold, and semiprecious metal crosses and jewelry that had been hidden there.

Weylyn couldn't believe the amount of treasure he was looking at. So this is what churchers covet and collect in their services on their sacred worship days. No wonder they feel the need to hide their services inside buildings of men, he mused.

The Elder pointed to the sleeping skins the men took from the house and instructed the workers to spread them upon the ground near the pole.

Pluvius glared at Elder Eghan. "What are you doing?"

"Securing this find until we turn it over to Commander Orrs," replied the Elder. "You have objections to that, do you?" His voice was one of experienced, powerful authority. Pluvius might take a dim view of a deputy such as Weylyn overstepping their bounds, but not so with Elder Eghan. Certainly there were lines even he would dare not cross, but Weylyn had often seen Enforcers back down from confrontation with the Chief Magistrate.

Pluvius frowned as the men filled the sleeping skins with the pieces of the treasure. In an obvious attempt to take charge, he found his Enforcer voice and thought of something to say with it. "Be careful with those crosses, men. They are sacred objects. They belong to the Great Church. I won't have them damaged. And make certain each piece, coin or otherwise, makes it into those skins!"

Pluvius wouldn't stop talking. "I'm truly blessed! God favors me above all others, because He has allowed me, of all the Enforcers, to find the Great Cross. The church will be pleased, most pleased with me for returning all this!" Reaching into his belt bag, he pulled out his favorite mushrooms and chewed heartily and watched the men work.

"Pluvius." Eghan leaned casually on his long walking staff.

"Hmm?" Pluvius reached for another mushroom. "What is it?" He did not take his eyes off the workers in front of him.

"Can you tell us, how large is the missing Great Cross?"

"Oh, well, it's large! About—" Pluvius extended his arms out to illustrate the approximate size of the cross when something obviously occurred to him. He was a comical sight to behold, mouth wide open, arms wide as he looked at the pole, seemingly measuring its length, width and girth, all the while calculating the size of the missing object.

Ironically, in all the excitement, Weylyn had assumed this pole held all they'd been looking for these last long weeks. The Elder had obviously formed another, completely different idea on the subject.

Pluvius dropped his arms limply to his side and muttered something under his breath, something which Weylyn thought sounded like a rather scathing expletive against the Enforcer's desert deity.

The men finished bundling the treasure. It had taken three sleeping skins to hold it all. The sun behind the thickening layer of clouds had touched the top of the western peaks. Soon what light they'd enjoyed would be gone for the day. The wind was still up and carried with it heavy dark clouds and a brisk chill.

"Where is it?" asked Pluvius. "Where's the Great Cross?"

"Now that's the question, isn't it?" The Elder pulled his short cape up tighter around his shoulders. "Weylyn, go inside and make us a fire. We've something to discuss."

The Elder motioned to four of his men. "I want that Pole put back up the way we found it, and cover the body, too." Looking at the others, he said, "Carry those three bundles inside then get back out here and bury the fellow up in the woods. When you finish, wait here for us. Be ready to ride."

Pluvius waited for the treasure to be carefully stored in one corner before he joined Weylyn and the Elder. When the last of the Elder's men left, Pluvius slammed the door behind them. "Tell me, Eghan. You know where the cross is, don't you?"

"Well, it doesn't appear to be here, does it?"

"I think you know where it is, and I think you'd better tell me," said Pluvius. "It happens I've recently come upon very reliable information relating to its whereabouts but it will take time for me to figure it out. You can save me that time by just telling me what I need to know."

"Ah, reliable information? And what might that be? Would you mind telling us?"

"You know I cannot share confidential information of that nature. Not about such an important and delicate subject as the location of the Great Cross. After all, I have my orders."

Weylyn thought he sounded smug, but that was typical for Pluvius. At least the Enforcer didn't say information would not be shared with a mere Celt, but Weylyn suspected that's what Pluvius meant. This churcher wasn't in the least bit thankful to Elder for finding his church's precious stash of wealth. In fact, Weylyn suspected Pluvius would seize every opportunity to take all the credit for its find and return.

Pluvius pulled more mushrooms from his pouch and offered some to the others, shrugging when they declined. "Well, no hard feelings, of course. I mean, I'd like to share what I know with you, but orders are orders." He paused to pop a small button, chew, and swallow before proceeding. "But I have an idea. Maybe in a roundabout way, sort of unofficial way, we can help each other. You know, I ask you a few questions and you can gather what you will about the information I've come upon. That way you can get what you want and I can get what I want. What do you say?"

"What is it you want to ask?" Elder Eghan inquired.

"Well, it's about something I, ah, heard recently, something about your old oracle glyphs. Those rune markings you Celts sometimes use as an excuse for real writing. I want to know the meanings of three of them."

"Which ones?" asked the Elder.

"Umm, well first, the symbol which looks like a circle with flowing horns across the top. Now I seem to recall it stands for the bull of fertility. I wondered if that were true and if it also, maybe, had other meanings."

The Elder Magistrate eyed Pluvius closely. He held his stare for quite a time before responding to the Enforcer's question. This line of questioning could get out of hand and might easily take a dangerous turn.

"Yes, true. As for other meanings, well, different symbols have many different meanings to many people. For instance, what does that symbol mean to you?"

"Me? Oh, ah, well—" His face turned red and he shook his head vigorously. "I know it is a pagan sign of the Horned One, the Great Satan!—and as such, barely speakable!" He quickly crossed himself, his right hand moving across the front of his body. The ritual finished, he ate another mushroom.

"What are the other markings you desire to know about?"

"Wait, not so fast. What could be another meaning of the, ah, you know, that one?"

"Well, it has been known to mark the spot of a place of worship, or perhaps a—"

"You mean like a pagan site for the worship of their deities?" Pluvius interrupted the Elder's telling, oblivious or unconcerned with his rudeness to an Elder Celt. His gaze wandered; he seemed to be seriously thinking about what he'd heard.

"I suppose so, yes. That mark has been used in that manner. What are the other two you are interested in?"

"One has a line straight down with two smaller lines, one on either side and a short way down from the top of the longer line. The other one has a straight line down, with two smaller lines pointing upward to the right." His voice trembled slightly. Pluvius did not appear comfortable discussing such things with two Celts.

"The signs you speak of are two of the many ancient stave signs. Again they have many meanings to many people. But I think the meanings you seek are the Warding Elder's signs of protection and of possessions. For example, the Druidic site that was here at Brennus Ford was not only for worship, but was also a sanctuary and offering site." The Magistrate spoke slowly and deliberately, watching Pluvius closely.

"Would the sign of the bull also have related to this site? Could those three together mark a location like Brennus Ford? It used to be the site of an ancient pagan temple, didn't it?" The Enforcer seemed to speak as much to himself as to the others.

"All three of the runic sites you mention would be applicable to the site that was here at Brennus Ford, so I suppose you might draw that conclusion," said Eghan. "Perhaps, if you just told us where you heard of these three glyphs, we could—"

"No! I told you, I have my orders!" said Pluvius. He looked away again from the fire and the magistrates, standing and staring off into some far inner-distance of his mind for some time before speaking. "If you two know anything at all about the location of the Great Cross, I suggest you tell me now!"

Eghan was warming his hands over the hearth. He looked away from Pluvius and into the fire; the Enforcer's rudeness didn't seem to affect him in the slightest. "Pluvius, I don't know where you can find the Cross. But I've thought long and hard on this, just as you and your fellow Enforcers have. Thanks to my able and hardworking deputy, Weylyn, and the valuable information he's gathered, I've been able to put together important pieces of this mystery that just might indicate the location of that which you so heartily and faithfully seek. Let me share that information with you and see what you think."

The Magistrate related information he and Weylyn had

gathered since the beginning, but he included only that which Pluvius would already know and added just the part about the iron banding and the story of the Romans concerning the barge. "It is the banding which gave it away, Pluvius. Weylyn's witness, Calvin, said the banding was being used in relation to the theft—at least according to Eiroy the Red. It is primarily that information which made me suspicious about this pole. If the story is true about Eiroy wanting the rest of this banding for a barge, then perhaps all you need to do is find the barge. The cross may be hidden within."

Pluvius stood there looking at them, at the treasure, at the fire. Finally, almost to himself, he said, "That explains why they asked us to be on the lookout for a barge. A barge owned and operated by a river man named Myrdoc. Of course! The Hierlaneum Enforcers had already figured it out! They just needed our help to find the barge."

"Do you remember the description of it?"

"Orrs said it was important but I didn't pay too much attention. Didn't seem likely it would help us find the treasure. I just figured they wanted us to bring in Myrdoc for questioning about hauling illegal goods for a Hierlaneum merchant. Why?"

"Well, the Griffyth fellow up there in the woods looks a lot like the man Orrs described to me as owning that barge."

A thought came to Weylyn. "Pluvius, what was the name of the barge we saw moored at the Brennus Ford pier?"

The Enforcer looked at Weylyn. "That ugly white one? Oh, let's see." They saw it cross his face. "Oh, my God!" exclaimed Pluvius. His jaw dropped, mouth open, eyes wide.

Weylyn knew it. There was something about it. He'd known it when he saw it. But he wanted the Enforcer to verify it. He had to ask. "It was the Elvira Domino, wasn't it?"

"Yes!"

Trinkets, Tin. Silver, Gold
Small & Mighty to Behold.
Value, Freedom. Fear, Hate
Great & Petty in Rebate.
Careful All what's on our plate.
We draw our plans upon life's slate.
Value, Freedom. Fear, Hate
Great & Petty in Rebate.
Trinkets, Tin. Silver, Gold
Small & Mighty to Behold.
Seek the Truth, be so Bold.
We find the Spirits have Foretold.

36

October 16th in the Roman calendar
Early Morning
Eleven days left in the Celtic Tree Month of Gort

The arguments that evening had been heated, almost brutal in their intensity. Pluvius was so angry he all but foamed at the mouth. He'd insisted the treasure stay right where it was, on the floor of the house of Griffyth, or whatever the name was for the man who lived here. The Elder Magistrate insisted the treasure accompany him and his men back to Elshorn. And the move, considering the rapidly approaching storm, should be sooner rather than later. There was no time to spare.

The Enforcer refused to leave the area without searching the barge tied up at the pier. His other option was to gather a crew and take it back to Cross Abbey where, if it did contain the Great Cross, it would be under safe and capable guard by Roman churchers. It had been yet another insult to the Elder and his Celt brethren.

Pluvius was in a real bind. He wanted to assemble Eghan's men and search the barge, but he hadn't wanted to leave the treasure they'd already found. And Elder Eghan had insisted if the treasure left the house, it would be put in his chariot, accompanied by his guards and taken safely back to Elshorn for safekeeping until Orrs arrived to collect it. That had been Orrs' charge to Eghan should he find any part of the treasure, and the Elder had no intention of turning the treasure over to Pluvius.

Pluvius tried to stay the course of his argument, but even he, after much debate, had to concede with darkness upon them and the storm moving in that he should wait until daybreak. He would not wait in the house. He was determined to make his way into Brennus Ford and gather a group of men to either help him get the barge up to Cross Abbey or Elshorn or help him guard it through the night.

Elder would have none of Pluvius' idea. "The road to Elshorn is safe for us to travel. It is imperative we travel quickly. We should not tarry here. The more we delay our departure, the more likely it will be that word gets out we have the treasure. You are going to arouse suspicion if you go through the Ford gathering men for your project tonight. You know how people will talk; they will ask questions, become suspicious of your goings-on. That will not only increase the danger of exposing the treasure—both what we've found but what you may find on the barge. You have my promise we will keep it safe in Elshorn until it is claimed by your boss, Orrs," said the Magistrate.

"But I can't just let the barge sit down there all night, unguarded. Someone may take off with it, take off with the Great Cross. How foolish I would look for not doing my duty because it was too cold, too stormy, or too dark! Never! The village will be happy to help me. Most are God-fearing people, Romans with high standards. They'll help me when I tell them it could mean the rescue of our Great Cross for His Majesty!"

Elder Eghan and Weylyn looked at each other in silence. The barge had sat there already for no telling how long. Its owner, in all likelihood, lay dead at Griffyth's. It wasn't likely the barge was going anywhere unless the Enforcer moved it. They knew they would never be able to dissuade Pluvius from his plans with the barge. He had the authority and power to raise the village to provide help. They knew, too, it would be a huge mistake to reveal the possibility the barge contained the Great Cross. It was an even greater danger to reveal the finding of the other treasure before it made its way safely into Elshorn.

The road from Brennus Ford, usually safe to travel, might grow extremely hazardous tonight if certain elements in the area knew about the treasure. While the Elder knew he and his cargo could travel with a degree of safety under the watch of his six guards and Weylyn, one never knew what the dark forces could mount against them for such a large amount of profit.

"Very well, Pluvius. You do what you must, but expect we shall do the same. You are welcome to come with us or stay behind—that choice is yours. We leave for Elshorn now," said the Magistrate. He told Weylyn to have the men load the three bundles. They would make for Elshorn with all possible haste.

"Very well, Magistrate, but mark my words, if any of those precious, sacred belongings of the Great Church come up missing, you will be held personally accountable. I want you to send Orrs and his men immediately to help me. I'm going to secure the barge and make certain no one gets away with the Great Cross again!" With that, Pluvius had left them and headed back down the road to the pier at Brennus Ford.

*

Except for the driving sleet brought in by the storm, the trip back to Elshorn was cold but otherwise uneventful. They were all exhausted by the time the treasure had been secured in the storage room of the Magistrate's Longhouse. Teg had moved his sleeping pallet over and with two servants remained to guard the treasure.

Weylyn remembered going back to his bed and collapsing into a deep sleep but he recalled nothing else. He'd slept like the dead. He couldn't even remember any dreams. He was up and awake before the morning bell and back at the Longhouse helping the servants stoke a fire in its hearth. The Elder, too, had risen early, washed and was ready for the morning meal. They were both tired from the grueling events of yesterday, but charged with energy thinking of the treasure they'd been able to find. There was much to discuss.

"I guess your next duty will be to ride over to Cross Abbey and fetch Orrs. At least let him know that Pluvius requests his presence at the Ford," Elder said to Weylyn.

Weylyn smiled and said in jest, "I thought my job was to find Fionna!"

"Oh! I didn't tell you, did I?" Eghan was busy at the hearth preparing the hot herb drink they would have with their soup and dark bread. "I knew there was something I meant to tell you. There was so much happening so quickly yesterday, I forgot. Well, no harm done I suppose.

"I found Fionna myself. Well, to be more precise, we ran into each other at Carew. It was she who approached me and introduced herself. We were both waiting to reenter the valley through the Fortress gates. She told me after she'd left Hierlaneum, she'd not gotten off the boat at Dynsmore or Cross Abbey. Instead she secured passage at Dynsmore farther down river to Carew. She had just visited the sanctuaries at Highdyn Hill when we met. I asked her to accompany me back to Elshorn and she agreed."

"Where is she now, Elder?"

"Back home by now, I should think. When we reached the Brennus Ford road I sent her on to Elshorn so I could attend to my investigation at Griffyth's."

"Did she find her grandfather?"

"He's still missing. We need to find him."

"Elder, did you get a chance to question her about the rune buckle? Does she have it? Does she know where it is?"

"No, she doesn't have it. At least, that's what she told me. You didn't find it with the body on the mountain, I take it?"

"No. I have a theory about that, Elder. But first, I must tell you what Pluvius told me before we arrived at Brennus Ford. He was waiting here at the Longhouse when I returned from Aife. He had information for you from Cross Abbey."

Weylyn briefed the Elder Magistrate on the pending arrival of both Orrs and the Centurion's forces. He shared all he'd learned about Parzifal. "It's quite possible he's come to the Brendan Valley, looking for both Fionna and the rune buckle."

"That is distressing news, distressing, indeed. It could bode dire consequence on two accounts. Fionna and her family could be in grave danger. But we may face an even bigger problem, one affecting the entire valley. When I was at Highdyn Hill I discovered that Celtic forces were being amassed, armed, and stationed at the fortress at Carew."

"What? Why?"

"Queen Maeverorix has been told to expect the delivery of the sacred amber and the sacred gold of the Great Cross. They were fully aware of its theft, and they very much want it back in Celtic hands. Can't say I blame them. I could not learn any names of those involved, but they were Celt, of course. The Druidic guild anticipates complications with the object's return.

"The Queen sent envoys to the Empire warning any intervention to stop the return of what was rightfully theirs could result in renewed warfare. I fear the movement of the Centurion's forces into the valley might send the wrong signal to the Queen."

"So the Great Cross is still here? Still in our valley?"

"Yes, I should think so."

"Do you think the coming of Axenus has something to do with Queen Maeverorix's diplomatic envoy?"

"I believe so," said Elder. He waved his hands at the hearth. "Let's eat and you can tell me your theory about the buckle."

"This has all seemed to me like a long, twisted ivy vine, Elder, wrapping and spinning about itself with so many twists and turns. Everything seems to spring from the rune buckles and their connection to the missing Great Cross. I think Eiroy the Red was followed to Elder Fey's by the men trying to find the rune buckle. The Hierlaneum merchant Pax Catus somehow found out Eiroy was off to Elshorn to find his brother. So, Pax sent one of his men—Aod—to get the buckle and retrieve the treasure. But that failed with the killing of Aod by Eiroy. Who, then, was there to follow Eiroy to Fey's? Considering all I've learned, it had to be the assassin, Parzifal."

"Why him?"

"Because the Centurion Axenus and Enforcer Warius told me of his methods, his signature kills. His victims are tortured or beaten, and their throats are always cut. The other members of the gang have all been killed. Other than Sergio, who died under Enforcer interrogation, the Enforcers haven't said how exactly the others died. I think they may have been set upon by Parzifal. If so, they may have revealed to him what they knew of the theft and the ones who stole it. It's probably where Pax Catus' men got the information on where to look for Eiroy, including the location of Eiroy's relative, Fey."

Weylyn paused to drink, then continued. "But I think the biggest source of information on the Red's relatives, including Elder Fey, was the Rodas where Eiroy lived. Calvin said Eiroy mentioned his relatives several times. I think Titus picked up that information easily from casual conversations, and then sold the information to Pax or anyone else who would pay him."

"Anyway," Weylyn continued, "when I dug the debris off the body of Fey yesterday, his throat had been cut, just like something this assassin would do. He had been beaten severely, too, probably while being questioned about the treasure."

Elder Eghan had been listening intently. He reached for his tisane, took a drink and set the cup back down. "How do you explain the ritual of the Death Hearth?"

"I think Parzifal did it."

The Elder was astonished. "A Roman assassin performing one of our rituals? Preposterous!"

"Much of the ritual, at least the basic, general requirements are common knowledge, even among the Romans, apparently. I think he learned it from one of Fey's relatives in High Point—ironically, Fey's sister, Brennarix."

"You actually believe this?"

"Elder, hear me out. You see, she is not only a healer but a teacher. She told me she teaches anyone who will listen and pay—Celt, Roman or anyone—the history and basic customs of Celts, and specifically, the teachings of the Elder Faith. She does not openly practice the faith, that would be illegal. And she does not teach the specific rituals, but she teaches the philosophy. And Parzifal is not a Roman—he's a Celt. He'd been learning our ways from her."

Weylyn paused to drink before continuing. "But no matter how he learned the ritual, I think it was Parzifal who did it. I think he killed Elder Fey after he discovered the Elder didn't know anything about the treasure. The assassin wanted no witness, so he finished off Eiroy, ransacked the place, and hid the fact he'd ever been there by applying what appeared to be the ritual of the Death Hearth. That would give him time to look for the stolen goods without stirring up any local interest in the whereabouts of Elder Fey. And, as a Celt, it would give him time to search the area without interference."

The Elder didn't look pleased with this latest theory. He set his empty bowl to one side and sat there brooding and thinking while holding his hot tisane. Weylyn finished his meal, including his drink. When some time passed with no comment from the Magistrate, Weylyn prepared another drink for each of them.

Finally, Eghan sighed deeply. "If we follow your theory, then where is Eiroy the Red's rune buckle? Fionna doesn't have it. Does Parzifal? And the next question which comes to mind is what would the assassin have done with the rune buckle if he'd found it? Would he try to find the treasure or would he have taken it to his boss, whoever that might be?" He gently tapped his fingers on the table as he tried to think the puzzle through.

"I know, Elder. That has me confused, too. The Centurion Axenus gave me the impression the rune buckle has yet to be found. And, as for Parzifal's boss—the merchant Pax Catus—he has no use for the buckle. He's dead."

"Fionna's grandfather might have the buckle, but we cannot find him. There is the possibility her grandfather is dead and buried, too, just like Eiroy and Fey."

Weylyn finished preparing the drink and sat back down with the Magistrate. "You'd think with the existence of two of those buckles we could at least find one of them."

"Actually, I think that one piece of the puzzle is solved. We already know where to find Eiroy the Younger's rune buckle."

"We do?"

"Yes. We solved that mystery yesterday evening."

"We did?"

"Remember Pluvius and his so-called reliable information? I've been thinking," said Eghan. He proceeded to share his thoughts about the Enforcer's assurance there was nothing to be found at Griffyth's place, his obvious discomfort when the search started, his lack of enthusiasm as they dug the pole, and his seeming indifference to the body found. "I'm just wondering if this reliable information came from a certain rune buckle."

"But where did he find it?"

"He didn't find it, he took it. He cut it from the body of that Griffyth fellow, or Myrdoc or whatever his name actually was, after he killed him, of course. He had time to make it to Brennus Ford and get back here long before you or I returned.

He knew about Griffyth's place. He was there when I briefed Orrs on your discovery that Fionna had been there looking for the Younger. It was the day Orrs gave me directions to Eiroy's place in Hierlaneum. The ones I gave you, remember?"

"Then Pluvius knew the treasure was there, at Griffyth's?"

"He probably hoped it was. After all, that's where he found the buckle. He couldn't figure out its meaning, though. That's why he was so excited when we found the first part of the missing treasure and why he was so eager to question us concerning the glyphs. Remember how Pluvius talked of how he heard about those runes? The way he described them tells me that he saw them rather than heard of them. Almost certainly his reliable information came directly from the Younger's rune buckle. Pluvius wants the Great Cross. More importantly, I think, he wants the glory of the find for himself."

"Yes, he's said as much to me. Well, if Pluvius killed Griffyth, who killed Eiroy the Younger?"

"Griffyth, I should think. At least, that was the name he used in the valley. His bargeman's name, the one he used on the river trade through Hierlaneum, the one used in his dealings with the merchant Pax Catus, was Myrdoc. Orrs will be able to verify if our Griffyth is indeed Myrdoc. He certainly fits the description. Anyway, I believe he found and killed the Younger, took the rune buckle and was waiting for orders from Pax or someone on what to do with it. He certainly was waiting for something, and the treasure was still there."

"But Pluvius found him first," said Weylyn.

"Yes," said the Elder. "Pluvius found him first."

Spilt Milk soaked into the ground.
Bruised fruit blackened all around.
Mold upon the morning cheese.
Required tasks go unachieved.
The day wears on and on some more
'Till Fate comes knocking on the door.
Delivered there upon the step—
Past the threshold where Normal's kept—
Come the Gods of Chaos mumbling amid frowns,
And turn Life's apple cart upside down.

37

October 16th in the Roman calendar
Early Afternoon
Eleven days left in the Celtic Tree Month of Gort

The day should have been a flurry of activity. It was not. The sky turned dark, overcast with heavy gray clouds. The temperatures, hovering at the freezing point, were accompanied by a gentle snowfall. Weylyn shared a midday meal and drink with Teg and Elder Eghan. Weylyn had wanted to discuss the runes Pluvius had been so interested in, presumably from one of the buckles, but the Elder was not interested. He looked very tired, and admitted it. He commented on not getting much sleep the night before, saying he was exhausted from the previous day's happenings. They checked the treasure, then stood watch while the guards had their meal and drinks. Satisfied all was well, the Elder excused himself, saying he needed more rest and gave orders to be awakened only if it was of extreme importance.

Teg had one of the servants build up the fire and keep it up while the Elder slept. "Get some dried beef, nuts, barley from the storehouse and prepare a kettle for the evening meal. Make enough for everyone here. The Magistrate will be hungry again when he awakes."

"I'll be over at the tavern if you need me," said Weylyn.

Teg gave him a big, knowing smile and raised his hand as if waving him out of the room.

Weylyn was anxious to see Adrianna again. It had seemed like forever since he'd gazed into her dark, beautiful eyes. He walked into the tavern, anticipating a quiet visit, only to discover Adrianna had worked herself into a fit.

"It's all over the town how you've been chasing that little Celt girl. Fionna. You even followed her to Hierlaneum. I suppose you had a good time down there?" She broke down in tears but continued her ranting. "You won't go to my cities with me, not even to visit, but you'll run off there with one of your Celt girls? How could you?"

He tried to reason with her, to explain it was his job to go to Hierlaneum, that the Elder ordered it, that he'd even thought of her often while he was there. But she continued to hurl hateful accusations at him. She was especially angry he hadn't said good-bye before he'd left. His apologies fell on deaf ears. Frustrated, he finally gave up and left the tavern, with Adrianna hurling insults after him.

"Didn't go well, I take it?" asked Teg, observing Weylyn when he returned to the Longhouse and plopped himself down on one of the benches near the fire.

"I don't want to talk about it."

The sound of horses and commotion out in the street had Teg hobbling over, opening the front door and peering out. "We have company," he announced. "It's the Commander. Go see what he wants. I'll wake Elder Eghan."

Brought out of his brooding over Adrianna, Weylyn went to greet Orrs and his contingent of twelve men. "Axenus and his troops have been delayed in Dynsmore by the storm," Orrs told him. "I expect they'll be here by early afternoon."

Weylyn brought Orrs up to date on the events of the day before. "And Pluvius wants you to join him at Brennus Ford. He thinks he's found the Great Cross."

The Cross Abbey Enforcer was clearly pleased by the news. "I'm eager to see what you've found. I'll wait here with the treasure for the arrival of the Centurion, but I'll send my troops to the Ford to assist Pluvius," said Orrs as Elder Eghan made his way into the room. "Your news couldn't have come at a more opportune time, Elder. It will be both an honor and a relief to present the treasure to the Centurion Axenus. I don't mind telling you, this has been the most frustrating of ventures. I'm glad it is over. Combat is less stressful."

They led Orrs into the storage area to view the treasure while Elder explained the circumstances of the find, omitting his theory about Pluvius taking the rune buckle from Griffyth. Orrs was suitably impressed with the horde of valuables and confirmed it was part of the goods taken from the Cross Abbey shipment. He commended the Elder and Weylyn on their efforts. He assured them the Prefect and the Bishop would be properly briefed on their diligence, loyalty, and efforts to reclaim the goods for the sake of the Empire.

At Elder Eghan's request, Orrs described the barge operator, Myrdoc, again. It certainly fit the man calling himself Griffyth. "It wouldn't surprise me if he had been using two separate names. It's a common practice these days," said Orrs. "One honest name for the Empire, one for the other times they need it. What good can one say about a bunch of thieves anyway?"

Back at the hearth, they dished up helpings of stew and enjoyed a quick meal before the Enforcer excused himself. "I've got to go to the Customs office here before Axenus arrives. I don't want Pluvius taking that barge down river to Cross Abbey. If he tries, I want the dockers to stop him here at Elshorn. It's important the Great Cross be presented to the Centurion along with the other valuables. I do not want this exchange bungled.

Frankly, I'll be relieved to wash my hands of this whole mess. The sooner the goods are turned over to Axenus, the better. I just hope Pluvius hasn't already put the barge on the river and made for Cross Abbey."

As the door closed behind the Enforcer, Eghan commented, "He won't be the only one happy to put this whole affair to rest, but I have a feeling something else disagreeable will happen before this affair is ended."

"You mean with Pluvius, don't you?"

"Could be. Remember how he was acting last night? Pluvius seems to spend his time walking in the twilight between rational consciousness and emotional recklessness. As if some evil churcher spirit dances him on a string between this and the Otherworld. It is scary considering the amount of power his office wields. I had disturbing dreams about Pluvius. They kept me awake most of the night, thinking. I can tell you this, I don't even want to consider what might happen if he doesn't find the cross on the barge," said the Elder.

"Elder, why didn't you tell us about Myrdoc and the barge?" Weylyn asked.

The Magistrate looked at his apprentices then back down at the hearth's fire. "I suppose it didn't occur to me. After all, your job, Weylyn, was to find Fionna de Aine and her grandfather. And you, Teg, were hobbled with that injury of yours. But in retrospect, it was a mistake not to tell both of you."

Weylyn was a little embarrassed the Elder seemed to be apologizing. He steered the conversation back to the Enforcer. "Pluvius has always seemed a bit off center, but he's never acted outside the rules of the Empire. He may be eccentric, but he wouldn't take the cross for himself, would he?"

"I wouldn't put it past him," said Teg.

"For himself? No. But this affair seems to have changed him, and not for the better, either. I think it best that caution be our course for the time being. He's become even more fanatic, more outrageous. The way he acted, the look in his eyes when he knelt and ran his hands through the treasure—he was a man possessed. I just hope he's possessed with doing his job and not something else."

"Something else?" asked Teg and Weylyn in unison.

"Oh, I don't know." The Elder shook his head, sighed and closed his eyes. "I guess I'm still tired. But, yes. Actually, I didn't want to give much thought to the intrigues of the Romans. Especially since it concerns their treasure, their Great Cross. As I told you early on, the business of Roman churchers is not something we should meddle in. Our job is to protect the people of our valley. Unfortunately, this whole thing spilled into our lives, harming our people and further contaminating us with churcher death, lies, and deceptions. Now we have one of the Emperor's Centurions and his forces marching our way. Our people beyond Carew are massing for an attack into our valley. That will be tragic, most destructive and very dangerous. The more I've learned of this affair the more I don't like it. But mine is not to like or dislike. It is to consider the facts as we know them and maintain order."

"The facts, yes," said Weylyn. "For instance, the stolen shipment originated in Cross Abbey. Who would have been in a position to know when the shipment was to be made and how it would be guarded? Who would know if it was going by land or by river?"

Elder Eghan's eyes were still closed, his hands holding his cup against his chest. "That priest in Cross Abbey would know. And the Hierlaneum Prefect's men would have certainly known. It was their troops guarding the shipment."

"Axenus told me he thought it was an inside job, a power struggle between churcher priests."

"Teg and I got a similar story from Orrs," said the Elder. "But it was his suspicion someone from Hierlaneum planned the theft to make the Cross Abbey priest look bad in the eyes of the Great Church, not the other way around. As far as I know, though, there's no direct proof of what the original plan had been. If anyone knows, they certainly haven't shared it with us."

"And likely never will," added Teg.

Weylyn thought about that. It seemed so incredibly tangled, a giant spider's web twisting, turning, always sticky enough to trap even the best thought-out logic. "What if the Cross Abbey priests made the arrangements? Wouldn't that be the ultimate in deception? Who would have thought they'd make themselves look bad in the eyes of the High Cleric by losing something most precious to them, this Great Cross? What better way to gain the upper hand over the Hierlaneum Bishop than to recover the treasure and disclose it was taken by the thieves of Hierlaneum—namely the merchant, Pax Catus and his little band of rogues? That would be the link to the Hierlaneum Bishop, enough to sully his reputation with The Grand Cleric of the Great Church in Rome," said Weylyn.

"Are you suggesting the Cross Abbey priest ordered his own men killed?" The Elder raised his head, opened his eyes and looked directly at his apprentice. Clearly, Magistrate Eghan was having difficulty believing what he'd just heard. He guffawed, mumbled briefly to himself before asking, "What is your proof of this?"

"I don't have any real proof, Elder, just suspicions. But we have information to connect Cross Abbey with the theft. The shipment originated there, with no real guards escorting it. Now we have a Cross Abbey Enforcer, Pluvius, carrying on. And if your suspicion is correct, he murdered Griffyth for one of the rune buckles. He wouldn't even admit to doing it. He knew full well we couldn't have done anything to him even if we saw him commit murder. He was recovering evidence to solve the case and fulfill his duties to his Prefect. He would have been acting under full authority within the laws of the Empire. So why did he hide it?"

"Well, I don't know. Do you?"

"No, but I agree we need to be cautious around Pluvius until this is settled." Weylyn's cup was empty. "Can I get you another drink, Elder? Teg?"

Teg shook his head. "I need to get back on guard with the treasure." Saying goodbye, he hobbled out.

"I'll have another." The Elder handed his cup over and stretched out his arms and back, twisting neck and body this way and that to relieve the pressure of his aching muscles and bones. "At this point, I really don't care who started this whole mess. I just want to be rid of it."

"I hope they find the cross on the barge, give it to the Centurion, and leave our valley as soon as possible," said Weylyn. He put the black pot of water back over the fire, laid the dried herbal leaves and ground roots on the hearth board and waited for the water to reheat. "Elder, what did you make of the runes Pluvius described to us last night? Was he on to something? Could those runes mark Brennus Ford as the hiding place of the Great Cross?"

"Hmm," considered the Elder. "Possible, yes. If one merely takes the basic meaning of the three it is possible, as Pluvius did, to deduce the Ford as the site called for in those three glyphs. At first blush it seems to make sense: the bull as the sign of Cernunnos, the chief God of the ancient site; the protection glyph representing the Circle of Protection which used to be an integral part of the ancient Brennus sanctuary site; finally, the third glyph representing possessions. And there were offerings made regularly at that site. Seems simple enough," said the Elder. "Then again, the sacred site at Brennus Ford contained no altar to Cernunnos, who is most often represented by the sign of the bull."

Weylyn sat watching the pot of water over the fire. He contemplated what the Elder said. "Seems simple, indeed. Yes, so simple even Pluvius figured it out."

"Good point."

"Why would they have gone to all the trouble to cast those buckles to secretly mark the treasure, and then hang around it for so long? You figured it out and didn't even have one of the buckles to guide you."

"Well, I had very good help. If it weren't for the information you provided, I don't believe I would have ever thought of it," said the Elder. "And that pot will never boil if you're going to watch it all the time," he said with a chuckle.

Weylyn sighed. "You are right, Elder, but like most of this mystery, it just doesn't make sense."

"What? Of course it does! A watched pot never boils."

Weylyn returned the jest with his own smile. "No, Elder. You know what I mean. They cast the buckles to mark the location of the treasure, then hid the treasure away. Why do that and hang around?"

"Who knows what runs through the minds of the dishonest? When their plans started falling apart, when people started dying, maybe they panicked. Who knows? Perhaps with both Eiroy the Red and Younger dead—in fact the entire lot of the thieves gone—we may never know the truth of what happened. Of course, that may be the intent of the ones who planned this whole thing in the first place," said the Elder. "Kill off everyone involved so there will be no link back to the instigators. I can tell you, if the Bishop and the churcher priests are the ones involved, they'll be successful in their endeavors to cut the link. They have the willpower, manpower, and political power to make it happen."

"You know Elder, besides the Red's buckle, we have another puzzle we should consider."

"What's that?"

"The runevision. It was what led us to the location of the treasure in the Greeting Pole. Is it possible the runevision may contain more clues we could use to locate the Great Cross?"

"Hmm," muttered the Elder. "Yes. You are right. The vision led us to the house at Brennus Ford. But it also contained the Place Marker rune, the sign of the elk's horn. That rune is not associated with Brennus Ford."

"So you think the Great Cross is not at Brennus Ford?"

"It doesn't seem likely, given the Place Maker rune. But then, that doesn't seem like it would give us much of a clue to who might have started all this in the first place. Could have been the priests or the Bishop," said the Elder.

"True. However, no matter who planned this, I doubt they ever imagined a Centurion and his forces would be sent all the way from Rome to investigate. They probably thought the treasure would have been safely returned long before news made it to the Supreme Prefect."

"I see your point. Just one question, though," said the Elder.

"Yes?"

"Are you boiling that water away or are you making drinks?"

Weylyn grabbed the pot and swung it from the fire. Neither said a word while he set to work preparing the hot drink. He added a good portion of dried herb mixture to each cup and ladled in the steaming water. He handed Elder a cup and joined him on the hearth bench. Both sat quietly as the concoction steeped. Suddenly, their tranquility was interrupted by shouting from the street.

"Elder! Elder Eghan, come quickly!"

The Elder and Weylyn no sooner set their cups on the hearth and rose from their seats when the front door of the Longhouse was flung open. It was Orrs and another man; the looks on their faces said something was gravely amiss.

"Eghan, I need those men of yours. It's Pluvius—"

"Magistrate! They're burning the village, killing us all! You must help us!" The man with Orrs shouted hysterically. He was shivering, barefoot, clad only in a dirty loincloth. "They killed my boy, my wife—" He broke down and couldn't finish.

Weylyn helped him to the bench beside the hearth. He offered him the cup of hot tisane. "Drink this," he urged. "I'll get you something warm to wear."

"What's going on? Trouble?" Teg asked as Weylyn hurried into the storeroom.

"It's Pluvius. I think he's gone crazy," said Weylyn, grabbing a robe from its peg on the wall and, rushing back to the main room, placed it over the man's shoulders and back.

"What is this all about?" demanded the Elder.

"This man came into the Elshorn dock on a small boat shouting for help. Said they were burning his house, everyone's house. He demanded to see you." They looked at the poor soul slouched next to the fire, barely able to hold a cup, his body racked with shivers.

"I think, Orrs, you'd better explain," said the Magistrate.

"I can't explain it. He says Pluvius has gone berserk—"

"I told you!" shouted the man. "That Enforcer, he's gone mad! Brennus Ford, our homes! He's, he's …"

The Elder moved to his side and placed a hand on the man's shoulder. "Calm down. We can't help you if you don't tell us what's happening. Take deep breaths. Drink. It will help warm you up."

"It's crazy! He's gone mad!"

"All right, all right. Start from the beginning and tell us, as calmly as you can, what happened."

"The Enforcer—he rousted a bunch of us from our homes last night. He was all excited, said he needed men to drag a barge out of the river. We were all reluctant because it was late and cold, but he was an Enforcer." He looked up at Orrs then back to the Magistrate. "It took hours in the freezing storm. When we hauled it on shore, he ordered us to guard it, set up shifts through the night. He never slept." He paused to swallow more of the hot tisane. "Then, at sunrise, he ordered us to take the barge apart."

"Did he tell you why?" asked Orrs.

"He kept shouting over and over, it was God's will, for God's glory! The Savior of Galilee would soon bless us all!" He looked up at Orrs with a hate in his eyes that made the others cringe. "But I can tell you, if this was the work of your lord, then truly it is he who is Satan!"

Orrs ignored the comment. He wanted the facts. "When you took the barge apart, what did you find?"

"Nothing! Nothing at all. And that was what really set him off! There we all were, out on a cold bank by the pier, pieces of the barge scattered everywhere. We stood there and watched, cold and hungry. He forbade anyone to leave. He went through every piece, examining every one himself. He had a wild look in his eyes. He told us to strip and smash every length of beam and plank, to search inside each piece! It was insane!"

"What's all this about burning the village?" Orrs demanded.

"A large crowd had gathered throughout the morning, our wives, children, relatives, all watching the insanity. When we found nothing, when we'd finished the total destruction of the barge pieces, the Enforcer started shouting sermons at us. Condemning all of us to burn in your Hades." He glared at Orrs. "We had no idea what he was talking about. We all started shouting back at him, demanding to know what he wanted. He only grew angrier, threatening our lives, our village with destruction if we didn't cooperate. But still he wouldn't tell us what it was he wanted--except to conform to God's will." The man stopped talking and dropped his head down. He set the cup on the stone hearth.

"And the burning?" asked Orrs.

"That started when the soldiers came."

Orrs and Eghan looked at each other. They knew the man was referring to Orrs' troops.

"The Enforcer ordered us all out onto the pier. He placed two of the soldiers to guard us before he and the others started searching all the homes and buildings. They burned everything when they were through. When we heard him give orders for some of the soldiers to dig up and search the graveyard, we panicked and ran. We tried to get away. Many were slaughtered in the process. My wife, son, they—" He broke down once more. "That's when I got into the boat and escaped to get help."

Elder Eghan glared at Orrs. "This is outrageous! We must stop this at once!"

"I agree. I'm afraid I must insist on those men of yours," said Orrs. "I invoke the power of the Emperor. I don't like having to do it but I need those men."

"And so you shall have them. We'll leave together," said the Elder. "Weylyn, take care of this man and when the Centurion arrives, send him immediately to Brennus Ford."

"Yes, sir."

"No!" shouted the man. "I will go with you!" He jumped up, wrapping the robe about him.

"Very well, then. Make haste! Orrs, if you would, go to the stables, tell them to prepare my chariot and get this man one of my horses. I'll join you there in just a moment."

"Right," said Orrs. He and the man left the Longhouse.

Elder turned to Weylyn and held up his hand, palm out—a signal for his young deputy not to say anything, not to argue. "Come with me."

He led the way to the storeroom. Tersely, Elder issued his orders to the men guarding the treasure. They were to report to the stable, get their horses, and be prepared to ride to Brennus Ford with him and Orrs. He'd brief them on the way.

When the others left the Magistrate turned to Weylyn and Teg. "I know you both want to ride with us, but you must remain here on guard. Weylyn, you know what to tell Axenus. It shouldn't be long before he and his men arrive. Tell him what has transpired and Orrs requires him immediately at the Ford.

He'll understand. But do not tell him anything about the treasure we've found. With a force so large it may be dangerous to reveal we hold so many valuables. Time enough to tell him after we've dealt with Pluvius. One more thing. I need you two to do something very important as soon as I leave."

"What's that, Elder?"

"On the chance this is a ruse to get us to leave the treasure unguarded, I want you to move it to Weylyn's sleeping place. Break the three large bundles down to smaller ones and hide them in the overhead loft where we keep the old drying baskets and pelt stretchers. Tie them to the rafters with the bundles of herbs. They'll practically be invisible there. Understand?"

"Yes, Elder," said Weylyn.

Teg nodded his understanding.

"I'm off to Brennus Ford. I fear otherwise, but I pray we aren't too late."

It came and landed at his door,
the message from the visitor.
She came to him with vital news,
with facts of interest to peruse.
But busy as we often get
important things can often slip
by our thoughts and through our grip
when Interruption flaps its lip.

38

October 16th in the Roman calendar
Mid-Afternoon
Eleven days left in the Celtic Tree Month of Gort

Teg helped Weylyn divide the treasure into smaller bundles and carry them to Weylyn's room. He hobbled back to the Longhouse to stand guard while Weylyn moved the bundles up to the loft. The thin hemp they'd planned to use to tie the bundles in place wasn't strong enough, so Weylyn distributed the goods among several of the large woven willow baskets kept in the niches along the ceiling beams. Task finally complete, he climbed back down from the small loft and dusted himself off.

There was a knock on his door. Weylyn opened it to find a young Celt girl with dark eyes and light brown hair standing there. She wore a red fox cape. "Fionna!"

"Greetings, sir. May I come in, please?"

"Yes, certainly." He opened the door wider and stepped back to allow her entry.

"I hope I'm not bothering you. I went to the Longhouse for the Chief Magistrate but he's not anywhere around. Teg said you were back here." She had her back to him, staring around the small one-room house.

"Elder has ridden to Brennus Ford on urgent business. I was just heading back to the Longhouse."

"Oh," she said.

"What is it you want, Fionna?"

"Kelwin has brought word from Aife, from Cullen and his father about the dead man you found up on the mountain." She placed a hand on his arm. "It wasn't Elder Fey but Cullen's father recognized the man. He'd seen him before."

Weylyn was confused. "Who was it then, if it wasn't Fey de Parke? Did they tell you, do you know?"

"I don't know his name. Angus said it was a bear hunter—one of two men who had been hunting near the area around the time of the last Equinox gathering. Some of the men who went with Angus thought, at first, he'd been killed by a bear and fell into the crevice where you found him."

"What did Angus think?"

She dropped her head for a moment and took her hand from his arm. "Kelwin told me Angus says—and they now all agree—the man was murdered."

Weylyn's mind raced. Then he remembered. On his first visit up to look for Eiroy, Angus told him of two hunters, strangers to the mountain he'd seen in the area. Who were they? How did one come to be murdered and stuffed in the mountain crevice? He couldn't believe it was a coincidence that the murdered hunter wound up in the same immediate area at the same time as Eiroy. There must be a connection, but what?

"Elder Eghan told me how much trouble you went through to find me," she said. She looked back up into his eyes. "I want to apologize for that. I didn't realize you'd followed me all the way to Hierlaneum."

He shrugged. "You did lead me on quite a chase. You should not have traveled so far by yourself," he admonished her. "That was dangerous. You should never travel to a city like Hierlaneum without escort. Next time, take a friend or relative with you, all right?"

Fionna dropped her head again and said meekly, "Kelwin's father operates a barge that runs to Hierlaneum. I was safe with him." She raised her head. In a stronger voice she said, "I need to speak with you about something very important."

"Fionna, I've got to get back up front to the Longhouse. Would you like to come with me and have something to eat? I'm waiting for the arrival of someone from Cross Abbey."

"Will we be alone? Just for a few minutes. Please!" She moved closer to him, reached up and clutched his arm again. "There's something we need to talk about. It's important we be alone."

"Let me ask Teg to come over here and watch my place. We can be alone in the Longhouse for a while." He stopped as he realized she was looking at something. Alarmed, he spun around and saw Adrianna standing in the open doorway.

"I knew it!" she shouted. "I knew I'd find the two of you together. Fine! Have her then! We are finished!" she shrieked. Face red with anger, Adrianna marched off.

Weylyn, stunned for a moment, finally regained his senses, ran to the door and looked out. "Adrianna! Wait!" But she'd already rounded the corner and was out of sight. "Curse the gods of chaos!" blurted Weylyn. He turned and saw Fionna standing behind him. She was staring at him, giggling and trying to cover her smile with her hands. He felt his face blush hot. Ignoring her, he made his way toward the Longhouse. He could hear Fionna running along behind him.

"Wait! I really do need to speak with you," she yelled after him. "It's very important!"

He turned the corner of the front of the Longhouse. The chestnut-brown mare with one white ear and white tail was tied to the tether pole. He looked up and down the main street but

Adrianna was nowhere to be seen. He was about to cross the street when he heard the sound of many horses. It was Axenus and his forces. He saw the Centurion just behind his standard bearers. Riding next to him was the Enforcer Warius. Beyond them, on the horizon over the distant river, he could see plumes of smoke rising from the direction of Brennus Ford.

"Weylyn! I really need to talk with you," shouted Fionna. She came around the corner and stopped when she saw the large Roman force approaching the Longhouse. Fionna grasped the sides of her cape, pulled it tight and fastened it again with her brooch as she walked over and stood next to Weylyn.

Teg opened the door to the Longhouse. "What's going on?"

"Teg," said Weylyn, "can you get over to my place please?"

"On my way," he said, closing the door.

The force was bigger than any Weylyn could remember seeing at any one time in the Brendan Valley. There may have been this many Roman soldiers during the search for Eiroy, but they'd never been all in one spot at the same time. Axenus had close to three dozen well-armed soldiers of the Empire with him, as well as a dozen or more mercenary fighters consisting of Roman, Celt and others. It was an impressive sight.

Weylyn searched the crowd, looking for Adrianna, but it was impossible to see through the gaggle of horses and men around the Longhouse.

Axenus rode up and raised his arm in salute. "Greetings, Weylyn. It's good to see you again. You seem to have recovered from your collision with a horse."

"Thank you, Axenus, I'm fine. Good to see you again, too." He greeted Warius next. The Enforcer grinned as he noticed Fionna. "Ah, I see you've found your Celt girl."

Weylyn hoped Adrianna hadn't come out to hear that.

The Centurion smiled at Weylyn then looked at the young girl. "I take it you must be Fionna."

She dropped her head but didn't say anything.

"Ha!" said Warius. "She's a bashful one! Well, Weylyn, does she have a certain piece of bronze we've all been looking for?"

Fionna turned quickly toward Weylyn, then up to look at the big Enforcer, then back to Weylyn.

The Centurion gave his Enforcer a stern look and looked around the troops gathered there. They were listening intently.

Weylyn remembered the Magistrate's orders not to mention anything about the rune buckle. He decided to ignore Warius and kept his eyes on Axenus.

The Centurion returned his attention to Weylyn. "Forget about that for the moment. Where's Magistrate Eghan? I'm looking forward to seeing him again."

"Elder Eghan bid me wait here for you with urgent news. We received word this morning that the Enforcer Pluvius of Cross Abbey thinks he's found the location of the Great Cross."

"Excellent!" Axenus exclaimed.

"You may not think so after I've told you the rest," Weylyn said grimly. "Elder Eghan and Commander Orrs have gone to Brennus Ford and urgently request you join them. Pluvius has taken some of Commander Orrs' men and is searching and burning the whole village, killing its citizens, even digging up graves looking for the Great Cross. We learned the news this morning, when one poor soul escaped and came for help."

Murmurs of disbelief and shock ran through Axenus' force when they heard Weylyn's tale.

"I feared something like this would happen," Axenus said.

"Sir, the road to Brennus Ford is—"

"No need for directions! I remember the road well. We must hurry." He turned his horse and told Warius to order the men around. They would ride to the Ford at a full run.

Weylyn stood there watching them depart. He wanted to see them all leave and, after that, he'd hurry over to the Five Fingers to straighten out the misunderstanding with Adrianna, but he was distracted by a tugging on his sleeve.

"I must speak with you, Weylyn. Please!" Fionna begged. She opened the door of the Magistrate's Longhouse, holding it for him to enter.

He looked at her, dropped his shoulders. "All right, young lady, but this had better be good."

Ruin Stones

The broken Circle lay upon the mounds,
ever centered on the Sacred Grounds.
Once it marked the Worshiper's Return,
the Ascent of Time, the Elder's Turn.
Now tumbled into scattered, sad demise,
by an evil that would not compromise.
Smart are they who never miss this.
A lesson missed by all the blissless.
Destruction, Renewal, In-Between,
To those aware, All is seen.
Look! Scattered about, the ruined Stone—
for humans' sake, their Truth is known.
Cycle in and Cycle out,
Praise it all and dance and shout!
The Patient Oaks, they know it too;
as they breathe for me and you.
So, raise your voices to the tune,
Celebrate the Sun and Moon.
Beat the drums, blow the fife,
Happiness for all that's Life!
Mercy, mercy Stars above,
The Dark of Evil is void of Love.

39

October 16th in the Roman calendar
Late Afternoon
Eleven days left in the Celtic Tree Month of Gort

They huddled together among the stones, waiting for a man Weylyn had long thought dead. The large gray slabs within the ruins, once flooring for the ceremonial protective ring of the ancient Elshorn temple to Cernunnos, were cold and icy to the touch. Weylyn shivered, crouched on his heels near a pillar stone which stood next to a partial, small stone wall. He hated being cold. The only warmth was coming from the body of the young Celt girl. Fionna sat there with him along the wall, huddled against the chill of the late afternoon wind.

The sky was heavy with clouds, the light already growing dim. There would be no stars visible tonight; the crescent moon would not show itself. In just over an hour, the winter darkness would cover this place. The blanket of obscure visions tonight would be as murky as the veil which had covered this mystery all along. No matter how many times he replayed Fionna's conversation in his mind, he still found it incredible.

"It is important, sir. It's my grandfather. As I've said, he's come home, back to Elshorn. I've received a message from him to meet this evening at the old Elshorn temple," she'd said.

"Are you certain the message was from your grandfather?"

"His friend Elder Bealantin gave it to me. He was at my mother's when I arrived from Carew. He said my grandfather was anxious to see me. He's afraid."

Weylyn thought that, at least, made sense. "I don't blame him."

"He promised to explain when he saw me tonight."

"Why now? And why in the ruins?"

"Elder Bealantin said they were leaving tonight, and if I wanted to see my grandfather it needed to be now."

"And you want me to go with you?"

"I thought you or Elder Eghan should be there. Elder Fey is with them—"

"Wait! Elder Fey is alive?"

"Yes," she'd said impatiently. "Elder Bealantin said they have what you're looking for. They have the rune buckle."

So now it was they sat in this place where Fionna had been told to wait. Weylyn was anxious to hear just what Elder Petroytrix and Elder Fey de Parke had to say for themselves—an explanation Weylyn thought long overdue.

"What's that? Listen," whispered Fionna.

They heard the sound of horses. Weylyn eased around the pillar, careful to remain hidden. He looked to the west down the old, narrow roadway winding through the ruin and saw three men on horseback. "It's them. I recognize the lead rider from the tavern. It's Elder Bealantin."

Fionna jumped up, ran past him and out of their place of concealment. Weylyn stayed where he was, watching.

"Grandfather!" she yelled. "Grandfather!"

The three stopped momentarily, apparently startled by her sudden appearance. The second man in line slid gingerly down from the horse. With a big smile he held his arms out to the girl running toward him. "Fionna, my dear!"

"I missed you!"

"And I missed you, too. I missed you a great deal, my dear."

"Why, Grandfather, why did you go away?" .

He gently pushed her away, holding her at arm's length. "Come. We've got important work to do, my dear, and we must be quick about it. There is no time to waste. There is great evil in the valley tonight and we must hurry to beat it. While we work, I will do my best to answer all your questions."

Weylyn stepped out from behind the pillar. "I hope you'll answer all of my questions, too, Elder."

His sudden appearance alarmed the group. The two men still on horseback drew short swords. The horses danced nervously. Petroytrix pulled Fionna behind him and drew a dagger. "Halt! Or you'll be cut to ribbons!" yelled Bealantin.

"Then you'll be cutting a magistrate. I don't think you want to do that. I'm Weylyn, deputy magistrate to Elder Eghan of Oaks." He walked toward them. "Put your weapons away. I mean you no harm."

The men looked nervously at each other.

"It's true, Grandfather, I asked him to come."

Petroytrix dropped his head, slowly shaking left and right. "Oh, child, I wish you hadn't brought him with you. You shouldn't have."

"But why not? Elder Bealantin said you were frightened. Maybe Weylyn can help."

"Enough of this," shouted Bealantin. "We don't have time to waste. Come!" He urged his horse forward and ignored Weylyn as he passed. Fey de Parke followed.

Petroytrix put his dagger back in his belt, grabbed the reins of his horse with one hand and the arm of his granddaughter with the other. "Come, child." They walked past Weylyn and as they did, Petroytrix looked at Fey. "Tell them."

Fey nodded and said, "We go to the well of Cernunnos. I'll explain all I can on the way."

And so Elder Fey de Parke told his story, explaining what had transpired since Eiroy the Red fled the scene of the murder of Aod that evening in Elshorn. He made it to Fey's for healing and to confess his part in the theft of the treasure. Fey left his nephew alone to venture down the mountain to exchange his herbs for fresh linen bandages for Eiroy's wounds. When he returned, Fey saw two strangers, both Celts, at his place. Sensing something was wrong, he stayed out of sight and watched while they broke into his house, ransacked it and dragged poor Eiroy outside. He watched in horror as they brutally interrogated the wounded man, demanding the whereabouts of the treasure.

Fey had overheard the younger, larger Celt tell Eiroy his fellow thieves had already admitted the existence of the rune buckle before he'd killed them. Eiroy wouldn't cooperate. The large Celt wanted to kill Eiroy and the older Celt tried to intervene. He wanted them to take Eiroy away, back to Hierlaneum. Their disagreement disintegrated into a deadly fight which resulted in the death of the older Celt. When Eiroy wouldn't give him any more information, the large Celt killed him, too.

Fey de Parke said he'd watched in disbelief and horror. He described how the man removed the bright ribbons from his Greeting Pole and replaced them with black ribbons—making the home look as if a death hearth ritual had been performed. Then the killer cleared away all evidence of violence from the scene. "As you might imagine, I was numb with fear. I sat there in my hiding place, clutching the piece of bronze Eiroy had given me for safe keeping. I was lucky the man was too busy with other things to search the woods for me. Or else I too would be buried on that mountain."

Petroytrix hugged Fionna and reached into his belt pouch, removed a buckle and handed it to her. "We don't need this any longer."

She examined the rune buckle and then handed it to Weylyn.

"He had black ribbons with him?" asked Weylyn. He briefly examined the piece before securing it in his own belt pouch.

"Yes. He must have planned to kill my nephew all along."

"What happened then?" Fionna asked.

"Well, it was late that afternoon, I watched the man take the two bodies on horseback up higher into the mountains. That's when I decided to leave."

"That's when he came to warn me and Bealantin," Petroytrix added.

"I knew the buckle had something to do with the stolen goods," Fey admitted. "Eiroy told me things intentionally, and some I heard as he ranted through his fever. He told me about the churcher's Grand Cross. The one made from sacred Celtic gold with the fabled amber of our Mother Goddess, Arianrod. He told me of his plans to return it to its rightful owners, to free it from its blasphemous captivity among the churchers. But Eiroy was never specific about the buckle's importance. I didn't figure that out until much later with the help of Bealantin and Petroytrix. Understand, we don't wish to harm anyone. But I must tell you it is the last promise I made to my nephew Eiroy. I will do everything possible to see the goods returned to our people. Arrangements have already been made."

"Elder Fey, why was Eiroy the Red looking for his brother in town that evening?" asked Weylyn.

"He'd been to the house at Brennus Ford and through the village but the Younger was nowhere to be found. Since both used to like to drink our valley wine, the Red thought perhaps he'd find him at the tavern. He'd spotted Aod earlier around the docks and knew he was being followed. He feared for his life and he wanted to find the Younger quickly."

Between the large statue of Cernunnos and the old, large stone well, Bealantin and Fey dismounted. Petroytrix dropped the reins of his horse and untied a catch loop and dropped a long coil of rope from the pack he carried behind his saddle. He cut off a length of it, put his sword away and held the rope length up to show Bealantin.

"What are we doing here, Grandfather?" asked Fionna.

"We're retrieving two very precious, sacred objects so we can return them."

"Magistrate!" said Bealantin. He stood looking up at the stone statue of one of the female nudes, pointing his sword at its face. "See this handmaiden? You want the treasure? So do we. Come give us a hand and we'll get it."

Weylyn walked over to Bealantin and looked up at the statue. He couldn't believe the Great Cross was hidden within. He wondered if it was buried under the statue's massive stone base. If so, they'd have to use the rope to pull over the stone carving.

He didn't know which came first, the hair standing up on the back of his neck or the cold steel of the Elder's sword pressing against his throat.

"Actually, sir, we want both your hands. Put them behind your back and through the legs of that statue, and don't give us any trouble. You're right, we don't want to hurt you. We just need to make certain you don't interfere with our plans. We are in a hurry and have no time for argument. Understand?" He pressed the blade further in against Weylyn's throat.

"Elder! What are you doing?" yelled Fionna.

Fey grabbed Fionna gently by the shoulder. "Quiet, my dear. We aren't going to harm him. Just keep him in one place for a while, until we finish what we came here to do. You may set him free after we've gone."

Petroytrix tied the young magistrate's hands behind him to the legs of the statue. Weylyn felt the cold, trembling fingers of the aged Petroytrix as he fought the rope, tying the knots as tight as his gnarly, shaking hands could make them. "There you go, young fellow," said Petroytrix, "that should keep you safe enough for the time being."

Bealantin returned his sword to his belt. "I truly apologize for this inconvenience. Don't take it personally. It's just that I know you'll try to stop us if you can. I don't blame you. It's your job and you are sworn to uphold the law. We honor that. But we three have also sworn an oath, an oath to right a wrong for all our people, our Celtic brethren. A chance to return what is rightfully ours, as Celts, where it can be appreciated for what it truly represents. You just relax, and Fionna will release you as soon as we leave. You have our promise."

The three elders went to the edge of the ancient well and peered down. Weylyn could hear the faint echo as they spoke.

"Looks worse in the darkness than it did in the daylight, doesn't it," said Fey.

"Yes, of course it does," replied Petroytrix. "Well, Beal, my friend, looks like you draw the short lot once again—but only because you are a year younger than us."

The three men laughed.

"All right, but this may take longer than I thought. It looks different than in full daylight."

"What are you going to do?" asked Fionna. "You're going into the well? Why?"

"Because, my dear, that's where the treasure is hidden," explained Petroytrix.

"I'll go," she volunteered. "What am I to look for?"

"No! No, it's too dangerous. Elder Bealantin has been down before, he can do it again. He just needs to take his time."

"She has a good point," Fey said. "Time is something we don't have a lot of—not if we're to make it to the boat in time to sail to our meeting point down river."

"Quiet," scolded Bealantin. "We can't endanger our plans by telling them everything." He looked down into the well.

Fionna leaped atop the large perimeter well-stones, moved one of the oak buckets to the side and turned her back to the hole. She got down on her knees, then onto her stomach and let her legs fall into the opening.

"Here! No! I'll have none of that, Fionna. It's too dangerous," said Petroytrix. "Get off there right now!"

She seemed to pay no attention to her grandfather. Instead, she gripped the outer edge of the stones and guided her right foot down until it found a grip in one of the hand-holds. Before the three Elders could reach her, she'd already grasped the first set of iron hand-holds and climbed down out of sight.

"Fionna!" yelled Petroytrix. He looked over into the well and down into her upturned face.

"I'm fine. This is easy. Easier than the cliffs I climb above your house. Tell me what I'm looking for. Hurry now. You said you don't have much time."

Bealantin seemed most happy with the opportunity to turn the task over to Fionna. He and Fey hurried to get the rope. Fey took his end to the well, while Bealantin tied his end of the rope to the nearby large statue of the partially-antlered Cernunnos.

"Here, take this end. Wrap it around you in case you slip."

"I don't need a rope."

"Yes, you do, Fionna," explained Fey. "It isn't just for safety. At the bottom, just below the waterline, you'll find a large burlap bundle wrapped in rope. Tie this rope to one of the many loops you'll find on the bundle. When you get it secured, give us a yell. Understand?"

"Yes." And down went Fionna into the huge dark well.

It seemed an eternity. Weylyn watched the three as they peered into the opening. Occasionally, they'd call to Fionna for a progress report. Finally, she yelled, "All right. Pull!"

Weylyn watched as the three Elders pulled, struggled, paused for a moment and pulled again. They weren't making any progress. He heard Fionna yell again. "It's stuck. Wait."

Another length of time passed. The Elders had let go of the rope and again peered over the edge of the well. Momentarily, her head popped back up over the rim. "It's tied to one of the large iron wall loops. I can't get it free."

Petroytrix asked, "Could you cut it with a dagger?"

"Yes, I think so."

Fey pulled his dagger from his belt and handed it to her.

"Be right back," she said. She put the blade into her mouth and clenched it with her teeth. She disappeared once again into the depths of the well.

Weylyn had been trying to loosen the rope from his wrists, which had grown numb. He had to keep moving his hands and wrists to keep feeling in them. He managed to finally get a little maneuvering room and felt the ropes loosen slightly. He tried working the knots loose. The Elders had lost interest in him totally; their full attention was on Fionna and the well.

"Got it! Pull now!" Fionna's words echoed eerily from the depths of the well, sounding like a spirit's voice hearkening from the depths of the Celtic Otherworld.

The three Elders pulled once again. This time they had movement. Slowly and with a great deal of effort, moans and grunts, the three aged men hauled the bundle to the top of the well. They rested it on the edge and then rested themselves while Fionna climbed back up to the top.

Weylyn struggled with the rope and its binding knots. He thought he was making progress but he knew he didn't have much time if he were to secure the treasure for Elder Eghan. Then it occurred to him, why bother? After all, didn't the amber and gold really belong to his people? It was stolen from them in the first place. He thought of the Roman churchers like Pluvius and Titus and the others he'd encountered. He remembered the runevision and the sign of the elk's horn—the horns worn by the deity, Cernunnos. Elder Blaine's vision had been accurate.

He studied the men at the well. Three honorable Elders were trying to correct a wrong by returning the piece to its rightful owners, its rightful place with the Celtic people.

What were his orders from the Chief Magistrate? Find Fionna. Locate her grandfather. He'd done both. He'd briefed Axenus. His immediate specific duties from Elder Eghan were complete. All he need do now is maintain order in the valley. That was the Magistrate's directive. At the moment—aside from being bound—he didn't see any disorder here. They said he'd be released when they finished. He believed them. They were honorable Elders. He stopped struggling with the rope and watched them. They were cutting an opening in the burlap bundle. Fionna was still in the well, her body only halfway out. He could see her smiling as the men complimented her on a job well done.

A portion of the burlap cover was cut away between the ropes. They were looking at the large piece of Celtic amber secured to the gold filigree cross of the churchers—gold stolen from the Celts.

"Oooh!" said Fionna. "It's beautiful! I've never seen such a large piece of amber!"

"Look closely, my dear," Petroytrix said. "You'll see the face of Arianrod, the Mother Goddess. And that is Celtic gold she's mounted on, poured from the sacred cauldron of the Druids."

They pried the piece of amber from its pronged clasps on the cross. Bealantin wrapped the amber in felt and secured it in the leather pouch hanging over his shoulder. Meanwhile, Petroytrix and Fey cut away the burlap strips from under the rope securing the t-shaped cross.

"Filthy blasphemy!" said Petroytrix. "To misuse our sacred gold in such a way!"

"Save it for later, my friend," said Fey. "Let's cut it loose so we can get it out of here. Fionna, give me the dagger."

"Yes, Elder. It's in my belt." said Fionna. One foot dangling in the open space of the well, the other in one of the inner hand-holds, she held one edge of the cross for balance and reached down to get the dagger.

Weylyn thought he heard a movement behind him. He turned his head as far left as he could and as he did he heard a quick whoosh sound, a thud and one of the Elders scream in pain. Weylyn turned back just in time to see Elder Fey collapse against the cross and then fall to the ground, a dagger lodged in his back. Fionna screamed as she was knocked backward into the well. The heavy piece of gold followed Fionna down into the well, its attached rope making a terrible noise as it sped across the stone and down into the depths of the well.

Weylyn struggled furiously to free himself when a large man stepped into the clearing. He wasn't wearing a dark cloak and hood this time, but Weylyn recognized the assassin, Parzifal.

"They're on to us!" Petroytrix yelled. "Go! Quickly! Run, Bealantin, run! Secure the sacred gem of Arianrod. I'll hold them off." The Elder, his old hands trembling, fought to free his short sword. The blade never cleared. Parzifal walked straight up to the Elder and with one blow from his right hand struck him hard across the jaw. Petroytrix fell hard like a sack of dried barley thrown against the well stones. He didn't move.

Weylyn struggled against the rope and knots. He could feel the blood from cuts on his wrists.

Two of the horses spooked and bolted from the area. Bealantin managed to mount his horse but held only one of the reins. The horse was dancing and jumping uncontrollably as its rider attempted to secure both reins. A second dagger struck Elder Bealantin in the upper left side of the back. He screamed in pain, kicked his horse, urging it on. The big mount lunged forward and ran full speed down the old temple road, its rider clinging precariously in the saddle.

Parzifal pulled his own sword and walked toward Weylyn. "They got you tied pretty good, huh? How stupid of you. I saw how they lured you over here and out of the way. You are entirely too trusting. You are wrong to trust Celts just because they are Celts. Even Celts have the dishonest among them."

"Like Eiroy the Red?"

Parzifal nodded. "That's why I killed him. The fool couldn't foresee what was to be his fate; but you, a magistrate, should have seen it coming. I would have." He smiled an evil smile. "But then, a lesson for you is a lesson wasted now, isn't it? You'll never get a chance to use it."

Weylyn stared into the face of the big man. The assassin was clad in leathers, with big fur-lined leather boots and a fur hat covering his head. The hat's long earflaps were tied under his chin and covered much of his face, but Weylyn could see the bottom end of what must be a large burn scar on his left cheek. Eiroy really did stick him just as Calvin said, Weylyn thought. He realized Parzifal was staring at him.

"I've been thinking, I know you from somewhere, don't I?"

"You almost killed me with your horse on the docks in the Celtarium, outside Hierlaneum. You ran me over with your big black horse." Weylyn continued to struggle against the knots.

Parzifal lowered his sword. "Was that you?" He laughed. "How fortunate for me I didn't kill you then. If I have trouble pulling the gold back out you're going to help me. Then, if you're lucky, I'll toss your body into the well with your little girlfriend. That would make the tavern maid Adrianna very happy, I think. That's right. She and I had a nice little talk. Tell me, does she chatter so much when she's in a good mood?" He laughed again.

Weylyn lost his temper and kicked at the big man, trying to hurt him.

Parzifal avoided the kick with ease and continued laughing. "Pathetic! I told you, I can see things like that coming. I hope you pull rope better than you fight."

"Elder Bealantin got away. It won't be long before he will have troops down here. You won't escape."

"Ha! Nice try. Didn't you see? I never miss. The old man won't make it out of these ruins before he falls dead off his horse. After I get the gold and take care of you, I'll retrieve the amber. You know as well as I do that there are no soldiers left in Elshorn to stop me."

Weylyn continued to work the last knot. He wanted to keep Parzifal talking. He needed to give himself enough time to get free or give Bealantin time to get help—if that was possible. After all, Parzifal was right. The forces were in Brennus Ford. He knew his chances were next to nil against the assassin. The man was big and strong. Worse, he was very good at killing. Weylyn tried to think calmly, tried to think of what he was going to do when he freed himself.

"Those pieces don't belong to you," yelled Weylyn. "They belong to Celts. They rightly belong in the Celtlands, not hidden away in a vulgar human churcher building!"

The big man, his face dark with rage, glared at Weylyn. "I am Celt! Look at me! I'm not Roman, not a churcher! I'm Celt, just like you!" Parzifal yelled.

Weylyn realized he had touched a nerve deep, deep inside the man. He watched Parzifal fight to regain emotional control.

The assassin took several deep breaths and stepped closer to Weylyn. "You and I appear to have something in common besides Adrianna." He laughed his evil laugh again. "I'm taking these pieces to Highdyn Hill and presenting them to her highness, Queen Maeverorix. For that, I expect to be granted lands and freeman status, to live my life as a Celt should, free! Too bad you won't be around to enjoy it with me."

The assassin watched the young magistrate struggle to free himself. Parzifal laughed. "It won't do you any good to get free. If you do, you'll only die sooner. You can't beat me in a fight. Remember, I can see every move coming." With that, the big man turned and walked through the growing darkness toward the well of Cernunnos.

Weylyn felt the knot finally loosen and fall away. He was free, but free to do what? He rubbed his hands together. They weren't back to normal, but most of the numbness now was due to the cold, not the loss of circulation from the binding rope.

Parzifal reached the edge of the well, picked up the trailing rope from atop the stone and pulled on it. "Still attached. Good." He laid his sword on the edge of the well stones. With both hands he pulled hard on the rope. It wouldn't budge.

"I might need your help after all," he called. "It seems to be stuck on something." Parzifal braced himself with his right hand, leaned over the well, and stuck his head into the pitch dark opening while pulling on the rope with his left hand.

There was only one thing Weylyn could do. It was his duty to keep order in this valley and this man had violated that order by killing four people in mere minutes. He sent a silent prayer for strength to his totem, the wolf, then pulled his dagger and crossed the space between him and the assassin.

Suddenly, the big man jerked straight up from the well. He let out a horrible, bloodcurdling scream of agony and pain. "Ahhhhhgghh—" He whirled around, his left hand trying to grasp something protruding from his left eye. Parzifal continued to scream as he managed to pick up his sword and wildly flail the air.

Weylyn charged the big man and jabbed his dagger into Parzifal's heart. The assassin dropped his sword and reached up to grab the wound in his chest.

Weylyn felt the hot blood of Parzifal cover him. He pushed the man backwards and the assassin dropped to the ground. Weylyn staggered, trying to catch his breath. He wiped the blood from his face, fought the urge to vomit, and waited for his heartbeat to slow to normal. The once seemingly invincible man twitched there on the ground. Weylyn watched as the last of life's energy left Parzifal.

"Is he dead?" Fionna's head appeared, just above the rim of the well stones.

"Fionna? Fionna! Are you all right? I heard you fall."

"I caught myself just a little way down. There are all those hand-holds and iron rings to grab—easier than catching myself on the cliffs when I used to slip. You want me to undo the bundle's rope? I wrapped it several times around one of those iron rings so it wouldn't slip any deeper into the well."

Weylyn straightened up and looked at the carnage around him. When he finally caught his breath he said, "Fionna, I'm glad you aren't hurt."

With his boot, Weylyn kicked Parzifal's left hand off his face. He peered down at the assassin and saw, protruding from his left eye, a bronze likeness of a wolf's head—the top part of Fionna's brooch pin. She'd driven the six-inch long pin through his eye and into his brain.

"You didn't see that coming, did you?" Weylyn muttered.

He knew he'd have to go look for Bealantin. The wounded Elder was probably down there among the ruins, dead or dying. He checked Fey. He was dead.

Fionna climbed up from the darkness, across the top of the stones and scrambled to the ground. When she saw her grandfather she broke down. "No!" She went to his body and rolled him slightly to see his face. He would never see her again outside the Otherworld.

Yesterday,
Younger then, with much to learn.
Today,
Wiser now, where the lessons burn.
Tomorrow,
Hopeful still, for dreams that yearn.
The Past?
It happened Yesterday.
The Present?
Lived in our own way.
The Future?
Ah, well, who can say?

40

October 17th in the Roman calendar
Late Evening
Ten days left in the Celtic Tree Month of Gort

"Fionna," Weylyn said, "find your friend Kelwin and ask him to bring his cart. Say nothing about what's happened here tonight," he cautioned her. "Tell him only that it is magistrate's business and that I need his help moving something to the Longhouse. I'll wait here." He didn't like the idea of being so close to the dead, but he couldn't leave the treasure unguarded, and he could hardly ask the girl to stay.

"Grandfather—"

"We'll see to him," Weylyn promised. "Let's get this back to the Longhouse and tell Elder Eghan; he'll know what to do."

Nodding, Fionna hurried off and returned in short order with Kelwin. The lad looked horrified by the scene at the well but wisely asked no questions as he helped Weylyn secure the heavy bundle in his cart.

Weylyn's hopes of finding the Chief Magistrate alone in the Longhouse were dashed when he saw the Elder sitting with

Axenus at the table in the great hall. After a hurried conversation in which Weylyn offered the barest of details of the assassin's attack, Elder Eghan immediately sent several men to the sacred well to see to the dead, and sent Kelwin off to bid Fionna's mother come to the Longhouse, where Eghan would himself tell her of her father's passing. Weylyn and Axenus carried the bundle into the main hall while Elder Eghan settled Fionna at the hearth and set the water to heat over the fire.

"Time enough for talk later," Elder Eghan told Weylyn. "Why don't you get cleaned up while I attend to matters here?"

Weylyn excused himself, acutely aware that his clothing was stained with the assassin's blood. He promised a full telling later to Teg, who was still in Weylyn's room guarding the treasure recovered from Griffyth's place. He returned to the main hall to find Elder Eghan speaking to Moyna de Aine, who clutched Fionna tightly and sobbed as she heard about the circumstances of her father's death. Weylyn noted Axenus waiting discreetly at the far end of the room and joined him.

"I'm looking forward to hearing how the Great Cross came into your possession," the Centurion said softly.

Weylyn shivered. "If you don't mind, I'd like to wait until Elder Eghan can join us." As he spoke, he saw the Elder escort Fionna and her mother to the door and heard him instruct Kelwin, who'd waited outside, to take them home in his cart.

With a deep sigh, Elder Eghan returned to his usual place by the fire and gestured for Weylyn and Axenus to join him at the hearth. "Now, young man," Elder said with a stern glance at his deputy, "I think you better tell us just what you and that young girl have been up to."

Taking a deep breath, Weylyn plunged into the narrative. "Fionna came here this afternoon, saying she'd received a message from her grandfather to meet him tonight before he left for the Celtlands. She thought her grandfather was in danger and wanted one of us to go with her."

"Who gave her that message?" Eghan asked sharply.

"It was Elder Bealantin, a friend of her grandfather."

"Ah. He and Petroytrix have been friends for many years."

"I saw them both, at the sacred well of Cernunnos tonight." Weylyn glanced at Axenus, wondering if he should have mentioned that in front of the Centurion. He was relieved when Axenus made no comment about pagan deities and merely gestured for him to continue. "And there was another Elder with them. Fey de Parke was there—"

"Isn't that the relative of Eiroy?" Axenus interrupted him to ask. "I thought he was dead."

"So did we," Weylyn told him. "That was the other message Fionna brought. One of the men who went up to retrieve that body recognized the dead man, said he'd come hunting bear around the time of the Equinox. And tonight, Elder Fey told us he'd watched two men torture Eiroy. There was a fight, and one of the men killed the other, then killed Eiroy."

Weylyn paused to gather his thoughts. "Tonight, Parzifal boasted about killing Eiroy. I'd say the body we found on the mountain was his partner, the one who helped torture Eiroy."

"From what my sources tell me," Axenus murmured, "that would be Brutovius. He's the only one of the thieves we haven't accounted for."

"Well, that settles part of the puzzle. As to the rest of it …" Weylyn told them everything that had transpired since he and Fionna went to the sacred well, straight through to that final, terrible attack by Parzifal. "She's a fighter, Elder," he finished with admiration. "If Fionna hadn't come charging up out of that well, I don't think I'd be sitting here telling you this tale."

*

A week passed. Weylyn's sleep was disturbed by nightmares in which he relived those final grisly moments at the sacred well of

Cernunnos. His days had been full of routine chores, as if Elder Eghan thought it best to keep him too busy to brood. There had been time, though, for Weylyn to accompany Moyna de Aine, Fionna, Druce and others to the funeral ceremonies of Elder Petroytrix. He'd promised Fionna he'd be there, and was glad he'd been able to fulfill that pledge.

Axenus and his forces had ridden back to Hierlaneum with the Great Cross and other treasure in tow—a triumphal victory of sorts. Their bounty was a little lighter without the piece of Celtic amber. They hadn't located Elder Bealantin or the amber. His bloodstained horse was found wandering along the banks of the Moryn Gweneth. A search of his home in Elshorn turned up nothing. In a skillful display of diplomacy, Axenus had decided Bealantin—who was probably mortally wounded—had fallen into the river and drowned, taking the precious piece of amber with him. Elder Eghan and Weylyn knew it was more likely Elder Bealantin had successfully made his rendezvous with the boat of Queen Maeverorix. They understood, though, what Axenus was saying. It was a compromise by the Centurion in exchange for the atrocities committed by one of the Empire's Enforcers.

The rune buckle of Eiroy the Younger was found in Pluvius' possession, just as Elder Eghan had suspected. It was turned over to Axenus, along with the one Petroytrix had given to Weylyn. Pluvius himself was escorted back to Cross Abbey under the care of Warius and a contingent of the Centurion's men and would be assigned new duties some place far from any of the Celtic lands. Nothing other than a territorial transfer, of course, for his outrageous behavior at Brennus Ford. After all, he was only doing his duty to the Empire and the Great Church, albeit a duty most overly vigorous and deadly in its execution.

The Centurion sent an envoy to Carew in the company of Elder Eghan and Commander Orrs to deliver a message to the Celtic Queen Maeverorix. Weylyn had been in the Longhouse when the document was drawn up. The envoy was to tell Her Majesty no further attempt to locate the amber would be made by the Empire. The gold and other treasure would be returned to the Great Church. If, by some trick of fate, the amber should happen to surface out in the Celtic lands, it would be considered an act of God and would not be disputed by the Empire. An admirable diplomatic compromise, Weylyn decided, to avert military conflict.

Such were the thoughts that filled Weylyn's head as the young magistrate headed back to Elshorn after a trip up the mountain at the request of Elder Eghan to attend the funeral services for Elder Fey de Parke. If the man's spirit lingered anywhere, it wasn't at his dwelling, where the remnants of death had been swept away and now stood clean and tidy, awaiting new occupants.

Wintry weather had once again descended on Brendan Valley, leaving Weylyn shivering despite his thick cape and warm hat. He hated being cold. He looked forward to getting back to Elshorn and settling somewhere warm with a hot drink and friendly company. He'd grab Teg, who was no longer hobbling around, and head to the Five Fingers Tavern. With the soldiers gone, the tavern was once again a quiet place.

And he'd have to go back there sometime, Weylyn told himself. He'd been there, just once, since that fateful night at the well. He'd tried then to speak to Adrianna, but any hope of reconciliation, any future they might have had together, was lost in a whirlwind of hateful accusations, curses, and bitter words. She wouldn't listen to reason. Her final words still rang in his head, no matter how he tried to shake the memory away.

"One day soon our soldiers will rid this valley of you wicked Celts," she'd taunted. "They'll smash your pagan temples and burn your homes, just as the great Enforcer Pluvius did at Brennus Ford. Oh, yes, we've all heard the news. He is a true soldier of our Great Church, a real man."

"Innocent people are dead because of him!"

"They defied the Great Church," she'd said flatly. "Good riddance to them—and to you!"

Her words about Pluvius, her obvious approval of his murderous ways, left him colder than any winter wind biting into his skin. He wondered how he'd ever thought he could love someone like her, someone who loathed everything that was important to him. Elder Eghan and Teg had been right after all. The affairs of churchers were no concern of a Celt.

Maybe he'd wait a little while longer before visiting the Five Fingers again, he decided as he entered Elshorn. He'd go to the Longhouse, have a hot drink, and see what task Elder Eghan might have ready for him. As he approached the compound, however, he was surprised to see Teg talking with two other deputy magistrates in front of the Longhouse. "What's going on?" he asked.

Chad, the deputy magistrate from Carew, shrugged. "All I know is that Elder Eghan summoned us. We've been waiting for you and York—ah, here he comes. What took you so long?" he called out. "Did you try to swim the Moryn Gweneth?"

"Only a fool ready for the Otherworld would attempt that," York retorted. "No, I was held up by some travelers from the placid sea. They brought news of sickness in the Empire."

Finn snorted. "There's a sickness there all right," he said. "They're all sick in the head, if you ask me."

The others laughed, but Weylyn, remembering Pluvius' evil deeds, didn't think it was a laughing matter. He was about to say so when the door to the Longhouse opened. Trooping inside, they found Elder Eghan and another man deep in conversation beside the hearth.

The Chief Magistrate gestured them toward the long table before the fireplace. "Help yourselves to food and drink," he told them. "And when you've refreshed yourselves, we will talk. I've summoned you to hear something important, something that may in time affect everyone here in Brendan Valley." He nodded to the man seated beside him. "I believe you all know my old friend, Blaine."

"Gather round, young magistrates," invited Elder Blaine. "I have a story to tell …"

The Celtic Elder Faith Year

Samhain (SOW-win):	Eve of November 1st
Winter Solstice:	December 21st
Imbolc (IM-volk):	Eve of February 1st
Spring Equinox:	March 21st
Beltane (BEL-tain-yuh):	Eve of May 1st
Summer Solstice:	June 21st
Lughnasadh (LOO-na-shav):	Eve of August 1st
Autumnal Equinox:	September 21st

The Celtic Tree Calendar

Luis (Rowan):	January 21st – February 17th
Nuin (Ash):	February 18th – March 17th
Fearn (Alder):	March 18th – April 14th
Saille (Willow):	April 15th – May 12th
Huath (Hawthorn):	May 13th – June 9th
Duir (Oak):	June 10th – July 7th
Tinne (Holly):	July 8th – August 4th
Coll (Hazel):	August 5th – September 1st
Muin (Vine):	September 2nd - 29th
Gort (Ivy):	September 30th – October 27th
Ngetal (Reed):	October 28th – November 24th
Ruis (Elder):	November.25th – December 22nd
Secret of the Unhewn Stone:	December 25th
Beth (Birch):	December 24th – January 20th

The Runic Half-Months

Eoh (yew tree):	December 28th – January 12th
Peorth (womb, dice cup).	January 13th – January 27th
Elhaz (elk):	January 28th – February 11th
Sigel (sun):	February 12th – February26th
Tyr (cosmic pillar):	February 27th – March 13th
Beorc (birch tree):	March 14th – March 29th
Ehwaz (horse):	March 30th – April 13th
Man (humans):	April 14th – April 28th
Lagu (flowing water):	April 29th – May 13th
Ing (expansive energy):	May 14th – May 28th
Odal (home, possession):	May 29th – June 13th
Dag (day):	June 14th – June 28th
Feoh (wealth):	June 29th – July 3rd
Ur (primal strength):	July 14th – July 28th
Thorn (defense):	July 29th – August 12th
As (gods):	August 13th –August 28th
Rad (motion):	August 29th – September 12th
Ken (illumination):	September 13th – September 27th
Gyfu (gift):	September 28th – October 12th
Wyn (joy):	October 13th – October 27th
Hagal (constraint):	October 28th – November 12th
Nyd (necessity):	November 13th – November 27th
Is (stasis):	November 28th – December 12th
Jara (year):	December 13th – December 27th

ABOUT THE AUTHOR

Jack R. Cotner is an author, poet, and artist. His publications include *Storytellin': True & Fictional Short Stories Of Arkansas* and *Mystery of the Death Hearth* (first in the Runevision Novel series). His work is available in paperback and e-book editions. Visit jackronaldcotner.wordpress.com for more.

www.ingramcontent.com/pod-product-compliance
Lightning Source LLC
LaVergne TN
LVHW020529100826
845148LV00010B/1398

* 9 7 8 0 6 1 5 6 7 1 6 7 3 *